NORTH COUNTRY
An Anthology of Contemporary Writing
from the Adirondacks
and the Upper Hudson Valley

Edited by:

Joseph Bruchac
Craig Hancock
Alice Gilborn
Jean Rikhoff

Publication of this anthology has been made possible, in part, through a Literary Publishing Grant from the Literature Program of the New York State Council on the Arts.

ISBN 0-912678-65-8

Library of Congress # 85-70358

FIRST EDITION

Typesetting by Sans Serif, 2378 E. Stadium Blvd., Ann Arbor, Mi. 48104
Printed in the United States of America.

Cover Photograph by Jack Lynch

ACKNOWLEDGEMENTS

In all cases, unless otherwise noted, permission to reprint previously published work in this anthology has been granted by the individual authors. We wish to express our gratitude to those magazines and presses listed below. Their commitments to literary excellence and the many voices of new American writing deserve attention.

Lawrence Allen: all selections from *Three Adirondack Poets*, The Loft Press.
Joe David Bellamy: *Blueline* for "The Message."
L. J. Bergamini: *Blueline* for "Departure," "Climbing Hurricane," and "Sisters." *The Christian Science Monitor* for "Climbing Without Ropes," and *The Windless Orchard* for "Skier's Dusk."
William Bronk: all selections from *Life Supports*, North Point Press.
Joseph Bruchac: *Blueline* for "Card Players and the Stars Above Paradox Lake," *The Glens Falls Review* for "Carrying Children," and "Last Day of the Season, Guard Tower # 4," and *Groundswell* for "The Fox Den."
Don Byrd: all selections from *Technics of Travel*.
Joe Cardillo: "Abandoned" is from *A Legacy of Desire*, 1983. All other selections are from *Turning Toward Morning*, 1984.
Catherine Clarke: *The Greenfield Review* for "Coming Back."
Paul Corrigan: *High Rock Review* for "The Vet's Club." *Blueline* for other selections.
George Drew: *Antioch Review* for "Either You Fall. . ." *Blueline* for "Pinnacle Farm," *Dacotah Territory* for "A Short Unhappy History of Uncle Frank," *Yes* for "To a Fisherman," and *Beloit Poetry Journal* for "The Drowning of Christopher French."
Jeanne Finley: *Conditions* for "Widow," and *High Rock Review* for "The Wandering Jew."
Jim Flosdorf: *Blueline* for "Osprey," "Taurus," and "Canoe Makers."
Eugene K. Garber: for "The Bird Watchers."
Alice Wolf Gilborn: *Blueline* for "Of Time and the Road" and "Out of the Blue." *The Greenfield Review* for "Portents."
Cynde Gregory: *Groundswell* for "Uncanny Beauty." *Blueline* for "Camping with Chloe."
Craig Hancock: *Blueline* for "The Owl," *The Greenfield Review* for "Teaching at Coxsackie Prison," *The Glens Falls Review* for "The Hunters" and "Wood Gathering."
William Hathaway: selections from *Fish, Flesh & Fowl*, LSU Press.
Kay Hogan: *The Glens Falls Review* for "Little Green Girl."
Ina Jones: *Blueline* for "The Fox."
Lawrence Josephs: *The Greenfield Review* for "Schroon Lake."
Sherry Kearns: *The Glens Falls Review* for "Calves Pen on Lake George," *Blueline* for other selections.
William Kennedy: *The Glens Falls Review* for "An Exchange of Gifts."
Maurice Kenny: "Sacrifice" from *The Smell of Slaughter*, Blue Cloud Quarterly Press, "North" and "Land" from *North: Poems of Home*, Blue Cloud Quarterly Press, "Picking Blackberries" from *The Mama Poems*, White Pine Press. *River Styx* for "Sitting in the Waters of Grasse River."
Walter B. Lape: all selections from *Three Adirondack Poets*, The Loft Press.

Elizabeth Lortie: *The Glens Falls Review* for "McCrea Street Elementary."
William Losinger: *The Glens Falls Review* for "Love on the Run."
Mary Ann Lynch: *Blueline* for "Aunt Hannah" and "Railroad Place."
Judith McDaniel: all selections from *November Woman*, The Loft Press.
Martin Nakell: *Groundswell* for "Train," and *Blueline* for "How It Will Be for You."
Mark Nepo: *Colorado-North Review* for "King of the Jews," *En Passant* for "Rusted Pail," *Washout Review* and the New York State Museum anthology *Collected Words* for "A Guide to Rock Climbing."
Kate O'Connell: *Blueline* for "David Smith" and "Autumn Elms," *Poet* for "At Globerson's Corner," and *Poets On* or "Listening to the Goldberg Variations."
John Quirk: all selections from *Three Adirondack Poets*, The Loft Press.
Joanne Rickhoff: *David Smith, I Remember* was originally published as a chapbook by The Loft Press.
Michael Rutherford: *Teachers and Writers Magazine* for "Toiling I."
Joanne Seltzer: *Blueline* for "At Big Moose Lake," *River Styx* for "The Case of the Pickled Woman," *On Turtle's Back, a Biogeographic Anthology of New York State*, edited by Dennis Maloney, White Pine Press for "Waiting to Watch the Bears," other selections from *Adirondack Lake Poems*, The Loft Press.
Jordan Smith: all selections from *An Apology for Loving the Old Hymns*, Princeton University Press.
Ed Tick: *The First Anniversary Journal* of the Hudson Valley Writers Guild for "On Regionalism."
Paul Weinman: *Groundswell* for "Traced By Blood," *Puckerbrush Review* for "In Early Driving," and *Wellspring* for "Got so Grandma."
Ron Welburn: *Groundswell* for "Mohawk Memory."
Russ Williams: *Blueline* for "Night Fisherman," and "Long Rod." "Howard Has Never Been to Brant Lake" appeared in the New York State Museum anthology *Collected Words*.

WRITING FROM THE NORTH COUNTRY:
An Introduction

Though mention of New York conjures up images of city landscapes for the majority of people outside of the Empire State, those
who live within its borders know that it is a place of almost infinite
variety. From the Great Lakes to the Atlantic and from the St.
Lawrence to the Finger Lakes it would be hard to find a greater range
of geography in a single state. Among other things, one of the largest
parks in the world, bigger than many European nations, can be found
within its borders in the forever wild Adirondacks. This area goes
from the edge of the St. Lawrence Plains down south past Lake
Champlain which my Abenaki ancestors called *Petonbowk*, the
"waters in between." It edges the Hudson River down through that
area which was once a Dutch trading outpost the Iroquois called
Skenectati, "Beyond the Trees." The Adirondacks and the Upper Hudson Valley, this is the area we called The North Country. Up here the
old wild rivers flow and the Hudson begins as a stream crystal clear
and shallow enough at its upper reaches for a deer to splash across
where it is joined by the Cedar River or a canoe paddle to scrape
against the ancient bedrock at Blue Ledges not far from Warrensburg.
There are cities, true, but none of them that seem bigger than the
heavily wooded hills around them or the river that flows through
them.

Growing up in this part of the country, I can never think of New
York myself without seeing the High Peaks, hearing the high whistle
of red-tail hawk, or feeling the wind whip the snow across my face as
my snowshoes web their way across an abandoned field. Though
Fenimore Cooper romanticized and often erred in his depictions of an
earlier age of this countryside in *The Last of the Mohicans*, I recognized
this place in his words when I was a child and understood the love of
his Indians and scouts for the land. Much of my own writing has been
as rooted in this landscape as a cedar is in a fissure of granite. Such
trees don't often grow very tall, but they are harder to dislodge than
those growing in what seems to be a richer earth. The Adirondacks
and the upper Hudson Valley are a hard land to lodge in at times --
like tonight when the late January wind has brought freezing rain and
snow that has unstrung wires and left thousands without power. But
the hardness makes it clear what living here means. If it were too easy
it wouldn't be worth it.

The inspiration for this anthology came first of all from this land, rocky and thin-soiled, its growing season short. It has made for tough voices, as well as voices sensitive to those moments of grace we might see in the flare of a cardinal flower by a brook in high summer. As is true for many parts of the United States, there has been a burst of what might be called "regional writing" in the North Country in the past ten years or so. As the variety of voices in this collection shows, not everyone writes the same or about the same things and some of their writing shows little outer evidence of place. Their presence in this region as residents, not summer visitors, was one criteria for inclusion. The other criteria was excellence -- as judged by a group of four editors all of whom are based in the North Country.

Writing in this part of New York, of course, is nothing new. Not one, but three Artists Colonies, are in this area, venerable Yaddo and the newer Millay and Blue Mountain Lake. And the long careers of two of our best known "area writers," American Book Award Winner Bill Bronk, who managed the family lumber yard in Hudson Falls while writing his poems, and Pulitzer Prize laureate William Kennedy, whose chronicling of Albany goes back several decades, are both examples and exemplary. Perhaps it is only that there are more of us writing in this region now and more of us aware of each other's work. Such relatively recent developments as The Hudson Valley Writers Guild, the Council of Literary Sponsors and the Greenfield Review Literary Center Newsletter have served as further connections and conduits. William Kennedy's brainchild, The New York State Writers Institute at Albany, has begun taking great strides in both bringing world-famous writers to the area and assisting the local artists. In addition to *The Greenfield Review, Blueline, The Glens Falls Review* and *Groundswell*, there are half a dozen literary magazines which have come into being since 1984 in the North Country and there are more than a dozen active literary presses.

So things are now. It is hard to say what future years will bring, though from the evidence of the submissions we received for this collections there will be much more writing to come from The North Country. Though more than 50 writers are represented, more than twice that number were rejected. Though many of them sent strong work, we decided only to include those about whose writing we were most in agreement. If this same anthology were to be edited a few years from now, I am certain that many of those who were not included would be found within its pages.

Joseph Bruchac
Greenfield Center, New York
Snow Moon 1986

CONTENTS

Lawrence Allen

BIOGRAPHICAL DATA

Birthplace . . . Lockport, New York
Birthdate . . . March 12, 1945
Married . . . Christine
Children . . . Jason and Lindsay
Residence . . . Lake George, New York
Occupation . . . High School/College English Instructor
        Lake George Senior High/Adirondack Community College
Summer Occupation . . . Captain: M/V Ticonderoga, M/V Mohigan

PARTIAL LIST OF PUBLISHING CREDITS:

Three Adirondack Poets (Anthology)
The Writer
The English Journal
Greenriver Review
Blueline
Cape Rock Quarterly
Various Other Literary Magazines

1

I am happily a North Country writer. The Adirondack Mountains provide me with an endless backdrop for my work—one that is uncommonly serene, free from the hustle of city life. As I look back, I think that poetry has always been a good part of me as long as I can remember, but it has been a part that has brought along its share of pain and frustration as well. When lines don't work and images fall into disjointed bits and pieces, I try to leave it all behind, pushing it into a distant corner of my desk and then turn to other writing forms. Yet always—always there is that poem rattling around somewhere in the darkest corners of my mind, just waiting until I let it out again—and I always do.

I love poetry for two reasons: imagery and sound. If the heart of the poem is its imagery, then its pulse must be the sound, and without these two interlocking parts the life force of the poem is sadly missing. Of the two, imagery is more important to me, and I would never knowingly create an image which does not, as Pound suggests, present ". . . an intellectual and emotional complex in an instant of time." When I am moved by a particular poem, anyone's poem, more often as not it is because I can sit back and say, "I've seen that picture and I know exactly what the poet is trying to show me." Sound, like imagery, can never be neglected either. For me, the perfect line, if such a thing can exist at all, has structure and sails smoothly along the page, joining and reinforcing my ideas and images. With the devices of sound, a poet can focus the reader's attention to detail and he can add limitless variations; moreover, he can break the all too predictable patterns where needed and perhaps lead the reader to make new discoveries about words and ideas he might ordinarily miss. In the end there is always a quiet satisfaction when I read my final draft aloud and the lines sing right back at me. When they do, I know it's as right as it will ever be.

On Returning to Bear Pond

When I was sixteen
you were eternity,
graced with the elegance
of singing stands of shadowed
pines and muted birches:
a slate of cold black water
that came from under the world
to run down the glacier lines
of the mountain's chiseled face.
Like my father before me
and his before him, I dipped
my paddle a thousand times
one way and back again, while all
the time my youth ran clear-eyed
and I was knee-deep in summers
that tumbled over one another
like a bushel of runaway apples
spilled across the cellar floor.

Summer Storm

A heavy-shouldered sky descends
To lean upon the western peaks.

The wind sweeps down the valley floor
To bend the stands of birch and spruce.

A sheet of rain begins to drive
Across the newly planted field.

The clouds are shelves of slate that turn
A summer afternoon to night.

I hear the sky begin to break;
It crumbles now directly overhead.

The lights go dim and shadows spill
Across the kitchen countertops.

The curtain ghosts flap in and out
Their wooden haunts of window sash.

And still I have no fear—until
I see an axe of lightning cleave

The Christmas pine beside the porch
And hear the wrenching of its roots:

The very one my father dug
And planted on the day he died.

Discovery

Far back along the mountain's middle, some
Good distance from the common walker's route,
There snakes a wall of piled stone with cracks
Of green-apple moss marked thick with scores
Of maple shoots and mushroom stalks. It's four
Stones high or more, depending where you count.
You run your eye along the wall and see
It jounce away until it disappears
With casual patience somewhere deep within
A waiting thicket to emerge again
Quite unconcerned for Nature's overgrowth
Of forcefulness. It gaps in several spots
With stones slipping down the leaf-strewn slope (not
Unlike a jack-o-lantern's jagged smile).
Then wide it swings around a grove of pine
Until it runs the slope to flat and back
To slope again where it tumbles to
A halt, a rampant mass of piled stone.
It is here that man has pushed his lust
To civilize, penetrated the mountainside,
And built a road that lizard-flicks away,
To meet with other roads, I suppose. I
Cross and find a rabbit warm against the
Cool pavement on the other side. And when
The fence picks up once more, I break away
And bend to hills beyond, forgetting that
I set myself to find the fence's end.

Garden Dreams

Last year's garden shrugs off
Winter's ice grip and
Will not die. The few missed
Onions send forth shoots of
Green, flags from beneath the
Melting snow, and even
Clumps of chard begin to
Grow again, recalled to
Life amid a background
Scaped in white and played with
Sweeps of mitigating black.

In the house we find our
Thoughts are buried deep in
Garden dreams of what will
Be, but surely not in what has been.

A Change of Seasons

Like a woman dressing for the evening,
Hiding signs of age with soft and gentle
Strokes of blush and shadow lines that trick the
Eye and hint of bold and sweeping youth,
Painting over years one by one, leaving
All to reminisce about her past and
Captivating charm and how she quickened
Pulses to a stir without the slightest
Care to those who stood and wet their lips with
Eager tongues if she but brushed their hand:
Autumn slips the line to winter, fighting
All the while an image of a face grown
Old and unfamiliar in the mirror
Of the pond that has turned itself to ice.

photo by S.E. Ekfelt

Joe David Bellamy

Joe David Bellamy was born in Cincinnati, Ohio, and has lived in upstate New York for the last fourteen years, in the small village of Canton, where, for roughly a decade, he was editor of Fiction International magazine and press. Canton is located in the far northwestern part of New York state in the relatively flat, wide valley of the St. Lawrence in a region nearly midway between the river and the Adirondacks.

During 1974–80, Bellamy ran the Fiction International/St. Lawrence University Writers Conference at Saranac Lake, which brought writers such as E. L. Doctorow, Joyce Carol Oates, John Hawkes, Margaret Atwood, James Tate, Ann Beattie, Russell Banks, Jayne Anne Phillips, and many others to upstate New York. He also founded the St. Lawrence Award for Fiction, an annual $1000 prize presented from 1973–83 to recognize authors of outstanding first collections of short fiction.

Bellamy's books and anthologies include: The New Fiction (Illinois, 1974); Superfiction (Random House/Vintage, 1975); Olympic Gold Medalist, a collection of poems (North American Review, 1978); and American Poetry Observed (Illinois, 1984).

He has published fiction in Mississippi Review, Prairie Schooner, North American

Review, Ontario Review, Ohio Review, *and others; poetry in* Paris Review, Iowa Review, Poetry Northwest, Southern Poetry Review, Ploughshares, *and others; essays, reviews, and interviews in* The Atlantic Monthly, New American Review, Partisan Review, Saturday Review, Chicago Review, *and the* New York Times Book Review.

He has been a recipient of grants from CAPS and from the National Endowment for the Arts and is a member of the National Book Critics Circle and past chairman of the board of the Coordinating Council of Literary Magazines.

The Message

I carve a slow neat path out
to the wood stacked like aging wine
dry and magnificent as ripe grain in the barn
scraping the steps with my red blade
snow sparkling in the cement crevices
billowing now like tiny air-borne diamonds
and the wind flapping the wolf's-hair of my hood
the distant fence aglitter with frozen light
the white birches stiff in their icy shells
bright shadows of chimney-plume rising
like a signal-fire across the yard

Jogging at Evergreen Cemetery

1.

I have just run three miles faster than a man my age
was meant to run, legs lifting higher, higher, flying
along deserted country roads between cornfields and
the stares of puzzled cows. Now, hot and breathless
at Evergreen Cemetery, I coast into shade and five
acres of gravestone markers. We come here, Theresa
(the dog) and I, for the luxury of seclusion, the
smoothness of the running, for the companionship.

It is a private place, unplowed but navigable in
winter, peaceful any time of year, a long, sloping
figure-eight of blacktop winding through a pine forest
thick with headstones and, as you run, the names
of the dead flash past: Elizabeth   John   Father
_____ and beside him, _____, his wife,
each name, each stone, like a blow to the chest,
like a wound . . . the large family stones
clustered about with smaller ones.

I am trying to put off the day, I suppose,
by a willed toughening of the capillaries,
when I will join them here. The residents
might take that as impoliteness, I'm afraid, or
at least, as presumption; but, by now, they
have grown accustomed to me, my earthly form
like a fond memory, my cockamamie determination to
continue a ritual so patently foolish and
out of place here that it might signify for
all human endeavor. No, they are not offended.
They are smiling at me now, smugly but wistfully,
as I glide along the winding cemetery road.

If there is such a thing as communing with the dead,
this might be a way to do it, by breathing deeply
as you are now, by holding in your mind the ideal,
the full empathetic awareness of . . . .
By saying, "I hear you," so to speak, to the utter silence
of the place, the freezing and the thawing of the sod, the

sprinkle of brown needles on the scalloped ledges of
weathered marble, the lichen growing year by year,
penetrating the rock like a system of veins, the water
seeping in, bubbling out in the spring, erasing the faces
of the stones, then the stones themselves, and the bones
underneath are turning to powder faster still, so many
bodies, so many lives—more lives
than one mind can hold in its grasp.

If you could hold these lives still long enough to
grasp them, how many could you hold onto at once
without your skull bursting from the effort?
Open up your mind. Feel the lives
entering it—the ones never understood, even by themselves,
the ones who died in mid-sentence without time to update
their wills or insurance policies, the ones whose love was
terribly needed by someone still living, the ones so much
more deserving of grace or comfort than oneself but who
never received it, the ones whose triumph was some act of
hideous inhumanity, the ones whose real monuments were
invisible and anonymous but more lasting than the stones.

2. Maps

Telephone wires mark the edge of the world of the living,
grids of lines framing random maps of space and sky. You
would have to stand on your head on the lawn, bring yourself
to their level beside the ancient stones, press your
ear to the pale marble, feel the imprint of their names
against your cheek, to see Heaven through that window.

Slowing to a walk, breathing hard, cooling down, I glance
at the bright roadsign beyond the ledge of evergreens:
Canton 1, Potsdam 10: the geometrical precision of our place
on the map, the misleading reflex of thinking we can know
our true location, as if this single formulation in the
endless fecundity of space could represent a key to anything.

The frustration of confinement here, trapped in a box,
labelled like an unidentifiable specimen, or an unexplored
space on a map, your legs sprouting shoots, pressing for
years against white satin, dividing, inching into every
crevise, desperate for the smell of earth, the touch of ripe
loam and the live universe of cellular profusion fuming and

caterwauling outside the coffin walls, the furious labyrinth
of roots branching and crisscrossing like an underground
telephone system connecting every point on the earth, every
space above or below or within, like a map of the spheres,
revealing like an x-ray, electron within atom, molecule within
compound, planet within solar system, star within galaxy.

3. Semper Fidelis

Corroded stars and bronze eagles screaming, faded flags
next to bunches of plastic flowers: I think of old men,
in dying, who turn to symbols of military honor.

Even my father, a man in his sixties who had nightmares for
years about his wounding on Okinawa but kept his medals and
Purple Heart tucked modestly away, chose a military funeral.

The Pentagon had flown him to Alabama for a heart valve.
Later, deathly ill, he waited for three hours in some
hallway to see doctors at the Veterans' Hospital.

For years, the print on the wall above his desk: the
Marines raising the flag at Iwo Jima and the inscription:
"Here Marine courage and skill were put to the supreme test."

My mother and I standing at his graveside in Ohio in the rain
while the Marines fired three shots into the grey sky
and lifted the flag from his coffin and folded it.

"By order of the Commandant of the Marine Corps and the
Secretary of the Treasury," one said, "we present you
with this flag on behalf of a grateful nation."

4. Epitaphs

> "Let's talk of graves, of worms, and epitaphs . . . "

This granite shaft, the tallest in the cemetery — what
does it signify? Monumental ego, or once-healthy capital,
at least — an obelisk rising thirty feet high. But beyond
the name, no words, no words of any kind. Why sink one's
wealth into a stone and then not speak: advice to the living
or praise for the dead, what caused the end to come, or what
deeds made the life worthy of such a slab? Even in death,
it seems to say, I was more mighty than my peers.
But here such arrogance seems an empty epitaph.

What can one say of death? "This man was born.
He lived this many years. After that, he died," or,
"Here lies one whose name was writ in water?"
(And if Keats' name was writ in water, where
does that leave the rest of us?) "Death found
him at his post," one inscription reads, the stone
embellished with a long marble hand, forefinger
perpetually raised, pointing heavenward. But, mostly,
these local folk seem not to believe in epitaphs.
Death has left them speechless, or else, a reticence
seems to them more fitting: a name, dates, little else.

If thought and action might serve as epitaph, the
inertia of their lives might still circulate like ions
in the air, and they are a part of us now, here, a pall
of thin smoke visible in the clearings and the eerie pencils
of buttery light filtering through the trees.
If not, what do these stones signify?
Nothing at all.

5. The Graveyard at Dusk

For years there was nothing across Route 11
from the Evergreen but a wide field of weeds.
Now the stones seem to line up at nightfall like cars
at the drive-in, each straining in the violet light
for a better view of the Super Duper, Pizza Hut,
Kinney's Rexall in its fluorescent splendor.

And the distant towers of the Agway feed plant like the
necks of aging dinosaurs listening to one another, or
a failed experiment in colossal praying mantises,
abandoned as impractical but left on view to warn the
world, passing families out on a Sunday evening, secure
in their complacency, of the folly of grand schemes.

I am surrounded by gravestones, phalanxes of marble
that tilt with the curving plane of asphalt at each lunge.
The tall pines wheel like ballerinas, their shaggy arms
swirling in the light, their scent wafting through me and
up above the clouds. At dusk, the graveyard comes alive.
A semi shifts loudly and whines northward out of town.
The names of the dead fade slowly into the dark.

L. J. Bergamini

Laurie J. Bergamini has spent every summer of her life in the high peaks of the Adirondacks and has been a full time North Country resident for the last five years. She is a sometime English teacher and has just completed her Ph.D. in Medieval Studies from the University of Connecticut. She lives in Lake Placid with her husband and two children where she skiis, gardens and writes. Her poetry and essays have been published in Blueline, Dark Horse, Windless Orchard, *and* The Christian Science Monitor.

Sisters

In the summer, within the blue cup of mountains,
In the midst of everlasting: wild strawflowers;
With insect sounds, cricket and cicada,
We wandered over the toppled meadow hay.
Bird songs, particularly the white throat's
Marked the hours of fading afternoon
Until we, two small sisters, you with long legs
And long curls, a lithe and elfin child
And I, younger and plumper, wandered home over the meadow
In twilight, into the trees, over the leafy track of an old tote road
Used a century before for dragging Adirondack timber,
Where, for us, time literally stood still.
We knew the woods only in summer,
So that they were, during our childhood,
One long sweet Eden perenially reviewed.
I walked the tote road with you, awed that you knew
both the names of flowers and the right way home,
I see them still along the grassy track, as we
Wandered east in the sunset's glow:
In the woods, Dutchman's breeches and British soldiers,
A rare pink slipper, quick-darkening Indian pipes;
In the meadow, Heal-all and Queen Anne's lace,
Gentle mountain aster.

Now, in our summers beneath the same blue mountains,
I watch our children, as lean or plump,
(Depending on the child and on the year)
They wander down that ancient logging road.
And as we, now matrons of this graceful brood,
Guard the summer hearth, lay the table,
Set our wanderers' food upon the board,
And in the twilight wait for them to issue home,
I am touched by echoes of our childhood passed.
I hope for them the clear memory of summers shared
Beside a stand of blue Heal-all, beneath a sturdy mountain ash,
The sweet and subtle smell of pasture lace,
And hours within the white throat's call.

Climbing Hurricane

I was five on a dawn hike up Hurricane Mountain,
Too old to be carried through the white pines and spruce
That obscured the sky, hid the scope of the trail and
Haunted the damp, morning air with resin.
So, first scratched by raspberry canes and dead branches;
Then tripped and bruised by rocks above the tree line
(But fearing most of all to be left behind),
I whined up the half-light, two thousand feet to the rocky top,
An unprotected and windy perspective on the high peaks.
The morning mist we'd climbed through melted into wisps
Above a green matrix of farm, pasture, wood and mountain,
A realm extended, clarified by the rising sun,
Its illuminating memory, since that moment, a wordless vision
Of the world unfolding, inalienably mine.

Departure

In the young man's muscles that work themselves along
Your sixteen-year-old arm when you wave;
In the easy way you leave home,
Slamming the kitchen door that never stays shut;
In the embarrassed distraction of your embrace;
In the ritual handshake with your father
(Facing each other, you each swing a right arm out,
Then down, until your hands meet in a gentle slap.
"Well, Mike," he says, and places his second hand over his first,
Which still holds yours, "I guess it's time to go"),
You signal your departure.

I stand on the kitchen steps like a stone and watch you drive off,
And think that if I were an Italian peasant like my grandmother
(Who kept chickens in her yard,
And tended goats on the eroded hills of Campagna,
Who watched her sons leave, one by one, for America,
Never to return),
I would fling my apron up over my head and weep.

Climbing Without Ropes

Climbing Giant Mountain on a clear August day,
I saved your life on impulse.
I reached out and caught your belt
As you slid down the rockface past me.
You seemed to be on your way to join
Your wife resting in the conifer scrub
Five hundred feet down.

Until that moment, we had been the most diffident of friends.
But, as we hung there, caught like insects on the
Updraft of a sudden, shared desire—
Unsteadily suspended between the
Mountain's gravity and the clarity of
A cloudless summer sky—
Life together seemed ineffably sweet.

Miraculously I found friction in the rock
Where there was only stone smooth as glass,
Enough traction to save us both.
Years later I cannot think of our diagonal ascent
Without the evocation of that moment's
Sweet salvation, without a memory
Of the blueness of that August sky.

Skier's Dusk

Just after the sun has set, the alpenglow departed,
In the quarter-hour before nightfall, everything is clear.
Each mountain stands distinct, detailed,
Yet part of a range; the snowfields roll away
From where I stand on my skis,
Near the edge of a conifer copse.
There is no color now. We are all,
Fields, woods, and woman, a pattern of white and black.
It's difficult to ski unblinded by the sun,
Unguided by its dark projections,
But I can count the branches of a balsam two miles off,
Discern the planes of mountain ledge,
Locate the hidden pasture edge,
During this brief time before nightfall in winter.

photo by Ann Hagen Griffith

William Bronk

"I was born in the Town of Fort Edward, NY in 1918 and have since lived nearby in the Village of Hudson Falls. I went to public school there and later to Dartmouth College where I was a student of Sidney Cox and graduated in 1938. The next year, I left Harvard graduate school after one semester to write The Brother in Elysium which I finished in 1946. It was finally published in 1980. After four and a half years of service in the army during the second world war, I taught briefly at Union College in Schenectady. Starting in 1947, I made a living in a retail fuel and building-materials business which my father had operated before he died. I continued this until 1978. When Cid Corman started his ORIGIN magazine in 1951, I published some poems there and subsequently had poems in each of its four series. Corman's Origin Press published Light and Dark in 1956. The San Francisco Review – New Directions Press published The World The Worldless in 1964. After that, James Weil, at Elizabeth Press published several collections culminating in Life Supports in 1981. A trade edition of this book was published by North Point Press which printed a Collected Prose in the fall of 1983 under the title Vectors and Smoothable Curves. In 1985 Red Ozier Press issued a collection of new poems, Careless Love and Its Apostrophes.

18

Waterland

Water, as much as land, is what it's about,
water, as much as air, the bearer of life,
water upon whose face the Spirit of God
moved at the first beginning, water the link
and water the final dissolver: we come from there
and flow away, staying a little on the land.

Here, in this State, we lean against Erie in the west,
on the north, bear against Ontario and its flow
to St. Lawrence. Champlain links to Canada,
Vermont in the east. The hand of the Finger Lakes
clutches the center and those great rivers—
Mohawk, Hudson, armatures to support
the clay of the State's statue, Delaware points
toward the tall city—the Bronx, river-edged,
Richmond, Manhattan, afloat on the estuary,
Brooklyn, Queens, on the Island. Here, is now
the capital of all the world and here
we front the water whence, long ago, as life,
we came and that particular ocean whence,
later, immigrants, we came to a new world,
as once, Hudson came, entering,
as into a newness from the sea, the Upper Bay.

My grandfather worked in a shipyard in New Baltimore
making new craft to traffic the river to New York.
Today, near there, as on a river, we launch
again a newness over the river land.

Citizens, we live on the land and build
on the land and love that land as well we might.
But we are mostly water. Water links
us, links us to one another, links us to life.
Let the links be in the land. Let all the land
pay homage to water. Let all we build be life.

Home Address

We always lived in a big house,
bigger than we needed,
and none of us could seem to understand
the way the pieces went together
or why the rooms were planned
the way they were.

We tried to fill the house as best we could.
Idly, fingering the contours of the wood,
we tried which way to fit them to the hand,
but the fingers always failed to understand.

The garden grew more tangled year by year.
We remodeled; nothing helped us; we despaired
of making the house look right, of ever living there
in comfort. There were drafts across the floor.
And, in the winter, coming alone from school,
we waited outside till there was at least a light
and someone else inside. We hated the night.
We hated the big, disordered, incongruous house.
It was beyond our power. But we stayed on there.
We lived an order different from the walls.
Leaving an empty room to disrepair,
we laughed a little, seeing the crooked halls.

Skunk Cabbage

Because it is soon, it has a private and quiet
spring. Before the birds come, before
another leaf or flower, it flowers; and bees
come there and enter and leave, thick
with pollen. Foetid, even in the thin chill
of a wintry spring, it stinks of livingness,
rawness. Its color also is of skin
rubbed raw by wind, by cold, by sun,
and the flesh showing through. It is the flesh
responding to warmth, to sun, to the first spring.
It looks like tenderness, the way it curves
upward and beaks over to cover within.

Life Supports

Life keeps me alive: all its tubes
and wires are connected to me and give support
in ways that life determines for my needs.
On a bed of earth, in house, its calendars
and clocks are programmed to me: the various airs
of mornings, evenings, noontimes, in and out;
the seasons turn and come again and turn
and come again. Issue by issue the news
runs by, describing events and non-events,
reports sometimes of me, others I know.
Food, of course, often. Salty and sweet,
soluble, and other solutions at times
— corrective fluids needed to restore such balance
as may be lost. I am aware though I
not seem to be. Hard to believe the surge
of current through my angers, ecstasies
and frights sometimes at crises: a faulty tube,
power-outages, not long, but I cried
to be restored. The dials and switches wait.
No god comes near me. I am alone.

Local Landscapes

The referent of worldly qualities
by which I mean the goods of this world
whether it be beauty of body, keenness
of mind, or any grace whatever, besides,
is not to this world but to somewhere else
unaffected by qualities or acts
of them, deaf-mute, sufficient to itself.

For a little time the world, at least, responds
to worldly qualities: cleverness,
invention, bolds and graces of various kinds.
Before their collapses happen, they make us think
the world's mechanisms will carry us.

We have the idea of homeland. As others before
and after, or in other worlds, I have loved
my native places as if, without them,
I should be lost, having no real place.
But our homes are contrivances, coverings
for emptinesses. Our local landscapes
acknowledge our unarrival, are brochures of desire
and postcards from there. They tour an untraveled space.

Flowers, the World and My Friend, Thoreau

It no longer matters what the names of flowers are.
Some I remember; others forget: ones
I never thought I should. Yes, tell me one.
I like to hear that. I may have forgotten again
next week. There's that yellow one whose name
I used to know. It's blossoming, secure
as ever as I walk by looking at it,
not saying its name or needing to.
Henry, it's true as you said it was, that this
is a world where there are flowers. Though it isn't our truth,
it's a truth we embrace with gratitude:
how should we endure our dourness otherwise?
And we feel an eager desire to make it ours,
making the flowers ours by naming them.

But they stay their own and it doesn't become our truth.

We live with it; we live with othernesses
as strangers live together in crowds. Truths
of strangeness jostle me; I jostle them
walking past them as I do past clumps of flowers.
Flowers, I know you, not knowing your name.

photo by Carol Bruchac

Joseph Bruchac

I was born in 1942 in Saratoga Springs in October, the Moon of Falling Leaves. My writing and my interests reflect my mixed ancestry, Slovak on one side and Native American (Abenaki) and English on the other. Aside from attending Cornell University and Syracuse and 3 years of teaching in West Africa, I've lived all of my life in the small Adirondack foothills town of Greenfield Center in a house built by my grandfather. After returning from Ghana in 1969, my wife Carol and I started The Greenfield Review and the Greenfield Review Press. We have a special commitment to multicultural writing, especially poetry.

I write poetry, fiction and some literary criticism and have been fortunate enough to receive recognition in all three areas. I've won, in the last two years, a CAPS poetry fellowship, a PEN Syndicated Fiction Award and a Rockefeller Foundation fellowship to do a study of themes of continuance in Native American poetry. My poems have appeared in more than 400 magazines in the U.S., Canada, England and Africa and I'm the author of 20 published books and chapbooks of poetry and fiction. My newest ones are Remembering the Dawn, a chapbook of poems from Blue Cloud Quarterly Press (1983) and No Telephone To Heaven, a novel based on my years in Africa which will be published by Cross Cultural Communications Press of Merrick, N.Y. In the last few years I've been doing a great deal of story-telling, focussing on northeastern Native American tales and traditions of the Adirondacks.

I've also done a great deal of work over the past ten years in teaching and helping start writing workshops in American prisons. I believe that poetry is as much a part of human beings as is breath—and that, like breath, poetry links us to all other living things and is meant to be shared.

The Fox Den

It is a Sunday afternoon in mid-spring. The air is hot and still, the day unseasonably dry. The rains which usually fill the streams of the Adirondack foothill slopes have not come. In the small valley formed by the flow of the crick, the water is quick over tumbled stones, yet shallower than in the years of the recent past. The steep slope to the west of the stream is topped by a great white pine tree, one which has stood for more centuries than the stream below its arching branches has known the name given it by white settlers: Bell Brook.

Two of the tree's roots arch out from the bank, almost like the buttresses of a cathedral. Between those roots two men stand, shovels in their hands. Neither of the men know that the hill on which they stand was formed more than ten thousand years ago at the end of the last Ice Age. Then, as the flow of the waters from the great mountains of cold slowed, scoured soil was deposited here as a terminal morraine.

The men have been digging into the fox den which opens, hidden from a casual eye, between those two roots. On the bank above them a collie dog sits, her tongue lolling out. She is lazily watchful, her paws around a large rock which now blocks the other entrance to the den. It is a piece of sedimentary rock. It holds within it deep memory of the time when all the land around was ocean. The shapes of sea shells and a perfectly shaped trilobite stand out on the surface, made darker and clearer by the saliva which drips from the collie's mouth.

The two men have been digging for half an hour and now they are resting. Sand sticks to their necks and their faces are blackened from the backs of their hands where they reached up to wipe away the sweat. My grandfather's dark black hair glistens with moisture. His eyes are quiet and bright as ebony. The dirt shows less on his dark skin than on the face of Harry Dunham, his brother-in-law. But Harry's face is brown also, burned tan by years of farming and working with the horses he loves and is always trading. They each take a deep breath, tap their shovels against a root to knock off moist sand, and begin to dig again.

Suddenly the vixen bolts from the den, right between my grandfather's legs.

"Jess, there she goes!" Harry shouts. My grandfather does not move. Instead, he whistles.

The collie leaps to her feet in a half circle and runs after the fox. Her belly is so low to the ground that she plows through the leaves. Her feet leave deep marks in the leaf mold and earth.

Thousands of tiny roots which hold the soil together as fine thread holds the pattern on a piece of embroidery are exposed. She grabs once. The fox snaps and dodges. The snarls of the dog and the high voice of the fox blend. Then it is over. The dog stands shaking the limp body. The black muzzle of the fox is stained with blood. The dog tosses the fox once, then again and backs off. The fox lies there on its side, mouth wide, eyes open yet without sight.

My grandfather reaches into the den. "She's killed em all," he says.

Trapped, hearing the scrape of the shovels, ranging back and forth between the blocked hole and the smells and sounds of men, digging frantically at the rock which blocked escape (her paws are worn bloody, pads raw from the rough stone), she went crazy and killed her litter.

My grandfather reaches in and brings out the small warm bodies of the little foxes. Then he shoves head and shoulders into the hole.

"This un's not dead."

He pulls out a tiny cub. Its throat is torn, but it whines feebly as he stands up with it in his hands.

"Might as well kill it now. It'll jus grow up t' kill yer chickens again." Harry hefts the shovel.

"I'm takin' it home to Marion."

Marion Flora Dunham was my grandmother's name before she married my grandfather. Flora Marion Bowman was my mother's name and her two first names were those of her grandmother. So it went back for generations: a Flora Marion birthing a Marion Flora whose daughter would again bear a grandmother's name. Other women might lose their names in marriage, but it was not completely so for the women of my grandmother's line, women who made the family decisions more than the men did, women who married men who — though strong and sure of themselves — had a quality of gentleness and quiet about them, a way of listening to their women as if hearing an ancient matriarchal voice from a past most other men forgot. So, when she married my grandfather, a man of little education and dubious ancestry, some were surprised, but to me, looking back at it over the decades, hearing my grandfather's soft voice, it seems that it was as it should have been. There was more to it than just a wealthy landowner's daughter marrying a half-breed hired man.

My grandmother sent her husband and her brother to dig out the fox den. The chickens were disappearing. That very morning the ·prized rooster, a Rhode Island Red, was taken. She'd seen the fox's brush disappearing into the sumacs at the edge of the field across Middle Grove Road just after hearing the squawks of the hens. Jess and Harry knew where the den was. Foxes had denned at the base of that pine for as long as Dunhams—or Bowmans (whether by that anglicized name or the older Abenaki of Abowmsawain)—had been in that country. My grandfather went the half mile up the crick and found red feathers and a recently gnawed bone on the mound of brown earth. He came back to get Harry and two shovels.

I see my grandfather walking into the kitchen with the fox in his hands. I hear my grandmother's voice, no hesitation in it.

"Flora, run get my sewing basket and the biggest needle." Then, the blood of the fox staining her apron patterned with tiny blue and purple flowers (blue and purple as the violets the men's feet brushed through as they walked the bank of the crick), she sewed its torn throat.

I hear my mother's voice talking about that fox.

"It played with a ball of yarn just like a kitten. Why, even the collie got to accept it. It'd run around her like a puppy, biting her nose and nipping at her tail while she'd pretend it wasn't really a fox at all."

They kept the fox in the house and it housetrained as easily as a cat, digging a little hole in the earth and scraping dirt back over it when it did its business. Some people came to see it, but a tamed fox was not such a big thing for many people in Greenfield in those days. That was the way it was then. People would, especially those who lived back more in the hills and on the more remote farmsteads, have wild animals for pets—most often raccoons or a crow taken as a fledgling from its nest. Wild animals could live for a time among humans. The boundaries were not as clear then as now. The magic of an age when everything in the natural world was known to have a voice and when some women and men could hear those voices—if not speak and understand them—was still present. It circled at nights around the farms where there were no streetlamps to keep away the dark and the sounds of cicadas and peepers and the call of the whip-poor-will and the nighthawk were louder than the roar of machines.

The boundaries were still there, though. One day Reddy crossed over one of those boundaries and there was no going back. He was shot as he was chasing chickens at the Middlebrooks place a mile down the road. When Truman saw the collar on him he brought him back to my grandparents and my mother. My grandfather buried him

on the pine hill above Bell Brook. He did not mention to my grandmother that a new burrow had been opened near the one they dug
out. Instead, he strengthened the chicken wire around the hen house.
No fox ever got in to take one of their chickens again, though twice
weasels came and my grandfather had to shoot them by the light of
the lantern as they stood, staring, mouths still red from the throats of
a dozen hens, their bodies small and snake-sinewy and brown.

Two years ago, on my 40th birthday, I walked the old fields.
When I came to the edge of the woods which follow both sides of the
stream bank like long arms I stopped. It seemed there was motion in
the sumacs and honey locusts which are reclaiming the northeast
edge of the field, colonists for an invasion of trees. A bird flew up
suddenly, wings flapping open like a Japanese fan, and then a small
orange dog followed it out into the field. A fox, I realized. Our eyes
met and it stopped. It was less than twenty feet away but it did not
run. Instead, it sat down. Then it yawned as both dogs and foxes
yawn, opening its mouth wide and turning its head slightly as it did
so. Its eyes turned back to mine and I began to sing. Its eyes half-
closed as I sang the song which a Pueblo Indian friend taught me. I
stopped singing and it got up from its haunches, moved a few steps
closer, then sat again. It looked up at me as if to say, "Well, isn't there
more to that song?" I sang again, the sun of that autumn day on both
of our faces. Finally, I walked away, leaving it still sitting there in the
meadow. I took that meeting as a kind of affirmation.

There was no collar around the neck of my fox, yet it was, for
that one moment and forever after, as close to me as the one my
mother and grandparents kept as a pet was to them two decades
before I was born. And when I walked this spring up along Bell Brook
to the old white pine, I saw fresh earth loosened around its roots.

Carrying Children

for Carol

It is an old game
all fathers must play.
Carry me up to bed, I'm asleep.
His body relaxed to the limpness of slumber.

Thirteen now, two-thirds my size
and though you protested,
I heaved him up two flights,
knees and stairs creaking.

I know how few such times there'll be
when both of us can play this way.
Just today he supported my weight on his back,
carried me, not yet from some ruined Troy
but towards a time some men see as exile.

So I carried him, marvelling
that it was not from some hut on fire,
some shattered city, where American bullets
bought on credit are exchanged
for the bright securities of blood.

Just before I dropped him
like a lumpy sack of potatoes
on his shrinking bed,
he asked, *If you can carry me, Dad,
then couldn't you carry a lot of weight?*

Enough for now, I said.

Card Players and the Stars
above Paradox Lake

Inside the cabin up the hill,
the slap of cards and clink of ice,
the scrape of chairs, sound of city laughter
as Aces, Kings and Queens hold back the night.

From the granite arm thrust into darkness
I look up at stars, no moon to be seen.
The Milky Way, that ancient sky arc,
is a trail across heaven, shimmering.

Random thoughts of the universe,
shooting stars are signatures of light.
The warmth which whirrs close to my face
is a hunting bat, not a dark comet,
down to graze moths from the surface of the lake.

The card players' voices are one grain of sand,
the constellations, those most distant shapes
our eyes will ever know, are more familiar
than that anger which flares up from a cabin
where words are hot about a pair
and a bobbing flashlight, briefer than a meteor,
begins to descend the rough stone stair.

Last Day of the Season, Guard Tower #4

All autumn, whenever he's had the chance
with sick leave or vacation time,
he's been out in those mountains
around the prison and although even
the Assistant Cook and the Director of Education
have gotten theirs, he still has yet
to take one shot and he knows it isn't fair.
The last day of the hunting season and
a scoped ought-six is in his hand, but he's
on Tower #4, won't get a chance to get his deer.

His eyes drift the edge of the big corn field
which flows, a frozen golden sea,
right up to the edge of the old North Gate
from the woods by the abandoned quarry
down past the lonely cemetery hill
where a few men left without kin still lie,
unclaimed by all but the State.

Then, as if stepping out of a vision,
a ten-point buck walks from that edge
and stands, head down, grazing the grass
twenty yards from the wall of the prison.

He blinks his eyes, shifts the gun in his grasp,
knowing what would happen if he fired a round
of that ammunition brought up into the towers
from outside the wall, each bullet counted,
then placed in the bag at the end of the rope,
recounted at the end of a shift.

Moving slowly as a sleepwalker he shifts
the gun until the butt's at his cheek,
scopes down, so nervous he sees only darkness
until he squints and finds the focus.
The deer's grey shoulder fills the field.

He breathes again, lowers the gun,
knowing how many other men have seen that deer

standing there free, freer than prisoner or guard
can feel on this November day, comes close
to thinking poetry then, throwing it all to the wind,
clicks off the safety, squeezes the trigger.

His shots echo, cannon blasts in his ears,
echoes answered with sirens and shouts,
lock-ins and a dozen counts before he appears
next day before the Inquiry Board
where he answers, red-faced, knuckles white,
that his gun discharged when it fell over.

He knows they know — as do all the others,
employees, officers, imprisoned men —
that he shot at a deer on the very last day
of the hunting season from Guard Tower #4,
that he shot at a deer, shot his whole magazine,
that he shot at a deer and missed it, clean.

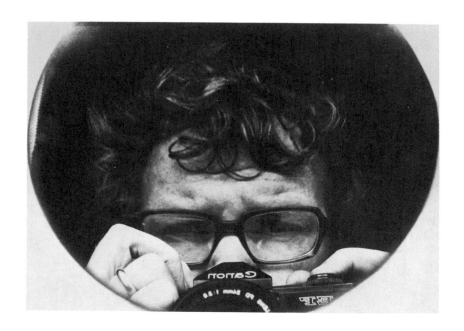

Don Byrd

Don Byrd was born April 24, 1944, in Springfield, Missouri. He moved to Albany, New York, in 1971, where he still lives with Marge and a daughter, Anne, and teaches at the State University of New York. His publications include Aesop's Garden (North Atlantic Books), Technics of Travel (Tansy Press), and a critical study, Charles Olson's Maximus (University of Illinois Press). The Great Dimestore Centennial will be published by Station Hill Press in 1986. He is in process of finishing The Poetics of Common Knowledge.

He believes that Reaganism is the death rattle of a dying culture and that, if humankind can avoid self-destruction by national rivalry and greed, the poets will seed still another beginning.

Technics of Travel

1. Spring

Turn
beyond rehearsal,
word
by word:
    forsythia in bloom

"fivesythia, sixsythia," Anne says,
untracked yellow petal urwörter,
dripping inside her song. Cheeks,
scalp at the part, sun-burnt,

and the sun has no face.
Fire, hours,
in the pine trees,
in the treacherous hills.

Her face is red:
it has no secret
it won't tell.

I have no technic
but need.

8.

The site of the second oldest settlement in the thirteen colonies,
called, at first, Fort Orange, Beverwyck, Rensselaerwyck,
Albany for ten years, then Willemstadt, before it became Albany
    again,
permanently Albany, 1674, after a feudal title of James II.

I feel tonight this place is still to be discovered.
"Crooked as an Albany Dutchman," a proverb of the English who
    prevailed.
Merchants and tradesmen are vipers whatever their nationality,
and it's usually the out-vipered who scream "crook,"
but the numbers of English were staggering. I come
from a pig-headed race, with a genius for bureaucracy,
a habit of relentless pursuit, and a language suited
to meditation wholly out of keeping with its character.

What did I mean, that it's to be discovered still?
that "to discover" is to change the world? not to settle it?

9.

I like routine, I am seldom bored, I spend days doing nothing.
If someone asks, I say I am thinking, and it's true
but that's nothing, as thinking does not change the thing thought
    about,
or if it does, it's worth than nothing: that is, I'm satisfied.

I like routine, I am seldom bored, I spend days thinking.
It changes everything. I'm making plans. Trotsky open before me:
"The historic ascent of humanity may be summarized
as a succession of victories of consciousness over blind forces."

I just went to cover Anne. I heard her coughing.
"Daddy," she said, "let's feed the cows." "We have no cows," I said,
but I had entered her dream, and now I don't know if I spoke
    truly.

"The Revolution still has no ritual, the streets are in smoke,
the masses have not yet learned the new songs."

I begin to get the point: "Okay, let's feed the cows."

11.

To Anne

The backyard is a swamp tonight. The alligator's teeth
are balloons, the cockatoos speak pig latin.
You've brought your own brand of civilization to it.

I don't doubt there's justice in this city of sand,
but the doll, her head buried, is a grim warning
against transgressions I can't seem to imagine.
Her legs reaching—given the scale—almost to the moon,
she is the Great Mother, her bulky loins open to the sky.
The small ones ranked around her are awed by her proportions
and precarious tilt. Though some go about their tasks bravely—
the dump truck driver for one is simply unaware,
Winnie-the-Pooh is as bemused as I am,
knowing neither the prayers nor the rituals,
not even certain whether it's a mystery or an accident.

12.

Gasping for breath with ritual complacency, barely able to speak,
"The air tastes good," she said. Bach organ on the radio,
and I took her nipple in my lips and ran my nose around her
    breast
in vague reply. E. Power Biggs was using my spine as a keyboard.
I was the instrument of angels, whose task it is
to glorify God day-in, day-out, some number of eternal hours a
    day.

Their labor is routine. They punch the clock,
drink too much coffee on the graveyard shift,
but they are not commodities to themselves or to God.
Here will and labor bend together in Divine Alienation.

I didn't have a thought in my head. I'd been used
and used well. I'd never been closer to God.
Before I could find a reply, she was asleep.
I wanted to say then, too late, "Give me a drink too."

photo by *William Muller*

Joe Cardillo

Joe Cardillo grew up in the Dairy Belt Region. He earned his B.A. from Siena College and his M.A. from S.U.N.Y. at Albany. He is a member of the Editorial Board for ESPRIT–A STATEWIDE MAGAZINE FOR THE HUMANITIES and coordinator of THE POETRY AND FICTION WRITERS' PROJECT. His book publications include A Legacy Of Desire (1983) and Turning Toward Morning (1984).

He has published hundreds of poems and over a dozen short stories in books and magazines around the country. In 1979, he recorded an album of Traditional American Music (for which he wrote and arranged musical and lyrical selections and performed on the dulcimer, violin, guitar, banjo, electric violin, and mandolin—instrumentation he still incorporates into many of his poetry presentations today). He has given readings and workshops throughout New York State.

Cardillo's work can best be described as reflecting both his rural upbringing and his experiences in the Middle East. "I really believe that the Middle East, especially right now, is one of the most emotionally awakened places in the world. If it taught me anything, it taught me that there really are things in life that people are willing to completely live for. And . . . that there are things in this life a human being will really die for. This is a concept a person living where I do most of the time finds difficult to understand—except for during Christmas . . . During Christmas, people are willing to die for parking spaces. The other thing it taught me was that no matter where we go in the world, people are the same. And that's true, but we are also going to find dissimilarities. Before we can even hope to begin to deal with people, we must not only recognize their human similarities, but their dissimilarities as well . . ."

"And of my country upbringing . . . It taught me that when the bone of my forearm is

flush with the limb of a tree, there is the possibility to remember what it is like to be a man; there is much respect owed a tree. And, that maybe after all is said and done, we will all have to rely on the creatures of this earth to remind us of who and what we are."

Cardillo teaches at Hudson Valley Community College and is an Assistant Professor of English and Creative Writing.

He is, now, working on a collection of poetry that is scheduled for release in the spring of '86. It will reflect a strong synthesis of East and West.

Courage

You say the
symbol
must be marked
in blood or land,
the cross, maybe,
X'd onto the souls
of men and women
who dare hold
their eyes to a
light that will
not diminish
until it has stripped
their faces to the
bone. Or radiated
their hearts to a
dead stop.

I say it is invisible.
Like the breath of
a woman passing
through the lips of
a man.

What you want is
a fast blackout.
Like the worm that
kisses the throat
of the cactus and
dies to save the
life of a stone.

Where Are We Going?

Remember
world was s[
water? How we ...
our mouths together,
tied them everywhere.
Before we tried
to crawl, our bellies
never really meant
to scrape the earth.
Before our eyes grew
lids to help us turn
our backs against
the sea, our bodies
never really knew
what it was like to
shake inside the wind.
But how, after all,
it was the wind that
carried the smell
of Judas, even then.
The first sighs of
meat and blood
forever forced into
shapes they could
never understand,
but someday pretend
themselves into
forgiving.

Annie, when I love you,
I can still taste
the salt beneath your
arms, inside your milk,
between your hairs.

Annie, last night
I dreamed a creature
still swimming miles
in the dark.
And he was laughing.

We Eat Together

We eat together
every night,
passing cups
that carry the
warmth of hands,
the smell of
different countries.

You talk of F-15's
slitting up the sky
at treetop,
of rifles your fingers
will steam on,

while the terrace
fills with the
sound of children
I imagine already
dead.
Pieces of voices
whipped around
the world
like the carrion
of a million
deja vu I could
gather in my hands
and spread across
your lips,
push inside your
nostrils and ears
until you stop
pretending
how different
we all are,
until you can taste
the sound
of your own voice.

Talking of Lebanon

. . . took 500 trucks
two months to
clean out the mess
of arms.
Illegal, all of them.
Terrorists no one
could imagine.
And all the shooting.
Cousin against cousin.
It never matters who.
How you'd laugh,
but it wasn't really
funny. 537 were
already counted dead
and maybe more.
How everyone has guns
and is afraid.
So people climb their
roofs at night,
and you can hear
them shaking,
saying something about
revenge, you say
people like us
can never understand.
But that a man could
shoot his daughter,
murder his wife
and go on living.
So people don't go
near the streets
at night because of
what could happen.
And how it doesn't
really bother you,
except for in the
morning.
When someone else is
always dead.

Abandoned

cold winds spit
pockets of

silence

everywhere

the house is

empty now

dead

she has gone

and winter

silently
piling up against
the door is

slowly freezing

me in

Faith

I loved
watching you
nurse
the squirrel
and
pour the shepherd
water you
might have had
yourself.
It was as though
a man
could learn
to square himself
off with
almost anyone
and with the
earth,
could want to
give back
a little more
than the rest
of the world
was always
taking.

Catherine Clarke

In 1948, in Saratoga Springs where my parents lived after leaving Brooklyn, I was born into a Roman Catholic, Irish American family of eight. I learned to write at Saint Clement's Grade School; school and horses occupied and gave me much of my childhood.

Eventually came studies in science at the College of Saint Rose, and some teaching; then an M.A. in philosophy at Boston University, and a cartoon strip, "Leaky River"; and then I finished an M.A. in the Writing Program at Brown University where my first chapbook of poems, Red Horse, was published by Copper Beech Press.

Teachers and friends always have helped me to see more and to find my way. In writing and in art these have included poet and scholar Herb Mason; sculptor Hugh Townley; and poets Edwin Honig and Michael Harper. Otherwise, all along, I have also kept circling the carpety pasture.

Now I live outside Saratoga, in Stillwater, uphill from Saratoga Lake and Fish Creek. I teach writing. My poems not yet written might or might not closely resemble older ones. Natural imagery still usually seems most expressive, for me, of preferred turns of thought. I will have to find, like the rest of the world, what will be natural in the coming years.

Mid-winter

Couldn't this be my day?
Then why are my arms as heavy as stone?
Half of winter has gone by
while the stars above have appeared to wait coolly.

I am eager for fortune to fall
but equally eager to dream myself one;
yet none of the fields I imagine are mine;
none of the hearts I imagine are here.

Since time will befall me, one of us lasting,
I want my days and nights to be long,
even though the vision is lonely,
as of a long road stretching before me.

Toward the New Day

If anyone asks, I will be the same,
always nearly where I began,
looking at day; then night
as if surrounded by day.

I have given up spinning aloft,
and now I belong to the cradling earth;
its bushes and woods are my coat;
its small birds and curious cows
are my daily delight.

I do not intend to work hard,
but to waste most of my time;
for the world does spin somewhere,
and I have found I love even the stones,
the trees, and the vagabond air.

On Nielson Road

On a bright day it is not a bad thing
to look back, seeing the road vanish
into a grey sky lying behind
the hill you are climbing.

Nor is it bad to hear
the brown dog beside you,
trotting soundlessly uphill,
leaving few faint white tracks
in white powder;
the whole hill vanishing forward as well
into an only slightly brighter sky.

Watching amid softly falling flakes
brings peace,
until some cold settles in
and unhumorously I think again:

I would not want to leave
this blue diamond of sky,
or brown and green cup of hills,
where I cannot see the hills,
or blue sky, or even the brown dog,
for cool white ribbons
of descending time;

that even this is only a glance
as if after a fleet run
over a shaky floor
to a windowsill promising more.

After Winter

for Margaret Clarke

I cannot imagine you going,
except without a hat
down Nielson Road
on the best of days.

You are walking slowly
past cornfields covered deeply,
so the sky is even more blue
over white, magnificent jewels.

According to Father Flynn,
angels might come to meet you.
This would be
at a point we cannot see.

Still, you and they
will be
deft breezes for me
on the brightest of days.

Coming Back

Oh it was dark where I went like a fool
falling my way to the bottom of all
those books, so strayed with wanting everything
the coming back is hard. Nothing happens,
nothing but rain at night on the slate roof
raising that green, and the water's face turns
blue on the long blue days, et cetera,
as usual, under the usual stars.

And what if I say this is all so odd?
Will kind eyes drop? Will everybody blush
for such a bad poem, hoping it's short?

I'm afraid to go down in the dark now,
but call me if wisdom comes to the door.
Wake me if love goes by like a loose horse.

Analogy for Hap

When I first worked I used
a speckled circus horse to carry children.
Cookie glided safely around a dusty ring
until she died slowly
after one distantly starred, dark night.
She didn't see us; or who knew what she saw?

Because she was kind and beautiful,
we thought she should be able to ride
quietly in night, as in a dark boat
sailing into night, then morning,
then to the shaded edge

of a bright, sweet scented field
where she could disembark,
and not only into a picture I could make
of a bright, sweet scented, buzzing field,
children, and a speckled circus horse.
And still I have found no brighter answer.

Paul Corrigan

Born in Millinocket, Maine in 1951. Earned my B.A. from the State University of New York at Binghamton (1974) and my M.A. from Brown University (1976) where I received an Academy of American Poets Award. In 1978 I was a recipient of a Creative Artists Public Service Award from the State of New York.

For several years I lived in the southern Adirondacks where I spent many enjoyable hours fishing, hunting and hiking. The North Country has figured into a number of my poems. It is nearly a dead ringer for the area in northern Maine where I grew up and I have felt comfortable writing about it. My seven years in the Adirondacks will always be a part of the body of experience that I draw from as a writer.

Currently, my wife and I reside in Norridgewock, Maine. These days I divide my time between working as a whitewater rafting guide and teaching poetry in New York State's Alternative Literary Programs in the Schools.

The Camp of the Cold River Hermit

(At the Adirondack Museum)

for Joe Bruchac

Built to hold warmth
on winter nights,
the bark roof peaks
at roughly six feet.
Above the door
hangs the thigh bone
of a bear, a talisman
against game wardens.
His table is wedged
between log walls,
his stool, a poplar stump
covered with deer leather.
Knives hang from knubs
on rafters, chipped china
lines shelves. A lamp
and snuffbox sit
above his cedar bed.

They have stolen his voice.
A button we press
brings it drifting
through the hermitage,
snared from his breath
so we may learn
what we can
of a man
keen to the flow
of water and wind.

It rises
from speakers
hidden
like the Cold River's source,
spilling only a little
of what it knows,
a brief drink
at a clear pool.

Raspberrying with My Mother

Her tin is brimming with berries
as it did when she was young
and I would pick berries beside her, paying
the price in berries for her pies.
Each July these fields supply her larder
but they are growing back to woods
and she must search among the firs
and birch that crowd the brambles out
to fill her peanut butter pail.
And so she does, quick as ever,
flicking berries into bright containers,
lightly squeezing each with thumb and finger
the way she holds her beads at mass
hoarding prayer as if it were ripe fruit
to be used later in a pie.
But I prefer to eat my pickings.
I crave the wild taste of fresh raspberries,
the soft fuzz that grazes the lips,
the tiny seeds that catch between the teeth.
Like a young bear I gorge myself
on tart gobs of tongue-staining fruit,
growing groggy on the excess
till the thought of dozing off
is more delicious than the pie
I'll get for gathering six cups.
But her sweet tooth takes her beyond this field
and she keeps seeing pies and tarts
and muffins rising in some oven,
lining some pantry shelf. She conjures them
from thin air like a mystic vision
to coax me into building up my stores.
"Are you here to pick or play
my son?" she'll say. And I admit
I share her taste for those unearthly things
like pies and shortcake or a bowl
with milk or cream and freshly gathered berries.
But I must come to some things on my own.

So when the crop is red and full
and falling off the branch, I look
no further than this berry patch
and, like some wild, woods-bred creature,
take only what I find next to my nose.

The Vet's Club

We've driven here from wars
with lunker bass, our tours
cut short by thirst, the dusk
filling our idle nets.

Locals slide in beside us,
paunches nuzzling the bar,
and whisper the lowdown on lures and bait.
Their lies mix well with beer.

One claims when cool spring rains
turn water chocolate,
his cross-eyed wabbler
takes tasty calicoes.

Another swears by rubber leeches
fished slow and zany. He winks
then slithers leech-like on his stool
while red-cheeked cronies roar.

Like bass in riled water
we all sit tight here,
chasing schnapps with beers,
our gills aglow,

the neon bar lights
catching our dying-fish stares.

At the Grave of the Unknown Riverdriver

Hellbent bravado broke the jam
that busted your skull that spring.
No known kin, you signed the payroll X
and went by Bill or Joe.
Whitewater's thrill was seasonal.
When spikes were winter-stored
the river roared through dreams.
Your flophouse room was bleak. Mice crapped
in your teacup, chewed your new cantdog.

The day the jam let go, gnarled tons
of spruce caught you mid-current, napping.
You bellyed-up downriver, blond hair aglow
in foam and they bundled you in burlap,
mouthing bits of scripture so your luck
would lie down with you here.

Now loons spin comic hymns above
your bones. Boy scouts shear new growth
that chokes you out each year
and paint your cross and white stave fence.
Men you might have known still mope
in nursing homes, arthritic remnants
of the rough-and-tumble, the river's
pounding strength a memory locked
in their old sinews, their shriveled arms.

The Boss Machine-Tender
After Losing a Son

When paper snaps in machines,
he pokes through greasy alleys, flashlight
beaming among clamoring wheels
and huge whirring belts.
He'll run himself ragged
getting sheets back on the reels,
shelving time for moments
when the clock ticks like a dream
of flawless paper. Then he smokes
his pipe in the office, and recalls
the smooth glide of his Old Town canoe.

He moves through waters
that sustained father and son
between slender, canvased ribs.
The two drift leisurely, machinery roaring
like distant white-water
inside his throbbing temples,
while somewhere back of his mind,
hidden like jagged river rock,
lies the night he shut down
machine number nine
to pull out his boy.

Old Woodpolers

Their forearm veins are thick as nylon cord.
They have calluses the size of quarters.
Their poles are sandpapered smooth,
the points honed sharp on an emery wheel
so a light poke embeds the steel
half-an-inch through pulp logs
passing on the current.

All the men are old tonight and quiet.
Stooped next to the troughs,
they arrange logs
in groups of threes and fours.
Their spare quick motions
have a fierce regularity
that never slackens.
They let the water
work for them,
never going
against the current.

George Drew

Who am I? What am I? The particulars don't matter: the ABC's of my life history. Like a poem, a man is the sum of all he is. He is the music, he is the ideas, he is the forms, he is the laws. He is the cosmos of himself. What does matter is this: as I enter my fifth decade, many years of which have been spent in the curiously dual role of being both midwife to and "mother" of the poem, I have only just realized what, for me, the poem truly is.

When I first listened to my unborn child's heartbeat what I heard was the interior melody of the seashell. That was at about three months. At seven I listened in again. This time the heart was loud and steady, proud in its announcement of a specialness—a clear arrangement already classic, wedded as it necessarily was to singleness, to the unique.

The making of poetry is like that heartbeat. At first the poem is indistinct, more a liquid pulse than a frozen note; more impulse than accomplishment. Then it happens. Clouds seem to part and there is moonlight carved of water, every wave a single syllable exploding in the ear, or along the shoreline of the tongue. There is, in an instant, clarity.

Once I said that poetry is the classical music of language; that it is the rows of black tuxedos starched and pressed. Nothing since has changed the truth of that for me. Perhaps this is because of all the empty space I suffered (as I saw it then) growing up with one foot planted firmly in the mockingbird-festooned landscape of the Mississippi delta, and the other in the flint and granite groundwork of the North. That kind of wildness seeks its opposite: the pure civility of measured feet and English-like landscapes of trope and rhyme.

But that is only half of it. There also is the wildness necessary to the clarity. As Frost so wisely saw and so shrewdly said on more than one occasion, the poem seeks after form to make itself detectable in the world, but not at the expense of wildness. In the tension is the wildness, the vital wildness without which no poem, nor no poet, defines itself. Today, as wildness disappears, and more and more of us confuse it with a spurious abandon, I have found it essential to remember, even as I listen to the heartbeat of the poem, the rush and tumble of its origins. Verandas filled with black tuxedos on a moonlit night in Mississippi are wonderful, but so is denim smeared with ashes in a cabin full of banjos in New York.

The journey to this knowledge, then, is my biography. It is who I am and what I am. It is all I wish to be.

A Short Unhappy History of Uncle Frank

Call him Cowboy. Back
when moons were gumdrops Grandma
kept in mason jars, *He's nuts!*
you'd say, not knowing what
to think about an uncle who,
on each arm like a bracelet, wore
a shopping bag, took meals alone
& worked himself into old age
at 50, crippled, short
of breath & racked
by hemorrhoids. No use
to say his lack of pedigree
protected him against the nobles
of this world: as he grew stranger,
it grew more familiar, shrinking,
like a sunset, toward its own
hot center. Now, as he

grows more familiar, it
grows ever stranger, shadows
lengthening where there's no sun,
doors warning ENTER AT YOUR OWN
RISK! Men are much like mutts:
stretched in the sun, their
shadows sometimes out ahead,
sometimes behind, legs pumping
after rabbits that they never
catch. Too late, you think
of how he had to sit
& watch as Grandma,
going yellow after Gramps
had run out with the future,
turned in like a nail & spiked
herself to death. The moon, for him,
was always yellow: think of that
& yodel to it as it founders
on the great white whale
of morning. Ishmael he wasn't.

To a Fisherman

November takes us like a hook,
but suits us well, compadre,
coming together every year,
this scraping of dry bottoms,
converging twin complexities.
Twenty years to draw us to
a common bait; but look, look
into the torrents of my eyes:
the architecture is superb. See
there, my erstwhile fisher of faith,
there swim the trout outsmarted
these twenty years, the big ones
speckled with adoration that
broke the surface, hoping to snag
your hook. And now no more deep pools,
no more the spawning run alone:
we will together face the mucus—
murdering sun, the shallows
in the terrible matrix of the bucket,
now netted in a common end.

The Drowning of Christopher French

1

He'd fallen in in the middle,
a good fifty yards from shore,
and from Whitaker's parking lot
it was a hundred yards to the lake:
across the road, along the edge
of the baseball field, and down
the service road to the beach.

So it was of course too late
from the beginning, given such
godawful cold — thirteen degrees
and an inch or two of snow
that crackled as you walked,
ice on the lake like a metal vest.

Sid showed good sense and stayed
rooted under a dying pine,
his eyes like burned-out lights
and his face a slash of white.
Above him the frozen branches popped.
Dragging a limb, I started out.

2

My Christ, it was cold out there!
I'd shucked my coat, and a stiff wind.
Crouched low, I shuffled, walked, ran,
the limb flipflopping like a broken leg.

The lake detached itself from shore,
the trees and rocks receded to a blur,
the ice began to spin. As best I could
I went a straight line to the rink.
From it I could see him thrashing,
I could hear his shouts for help,
the light cavorting about the hole
and next to him the red rubber ball.

At ten yards I could see his face.
At five I went down on my belly.
Pushing the limb ahead, I inched
to within a half foot of the edge.
My God! As if glass-blown, he was
encased in a thin skin of ice,
his hair matted against his skull
and from his forehead tiny shards
strung like lights on a Christmas tree.

I called, I offered him the limb.
He tried to grab it but, like
the webbed foot of a crippled duck,
his arm flopped this way, that.
Eyes were the only things that worked.
They were bluer than any I had seen,
transparent murals of bewilderment
and agony that hammered, hammered me.

Then something snapped. I tore
my eyes from his and looked left.
The ice! The ice was giving way!
From shore a voice broke in
and I withdrew. The cracking stopped.
Again I inched ahead, again the limb.
Too late. All I could do was watch
as he went down, the red ball bobbing
in the backwash like a fallen sun.

3

Across the ice three men approached.
As they came near, "He's gone," I said,
explaining, "Nothing anyone could do."
But one, whose face was flannel, said,
"My ass," and went down on his knees
and, like a legless man with stumps
set firmly on a dolly, shoved himself
ahead, then back each time the ice
began to crack. His name was Doyle.

I threw the limb down on the ice,
screaming at him, "You do it then!"
The others shuffled their feet,
averted eyes and counseled tolerance:
"That's how he is." I looked once more
at where the boy and I had been,
at Doyle still sliding back and forth,
at them. I started back to shore.

Pinnacle Farm

For Patricia

1

That afternoon we linked arms
and walked downslope from the house
through the shadow-labyrinth of pine
and lazed away the last moments
of sun and blue sky on the green
ground of the dead. Behind a stone,
we hid from the fat couple coming
our way on the gravelled drive
looping the graveyard like a bow,
titillated by them and the dead
into a hot huddle of arms and legs.

That evening we lay on the dark
plot of the sofa, fire clapping us
to a white completion of the afternoon,
and hid, in a patch of molten touch,
from the rectangular shadow-tongues
unrolling upslope into morning's red
departures. Bones cracked like stones.

2

Here I am dreaming again of large
locusts loose in the wheat. Downstairs,
her friend, the minister, mounts
the pulpit of my nightmare and orates
Ezekiel and his bones. Come dawn,
the North Country culls the wakeful
to a living dream ablaze with shapes.

By afternoon we're at the farm again,
the Adirondacks terracing the background
to a green epiphany, white blossoms
of wild strawberry moderating the
downslope sweep of green and uncut field,
copses of birch staking the perimeters.

All day we wander the thick underbrush
of brown boxes stored in the garage,
combing them for leftovers from
her other life. A husband and Bermuda.

Sunset. Pulsing like a dinner gong,
in the big brown bedroom ringed by books
we flare toward climax, fleshing bones
into conviction. Then it's to the field
and green applause, strawberry blossoms
wafering the bottoms of our feet.

Either You Fall in the River of Despair
or You Walk on the Water like Christ

He failed the last exam he took.
You know, the one on which you had
the parts of speech. One sentence
near the end made mention of a beach.
Evidently, that one he knew well.
Unlike the rest, it was correct.
The paragraph you were to analyze
concerned a boy who drowned when he
went through the thin ice of a lake.
From a score of fifty, he pulled three.

All I recall of him was Walker was
his name, and that he was named well.
He walked out on us many weeks ago.
He'd come a few times, then no more.
A name on a computerized roll sheet,
that's all. In fact, a very average C.
And that's an educated guess. You see,
he never handed in what was required.
And I'd not had the chance to ask
him why. Nor would have anyhow.

You say he was the friendly sort?
Good natured? And quick with a smile?
Perhaps, but that's no news to me.
For fourteen weeks he was a name;
and for eleven, for the most part
successfully avoided me. That's all.

Of course, I mourn a student's loss,
even the others', whom I didn't know.
Of course, I mourn a human loss.
Mostly, I mourn I can't mourn more.
In truth, if I feel pain it's more
like that seen smeared on a canvas,
or a page. It's more idea than fact.

As of this class, he's not turned up,
not in the lake nor on the shore.
Nor have they found the other three.
In all, they've searched for seven days.
They'll probably search seven more.
That he's not been found is no surprise.
What is is how the theories multiply.
Could they have drifted out? Could they
have struck out boldly, gotten lost
and fallen overboard too far from shore?

Who cares? The only thing for sure
is he is absent, probably for good.
Pure logic leads us straight to that.
All we've left is the boat where it
was found upended near the shore,
some foodstuff, oars, and a guitar
up to its neck in thick, green reeds.
A frisbee floating lonely as a moon.
Now open your books. Page fifty-three.

Jeanne Finley

I was born in the Adirondacks, grew up in Western New York, returned to the mountains, moved east to Massachusetts, came back once again to the mountains, and have lived in the Capital District for the past 13 years. I work as Assistant to the Directors of the New York State Writers Institute in Albany; I am also working simultaneously on a collection of short stories called Acts of Intimacy, *on a novel called* Children of Darkness, *and on editing a collection of poems,* The Powers That Be. *I find an inevitable crossover between the forms, which extends and redefines the bounds of each; the same is true, I think, for my "inner" and "outer" lives. Helping to administer literary programs, a very public undertaking, and writing, for me an intensely private one, compel and complement each other, are parts of a larger process. And so my written people and situations are also both public and private, actual and imaginary. I like to ground them in reality and then shamelessly lie about them. Sometimes the lie comes first; then the reality becomes shameless. To allow the fantastic into a commonplace situation, or to make a myth "everydayable", is what interests me most: those trans-formations where boundaries are chosen instead of resisted, when public and private knowledges can be elegantly manipulated into a world summoned on its own power. A world, a life, earning its right to exist.*

For me and for my people, "place" is a form to be chosen, explored, trans-formed. Maybe we're gypsies at heart; maybe we're exiles who can't remember where home is. I write about flux, loss, ghosts, impermanence — transits — and I write about family, tribes, recurrences, things that are graven in stone: boundaries. I find no duality in that.

Widow

for my mother

I wash the windows of their photographs,
sleep on my side of the bed,
play for all the village weddings
as if each one was my own. I teach the children
reading, adding; marking each small desk
with a nametag at the start of each September
I lose them all in June. My friends
remarry, die or move away but there are some
who phone or look me up
whenever they're in town . . . the mountains are so beautiful
in fall but in the winter
driving is a problem, there's a joke
folks crack up here, they say there are
two seasons only — July-and-August,
and the winter. When my daughter
was a little girl, before we moved
we lived in town, Al had the station and we'd watch
the cars packed full of summer people
swarming in Memorial Day; and three months later
to the Labor Day, out they'd drive, like lemmings.
I remember walking through the town
and seeing almost nobody. It was kind of sad
to see the litter that they'd left. I wasn't
driving then.

I hear this winter's
supposed to be a hard one.
The year turns over, New Year's already,
and it's funny how I see
my only child as snowprints
in my sleep, she never was
real happy here, they resented her when we moved back
because she was the new kid-which is crazy,

she was born here, and my mother
never wanting me to leave, wanting us
to stay near her, she would tell me over and over
I'd lose the baby way up there with no
doctor to come, or have it in the car, toward the end
we didn't know how sick she was, it must have been
that, she wasn't crazy, making apple pies
instead of pork for dinner, saying as she kneaded
don't pound it, see, just slip it
gently through your fingers
as though I was a little girl and hadn't ever
made a crust before;
and my sisters leaving home in winter
in a rush of love and fortune, one was quite
a singer, successful in New York
before she gave it up to marry Butts,
she's a widow too and when we get together
we do such crazy things and stay up way too late;
the other is an Army wife, lived all around
the world, they finally settled
in Virginia in a gorgeous house, I see them
once a year sometimes and my second nephew's
wedding—he's my godson—was so lovely. The babies
that I lost would be thirty, maybe more. Just yesterday

I had them clear away the snow
from the driveway, they plowed me in again,
I couldn't get out otherwise. I visit Jeannie
every long vacation, sometimes take
a longer weekend than I should, but what's the harm,
you only live once, right? and we always
have a good time and I always learn so much. I miss her
more than I should, those poems always
make me cry, I just can't help it. They want me
to retire and I want to know
from what? Al's been dead
six years and I still don't understand
why I ordered, on that gravestone,
my name and birthday next to his,

why I wake up in the mornings — late as usual —
and sometimes don't know where I am,
why my life keeps turning over
like a tire in the snow, spinning deep
into the mud, rocking back and forth, mother that I am,
patiently reshifting, trying to catch hold.

Haze

Waterfog. Here, south,
the Hudson breathes visibly
behind us, the air

unbreatheable. Skin of the eye:
valleys and columbine
purple in refracted light

as if the lens of landscape
that is everything we know
has itself filmed and thickened

in the heat. I'm thirty. We can't
swim or squint beyond
the shapes whose edges

fur in this ghost of haze that roils
downriver from the north,
the mountains I was born to,

my father's grave, my mother's
daily wait and half my life
glazed over in that place

where a white lid
closes
on everything I knew.

The Wandering Jew

*Outside Syracuse on the New York State Thruway, many travelers have
reported picking up a hitchhiker dressed in a long white robe and sandals
who disappears from the car after a few miles.*

You will always be alone.
Thumb and fingers
stretched like a menorah, you will see him
waving his whole hand slowly
in a benediction, a mandala.
He will have no rucksack, the last exit
twenty miles ago, the hills
tense and lush with summer; if you
stop, he will smile a smile of Leonardo's
shadowed at the corners, blur so slightly
as a fresco thick with pigment, you will
rub your eyes impatiently
(hypnosis of the sloping
stripe, the endless curve through
still another rotund valley) you will
turn to ask   *how far up the line?*

and he will be gone.

After, you will swear you saw
a fresh impression on the seat,
though you will tell no one,
and smelled a scent of perfumed oil,
though this would be impossible. And yet
his face comes back to you
(though you did not clearly see his face)
in dreams heavy with chiaroscuro,
in deep ponds in autumn, leaves fluttering and drowning
in a thousand years of hapless wings,
in half-remembered flashbacks
that paste to candle flames or rise up
grey in dark museums. And though
you formulate a list of questions

you will not see him again,
the road will wind through foothills like the catacombs,
you will always be alone.

Entering the Forest

for K.H., crushed in a logging accident

You are dead, Kenny,
your heels in the air
underground, making
roots. I see you on the school bus
saving me a seat, you're thirteen
and we are seers together.
I was the new kid then and you
were my mountain guide and escort, you knew
trees and birds and logging trails,
you knew seasons and soils, gossip,
weather, survival, all the teachers
and every backwoods tale ever cooked up
plus some of your own. I sat with you
every morning and every morning
you looked up from your book,
finger to your lips, pointed at the first light
over Third Lake, then talked me all the way to school
on the sound of a loon, owls' wings,
why I shouldn't worry at the snubs and silences,
as we rode
hands of pines against the sky
coming green out of the darkness.

We were improbable
on lunch hour downtown, you were 5'3"
and I was seventeen, in your hiking boots
you steered me across the snow-drifted street,
you city girls fall down in all the ruts,
in my hippie beads and fishnets
I sneaked a drink behind Jake's,
you watched for my father, we walked
south on 28 as far as we could
before the seventh period bell.

We never looked back, we were
always late, our fathers
chuckled over us and the town
made bad jokes, your brother
took me aside, said he couldn't figure
why I talked to you, a punk kid
with his nose in books, how he,
older and taller, would rather take me parking . . .

Kenny, it seemed
to always snow, it was
snow that scared me numb, having to survive
on what I'd stored. Those nights
I'd bury my face in the bathroom mirror,
powdered, plucked, already drunk,
eat silent dinner with my parents and the fishbone snow
in my hair, in my throat. My father said
be home early, not with those hoods
my mother said *eat, you're so thin*
but I said nothing,
drank all the way to the Woodgate Bar
and the snow spread slowly through me;
waiting, I'd call you, just to say hello,
just to hear your voice, find out
what kind of tracks I'd seen in the driveway
or whether it would snow again tomorrow.
Waiting for the friend of a friend,
always a lumberjack, blonde moustache
caked with snow; sometimes
we used the cabin behind Foley's
if the snow wasn't drifted high,
lit a fire, Canadian Club and the radio
tuned to Boonville static, if it was clear
Albany or even Montreal, switching back and forth,
whatever we could get. I never got stuck,
he was never local, you
were my innocence as I drove back
to the dark house on the mountain,
snow pasting itself like tongues
to the frozen chrome.

Kenny, my life's been the road out of town.
I've had summers, other winters,
my father's been gone for years.
I don't see my mother much
but today she phoned, told me you are dead
and I realize
I never saw you seventeen, never saw you
enter the forest, cut a path
with scholarships and goodbyes;
never heard from you at Cornell,
never saw you come back in the middle of the term,
quiet, strangely old, get married
to a local girl, begin to drink,
work for the State as a lumberjack —

when I dream of you, we are
walking 28 blindfolded and you are
holding my hand. Even now
there are some things
I cannot see, things I will not see;
even things, Kenny-tree, that neither of us saw
in our separate forests where we grow now,
your life one ring of a sapling somewhere,
mine an ax swinging wildly in the dark:
whether I can find the trail alone,
whether you made a mistake and cut too deep,
whether you heard the crack and ignored it,
whether you ran, or tried to,
whether it was the snow that finally dulled you,
whether you smiled at the light
as the forest finally broke you,
whether it was pine or oak,
whether you are
box, or beech, or mountain ash.

The Mothers and the Fathers

You will never meet them, except as metaphor.

They are locusts singing to each other
when the moon spills into the trees;
always in pairs, they are cedars
stretching their branches to you
from the edge of the road you are travelling.
On the beach
they are the stones you carry home,
chipping into sand, trailing your steps,
or mussel shells that open with the tide. You
are the membrane that joins them. They
are the limestone of years.

Faceless,
they are eyes:
in your headlights,
of your children,
behind the eyes of your mother and father.
You have always seen them
since you can remember seeing, and before —
before you knew the name that created you,
before you dreamed, or remembered —
in the water of your body,
then in the white sea that became your mother
when your body was no longer enough.
Later, you sometimes have photographs
pulled from your father's deepest drawer
but those faces are not who they are,
nor are the long German names
which mottle your tongue with consonants,
nor is the arc of your features,
that ghost in the mirror, when your mother
holds your face in her hands
and dies.

No. They are the language you speak
in the knock of your heart
on the limestone door of ribs,
in the vowels of your blood, in the breath
from the delta of cells.
You are the link of their dreams,
the circle of their bodies.
You live like a hoop,
rolling in their arms.

photo by Jack L. Goodman, Jr.

Jim Flosdorf

Jim Flosdorf was born in Philadelphia and grew up in Pennsylvania, spending many of his early summers in the Pocono Mountains. He has been a resident of Troy for seventeen years and teaches literature and creative writing at Russell Sage College. He has been active in neighborhood issues as president of his neighborhood association and by serving on the boards of other community service organizations. He is quite interested in Troy history and in efforts to preserve the historical and architectural heritage of the city. For twenty-five years he has been a summer resident of Lake Temagami in northern Ontario where he has spoken out for environmental issues and also pursued an active interest in canoe-tripping and photography. He is a member of the Hudson Valley Writers' Guild and an editor of Groundswell. His poems have appeared in Song, Blueline, Outpost, Minority Voices, Wind Chimes, and other publications. A book of his poetry, Temagami, was published in May, 1985 by Penumbra Press in Moonbeam, Ont.

*****

My grandfather was a preacher. One of my great uncles was a landscape painter, and another was the engineer who built the steps in the Rhinefall. Possibly these ancestral figures have had some influence on my writing and the way I see things. I wrote the proverbial first poem at the appropriate age of seven. It was titled "Spring," rhymed, and I think it is now long-lost. I don't believe I wrote another poem for about eighteen years, when I began writing sonnets because I had assigned students in a class in renaissance literature to try their hand at it, and I thought I had better try also. I wrote about a hundred before I finally gave up, discouraged and probably burnt-out by the form. It was some time before I began writing again, but by then I had shaken off the rigid constraints of formal poetry.

I find myself interested in expressing feelings about continuity, our closeness to the natural world, the kinship of creatures, our mutual interdependence and interweaving. This is likely to appear not only in my nature poems and poems of the north, but also in city poems and "civilized" poems, for I believe we have a responsibility to the community in which we live, and this should be fulfilled by active service in our neighborhood as well as in our writing if we are writers. Writing for me is also an exploration of the psyche, the recording events and scenery around me, and the evocation of fantasy. I would find it difficult to name contemporary poets who influence me; I think I hear many voices, and the problem is to sort out my own in the midst of the cacophony. I would say I am equally influenced by music however, by Paul Winter, and particularly the school of minimalism: such musicians as Steve Reich, Brian Eno, Dueter, Jarre, and Kitaro. Then too I find considerable influence coming from painters, Dali, Hopper, Wyeth, the Hudson River Painters and the Group of Seven, to suggest a few, also the art of the Pacific Northwest Coast Indians, and Inuit carving, which I enjoy collecting. I am currently working on a group of Troy poems and also a group of poems inspired by some of the Wiskedjak legends of the Ojibwa.

Cement-Man

Cement-man weighs down the back
of his boat when he passes —
the motor groans and casts a huge
rooster-tail behind the gray-steel hauler.

Cement-man spends his holidays
lugging sand, gravel, and mix,
stirring, pouring, shoveling,
smoothing, and patty-patting.

Cement-man is building a cement patio
at the back of his cottage
because his charcoal grill tips
on the old precambrian shield.

Cement-man built a cement dock
with solid steps leading to water
thus avoiding the mess of rocks
old logs, sphagnum moss, and laurel.

Cement-man likes his world concrete,
then he can feel it, and he knows it's his.

Behind the Wheel

This old barn alone in the field of hay,
with its gray, creased boards, leans
against the nails, against the sun.
Your feet, shade-struck, crush pungent mint
where grass crowds out post and threshold,
and the door hangs on one dark hinge.

You enter through the slit gingerly,
assailed by the musty, minty smell
of damp earth, darkness, and old grease—
these ancient autos always smell like this.
You open the car door; it bends and shrieks;
moldy upholstery, old wood trim, rusty metal,
all smell together, sour and bitter like sounds of
La Salle, Packard, Pierce Arrow, Terraplane—
dried ferns and stems in crystal, petals long-fallen.

Sit behind the wheel; you feel coil springs,
the crackling leather seat. Now try the switches,
wind the clock and set the hands,
shift the spark, throttle, push the clutch;
it crunches under foot; hit the brake.
Push, and the door gives grudgingly, groans,
a rusty runningboard may drop your feet to dirt.

Light glimmers through cracks and knot holes,
breaks in the roof, shingles gone;
swallows nest on the beams, with bats.
Become accustomed to the smell of age,
of rust and grease and ancient horse-hair,
your eyes will read the faded label on the radiator,
see through darkened glass a yellow disk,
on windows prints of hands, of noses, foreheads,
staring back where you reflect.

Slipping out again, into the brilliance,
is a kind of death.

Mel

On a balmy early-spring day
he set out across the ice
by skidoo, speeding
on the white surface
skis humming over snow bumps
and pressure-ridges, spraying
through slush at thirty miles an hour
racing around the bend of the island—
he never saw till too late—
ice feathering to dark hole,
going so fast he and machine
leaped from crackling edge
into the middle of night with spray
like a trout rising on a summer's day—

but the water took him gently,
tugging, filling the arms and legs
of his suit, slowing his flailing,
slowing his frantic hands at the ice-edge,
slowing the head, bloody, butting the glass-thin
ice searching for strength, slowing
the racing heart, slowing the flow of air
to the fainting lungs, as
slowly he gives in,
slowly drifts
downward,
like the feather of a gull,
and rests at the bottom,
finally.

Taurus

Her bony back is pointed
and spare. I ride
surprised the way the bones
dig into my bones,
legs around the barrel
of her stony ribs.

Two thin cows scrounge
the rocks and weeds.
We three in the old orchard —
one to hold feet and boost,
one to steer the somnolent
beast, and I astride.

The boy who knows, goes behind
and cranks to make her start.
She sets off, a rough jog,
I bouncing, bone against bone,
for the closest apple tree,
barren and old, to scrape me off.

Under its long, bony arms
I fall on the rockfilled slope.
The hands that squeeze the milk,
tired from working on the road,
will find it sour, tonight.
But we don't care.

Canoe Makers

Quickly, deftly out of the steam chest
a rib extracted,
and with a hasty grace
they bend the supple wood
over the mold and tack it down,
over and over, growing skeleton,
nailing it to backbone
in the old way.

Muscle and tissue planks lift off the mold
like a dragonfly slipping from its crysalis,
a skin grows, breathes
again. As it swims among brother
pike and bass, cedar and ash,
they nod to each other,
exchange greetings.

Osprey

for Doris Allen

I tell you today of the osprey
that scared the duck in its dive,
how at the sound I twisted to see
a great hawk rise from the water
and balance, like a ballerina on one toe,
at the top of a slender spruce,
and dive, swoop, and perch again,
wide wings adjusting a tenuous
equilibrium with each bending tree tip

and you tell me of the day you fished
a secret bay,
three bass in the bottom of the boat
when the great bird hovered and dove
and stopped just over your head,
rose, hovered, and dove again,
the fearful attraction-repulsion,
a flurry of white feathers,
bandit-masked face, sharp black eyes,
and black hair, the silver fish,
outstretched claws—
everything stops,
hovering
in a wingbeat

until breath returns.

Eugene K. Garber

A Professor of English at the State University of New York at Albany since 1977, Eugene K. Garber was born in Birmingham, Alabama. With a Ph.D. in English and Creative Writing from the University of Iowa, he has been the Director of the Capital District Writing Project (a site of the National Writing Project) since 1978. His honors include a National Endowment for the Arts Fellowship for 1978–79 and the 1980 AWP Short Fiction Award for his collection of stories, Metaphysical Tales, *which was published in 1981 by the University of Missouri. He describes himself as "an avid fly fisherman, as long as everybody understands that avidity and effectiveness are more or less unrelated in this case."*

The Bird Watchers

They lived in a small house just back from the road on the west
shore of the island. When I first ferried down from town, it was as
though they had erected a great canopy of repose or carved it from
some secret bay of silence and set it invisibly over their house. On the
day of that first visit I discovered its exact dimensions. In the back
and along the sides of the lot it pushed boldly against the edge of the
dark wood. In the front it converged gently just beyond the road,
ending at the base of a huge dying fir that clung on the talus of the
steep declivity that fronted the tidal flats. It was therefore roughly the
shape of an egg, and more than house high, for the wind curled above
the chimney without chilling us.

We made daring excursions—down a set of rickety old steps to the
flats to contest gulls for clams, out into the forest to a damp hollow
where elephant cabbage waved its rank fronds and tiny seedlings
sprouted on the mossy carcasses of feeder timber. They watched me
enter and exit and enter again the protected zone. They saw that I
discovered it but we did not speak of it. We shared my discovery of
the transparent grot silently.

And so, before dinner, though we had martinis and I wore a
glistening eye and though the old cat sat in my lap like a warm
messenger from their hearts, the ovum was not to be spoken of
directly. We must skirt. What were their plans, I asked. They wanted
to share, with the right kind, of course. They were constructing a
bird-feeder. She shooed the cat and he took me to see a table in
progress—a roof, a water basin, some troughs—I made out the general
outlines.

Later, over brandy, hot and bursting with incipient love, I made a
silly speech. I would be their bird man, flying from the frozen North,
from my broken marriage and childless house to their hospitable
feeder, if they would let me. "Icarian, but inaspirant of the sun," I said
pedantically, "low-flying, safely arriving." Of course they wanted me,
she said, showing beautiful teeth, slightly gapped, emblem of the
erotic carnivore. But I did not covet her. I swear it. I thought too
fondly of her delicious teeth in his soft flesh, for he was the soft one,
wide-bosomed, downy, with gray eyes that tempered the most tumul-
tuous sky. "I will fly down," I said. "Bell the cat."

And then I practiced a delicious abstinence, an aroused and
tantric celibacy, coitus semper incipiens, the source, the mad French-
man says, from Persia through the eastern sea to the Albigensians, of

all courtly loves and cults of the rose. It made me gay, passing the phone, touching it, not dialing, for a week and a second week. Then finally, lying in bed in a long concessive passion, I rang the number and watched the signal run under the sea along the deep cable woven with the images of fishes and the shadows of diving birds. Her voice came back lilting, close, as though it had been waiting just outside my window, hovering on the wind.

On the way down, the ferry was beaten brutally by the sea. Gulls screamed and wheeled brokenly. Islands heaved in the wake like animations of geologic evolutions, mountains aborning. My eyes swam and my stomach rolled. And so I arrived that Sunday in a dark mood. That, I assumed, accounted for my imagining a difference in the ambiance of the zone. It seemed slightly disturbed, from within. And indeed there was a great flutter around the feeder in the back — robins, sparrows, ravens, grosbeaks, and others I cannot name.

The main exhibit of that evening was their collection of bird skulls, which had not yet been unpacked on my first visit. They are yellow, you know, like old ivory, and delicately seamed, as though some fine craftsman had assembled them from carven parts. The nostrils are astonishingly wide, as though they drank great quantities of the wind. And there are deep sockets, too, for big bright eyes. My hostess might herself have been the master craftsman, so knowingly she handled each skull, cradling the fine jaw gently in her palm, avoiding the brittle slope of the skull at the base, a thinness among the small ones even to translucency. She had them displayed on a long shelf covered with linen as blanched and beautifully embroidered as a Christmas altar cloth. The sheen of the raised thread lured the eye into a vinous and flowered labyrinth and then lost it. She had made the cloth to set off and deepen the burnished ebur of the skulls.

Those bones affected me adversely. A joy to my ornithological friends, they were in my eyes more necrotic than beautiful, their fleshless pallor too distinct from the quick dart and eyebright of their recent lives. I turned away. The cat by the fire made a cavernous yawn with bright teeth and presently jumped up into my lap. My hostess told the memorable story of the owl skull, one of the largest and most interestingly configured of the collection.

Her husband was walking in a snowy wood at midnight under a gibbous moon. It was misty, she said, and warm, late in a long winter. The bare branches of the alders made a complex calligraphy against the sky, but the man was not inclined to read its mysteries. He walked slowly, in peace. And then suddenly he was aware of something descending on him. There was scarcely a sharp enough light for a penumbra of wings. But there must have been some mild shadowing of the moon, for he was certain that his first awareness was not of the noise. That came later—the deep plummeting of the great body, pierced by the mounting reedy scream of claws rending the air. The owl, with its faulty eyes, was stooping on him as though he were a small creature darting in the snow. The man crouched and dodged instinctively, but the owl struck his shoulder, and they tumbled together into the snow. The man lay senseless for some moments. When he came to he was frightened for his life, because it seemed to him that the woods and the sky had set upon him some dark avenger. For what crime? That he disturbed their peace with his light footfall? That he had failed to read their message in the shifting calligraphy of the bare trees? He stood up. His hat was gone, his head bare to the sky. The darkening moon seemed to whirl in a high cosmic dust. Beside him on the snow, happily, was a wide object. He lifted it, unfolded it. It was warm. He raised it over his naked head like a mantle, like a shield. He walked all atremor through the snow to his house. There the wife started back; then she laughed to see him playing bird man. Then she took the bird and measured its great wings and touched its cooling breast and slipped her finger amongst its curling claws, which made a little cage.

But all the way home on the ferry I could not make myself believe that she had told the story true. It seemed to me that the great bird had torn open the man's breast and eaten out heart and liver. And when she had taken from the man his mantle of bird, she had plucked his breast, sucked his blood, bleached his bones, and preserved his skull on linen. Though he had sat beside me at the table and our faces had flushed with brandy, I could not hear his heart. I listened. The downy breast was as silent as the moon-filled wood. Only the hot old cat roared in my lap like a tiny furnace. Too much liquor, I said to myself, compounded with loss of mate and child, with a wild March sea and a misted moon. But I could not sway my heart with reason. I swore I would never return to the island.

I returned. In fact, in the weeks to come I was a regular Sunday guest. The skull collection grew apace. The cat, fed progressively less, soon recovered her ancient wile and made swift depredations on the feeder, which was always kept in good supply of water, mush, and seeds. And there were two other predators. As April advanced and the feeder swarmed, a great gray kestrel began to lurk in the back woods. He was wary, but occasionally they saw him float out above the trees on a high wind, spot his prey, a sparrow perhaps, stoop and strike. The burst of feathers, he told me, was like the flak in the old war movies — a little thump, a pleasant puff which broke up instantly into a gentle gauzy shower.

The third collector of skulls was an old eagle that took station in the high fir beyond the road. In the telescope he seemed to me lazy and stupid, potentially unproductive. He seemed to hang onto his high perch precariously. His eyes rolled shut and popped open comically like a foolish drunk pretending percipience. Occasionally his beak would open inconclusively as though he were maundering in the wind the distant triumphs of his youth. He hunched, ruffled, and shifted uneasily, stiff, probably arthritic. Then one day I saw him stoop. His golden eye lighted suddenly, his legs straightened, he wheeled out quickly and fell like a bolt on a gull laboring up from the mudflats with a fish. He ate selectively — the fish, the heart of the bird — brought back to his perch an indelicate string of entrail, mouthed it momentarily, then dropped it indifferently. The great eye rolled shut.

We did not need a gull skull, so that carcass was left for the tide to sweep. Otherwise we were assiduous, combing the high grass and the near woods for the remains of the kestrel's kills, searching the face of the cliff and the flats below the eagle regularly, and, of course, frequently checking the garage, where the cat ate her game. Perhaps one skull in twenty represented a new species suitable for the collection. These the wife picked clean, then hung them on the sun porch out of reach of ants and cat, sprinkled with a compound that helped hold the drying bones together.

Why was I here after I had sworn never to return? In town I was utterly lonely, as lonely as death. But death here on the island had an excitement, a savor, a collector's avidity. And do not forget the arching invisible egg that protected us. I could still feel it as I entered, a sweet membrane. And though destruction too had entered, it needn't be feared, for she was the queen of this magic zone and our protectoress — mine, his, the cat's — as long as we were faithful and serviceable. Her beauty shone on us brighter and brighter — her lovely teeth, her lucid flesh, her flashing fingers so nimble with needle and pick. The roses in her cheeks deepened under the climbing spring sun. Her hair, even in the stillness of the house, rose in a breezy excitement like the crest of a cockatoo. And he also was a great part of my fascination. His softness and his abstraction approached an absolute degree. I would find him sitting in the sun on the porch. Above him the drying heads turned lazily in an imperceptible breeze. From his hand curled the smoke of a forgotten cigarette. His eyes, like moons risen in daylight, were pallorous and peaceful. I began to believe that the stroke of the great owl, which I had thought so terrible, was in reality a gift of grace, a slow emptying of the heart, which his wife had nurtured carefully ever since. Inside, he would be as fair as her linen, as blanched. By this gracious bleeding his life grew infinitesimal, and we would scarcely notice when he slipped finally into the giant peace of that great owl-shadowed nightwood.

I, too, began to feel somnolent and blessed in her beauty. I conceived that it was not necessary to receive a midnight mortal wound like his, that it was sufficient to submit one's breast to the stooping of her sharp beauty. Better perhaps. For my going forth, I was sure, would not be into a cold forest, but into the great warm grot or egg of her heart. I thought of the golden egg that Love laid in Night, tiny chick of creation or little world worm coiled in the vivid warmth. Not to death I, but to the very beginning of life.

This was our progression, until one Sunday in late May I arrived to find the shell damaged, perhaps irreparably. I knew the moment I stopped my car on the road and entered the zone that there had been some terrible invasion. I felt it like a brokenness in the air, a bleeding of the harmonious peace of the house. She greeted me at the door, worn but determined.

"What happened?"

"The eagle struck."

The cat had seen a bird fall, broken and bleeding. She had pounced, unwary of the shadow of great wings coursing the grass. I understood the cat's lack of caution. That yard was her private game preserve. How could she fear that either kestrel or eagle, always before so careful to hunt beyond the protected zone, would ever even in hottest pursuit violate the house? But the eagle struck the cat, broke its spine and left it writhing in a rush of blood. The man ran out with a stick and beat the bird. In a rage the bird lashed the man, then flew up, entangled itself in the apple tree like a broken kite, and dropped dead. The man lay beside the dying cat, blind, stricken a second time by the fury of the skies. He had not spoken since. She took me to his bed. We whispered his name. But the mouth below the bandaged eyes did not move. Neither did the hands, which lay on his chest awkwardly splayed, like broken wings.

He will never move, although the house resounds with the clash of our flesh. I took her first in the high grass at the edge of the woods in hot June. She was virginal of course. The pain we shared was almost unbearable. She stitched my back and neck with her nails until my cries echoed in the trees. Sometimes even now she resists fiercely and tears my flesh. He pretends not to hear. Once I crept into the room and whispered in his ear, "Your wife's flesh, which you never tasted, is sweet." He did not flinch, not a flicker of wayward nerve. Perhaps he is a saint. Perhaps he is already dead. His flesh is shrinking to the bone. His breath scarcely moves a feather. I think of the painting in which the death's-head, the memento mori seems more alive than St. Jerome.

The harmonious membrane is all but gone. Only here and there at the edge of the woods can you feel its tattered presence, a shredded melody more felt than heard. I have ceased willing its destruction. I have come to stay, to possess her, house, all. I have broken her translucent flesh, bruised the delicate veining, and torn that golden hair in my teeth. I have thrown two wild tantrums and I threaten others. In one I smashed the skull collection and raked it to the floor like so much rubble. "Life!" I cried, "Life!" as I battered the bones. My hand bled on the fair cloth. Since then I insist we eat upon it. I have painted it motley with the spillings of wine and meat.

In my other tantrum I reduced the feeder to sticks and splinters. Now the birds dart again from bush to tree, wary of hawks. I walk in the back with my bag broadcasting seeds like a drunken sower. "Eat, birds! Eat, earth!" I cry. "Life, Life!" I cry. The golden egg that Love laid in Night is burst. The world worm has slithered loose. The urchick has flown, and others a million billion times since. "Life!" I cry. We live in a grand chaos of blood.

Alice Gilborn

Since 1979 Alice Wolf Gilborn has been editor and publisher of Blueline, a semiannual magazine featuring writing about the Adirondacks and other similar areas. She was born in Denver when mountains were more visible than buildings, and during her college years in Massachusetts often visited AuSable Forks with a friend who lived there because it was too far and too expensive to travel back to Colorado. She and her family moved to Blue Mountain Lake in 1972. "It was inevitable," she says. "I already considered the Adirondacks my second home."

Gilborn received a BA in English from Wellesley College in 1958 and in 1968 an MA from the University of Delaware in English and American literature. She has taught courses in writing and literature for North Country Community College, and her articles and poetry have appeared in Adirondack Life, The New York Times, The Greenfield Review and other magazines. Her book about her mother's collection of animals in Colorado, What Do You Do With a Kinkajou?, was published by Lippincott in 1976. As associate editor at the Adirondack Museum in Blue Mountain Lake, she has helped edit numerous books, catalogs and monographs and has coauthored a book, Museum of the Adirondacks, with director Craig Gilborn. Recently she completed editorial work on a major biography and checklist of the paintings of 19th century artist Arthur Fitzwilliam Tait published by Kennedy Galleries and the University of Delaware Press the fall of 1985.

Out of the Blue

They come out of the blue, two at a time, slicing the bright air in unison, so sudden and close that we stand stunned in the shattered calm of our afternoon as if a giant locomotive had just roared across the horizon. They come from bases outside the Blue Line, rockets on their wings, prong-nosed, twin tailed, A–10 attack planes slow for jets, built to sweep under enemy radar and deliver their lethal message to earth. The Adirondacks are their training ground, their mythical war zone. No matter how many times they come they transfix us with their beauty and power, but they leave behind a momentary sense of menace. If we had been lulled before by the quiet harmony of lakes, mountains and forests on a windless day, our peace is gone and the air now hums with dissonance.

In his book *The Machine in the Garden* (1964), Leo Marx explores in depth the intrusion of an alien technology into the realm of nature, or more exactly, man's ideal of nature. Marx begins with an example from Hawthorne's notebooks. Hawthorne has retreated to a hollow in the woods for the purpose of recording in minute detail the natural phenomena around him. In the midst of his close observations of leaves, twigs, the play of light and so forth, he is startled by the sharp whistle of a locomotive, immediately reminding him of the heat and bustle of cities, an intrusion of the commercial world and its machines into his solitude. His mood changes from one close to euphoria to melancholy. Nineteenth century writers and artists often used the railroad as a metaphor for progress, an emblem of power. Opposing them were those who viewed the "Iron Horse" with fear and skepticism. Hawthorne and others, including Emerson and Thoreau, paid tribute to man's technological advancement, but they also saw it as a danger, an invasion of privacy and the natural, if idealized, order of things. In his story, "The Celestial Railroad," Hawthorne's train never gets beyond purgatory.

The Adirondacks in the latter part of the 19th century sported their own railroads which helped open up the region and encouraged the growth of industries such as mining and logging. Entrepreneur William West Durant, anticipating great recreational development, built steamboat and rail lines in the central Adirondacks and made plans for extensions that would link widely scattered towns and villages by encompassing thousands of miles of wilderness. Durant's scheme failed, but progress had made its inroads. At the end of the century, however, with the establishment of the Forest Preserve by the state of New York in 1885, a counterforce emerged: the recognition of wilderness as a commodity in itself which must be protected by law from future exploitation. A provision in the Constitution of 1894 proclaimed state-owned lands throughout the Adirondacks to be held "Forever Wild."

A century later parts of the Adirondack Park as it is known today are still forever wild, but they bear the scars of man's intrusions. Signs of this technology are everywhere: automobiles rip across mountain highways, snowmobiles spin through woods on a web of trails, seaplanes drop hunters and fishermen into hidden lakes and ponds. Even in the core of the Adirondacks clouds filled with chemical particles from midwest factories rain acid on the water and the land.

Yet people continue to come here, drawn by their dreams of wilderness, not to exploit it but to find some necessary link between the natural world and themselves. Some want recreation in all senses of the word; others want to test themselves in the wild; still others are driven by the age old need to withdraw from the complexities of society and return to a simpler, Arcadian way of life. Paradoxically, the less spoiled a scenic area is, the more people wish to retreat to it, thereby diminishing its uniqueness. The Adirondacks has its share of escapees from New York City and other civilized centers espousing the same pastoral ideals that inspired the poet Virgil centuries ago.

Living in a region whose value is determined by how much of its wilderness is preserved, we are especially aware of the dichotomy between the primitive virtues of the past and the technological achievements of the present. To what degree are the two compatible? We drive our cars to trailheads and ride neoprene rafts down wild rivers. The French aviator Antoine de Saint Exupéry believed that the machine, the airplane in particular, would eventually unite all mankind by annihilating time and space. For him, the airplane was a means to an end, a mechanical tool in the service of humanity's spiritual quest to understand one another and join together for the common weal. As for the natural world, "the machine does not isolate man from the great problems of nature, but plunges him more deeply into them," wrote Saint Exupéry in the 1930s. Fifty years and several wars later we can marvel more than ever at the genius and sophistication of technology, but its service to mankind may not be quite what Saint Exupéry envisioned. If man's beautiful machine spells destruction with its contrail, do we want it plunging into our garden?

The Adirondacks may fall short of Eden, yet it is here in this forest preserve that men have a chance to make a covenant with nature and to find that hollow in the woods so necessary to the human spirit. Perhaps it is not possible in the 20th century to shed all the crustations of civilization, to die down to the root, as Thoreau put it, to revive again in a simpler form. But because a majority of legislators in 1885 took a conservative view of progress, we have a country in which to try. The red trillium by the trail in spring, the ripple of flame across the hills in autumn, the rosy glow on the mountain on a winter afternoon are brief and seasonal, but we don't need much to remind us that we live at the hub of the great wheel of nature turning as it has done for millions of years. Until the jets fly over.

Of Time and the Road

It began innocuously in mud season when a few trees along Route 28 bloomed overnight with orange, polyethylene ribbons. With blackflies came a scattering of surveyors who scratched their necks, peered through instruments and drew hieroglyphics on the pavement. By June the first machines arrived, testaments to man's mechanical genius yet cumbersome and oddly prehistoric, a yellow brachiosaurus of a bucket loader, a black stegasaurian dump truck. Still, the road up Blue Mountain was relatively quiet; we could hear the machines at work in the distance at the bottom or top of the hill and occasionally, miraculously, a loon yodeling in the clear morning air.

Technology changed this soon enough. The side of the hill was excavated, and the trees that held the earth were replaced by a bank of gray stones laid one upon another like a high New England wall caught in a wire cage. Driving became a challenge: one day we found ourselves inching along a narrow plateau with deep gulches on either side; the next, we were rerouted into a trench. The blacktop disappeared; ditches were opened, pipes revealed, water mains broken causing gulley washers; great jagged rocks which had lain somnolent since the road was first built were yanked from their burrows and exposed to the light, still wearing their protective fur of brown dirt. Flagmen — mostly women — herded vehicles along as if they were conducting a slow motion slalom, and we became as accustomed to driving on the left side of what road remained as citizens of Great Britain. Then one morning at 6:00 we were wakened by a drill that reverberated over the mountains and woods and lakes with the sound of a thousand jackhammers. Later the hill boomed, and a puff of dust the shape of the hole just created rose above the trees. No more morning loons—construction was at our door.

I learned a lot about waiting on the road last summer. I learned that my emergency brake was unreliable, and my brake foot quickly fell asleep when I was stuck in line. I learned the exact points along the half mile hill where my radio picked up Albany and where it generated static. I learned that the baby, harnessed in her car seat, could tolerate just a few motionless minutes before she squawked. I learned that it took ten minutes to load a truck, four minutes to turn it around, two minutes to start the line of cars crawling behind it. Captive, I watched the machines and their men as avidly as my young son had once pored over his Richard Scarry books: the graders and bulldozers, the operator who played the gears of his shovel as precisely as a keyboard, grasping a boulder here, lowering a blasting pad there; the burly proprietor of the green steam roller who ate his sandwich in its cab and took his midday nap at the wheel.

I also began to watch my fellow prisoners in line. What do people do when they have someplace to go and can't move? Most of them glare at the flagwoman, one or two try to run her down, another kills his engine, opens his door and steps outside to scout. My brakes won't allow me to do that so I chew off all the fingernails on my left hand instead. The couple in front of me lean away from each other, elbows on windows, and I imagine more than a few expletives are floating in the Adirondack wind. As time goes on, fidgeting stops and we all wait encapsulated in stony silence. A lone backpacker on his wilderness experience picks his way upwards among the vehicles and debris. Powdered rock and diesel smoke rise above the flame red maples; a cold rain slithers in the ruts. The young woman with her flag and orange ribbon on her helmet is muddy and shivering; I have ceased to envy her wages and the job that lets her be outdoors. For the moment she has the power—the rest of us are irrevocably locked in line, without another route or bypass, with no choice but to obey her commands and slip grimly down the mountain in a long metal chain. In that moment I know how it feels to lose hope.

But the feeling is ephemeral—I also know about time. Winter will stop the road work for better or worse; by spring the giant machines will be last year's shadows, and the cry of geese stringing north will replace the beep beep of a backing Gradall. The shoulders will grow green, and the road, new as a peeled snake, will wear on its back a fresh yellow stripe. When the dinosaurs forage on another hill my emergency brake will be fixed. Perhaps. Of time I am certain; of technology, never.

Portents

Something in the chain was broken
the bird bumping on the window
like a moth or night born thing
frantic for the inside light —
no owl nor hawk but a warbler
numb from fright in a dark land.
Yet days ago the geese came gabbling
down miles of icy air sixty
straight strung from tail to tip
hooked and certain of their aim.
Since then children found
in the woods the skeleton
of a dog, around its brittle
neck a rope, one end knotted
in the brush. Hunters stalking
bear stumbled on a plane
crashed twenty years ago,
a rusted husk, but of a body
not a trace, not a bone.
Squirrels black as pitch seized
the hemlock; the air changed.
Last night bird, bat, slapped
against the wall and froze.

There was a time when all things
strange seemed portents, when
mousing owls killed falcons,
horses broke their stalls
attacked their masters, Birnam
wood uprooted, crept to Dunsinane.
Bird, beast, forest mirrored
man's transgressions; nothing
then was accident.
Yet better to believe that ancient
order, in nature signalling some
massive wrong, than a world gone
gray and careless — where men
and dogs die undiscovered, birds beat
their futile lives against a glass.

Evening and Early Sorrow

for Sally

Always when I look at you
I see the shadow of your son
upon your face. Eyes dark
as moth's wings, his smile
a sudden bend of light.
Turned ten you let him
ride his birthday with your
friend in that sleek bright
hunkered down machine pressing
the mountain road too fast
until the missed curve seemed
like flight, the car a comet
looping through the trees.
Later you knew. Sirens
you never heard shattered
your skull, flames gutted
your heart. Yet you stand
here, black eyes circling my
own boy with his big hands,
pants an inch above his ankles
wanting out, wanting to go
if only for an hour. There
is nothing we can save him
from. He runs toward the sun
while we wait, bracketed
by ghosts, in the slow dusk
of his leaving.

photo by Tom Eckerley

Cynde Gregory

I am working on my dissertation, a collection of short stories, and expect to complete work toward my doctoral degree this year. I have fiction forthcoming in Black Ice, Groundswell, *(2 issues) and it looks like* Calyx, *although that isn't absolutely definite. I live a (currently) blissful life in the treetops with two non-talking parrots, which is good, because that way I don't get interrupted all the time. I am currently learning Irish step-dance, English clog dance, and African dance, and am planning a trip to Senegal probably in January to study dancing and drumming. During the school year, I teach creative writing and Appalachian clog-dance.*

Uncanny Beauty

Amanda's nightmares have begun to come more and more often. It reaches a point where she bolts upright in her bed nearly every night, hands rigid at her face, a low moan easing from her throat to saturate the air. The only thing that helps then is a visit to Lillian, her mother, who still lives on the farm where Amanda grew up. After that, she sleeps better for a few months before it starts again, as if some terrible ghost had been laid temporarily to rest.

Amanda can't know what I know about Lillian, or she would not rest so easily. Or perhaps I am wrong. Perhaps Amanda's own understanding eclipses my own, swinging like an arc of light from a place buried deeply inside herself and outward to contain her entire world. But if she knows what I have only just discovered, I think it must be a knowledge that has covered itself over carefully through the years and would require a great act, an unkind act of archeology to uproot it again. There can be no point in bringing the bones upward into light, they can tell nothing useful anymore.

It's been nearly a year since Amanda gouged her eyes. She has learned to get around by moving slowly, feeling the air as it courses by her cheek, listening for what she wants to move toward. Last Wednesday I took her to see Lillian in the little red pickup that belonged to Amanda before she blinded herself. She likes to listen to the familiar sounds it makes, the metallic bangs and grinds, the whirr as the motor races and I change gears. I like the truck because it is easier to haul around the toolchest and wood than in my hatchback. We left early in the morning. She slept for the first hour or so, her head thrown back against the hot red plastic seat, but when we began the climb into the hills she woke and shook down her long white hair. Her face was turned to the wind and her hair tangled wildly across her eyes and out the open cab window. Her face has gotten thinner in the last year. She looks now the way she used to when we were twelve. Sunburned nose, freckles, a spot on her cheek that won't tan. The sun glinted like milk in her teeth.

"I love you," I said, knowing it would make her angry. She does not know what it is to love, caught as she is in her own terrible pain. She does not know the terrible pain I feel when she pulls her hand away from mine, when she will not answer me with love of her own.

"I don't want to hear it, Lena." She turned her face sharply into the wind.

"I love you," I said again. One day she will understand what it means. For now, she rarely lets me touch her and when she does, she makes me use my entire body. Breast against breast. Thigh pressed on thigh, our knees locked, hands held, fingers twined. Our hair tangling. I can only stroke her long and patiently the way I want after a nightmare when she is dead in sleep and doesn't know I do it.

It was after two by the time we reached her mother's. Lillian stood slowly when she heard the truck, brushing off the bits of peat moss that clung to her knees. She always moves slowly, evenly, as if by putting out her hands to smooth the air she can ease the impact of event; even more, that she can turn things back upon themselves and change them utterly. Now, she swung her arms to the small of her back and arched into her palms. A dry wind fluttered aside the leaves on the lowest branch of the oak so that she slitted her eyes into the hot sun, wincing with the suddenness.

"Lillian," I called. Beside me, Amanda straightened, turning her face toward the garden.

Lillian lifted one hand from her back and waved it slowly to where we waited in the truck. Amanda began to open the cab door but I took her cool smooth fingers in my hand to stop her.

"Don't start on her again," I told her. She said nothing and in the absence of her voice I felt my chest tighten painfully. After a moment she swung down from the cab and onto the stony ground.

I sat for a moment longer while the sun beat through the dusty windshield and onto my face. Maxwell came and put his old head into her hand, grumbling and flopping his tail. Even the chickens darted across the yard to peck at the small stones she scattered as she moved slowly toward Lillian. The doctor wanted Amanda to get a seeing eye dog, but Amanda refused, saying the only place she ever wanted to go was the farm and she knew that inside and out. To her, Lillian said nothing, but to me, she insisted Amanda should have the dog. "She might be hurt by what she can't see," she muttered under her breath the last time we came. "Try to make her." I nodded, knowing I wouldn't because Amanda had me to see through and a dog would only take her further from what she needed most.

When Amanda reached the tomato end of the garden and stopped, I swung down from the cab and went around to the back. Lillian turned to face her, balancing on her hip a deep wooden bowl I had carved. It was brimming with fat snowpeas, green and moist in their pods. Ours have been gone for weeks, maybe because we live in a city, as Amanda says, or maybe because Lillian has a gift with life. Her garden flourishes, her chickens lay. Only the house collapses, imperceptible except through the years. I banged into the bed of the truck and hauled out the steel chest of tools. Lillian lifted one slow hand and shielded her eyes against the sun's glare to study my motions. After a moment, she raised her finger and nodded. I took it as a signal and slammed the toolbox loudly onto the tailgate, slid it from side to side so that the tools clattered noisily. Lillian and I want to know how much Amanda sees. She claims there is only blackness. The doctor has said she can see outlines and shadows. Even before she took the knife to her eyes, Amanda never seemed to look directly at things. The first time I told her I wanted her, when we were seventeen, she stared at me with the same placid look Lillian gives and I had the uncanny impression she was cutting something away from my words until she reached the final, essential thing; what I had not known was love.

I slammed the toolbox again, then sprang from the tailgate so that the truckbed groaned, covering the sound of Lillian's slight movements. As we watched, Amanda held out her arms, then swung them to her side and laughed. She took a step toward Lillian, and when Maxwell pushed in front of her and barked she did not let herself be deflected as she would had she not seen or sensed Lillian standing in the sun in her plaid housedress with the wooden bowl of snowpeas pressed against her hip. Lillian's mouth twitched into a smile beneath the shade of her hand. Maxwell barked and stepped against her again, and Amanda bent and shoved him aside.

"Fix my porch today," Lillian called suddenly to me. Amanda laughed and moved more surely toward her.

"I intend to. Fix some other things, too," I called back. Overhead, two swallows swung from the hanging barn door out of darkness and into light. We three turned our faces up, caught in the bright stillness that followed their song as the bird scissored up and vanished behind the house, and then Lillian covered the little distance remaining between her and Amanda.

"You look good today," she said, circling Amanda's waist with her speckled arm. They looked alike for a moment, freckled, peeling noses. But then they began to move toward me and I saw how pale Amanda's body was beside Lillian's, how thin and weak.

"Mother," Amanda began, as if she were going to ask a question and then changed her mind. They turned and began to walk toward the house. Lillian swung the bowl of peas against her hip as she walked and Amanda stretched her fingers down toward Maxwell's setter head. He nosed up into her palm, licking and grumbling.

They stopped by the truck. Lillian wiped her hands front and back against the yellow apron to get the rest of the dirt off her fingers.

She didn't seem old enough to be Amanda's mother, except for the wrinkles visible when she tilted her head back flirtatiously in the bright sun. Amanda did not squint, unaffected by the hot brightness that reflected off the house, the truck, the very air.

"Inside or porch?" Lillian asked.

"Inside," Amanda answered before I could speak. "I feel better in there. It's familiar."

"You don't know the porch by now?" I asked, careful to keep the irony from my voice. It was where we had sat, pressing our backs against the kitchen wall, listening to the hoot owl that mourned behind the barn, when I first loved her with my mouth and hands and heart.

"I haven't spent much time there since I was a child," she said evenly. "I'm not a child anymore."

They vanished into the kitchen, the broken door slamming loudly behind. I went up the stony path behind the barn, imagining them silent in the slant light of the kitchen without me.

Halfway up the path I turned to look at the barn. The sillbeam was rotted part of the way around and the flat slate rocks that were piled into a foundation had scattered. Lillian didn't care about the barn but Amanda played there alone all her childhood until she reached twelve and I moved down the road. Even now, she would feel her way to the worn red walls, touching them softly with her fingers as if the porous barnwood weren't the color of dried blood, but rather, a velvet left in the sun to age. Soon it would lean in upon itself and finding no support, drop into a sudden hollow chorus of boards. We would have to get Willard to come up in his pickup and bring his sons. Willard works for the chickens Lillian trades him. His sons come to stare at the moons my breasts make when sweat turns my teeshirt translucent and bonds it to my skin. They used to come for Amanda, before she gouged her eyes. They came one at a time when she was fifteen and sixteen; by the time she had turned seventeen they knew she would take none of them for a husband or anything else. In spite of her uncanny beauty, in spite of the birdlike way she moved, as if she could fly, they stopped coming.

I walked further up the path to sit on a large flat rock that hung over a narrow drop. Amanda and I planned to stay two nights and leave the following morning. The porch wouldn't take but a few hours to replace the bad clapboard and railing so Lillian could sit in her broken rocker with her feet up, drinking lemonade in the hot sun. There was a leak in the bathroom wall. Going into that wall would be a bigger job.

"Lena," Lillian called from the bottom of the path, leaning her strong arm against the barn. I had to stand on the rock and shade my eyes to see her. "You can come back. We've finished the first round." She waited while I swung down from the rock. As I jumped I caught a glimpse of a small outbuilding that had nearly collapsed, in a small grove of pine I had never been in. Maxwell spun up the path and past the rock, his long red tongue swinging wetly from side to side. The shed had to come down, too, before we left or it would fall in on itself and Maxwell or some other animal would catch a nail.

"Anything new this time?" I put my hand on Lillian's shoulder. She reached behind my neck and held my face against her cheek for a moment.

"Nothing." She squinted into my face. "How old was I when he left? Why did he leave? Did you ever see him again?" I looked at her, remembering suddenly that I knew her when she had not been wrinkled at all. Now, they were like shallow cracks in rock. "Lena, please take care of her," she said suddenly.

It was not a question, but I answered "yes," and felt that I had made the promise to her again. Lillian has always worried over Amanda, even before Amanda took away her sight; a peculiar thing, since for the most part Lillian moves through her life with an easy control that does not allow energy for worrying needlessly. I have been aware of it for many years, and it is not the explicable and expectable concern of any mother for her child; it is rather as if Lillian expects some day that Amanda will be taken from her entirely, outside the arc of her influence and her care.

In the kitchen, Amanda was already smoking Luckies. She usually waited until we three sat around the scarred round table with our lemonades condensing in the thin blue glasses. Lillian propped open the screen door with a milk bottle. At home I would have cared about the flies, but she had six or seven long amber strips of gluey paper hanging from the ceiling. Black fly husks pocked them, and crumbled pieces of cellophaned wings. Amanda shook out a Lucky for Lillian and one for me. Lillian's long dry fingers struck the match against the table top and the flame licked and blacked the end of both cigarettes. I took the match and drew absently on the tabletop.

"So I was five."

"Amanda," I began, but Lillian put her hand out to cover mine. "I just finished telling you," she said.

"So tell me again."

Lillian sighed. "He put on his coat and left."

"I don't remember that."

"You were too young to remember anything. It was February, the middle of a thaw. Uncannily warm. I was wearing a sweater that day."

"And he never came back." Amanda spoke with finality.

"Amanda," Lillian said, "baby, your father was a bad man. Sometimes he hit me. That day he hit you. It was the first time. And the last."

I closed my eyes hard to screen out the nausea that crept through my stomach. I saw it again and again, a faceless man, suddenly here where there were only women, hitting the side of Lillian's face with his closed fist. In slow motion, Lillian fell, again and again.

Lillian's voice brought me back. "I ordered him to leave," she said.

"But that's not why he left."

"I ordered him."

"He wouldn't leave though, mother, just because you said he must."

Lillian shuddered suddenly, though the heat in the kitchen was overwhelming. "He left." She said. "He left because he left. He couldn't stay here anymore."

Amanda tilted her head as if she was studying Lillian for a sign. The tight line of her mouth softened as Lillian passed her hand across her brow. Maxwell barked.

"Come here," I yelled to him through the open door. He came and laid his jowly flaps in my lap.

"Sell it," Amanda leaned forward onto her elbows. Her lashes glinted on her sunburned cheeks like snow. They were so pale they were usually invisible, but in this light they shone. "Sell the farm," she said again, and began to rock a little in her chair like she does when she has to go to the bathroom and can't.

"Why on earth would you want me to sell?" Lillian looked nervously at Amanda.

"I just wondered if you would."

"I can't." Lillian spoke quietly.

Amanda laughed, a tight sound that rattled like a stone.

"Why?" She sucked her front tooth.

"Because there's too much of the past here." I knew from Lillian's voice that that wasn't the reason, not really. I reached for the Luckies and lit one then went to work on the porch while Lillian began supper.

I worked for an hour or so silently, because Amanda had gone off to the end of the yard with Maxwell. Lillian worked in the kitchen as if absorbed by something beyond understanding. As I hammered she walked back and forth past the open door, setting the table, stirring the cooking vegetables.

After dinner, Lillian brought chairs to the doorway so they could talk while I finished the clapboard and put in a new support for the railing. Cicadas swelled in waves, seeming almost to bring a heat in their cries that was deeper and more oppressive than the close summer heat that pressed in all around us. I worked quickly, checking the boards for bug damage, making a heap of boards to burn.

"You'll have to paint it," I pointed out to Lillian after the clapboard was in place.

"Why should I?" she snorted. "Rest of the house hasn't been painted for years."

Amanda sat up suddenly against the screen door. "I remember the gingerbread," she said abruptly.

"Gingerbread's been gone for years," Lillian said, and Amanda slumped back against her chair. "You've seen it since it was gone."

"It's too dark to work. I can't see anything," I said at last. I hauled up the toolchest. Lillian and Amanda moved their chairs so I could get through the door.

"Are you done working?" Lillian's voice held an undercurrent of disappointment.

"I'll look at that wall in the bathroom. Just can't work in the dark anymore."

The pipes were filthy, covered with flakes of rust. I saw a likely leak right away and turned on the faucet. The wrench had a hard time angling in around the joint and though I threw my weight behind it, I couldn't tighten it enough to stop the leaking.

"Christ," I said to Lillian. "How old are these pipes?"

"Had the house plumbed that spring after Amanda's father left," she said. "I sold off some acres to Willard and had him do it along with the roof and some other work."

"He'll do anything for a trade," I muttered, and Lillian and Amanda laughed.

"Old scavange," Amanda muttered. "Like a vulture. Didn't we always have water?"

"Water in the kitchen, but no bathroom." Lillian turned her face from Amanda. I studied her profile, wondering why she got so suddenly quiet. She sat rigid, staring at something on the wall. Amanda said nothing and I sat back and put the wrench in my lap and waited.

After a long time, Amanda spoke. "We didn't always have the toilet?"

"No, there was an outhouse. But it was awful in the winter,

climbing up that hill, too far to go. I used to let you go in a bucket inside when it was cold."

"Outhouse," Amanda tightened her face in concentration. "I don't remember."

"You were too young to remember anything." Lillian looked at her. "And you didn't use it much. I had to go with you until you were five or so. I guess I usually just let you use the bucket or squat behind the house."

I couldn't remember it either. "Lillian, there's no outhouse here." I tried to picture it but couldn't.

"Amanda's father," Lillian's cheeks tightened, "built it a ways from the house. He was so unreasonable, that man. He said it would make us sick if it was near the house, said it would contaminate the water."

"Something scared me!" Amanda blurted, leaning forward on her elbows. Her mouth opened into a little circle.

Lillian jerked forward in her chair and stared at the wall. She got up slowly, then got a rag and brushed down a cobweb. "Yes," she said finally. "You must have seen a mouse or rat or something."

Amanda shuddered.

"Christ, Amanda," I said, trying to make them laugh, "no wonder you have trouble going to the bathroom." Neither of them seemed to hear me.

"You went there," Lillian continued, "during a thaw that winter. You just went without telling me. I guess I was distracted anyway, with your father suddenly gone. You never did it before. I heard you scream from the house." Lillian tightened her lips and suddenly I felt afraid. "Whatever it was scared you so bad you wouldn't go there anymore, and I didn't make you. I had the plumbing put in that spring."

"Rat," Amanda muttered, groping for a cigarette.

"Well, we don't have to worry about it anymore," Lillian smiled thinly. "How's the wall?"

"I don't think I can do this one, Lillian. Willard owe you any favors?"

Lillian stood, sending the rocker into a fit of convulsive jerking. She strode into the pantry and began to rearrange jars. After a minute she called out, "I've got ten peach preserves, half a dozen corn relishes and a hell of a lot of tomatoes. I'll have to spring for the pipe but he'll do the work for that."

"He works cheap," I said.

"He likes barter," Lillian said back and laughed.

Amanda pushed herself up from the table and started for the

104

stairs. "I'm going up," she said, and when Lillian stood to help her, she added, "don't. I can get there myself." She moved carefully and certainly toward the hall. We heard her take the stairs one at a time. At the top, she turned into the first bedroom, the one we always shared.

For a long moment, I felt Lillian watching me and I tried to avoid her eyes. She said my name once, low, and I looked at her full in the face. "Lena," she said, "What's going to happen to us?"

I said nothing for a moment because I didn't know quite what she meant, what answer she was looking for. She turned her face away from mine and stared into the darkness that gathered at the foot of the stairs. I felt a sudden urge to cradle her, but instead I said, "Don't worry. We're good at taking care of ourselves." She gave an abrupt laugh and then we said goodnight.

I don't know what it was that woke me. Amanda sat upright in the bed, her face and one shoulder pale with moonlight. Her mouth slacked open, and the moon fell across her tongue like light dappling stones below the surface of a stream. She uttered a sound, a half-sung moan deep in her throat. Her skin was covered with a light sheen of sweat.

"Amanda," I whispered. She did not hear, or if she did, gave no sign. I pulled my weight onto my elbow and watched as she unwound herself from the sheets and crept, naked, to the edge of the bed. She dropped her head down between her shoulders, like an animal sniffing something unfamiliar in the darkness. Her long white hair draped across her face like a screen, but it did not hold back the uttering, low and insistent. As she sat back on her haunches the moonlight seemed to swell her flesh.

There was nothing to do but watch the dream pass through her. Watch her move across the bed, watch the anxious spasms, her fists tightening and loosening. When the sweat had become a wet gloss on her skin, I held her as if she were my child and not my lover. I smoothed her hair, whispered into her ear. Although I wished for her sake these terrible nightmares would leave her, for my own I never wished it. It was in holding her afterwards as she trembled like a wild creature sleeping in my arms that I loved her best. As she dropped back into the heaviness of sleep and beyond her dreams, I stroked her until sleep took me as well.

By the time we got up the next morning, Lillian had already left. There was a note on the kitchen table saying she had gone into town for some canning supplies. We sat in the sunlight that slanted in the window, drinking coffee and not talking. After a while, I gathered my tools into the box to go pull down the outbuilding. As I started out the door, Amanda shook herself from her reverie and said, "Where are you going?"

"There's an outbuilding behind the barn I want to pull down."

"Behind the barn? Since when?"

"It's off the main path, behind a thorny patch. I'll be a few hours because I can carry down the good boards to use on the barn."

"Take me," she said, "I don't know of any outbuilding."

"I guess we never went there as kids because of the thorns. They're pretty thick."

"Take me," she said again. "I haven't been up that way in a year." She stood, shaking the hair out of her eyes. I shrugged and opened the screen door for her. We moved slowly and I had to run the steel box up to the rock and slide back down the steep path for her. We started to make the left turn onto what remained of the path. Amanda froze. She turned her face to the path below, as if she might try to descend alone. Maxwell wagged his low tail. My fingers found a soft bed of moss in the rock where we stood.

"You said shed. That's the outhouse," Amanda said flatly. She shook her white head in the sunlight and began to turn back.

"You can't go back by yourself, it's too rocky." I slid off the stone and scrambled to where she moved toward the bluff and the barn. She shook my hand off her shoulder, but when I took her elbow firmly in my hand she turned her face to me.

"No," she said simply.

"You asked to come. What are you afraid of?"

"I changed my mind." Her face was pale with fear and her mouth a thin line. I touched her white, white hair with my fingertips and she didn't pull away, so I put my arms around her waist and kissed her until I felt her heart against my chest. She shuddered after a moment and said, "There were rats there."

I took her arm to help her over the worst part of the overgrown path. When it leveled into a soft gray dust, she walked ahead without me to guide her, surefooted, as if she walked the path through the blackness nightly, knowing where to duck below a branch, where the path curved around a boulder.

We rounded the final curve with Amanda leading me by the hand. In the clearing, the sun felt suddenly hot on our faces. Amanda wandered to a mossy spot a little out of the sunlight and I began to work, pulling down boards with a hammer and catspaw. It became a rhythm after a while, pulling boards, pulling nails and making a rusty heap of them. The sun was hot on my back like the heat of a person standing close.

106

"I don't think it was her fault," Amanda called to me from the shade where she sat. "Even though she told him to go."

I had worked up a good sweat and stood to pull my teeshirt over my head. Amanda appeared to be almost watching me, her head tilted back against Maxwell's neck, her eyes opened so that they seemed to shine beneath the lid.

"I don't know," she said abruptly.

"What?" I grunted, pulling hard against a nail that was rusted and bent double.

"Anything," she answered. "I don't know anything." Somewhere a blackbird screamed.

After a while, Amanda came and crouched behind me, feeling the boards for nails. I handed her a hammer and she began to pull. It was like a dance for a little space of time, her rocking back and forth on her haunches, my arms flexing against the stubborn boards, pulling down what must be pulled down, the loud slap of board on board, Maxwell's tail thumping in the dust.

After the walls were down I began to dismantle the seat so nothing would fall in. I made Amanda support the sides as I pulled each section down. She crouched against the base of the seat, a knee pressed into each side, her face lowered in concentration over the opening. It no longer smelled like an outhouse, or like rats. It just smelled like rich soil. When I stood to lift the panel away from the rest of the seat, I glanced down into the opening. I gasped, and when Amanda looked up sharply, I knew by her face that she was entirely blind, as she said, that she saw nothing, not shadows and outlines, that she knew nothing and remembered nothing.

"What is it?" she asked, her voice trembling. I wiped the cold sweat from my hands and cradled her blind face in my fingertips.

"Nothing," I told her, "nothing at all."

I looked down into the opening one last time, then got the shovel and began to dig earth to fill in the hole. As I tipped the blade to let the earth rain down, I realized that even if Amanda could see a little, shadows and outlines, the oddly luminescent skeleton with a single perfect bullet hole in the skull must have looked to her like some unfamiliar and beautiful mushroom growing whitely in the rich black nightsoil.

Camping with Chloe

it is three o'clock in the morning.
I am afraid of bears.
I listen to the pine needles
rattle. *chloe*, I whisper
so that if you are sleeping
you won't hear. then louder,
chloe, it'll get the food.
you stir and mutter, *sleep, there's nothing there.*
it makes a chant inside my head,
fills my eyes and ears, the rough black fur
rubs my fingers raw. I feel its teeth.
the wet nose nudges. *there is, there is.*
at last I sleep, because I'd rather die
dreaming, but first I cry.
in the green glass morning I'm pleased
to see the box of broken food.
see? I sing, triumphant. you snort,
racoon, or something small.
a small bear then. but you are not convinced.
we feast on coffee and share the egg it left.

we dig holes in the loamy soil side by side.
we like this planting back
what we've consumed. we sing motown
loud and the birds back us up, yelling
in the trees.

this body is different than the one
I left in the city. this body leaps
and bounds in the light air, it dances
without my knowing.
you find where the earth turns boulder
and shoots up.
are we going to climb a mountain?
—*no. this is just a hill.*
I am from Illinois where the land lays down
like a sensible cat.
this rock and moss construction
is certainly a mountain.

I am glad when my fingers turn red
from scrambling. I have earned
the sudden joy in my blood, have forgotten
the terror of high uncertainty.
at the top, we swim naked
in a blue sky pond.
we catch clouds in our fingers.
the copper sun glints in our scales.
we slap our fins and tails, dive
for nothing but the joy.
up here we are gods, I tell you.
we and the sun and the pines that nod
and whisper back.
up here we are gods.

Louis Hammer

Louis Hammer has written five books of poetry and has been widely published in magazines across the country since the first publication of his work in Robert Bly's journal, The Sixties. He is a translator of poetry, a teacher of philosophy and creative writing, and editor of Sachem Press, a literary publisher.

His books include Bone Planet, *1967,* To Burn California, *1974,* Lying on the Earth, *1975,* Birth Sores/Bands, *1980 and* The Book of Games, *1985. With Sara Schyfter he edited and translated* Recent Poetry of Spain, *1983, a bilingual anthology containing the work of 24 Spanish poets. His long poem,* The Mirror Dances, *will appear in book form in 1986. A large selection of his work, along with an interview and critical article by Edward Tick, appeared in the second issue of* Groundswell. *He has also translated poems by Lorca and, with Sharon Ann Jaeger, has completed a translation of Rilke's* Duino Elegies.

Hammer has a Ph.D. in philosophy from Yale and teaches at Rensselaer Polytechnic Institute. Previously he taught at the University of Southern California, the Hebrew University of Jerusalem, Wellesley and Brandeis.

A BRIEF SYNOPSIS OF MY POETICS

My poetry aims to be experience more than to recreate experience. It tries to expose the gap in our lives between pleasure and joy and to orient our awareness toward the possibility of joy. In this way it tries to create an opening to the sacred by exploring the endless multiplicity of the sensed world and the hidden life in which we dream our animal existence.

STATEMENT ON SURREALISM*

I have never made any deliberate effort to introduce Surrealism into my poetry. I wrote and the surreal sprouted as if some ancient seeds had suddenly come to life. When I realized that my work had surrealist qualities (other people told me this; to me it was just my work) it was like coming to a strange city and finding friends but not a movement or dogma. It was like finding eccentric, slightly impossible friends whom other people feared, but who, you knew, would love you. In the gray academies of the fifties where I first began to write poetry, surrealists were reviled and mistrusted along with Nietzsche, Marx, Heraclitus and Elvis.

For me Surrealism is not an ideology, a movement or even a method. It is a commitment to being scared a long time by the complexity of matter and its spiritual force, to living in Dostoevskian worlds kept steady by silver tuning forks engaged in subterranean thought.

It is as though the sculptor made a mask and it became living wood which entered deep inside the face and then wanted to go deeper still into the kinetic silence of that lost space into which the world disappears from exhaustion each moment.

On the trampoline of Surrealism matter bounces to its inevitable height and there meets the machine of peace emptied of the immensity of thought.

The surrealist is an adventurer, a beggar, a gardener and a shadow whose life is left over from another epoch of destruction. He is an old man who doesn't mind getting wet in a cloudburst of silence. He is plated with gold, stuffed with ugliness and seeded with mercy. His laughter is scorched by flames from the double heartbeat of science and criminal beauty.

*Reprinted courtesy of Look Quick, No. 12, Winter '84.

Louis Hammer 111

Crow and Poplar

Huge poplar trees
limber as ghosts
drawing poisons from the blood
of the sky.

Only the old smoke
offers you comfort,
the old feathers
circling north.

A crow
in the life of the sun
is a weak system
of inertia.

The sky thickens
around the opening
of the pond,
arranging the birth
of the blood.

Every day we sign with the crows
to awake from our river.

Small Poem of Sleep

The mops come and sweep my breath away.
I dropped one lucky card on the floor
and it, too, is gone.

The moon is heavy on my shoulder
and the sun is circling in a wave of gold.

All along the bay
the trees stippled with light.

The blind are blind
because there's nothing
to look at.
The moss hanging from
forgotten trees,
the small snakes shining through the ferns.

I stood outside the room
and wept for all the facts.

A green arm holds me
and talks to me of pyramids,
a whole winter trembles in its cuff.

I like to hear music
when I'm unprepared for it.
It moves away like a snake
darting from a stone.

A Life without Images

Now my blood has stopped counting,
its wild clarity
begs forgiveness.

The sky clouds up,
darkens,
becomes a gray-green sea.

Into the vessels,
sweethearts of pain,
the sky squeezes rain, hail,
lightning, entropy,
night
and the bones of distraction.

I listen for the wind
at the sink.

The last law of physics
knocks around in the sky
without me.

The sea is weary of glass.

I sink in its ambiguous
dreaming wheat

alone

like a sky
that thinks.

Spring

A whole long winter
can come out of your heart
like wax from your ears
and there you are on the bus
in April
noticing how little of "man"
is in men
and how we are constructed
of something alien
like a paste of worms
or the smell of a radish
or exhaust from a diesel.

Spring is the time to say that you are alive
and to begin to rebuild yourself
out of the folly that has become your life,
to get out your camera
and try to take your own picture
as though you stood on the other side
waiting to hear the roar of a flood
that could upend you
and make you mortal.

Spring is the time to walk toward the infinite
like approaching your own bed
covered with a red quilt
and to believe that all color
is a nocturne of light
and we see only darkness
spread into infinite layers
until it is noble and worthy of man.

Spring is the time to tear up
the dead trees and the rotten sidewalks
and the papers that embroil you in disaster
and to cast the yarrow stalks that reveal
a silent place in your life
and to begin to remove the sound from your head
until it is totally gone
and your ears are free
to hear the whole world.

The Mayor

The Mayor stays in office
until he can no longer breathe.

It is not the garbage that is choking him,
it is not the exhaust from the refinery,

it is the fragrance of ground spices
coming from the hillside on an August evening,

it is the impatience of the young
turning the leaves
into sacrifice.

Watching the Sky

Our friend is watching the sky –
its steel, stone and powder.
He has put the earth
into a great blue vase
which he has filled
with crows and music.

The sky filled with black air,
sudden breeze, criminal justice.
Summer crashes on the boardwalk
breaking open immense eggs
containing whites of malignant virtue.
Water flows down the stairways to the shore
where the strobe sunlight whips the eyes of bathers.

There blood is an industry,
it stacks words, it folds time.
Snow – dense, lyrical, refractory,
stretching across the oblivion
that accompanies us like a piano score
sweet and patient as the earth

or this center from which the day springs
bringing an ark
filled with bitter seeds,
bitter as the harvester.
The mind works feverishly
around its freedom.

photo by Rebecca Thompson

Craig Hancock

Craig Hancock has had poems published in numerous publications, including The Green-field Review, Blueline, and The Glens Falls Review. He has poems forthcoming in Esprit and The Washout Review. He was General Editor for the first three issues of Groundswell. He is a founding member of The Hudson Valley Writers Guild, which he currently serves as treasurer. He is Assistant Director of the Office of Special Programs at the Junior College of Albany. He has taught courses at Coxsackie, Hudson, and Mt. McGregor Correctional Facilities and currently lives in Valatie, NY with his two children.

The Owl

Twenty below again,
cat's water dish frozen in the pantry
and the woodpile low. Time
to bring down the big, dead elm,
to call up Duke and his brother Willie,
who has a cable and a come-a-long,
enough practice with big trees
to keep this one out of the river.

The trunk was so big even the blade on Willie's
old pioneer left the center,
a bent chain link couldn't be coaxed through the winch,
and a hung up limb that dropped when we
were driving wedges hit Duke and Willie
and left Willie leaning his weight off the leg
he thought might be broken, shaking his fist
at the big tree he said he couldn't wait
to sink his saw teeth back into.

We winched her again, but the chain broke.
And you can't just leave an almost cut tree
for any stray kid to walk under when the wind comes up,
so we dropped her in the river.
The ice was thick enough to hold,
about two feet deep there
and all of it ice after weeks so cold
you had to be moving to survive.

And this, I swear, was worth it all:
a small white owl I'd never seen or heard
fluttered out of his hole as the tree fell,
having wanted to make sure, I suppose,
before braving the cold, perched on a nearby branch
and looked down.
What words are there for this?
As if the very spirit of the tree
had not fallen, but flown.

And Willie, even with his bad leg,
wondered if there weren't some way to catch it,
and Duke said, "no, it's a waste of time—
all of us looking at the bird and the bird
looking back—"we'll have to let it go."

Late February

In late February the sun's as warm
as October.
on a day without clouds or wind
I'm on the back porch
in shirtsleeves
shovelling ice and snow
that was loosened by the sun
and roared off the roof,
smashing a picnic table and bench.
For a moment the whole house was shaking.

Today I remember the hurricanes.
School would close, my mother would get out
batteries for the transistor and candles.
The dark and the wind
and the sudden rush of rain.
I prayed that it would be fierce,
that it would shake the everyday world
into a new shape,
that streets would be rivers
and shore homes driven
right off their stilts.
Once when the water rose
my brother and I—we must have been older—
went out in hip boots and rain coats
to lean against that wind,
pull leaves and sticks from the street drain,
and send a funnel of loosened water
clear down to the netherworld.

In moments such as this,
new words cry to be spoken.
Holding splintered pieces of wood,
bench and table legs,
as if they were a child's limbs.

Teaching at Coxsackie Prison

"Write in your own voice,
out of your own experience," I tell them.
But what is one to do
with such matter-of-fact brutalness?

"There are two ways of dealing with women in a citation like
this. One is by talking nice to them, like saying don't worry
about anything miss know ones going to hurt you everythings
going to be alright we're just here to rob the place. Most
of the time the easy way works, if it dose not, then you do
it the hard way. The hard way I don't like to use because
you have to stick a pistol in the women's face or slap the shit
out of her . . . Children are the worse because they panic or
scream."

And no doubt dream.

I think of my daughter, Rani,
hurt at something so simple
as a supposed friend not wanting
to play with her.
And Clai, who sometimes sees in my gaunt shape
and man's face
shadows
of the stepfather who shot her.
Clai, who expects me to want to hit her
when I'm angry.

"We shall pass this way but once,"
in roman lettering
over the grammar school auditorium,
and inside, between the parted velvet curtains,
a child's chorus of Christmas sounds.

Buck-toothed Mark Govoni,
one time best friend, pushes me
and pushes me all the way home from school.
And who was I, at twelve,
not to have wanted to fight back,
to have felt sorry for him
and lonely?

And what did I tell that prison kid
who has spoken so directly
a truth that unnerves me?
While the walls close around us.
About my son's need for gentleness —
and what would he make of it?
At fourteen weeks, gazing
at the opening and closing
of his own hands.

But listen, lay it out there,
it's alright, it's only the past,
only February, and a freak rain
driving the river right out
through its ice.
And at night, in the moon,
I drive home from prison class
and watch it rise,
huge ice chunks battering the trees
already straining for balance
along the bank.

Wood Gathering

Just enough snow to get the wood from the lawn
to the porch on the flat-bottomed sled,
a dusting, powder dry.
Windless, sun in the southern sky.

"I wonder if anyone wants a ride," I say,
every return trip, and Zach says, "I do."
"Everybody aboard," I say, and he says,
"but Daddy, there's only me."
Still, I stand at polite attention, usher him on board
like a streetcar conductor, make sure
he holds on tight, then get up speed as he laughs
and urges me on past the woodpile
down toward the river where we pause
on the bank and look out over the river's new ice,
thick enough now, maybe, to stand on,
clear as water, most recent, over the channel.
Such faith, that I'd take him out over the edge of the world
if I could, out over the brink of our mortality.

In an hour, a week's worth of wood out of the weather,
and behind that two, three weeks of reserve.
"This is the prime," I tell myself; "it won't last forever."
And I like the peace of reserves so much
I go out at night, not to the porch, but the lawn,
the stars so close, a haze on the waning moon,
searching for the darker, more seasoned wood,
beneath the light, the recently split.

"Green," we say, meaning closer to leaf, to life.

The Hunters

I love to be up on these autumn mornings
as the sun comes beyond the hill
and forms take shape as if the source
of their own light.
And the deer! Suddenly there
in the meadow, at the edge of the wood,
the same color in that vague light
as the autumn grass.
Two does and their fawns.
Only the does are still,
a month before hunting opens,
with head raised, ears tilted
toward any sound. If they bolt,
the fawns are fearful of being left
and bolt after. They cavort—
there's no better word for it—
around the cautious grazing of their mothers.

Tom told me once of seeing a dead fawn
in the forest, left by some hunter too embarassed
to sling it up on his car.
And post the land as well as we can,
some fool hunter who thinks he's at the end
of the civilized world will be there with his gun
as my daughter walks the dirt road
to the school bus. She sees the deer
most every morning, she says,
and if she's still they'll just graze there
until the school bus rattles them away
before it sways into sight.

She with those deer-like eyes.

The spring day washed
a thousand sun waves
across the shores of my sleeping,
and I woke at 7 a.m., guilty,
feeling it must be summer noon at least
to be buoyed on such brilliance,
and threw open the doors
to the wonder of an air
so warm and still,
letting in the first few mosquitoes
and a sleepy hornet
with the bird songs.

I expected to say it differently,
as poets usually do,
with sheep in the meadow, a woman
in my arms.
That's why it caught me
standing in a doorway,
a winter-hearted disbeliever,
like those bare trees
with their leaf nets drawn
while all that sun snuck by.

We need new names for it:
a name for the brown river
swollen with leached soil;
a name for the one clear note
the grass sings,
the one green thing in all that landscape
and oh, so simple.

Curtis Harnack

Curtis Harnack has lived in the North Country since 1971, when he became Executive Director of Yaddo, the artists' retreat in Saratoga Springs, N.Y. His seventh and most recent book was Gentlemen on the Prairie *(1985), a history of an English colony in the Middle West. He has written, in addition, three novels and one collection of short fiction; a memoir of his stay in Iran,* Persian Lions, Persian Lambs, *and an account of his rural Iowa childhood,* We Have All Gone Away.

The Dent

Lester woke with a start. Three a.m. on the digital clock.

"What's wrong?" Joan asked groggily.

"That's Tim." Tomorrow morning he'd sleep it off, never make church, and Debbie and Priscilla would cluck fondly about their eighteen-year-old brother, such a sport in the town's night life. Joan would shake her head and smile—all the women in the house doted on the handsome kid.

The car motor shut off with a tinny wheeze; the garage door slammed shut. His son entered the kitchen, paused in the dark to scavenge in the refrigerator, then, shoes off, crept up the stairs to his room.

In the cloakroom after church the men were talking about a hit-and-run accident, a pedestrian struck down in the dark near the Roundhouse nightclub on the highway—the man near death. A thought crossed his mind, but he stopped himself, for he wouldn't believe the worst of Tim just because Joan said he always tended to. But now, remembering last night, there *was* something contrite and unusual about the way Tim sneaked into the house, even if drunk—which he probably was.

When they got back home Lester examined the front end of Tim's car. A fairly good-sized dent in the right fender, which hadn't been there, certainly not the day before yesterday when Tim had washed and polished his bright blue auto—given him last month on his birthday. A cheap Detroit job, not enough steel in it to withstand the shock of hitting a man walking along the roadside.

"You coming Lester?—or what?" Joan called to him from the kitchen. "Girls, it's not summer yet. Don't leave the door open."

Tim didn't look up when the family entered the kitchen. He kept on reading the Sunday sports section, propped against a box of Special K.

"I see you got a dent in your fender."

His son's startled, guilty look wasn't reassuring.

"Yeah, I'll get it hammered out. Won't notice it."

"How'd it happen?"

"Parking lot. Somebody must've backed into me."

"When was it?"

"Yesterday."

"Why'ncha say something?"

"Lester—do you have to make such a fuss about a dent? And spoil our Sunday."

"I was wondering, Joan, that's all." He let it go at that, so they could all have the Sunday they wanted.

Next morning at the bank there was much talk about the hit-and-run. The police reportedly had some leads, including paint on the victim's clothes, which they intended to match with the suspect's car. If it *was* Tim, how in the world did he think he could get away with it?

If it was Tim, what accountability did his parents bear for having raised their son so that he turned out this way? Of course Tim was no doubt drunk, and he was notoriously impetuous. Probably thought he'd hit a dog. But by now surely he must know differently and should be stepping forward to own up.

Lester couldn't talk to Joan about it—they weren't close enough. Between them it had sort of wound down this way, for a long time now. Joan played her housewife role, put him in her cast. Gallantly she kept trying not to be bitter—ever since that dumb little affair of his five years ago with the girl in the bank. You couldn't get away with things like that in a small Upstate town, even though he'd been discreet about the assignations; they met only in New York City. But somebody saw them together and word got back—as it always does. After they'd thrashed it all over, Joan finally said she forgave him. Indeed, their lovemaking seemed more to the point; they were together in a sad, different way. But she never got over her deep resentment and transferred her primary interests to the children, leaving him emotionally isolated, somebody they could all walk around.

On Tuesday the injured man died. When the evening paper with its banner headline was delivered, Lester spread it out on the table in front of Tim. "My God, would you look at that!"

"Yeah." He kept shoveling in his food, without pause. A shock of black hair fell over his forehead, covering his eyes.

"They'll get who did it."

"Think so?"

"I heard—they already know. Just have to complete the evidence before making the arrest."

"Somebody saw it happen?" Joan asked.

"There were others in the car—they say. Somebody squealed."

"You'd think whoever did it would just fess up and take what's coming to him."

"Or *her*, Mom," from Priscilla.

128

"Sexist!" Debbie added. "Women have a right to be guilty of crimes, too."

"Get away with *anything*, some people think." He fell easily into his heavy father role. "Don't know what they teach anymore—in the home or school—about moral principles."

"Dad! You're so stuffy," said Priscilla.

"It's true."

"You always say everything's going to pot," said Debbie, for the sisters were often in rote response when it came to dealing with him.

If only they'd grow up and get over it! "I just wonder how the person who did that can live with himself—that's all."

"What's so surprising?" Joan asked. "That people expect to get away with things."

"That it happened doesn't surprise me. Dark road—the guy wearing black—the kid at the wheel drunk."

"What makes you think it was a kid?" asked Priscilla.

"It happened near the Roundhouse—a youth hangout. Even the guy who died was only twenty."

"What was he doing out there at that hour?" Joan said. "His wife pregnant and all. How come a night at the Roundhouse? He should've been home with her—then he'd still be alive."

"So he deserved to die, is that what you're saying? For stepping out on her?" Another layer of meaning had just been added, if only for the two of them.

"Don't be ridiculous."

Tim abruptly jumped up and left the table.

"Where do you think *you're* going?" Lester called, but the boy was already out of the room.

"We could think of pleasanter topics—with our supper, I should think," Joan said.

Lester heard the car start up. "Off somewhere again."

"He's *that* age! Let him be, why can't you?"

"Oh, I am."

Tim did not return until everybody was in bed. Next morning when Lester entered the garage to start up his BMW, he smelled fresh paint. Sure enough, Tim had had the fender of his car fixed last night. Probably in another town, knowing the police had sent out bulletins on the paint-type.

So it was true—Tim had killed a man! He closed the garage door as if shutting up an ugly secret. He decided to walk to the bank, needing time to regain his composure.

What in hell should he do about this? *Was* there anything? The kid would be arrested and he'd have to take his lumps like anybody else; the disgrace about to befall the family would be only what they deserved.

No, it needn't reflect on them; to have a son go bad happened anytime, to any parents. But poor Priscilla and Debbie, how they'd suffer in school!

If Tim were convicted and sent to jail—he was eighteen and there'd be no nambypamby juvenile business—the experience might be so awful he'd never recover. Lester had seen the stockade prison walls of Comstock and Attica; no middle-class, soft, protected boy like Tim could survive incarceration there. He wasn't tough enough, and altogether too good-looking—which would cause him a hell of a lot of trouble behind bars. Perhaps, if the case went before Judge Clellan, an attempt might be made to . . . And yet, cronyism—or the possibility of it was out. A man had died.

And the Roundhouse? They could have their liquor license suspended for serving a minor, when the legal age was nineteen. Johnny O'Rourke would never allow that to happen, not with his connections on every level, even beyond the county. But even to think of a cover-up was foolish, when the publicity had already carried so far.

Nine a.m. The officers of the bank filed into the paneled board room, under the portrait gaze of Lester's grandfather, who'd founded the bank—and across from the picture of his father, who'd made it the leading bank around because it survived the Great Depression without folding. First to arrive—Lester's brother Bob, head of a thriving appliance store; he might also have become a banker if he'd been able to get along with their father. He was a vice-president because of the family bank stock he owned. The two brothers managed to stay cordial if not close. Bob's wife was an alcoholic and the two of them stuck to themselves. Once the news broke about Tim, Lester knew he'd catch a flicker of sibling triumph, for Bob often gave him the business about having a too-perfect life, everything always okay. His brother was due for some pain, Bob surely felt; *then* he'd have a better sense of what life was like for others.

As the officers assembled, Lester kept his head down, studying the *Wall Street Journal*. Out of the corner of his eye he could identify them by their bodily shapes: the cashier, the staff accountant, the attorney Ed Bond, and faithful Miss Spiers, also a vice-president and very sharp on loans—she knew everybody's business. Now she was telling her neighbor, a developer and contractor, that the police were contacting the F.B.I. because of the paint-matching equipment needed. "But they know who it is already."

Spiers didn't, obviously, or she wouldn't be babbling this way. The teller said he'd heard several names mentioned. Lester quickly brought the meeting to order, even before they had a chance to sip the coffee which his secretary had just brought in. The Fed had lowered interest rates, and they had some important decisions to make this morning.

On his walk home for lunch Lester picked up a copy of the daily paper, off the presses at 12:30. Would anyone in the newspaper office wonder why he was so eager to buy a copy when one would be delivered to his home later on?

Big story on the victim. Not married to the pregnant woman after all. They were part of a hippie clutch who all lived together in rooms above the stores on Main Street. Arrested twice for selling marijuana but because of his age had gotten off without a prison term. He'd lived in town about eight years, place of birth and family origins unknown. Pretty much a drifter, somebody Lester would normally have little interest in, most likely contempt; but now that Tim had killed the guy he seemed to have joined the family. The pregnant woman had no money, no hospitalization insurance, or support coming when the baby was born. Her "old man," she said, had been out of work for over a year and their money was about gone. No wonder he'd headed for the Roundhouse to drink and forget!

Perhaps something could be done for the woman through the church—an anonymous gift of cash. That would be a start.

But it's Tim I've got to think about!

Lester knew he must decide—and quickly—what if anything he should do. The boy had had a few days to haul it all through his mind and squirm in his guilt. One ought to treat Tim as an adult and respect his right to come to a decision. Otherwise, he'd never grow up, always have the family safety-net under him. If Tim went to the police now, before they came for him, and confessed—given his age, he'd probably be put in the custody of his father on probation, with his driver's license taken away. The whole episode would be hard for Tim to live with, but this fall he'd enroll at Dartmouth or Williams (or Hobart, his third choice), start a fresh life with new friends. The scandal need not follow or cloud his days for long. Tim might even grow into a better man—awful as it was to think of—because he'd done this terrible thing. Adlai Stevenson once shot and killed a man and still almost became President.

Nobody at home for lunch. Tim and the girls usually ate at school and today was Joan's day for golf at the Country Club, followed by a few rubbers of bridge—to his mind an embarrassingly indolent way to spend an afternoon. No, she didn't find it boring—it was fun! Once he'd seen her from a distance in the middle of her golf and bridge set, all of them dressed in such sensible sports clothes, pastel shades, hair well-coifed; they seemed to have been wafted from a sorority lounge of time past. They were women of leisure and unashamed of it—in social standing at the top of the town. They served on charity committees and strove to keep the community up to the mark—worked for the hospital, the schools. They believed in doing good and doing it their own way. In the empty house, Lester fixed himself a sandwich, listened to the market report, and was back at the bank by 1:30.

Three more days it went on: Tim guarded, seldom around the house, missing meals; the women of the family maddeningly ignorant of the impending crisis; and only Lester brooding, watching, waiting for the full disclosure. Finally—up in their bedroom in the midst of one of Joan's long rundowns on exactly what happened at the garden club meeting, describing the peculiarities of the chairman, the laziness of the members, Lester suddenly stopped her: "Joan, Joan. There's something so much more important—so close by."

They were dressing for a dinner honoring the mayor, who had decided not to run again—everyone so relieved they got up this tribute party before he changed his mind. "Tonight—there'll be talk about the hit-and-run . . ."

She frowned. He now had her attention for the first time in weeks.

"I don't know how to say this, but you remember Saturday night? Three in the morning, when Tim got in? Drunk. He'd been at the Roundhouse. On the way home he ran over that man. Yes, I think he did. I saw the dent in his fender."

She was clearly shocked but recovered quickly. "Nobody can prove it."

"I don't know about that."

"Tim must think—it was a mistake. I mean . . . that he didn't. The dent could've come from anything, couldn't it?"

"You heard him say—he got it at the shopping center. But I don't believe it." He said the F.B.I. was helping the police analyze paint samples. "It's just a matter of time—they want to be sure."

Well if he *is* in trouble, I'm sure Ed Bond will get him out of it."

"That's not the point, Joan. We'd get him a good lawyer. But what does it say about *him*? That he'd hit-and-run and try to get away with it."

"How we raised him, you mean?"

"What kind of kid *is* he anyhow?"

"Your love should be able to go that far." Joan looked at him in the mirror as she sat doing the final touches on her face. "It's not conditional. No matter what he's done, he's our Tim, and I'm for him."

"But he *killed* a man—and is trying to—"

"A bum—yes. He ran over a drunken bum sitting in the middle of the road, probably. And wearing black. That's what the paper said. It's not Tim's fault."

"Why didn't he go to the police right away? The hospital says the man might've lived, if he'd gotten to Emergency quicker—before the bleeding went out of control."

"I hadn't heard that."

"Well, it's true."

"Now, you're not going to—interfere, Lester?"

"What do you mean?"

"You're *for* Tim, aren't you? You're not going to use this chance—against him, are you? She stood up to face him. "Because if you have anything like that in mind, let me warn you. I don't forgive or forget. Not anything."

"I know."

"You don't just raise a boy till he's eighteen and then throw him away because he's made a mistake. That's not what a father does, who's a *real* father. You've never been able to love Tim, and I haven't figured that one out—why, *why?*"

"I loved him—when he was lovable. But these years it's all one-way. We give, give. He takes, takes. Is that love? I don't think so. We've reared a selfish, dishonest kid who thinks he can get away with anything. Because so far he always has. But not this. *This* is different."

"It needn't be. There weren't any witnesses."

"Oh, that's not so. There were others in the car. The police know it's Tim—I'm sure."

"Then why haven't they arrested him?"

"They're waiting for the paint-tests to check out."

"I see. Well, I don't think I want to go to that banquet tonight." She slowly drew off the rope of pearls. "I'll look what we've got in the freezer for supper."

The girls were out for the evening at a friend's house and Tim had said he'd eat with the guys following track practice. Having the house to themselves, they did not converse in the mom and pop way they usually did when the children were present. Just the two of them

here, with their world scrambled again, not set. She stopped chivvy-
ing him when he made it clear he was waiting for Tim to act—that he
had to, since he was almost a man now. "However it goes, we've done
what we could. The rest is Tim's life."

She accepted that, feeling they'd built properly in the basic
ways—believing, still, in her son. He wouldn't let her know how
deeply he despaired over it. They had this one night at least when the
thing could be discussed, their parenting called to account. They
retired to bed early and made love.

On the day of the funeral for the victim, the newspaper ran a
guarded story, saying the suspect was from "a prominent local family."
Now when Lester met anyone in the bank he got darkly meaningful
glances. Even Miss Spiers turned very formal at the morning meetings
around the mahogany table. A stiffness had set in, no small talk. His
brother Bob eyed him closely, an attentiveness without compassion.
Lester knew that his best friend was still Joan. There wasn't anybody
in this room, at the Country Club, or anywhere, whom he could
confide in—about this. He'd lived his entire life in this town, where
he dare not trust anybody with intimate revelations, knowing it
would get around. Until this moment he'd not realized what a strange
way it was to live. He'd always assumed he had plenty of friends—and
of a certain sort and to a degree he did—but these relationships
weren't up to life and death issues. They didn't add up to much.

Ten days passed. No more daily front-page follow up stories, only
about every other day. What were the police waiting for?

Tim seemed pretty much his old self, but Lester and Joan saw
little of him these days before Commencement. He was busy with his
girl-friend, Cindy, who hung around the house—when Tim wasn't
over at hers. One Saturday night he didn't come home at all. The
family returned from church and found Tim in the kitchen; said he'd
stayed over at Cindy's house, "since it got so late." And blushed.

Lester let it go at that, remembering his own youthful escapades,
but Priscilla and Debbie were all eyes and ears. Later, Joan told Tim
she wouldn't allow such goings-on in *her* house and he'd better not try
it. With Lester, alone, she vented her fury at Cindy's parents. "I know
I'm being old-fashioned, but how could they've allowed it? What
youngsters do in private should *be* private. Not something for the
whole family. What do you think Priscilla and Debbie made of it?"

"Not hard to guess."

It was a heady, exciting, senior-in-highschool spring for Tim; and

Dartmouth, his first choice, accepted him. If only this cloud weren't hovering. Would the police make the arrest soon? Tim seemed blithe—as if he'd forgotten it, or figured he was in the clear by now. Lester guessed that one cause of the delay was the O'Rourke connection: the police chief was a cousin of the Roundhouse owner. Precautions had to be taken so that the nightclub wouldn't be shut down for serving liquor to minors. Took a little time to be sure all the right people had been gotten to.

As it turned out, the power of the O'Rourkes was even greater than Lester imagined. They would not risk having anything done about the hit-and-run. The police announced that they were convinced the driver was from another town or out of state. The highway patrol was now involved, but possibly the crime would not be solved for some time, if ever.

Joan was relieved when she read this in the paper. "Well, let's believe you were wrong. For the peace of our lives, let's believe it."

"The question is, what does Tim believe?"

"That's for him to live with."

"He's living with it very well—from what I gather."

"I think you were mistaken—Tim had nothing to do with it."

"I think our boy is . . . even less than I thought." Callous, more selfish, more arrogant, and now certain that if you played it smart you could get away with murder.

In early May the baby of the dead man was born—a boy. The papers made the most of it, but an update on the investigation showed that the O'Rourkes were holding firm. Everytime Lester ran into one of that family, he had to get hold of himself, not show a flicker of awareness or unease. But he could tell by their overfamiliarity, and a few slaps on his back, that they regarded him as now securely in their pockets, one of their own sort and obligated to their influence. It would be only a matter of time before they began to presume on their new relationship with him and press for extrafavorable treatment at the bank, count on his support on the planning board for zoning variances, who knew what?

After mass, Lester spoke privately with Father Cavendish in the vestry of the Episcopal church. The priest was an elaborate, snobbish man who genuinely believed that God and the right sort among his parishioners pretty much made up who would do—and yet he enjoyed going through the motions of concern for the poor. Yes, he would see to it that the unfortunate mother got this anonymous gift of $2,000, which would no doubt be of great comfort, if she didn't drink it all away—for wasn't it a little much, when $500 would be perfectly adequate? And the church was in so much need of roof repairs that the $1500 could go for *that*, if Lester saw it fit in his heart to do so. Lester ended up with a donation to the church as well as the $2,000 to the girl, and innocent Father Cavendish hadn't the slightest notion why Lester might be doing this.

However, the astonished mother got the ear of a newspaper reporter. Blood money, she called it, and wouldn't accept a penny of it. Father Cavendish came under pressure to reveal the source; even a detective came to question him (because it was expected of the police to do this). The priest was quoted as saying that the money came from an impeccable person of "very high standing" in the community, who acted solely out of sympathy for the unfortunate woman and her baby. But even his phrase recalled the earliest police reports about the suspect, and now everyone seemed to think a massive cover-up was going on. The state attorney general's office would be asked to investigate if the county district attorney continued to do nothing. Lester realized that if he'd let well enough alone, this uproar wouldn't be going on. So in a sense it *was* blood money, even though the perpetrator of the crime seemed so heedless of the consequences.

Tim was spinning, spinning in his last weeks of school, the prom night now—tonight—and Cindy on the other side of town would be dressed in a long formal gown, with an orchid, waiting for Tim to take her out for their special evening, one they'd always remember. Tim had rented a dinner jacket outfit, though he could have fit into Lester's tux—and he had the taste not to go in for a Mississippi riverboat gambler's costume, which so many of the locals liked to dress in when going "formal."

The whole house revolved around the importance of this night for Tim. He was allowed to sleep late (no classes for seniors, of course), and in the afternoon when he came home from wherever he'd been with his buddies, he occupied the upstairs bathroom for an hour and a half, though what he could possibly be doing in there except admiring himself, Lester didn't know. Finally Tim emerged, leaving the door ajar, and Lester went in to open a window to disperse the steam a little before all the wallpaper started to peel.

Joan knocked on Tim's bedroom door several times, asking if there was anything at all he needed, and brought him food. Then she and Lester and the girls ate supper, while Tim accomplished his toilet and got himself up exactly as he should look. But Lester doubted Tim would emerge in full glory quite this easily, for he'd never learned to tie a bow tie and no doubt was up there struggling with it in front of the mirror.

"Could you come up here once, Dad?"

"Sure thing." They were just leaving the table and Lester smiled at Joan, both of them pleased over Tim's vulnerability, still. "His tie," he said simply.

But when Lester opened the door he smelled the sweet stench of marijuana and saw the snuffed out joint in an ashtray on the dresser. "I told you, Tim, that's forbidden in this house."

"Christ, Dad, I wish you'd stop it. This one night."

"Your mother and I both object—we've made it clear."

"I know, I know, but I can't get this damn tie—no way!" He was perspiring in the starch-stiff shirt, standing there barefoot in his jockey shorts, muscular legs spread wide for the battle of the tie.

"Okay, calm down. Here, this is the longer end, you loop it under and over like this. Then take the shorter end and pull it through here. That forms the knot."

"Just do it. I'll never learn how. I'll never wear the thing again."

"Oh yes you will. It's not hard. Bow ties can be pretty sharp sometimes—just the thing." Now he had his son by silken ropes, right here, close to him, face inches away. Now surely was the time, if ever. "Tim, let me ask you something—that's bothering me. Maybe you know what. *Did* you do it?"

"What?"

"You know . . . the hit-and-run. You were at the Roundhouse that night and came home at three. I saw the dent in the car. I want to know—for my own peace of mind—*did* you do it?"

"I don't remember—anything much, about that night. I was so drunk."

"I know. But you'd remember something like that." Lester looked directly into his son's hazel eyes, but they didn't look back at him.

"Why bring it up—something like that? Why do you always have it in for me?"

"I've got to know. Because I live in this town, and I have to face the neighbors. You're off to Dartmouth and God knows where."

Tim pushed his father's hand away from his throat. "It's finished. I can do the rest."

"Tim, I want an answer."

"I don't *know!* I could've—maybe. I'm blank—on what happened."

"Did you hit something that night—or didn't you?"

Tim stepped away. A smile, almost smug. "We'll never know, I guess." He picked up the joint and re-lit it, inhaling deeply, shaking his head in pleasure at the buzz it gave him, then thrust it out as an offering in the ritual, cupped-palm way. "It won't hurt you Dad. Might do you some good."

Lester walked out of the room, heart pounding, but whether from anger or disappointment mixed with despair, he didn't know. He needed to be alone for a few minutes and sought the security of his den, next to their bedroom. The whole thing had gone so far beyond his son's life—and into his own—that he knew the outcome couldn't be left to happenstance. And certainly not to Tim.

At last he heard Tim leave the room, descend the stairs, and receive the plaudits of Debbie and Priscilla. Joan in the kitchen would give his shoulders a final lint-dusting before sending him off to his night with Cindy, the gang, drugs, and booze. It was normal; this was middle-class American life. His grown-up son kept telling him to grow up. But he meant something different by it.

Tim's blue car, very shiny and looking as good as it possibly could, stood in the driveway outside the kitchen door, the dent so skillfully pounded out and painted you couldn't tell at all where it had been. Not from ordinary looking, that is, but go underneath and you'd find the hammer marks. Paint flecks as evidence still waited in a lab somewhere—for someone to make a connection between a person's actions and life. Lester got up and walked down the back stairs, which led directly to the basement and outdoors—and waited there for Tim.

When he emerged from the kitchen, resplendent in his white-and-black, the shock of jet hair neatly in place, he looked like some playboy of the 1920's bent on hell-raising and dissoluteness. And if he smoked and drank as much as he clearly intended to, how long would it be before they got the phone call in the middle of the night from the hospital emergency room—a smashed car, crushed bodies?

"Tim—one more thing. I think you ought to know. The state attorney general's office has entered the case. I'm going to them myself. If you won't."

For a second Tim looked surprised, as if his father had slapped him, but he recovered quickly and jumped into his car. "Go ahead."

Joan frowned at Lester from the kitchen window, knew there had been "words." He didn't want to explain anything to her just now, so he walked down the drive toward the front of the house. Tim behind him started the motor, gunned it—and in a second was right there bearing down with terrific speed. Lester threw himself into the spiraea and felt the auto brush his pantleg as it went hurtling by. Tim laughed and called from the street—"Almost got ya, Dad."

For a moment Lester didn't have the strength to disentangle himself from the spindly branches of the shrub. Did Tim really mean to run him down? Or was it his sick idea of a joke?

Here he was in the bushes—and at an end. Nothing would be done about the hit-and-run by him or anybody, he knew. No making amends, no attempt to come to terms with how Tim could live with himself. One had to go on—like everyone else. And after a time it would be over.

He heard the front door open. "Dad! What happened?" called Priscilla.

"Are you hurt?" Debbie said, coming down the porch steps.

"Girls, girls, get me out of this."

They each took an arm and pulled him from the spiraea bush. He couldn't let go of their hands.

William Hathaway

I was brought to age in the Fingerlakes region of NYS, not the North Country and I've lived all over the USA—Iowa, Montana, Massachusetts, Louisiana. Since all I ever did in Madison, Wisconsin was get born there, it seems strange to read in bio-notes sometimes that I'm a "Wisconsin native." My parents came from Michigan and I don't think that people in my family have stayed put in any locale for more than one generation. But don't call me Ishmael. I try to actually "live" where I am, rather than merely quarter in some place where I serve an institution or profession. It's better to be more loyal to your locale than to your social class, I think, but my poems and general sentiments aren't particularly regionalistic. Local color, that ostentatious frolic all costumed in customs quaint & rustic, doesn't suit me well. And sectionalism, a paranoiac community narcissism that insists on the gospel rectitude of oppressive "traditions," has been a Big Evil in our history. I like the kind of regionalism found in Faulkner's novels, in Frost's poems—the stuff that gets folks all over the world nodding in agreement over the pages. I nod, for instance, over Hemingway's poignant understatement, "We were all a little detached . . ." in his story of psychic disconnection, "In Another Country." Regionalism is sometimes, too often I think, a disguise-word for a solipsistic and artificial redefinition of personal image—a desperate mis-application of language in a pathetic struggle to create a world small enough to feel comfortably attached to. None of the five poems of mine included in this anthology are about a comfortable sense of belonging, though I think the belief in Harmony, possible in each local moment, is essential for a sympathetic reading. I would contend that the thematic sense of these poems is accessible to a general audience of tremendous size.

140

Late and Early Geese

More often they pass over as ragged checkmarks
than those balanced vees of tradition.
The route's still north/south and sunsets
are sloppier, more paprika swirling in the sour
cream, than ever—what with the Mexican
volcano. A cartoon made me wonder why
their formation's never vertical, a stately V
for victory strut, derisive honks and a small
confetti rain of ejectamenta in its wake.
Sure makes you wonder how the shining Cross
positioned itself for Constantine, or if
those show jets buzzing the anthem at the Rose
Bowl are imitating nature. Well, it's quite
obvious. Sergeant Alvin York beaded over
twenty Huns, lined in a trench, on the lead-
bird principle. He got religion in a lightning
storm, just like Luther, and Gary Cooper
did a bang-up job playing him. But what
can a checkmark ever mean but "OK, right.
I gotcha."? We seem to greet these sings
of seasons' passage with more relief
than triumph lately, but their far calls
in early February startled me. I thought
some babies were locked and left like pups
in some cold parked car. But there they were,
such sad, insistent bleats. Over Myer's Point,
they banked East to circle once again our
bare, gray squares, white and brown in patches.
And because I knew that didn't mean a thing
beyond a second look, I knew it meant no good.

Greyhound/Science Fiction

A fresh bus in Syracuse filled fast
with squeaky-clean Kyotan Bourgeoisie.
Each mama and papa-san wore a bright
orange blazer, a turquoise company
badge on each hankie pocket. Ecstatic
squeals, gutterals, with snaps from
many cameras drowned the air conditioner's
endless, listless exhale. The tinted
windows, already trembling from the motor's
idle, were shocked by alien presence,
fauve reflections writhing round our heads.
So, he sat by me, the only other white
American aboard who talked his lingo.
And he would know right off the bat
if I knew we're visited by superior beings
from distant galaxies? Of course I did,

I said, for all the supperless hours,
the careening miles, loneliness of torn
vinyl and crackling intercom had addled
loose my one lick of sense. He told
a secret he'd told so many times,
his voice held an uncomprehending reader's
steady, flat despair. How the car froze
shut on a pitchblack, empty road.
How he and a wife now gone were beamed
up into the silver humming glow,
stripped and painfully probed by some
big-headed ones – all yellow and hairless.
How a disembowelled dog, its pitiful
human collar still dangling tags,
was spread in mute gore on a winking
table. How they awoke nude and broken
in the cowflop of some farmer's field.

No matter how insistently I offered up
my faith, the hopeless eye he fixed on me
would not glitter. He was cursed to tell,
not listen and the windy echoes whistling

through his starved heart would have drowned
out all answering cries across the bleak strand.
And what was I? A vain little peacock who
oh so casually dropped the titles
of my skinny volumes. And that raised him
to say he lacked the 'way with words'
to warn our world and I'd get ten percent.
This commercial vision enthralled him so,
he barely noted the busdriver's braying
hullabaloo when an oriental elder
stripped for pajamas in full aisle-view
thirteen miles from Binghamton.

But I told my new friend no: another earthly
story kept grinding in my brain. It seemed
too sadly predictable that golden strangers,
throbbing with soft light, would not come
to save us from ourselves, but to behave
just like our own geewhiz-flyboy scientists.
The true knowledge I hungered to discern
and tell is why as I "rode the hound"
from coast to coast I saw a fat woman
slap a weeping child in every midnight
station. And why can bookstores no longer
sell Conrad's journeys into the secret heart?

Why, I asked this man, does only 'how to jog,'
or, 'how to be rude with equanimity to sad
little men on buses, turn the cost-efficient
buck? And please tell me why worlds so far
away, only the beams of their extinct suns
persist, seem closer than Benares, where
mothers maim their own wee babes
like bonsai trees to improve success
in beggary? I told this witness how
I longed with all my soul to believe
in voices from blazing shrubs, in angels
and demons who swoop good simpletons
up aloft so their frantic feet would kick
helplessly for the fields they had just
cursed through a veil of sweat.

What was his reply to this unbaring
of my secret self? He turned his face
to its frozen double in the window glass.
He had more sense than to talk to creeps
on the public buses.

Tardiness Lecture

for my son Jesse

On my knees in the powdered dust
covering packed dirt under the see-saw
I put my face close to the earth
to watch two ants grapple to the death
of both. Ants were ants to me,
but one had an abdomen of burnished
copper, the other was all black, so I
guessed they held some ancient grudge.

Jaws locked at a fulcrum, they strained
and teetered in most serious silence
until the red one suddenly crumpled
into a still and curled thing. I was
a God. Indifferent, benign, I watched
the other limp some inches off, topple
on its remaining legs and also die.

When I raised my head back up
to my own world, vast and brilliant,
it was to terror. For only
the wind tumbled leaves and paper
scraps across the quiet playground.
My school seemed to hum like bomb,
a busy beebox, from its yellow windows
as I stumbled on strange legs to my fate.
My tongue was a dry stick in a dusty
crevice: useless in my defence.

She made me stand before the class
and jabbed her pointer at my head.
I could not contain my tears. Nor
can I remember what words spat out
of her writhing lips, but to this day
I always stiffen just a bit
when I hear that word "tardy" said.
Some meanly grinned, while others tried
with all their might to see the swirl
of woodgrain at the centers of their desks.
All through that longest day I longed
to blow my nose in the soft folds
of our nobly drooping flag, sharing
that public corner where she put me.

And now, in discourse, what lesson
can I give to you? For that is the serious
mode, it is supposed. That it is an insect's
life, fraught with struggle; we must submit?
Or will resistance (though it is a Sin)
at least bring dignity to recompense the pain?
Critics' questions. Which I do not disdain,
but these fools mark time with petty bells
and you had best obey, my boy—or else.

Watching the Fishing Show

The best part is when, trout or bass,
it hits the lure. While the pole
does its crazy pointing, like a bird-
dog following its dripping tongue,
or a dowser's rod in Oklahoma,
everything gets in balance. I mean
the pull on arms, shoulders, and back
exactly matches the give of water
cushioning the boat. Ancient Greeks
referred to this in different contexts.

But you must rush to turn off the sound
or the sportsman's bluff monologue,

a whisper sneering like the tough boy's
joke in church, will wreck it all.
He says "Beauty" often, but the way
the uncle who kept punching your arm
did, staring at your mother's behind.

The very best part is when silver
flashes wink back and forth next to
the boat and the tail begins to rip
little holes in the lake. You are
about to pull part of yourself up
into yourself. Hypnotized by its zig-
zag, you might murmur "hither,
thither and yon" to your own mind.
Who knows why? These words sound
like "winken, blinken and nod."

When the fish is boated, expertly
measured, and held up for the sun
to see, it is over. You become
as bored as their sober guide looks.
But it's not over! No matter
you've seen it hundreds of times,
it flabbergasts you as they release
the fish into the bouncing wrinkles,
slip it free with a careless flourish!

If you could catch such fish,
so many, so big—your wife
would come home from her sad religion.
Your children would quit drugs
to honor you, but to these beefy sports,
easy in their wealth of orange flesh
it is *por nada. Sprezzatura*: a big wink,
fat hand on your back, some dollars
stuffed in your shirtpocket. Let's
face it, nothing has been the same
since Momma brought the new baby home
from the hospital and that fish
could make all the difference.

A Crush

Do—Re—Me—Fa—So—Thunk!
Do-re-mi-fa-so-La—La—la-ti-do.
As if late August sun could not set
without the pitiless descent and climb
of those dismal rungs, her little brother
played our porch song nightly.

Whenever piano scales reach me, from high
curtain-waving windows or echoing halls
of sedate purpose, I smell that meatloaf
from the black screendoor with its feeble
television moon. Because when those dull notes
ceased, a cicada's drone from a tall elm's
droop took up that keen of dolar
and despair, until its whine was cut off
so hard before its natural peak, dusk
suddenly just hung in unabated yearning.
I wince at the memory of my high-pitched
jabber—a plea sobbing in every syllable.

For I adored the soft down rippling on
her jaw when she chewed gum. She loved
the lifeguard at the countryclub. Tab Hunter
hair, ivy-league smirk and blazer; he dropped
full-blown from birth in a red convertible
onto our town's sleepy street, like Hercules
serving a casual summer's penance. Certainly
a monotonous clang of horseshoes from distant
lawns never tugged a discordant ache in *his*
fresh heart. I loathed my skinny arms in short-
sleeves, my timid, sweet-cheeping soul.

If the evening breeze carried his carhorn's wolf-
whistle from far-off avenues to where we slumped
on her porch stoop, a flickering lustre cleared
blue fathoms in her eyes. God, how my teeth
needed to bite the pout of her lower lip!

But one night beneath buzzing streetlamps, I
kicked a soup can home and never did go back.
I don't know why. The clankey-clank-
clank of that can had an angry ring I liked —
more my kind of song than the dreamy moans
of trains that got Dick Nixon scheming in *his* bed.
I knew what those blade-thin beams from parted drapes
on crewcut lawns wished for me: a depression, a good
war for a boy who yipped back at their unchained dogs.

Kay Hogan

Born and raised in The Bronx, New York, I have spent my married life in Saratoga Springs where I reside with my husband and five children. Although my genre is Irish Short Stories and my Irishness and Catholicism remain an integral part of my writing, I write also of women, children and relationships.

My publication credits include Descant, Expressions and The Glens Falls Review. I have completed a one-act play and am now working on a collection of Short Stories as well as a novel.

Both city transplants, my husband and I have become "pause people," taking time to stop and experience the beauty that is Saratoga. It is here I have found time and space to begin a writing career. Both, have brought much joy.

Little Green Girl

Mary loves late summer, that inbetween time, too late for planting, too early for closing windows and settling in. From the kitchen window she sees trees still full and green with only a hint of burnt around the edges. A quiet waiting time.

"I have to sell candy bars." Her daughter bounds into the kitchen—interrupts her reverie. "The cheerleaders have to sell at least forty candy bars, and we have to do it today. Sarah and I are going now. Okay, Mom?" All said in one quick breath. Don't they ever pause? ever? She looks tall today, Mary thinks, watching the blonde hair bounce with each inflection. Mary recalls the little girl in bright pink, her favorite picture, remembers all those long walks. "Have I told you that I love you," she says over and over. They both laugh. Yes, that is her favorite picture, her favorite time.

I hate cheerleaders, Mary starts to say, but remembers she's said that before and before that. Visions of girls—big girls, small girls gyrating, leaping, orange and gold, pom-poms, glittering sequined Dallas Cowgirls, fuse with other girls, other gyrations. She sees the slave dancers of old, their soothing curves, stirring, while men watch: always men watch.

"Stay close to home," she pleads, but knows forty sales will have to take her daughter far away.

"I know, Ma, I know. And don't give anybody directions if they ask. Mumble and move on."

Mary laughs despite her nervousness.

"Walk close to the houses, away from cars."

"Okay, Mom. I love you."

I love you. It comes so easy. Those quick hugs spurt out of nowhere. "I love you, Mom; I love you, Dad." At ten, her body is no longer a neutral size eight. She fits into her clothes now, the slight curves just beginning. Mary senses that the inbetween time is almost over and her watching words tumble out, and fear too. Lately her words ring with caution.

"Where's Kath? Who is she with? You can't stay out after dark. Boyfriends? Never—well, not for years." An ache springs up. Mary knows the pink bubbles and white lace Communion days are gone. All gone. She misses her already.

"What time is it?"

"You just asked," Jim says. "She's only been gone half an hour. Don't start worrying," and his voice sounds heavy with worry.

When did it start, that worry time? Was it when Kathleen was younger? No, ages ago, when someone worried about her, when she was the little girl.

"Mary, be careful on the roof. There was a man," and the voice trails off. "Be careful in the park." She still remembers the park and the carriage, especially the carriage. She and Johnny Keenan push it up the big hill. They laugh and push while the babies, her brothers, sleep quietly. A man, tall and old, moves toward them. He smiles, talks to Johnny in a soft voice. "No," Johnny says, "No." Later Johnny tells how the man wanted Johnny to leave the park if he gave him five dollars. He likes girls, he says, especially, little girls. "Five dollars, wow, that's a lot of money." She likes Johnny, but wonders how he knows about man and things. Mary begins to worry about men. She is six years old.

The clock ticks loudly. Busy, busy, keep moving, Mary tells herself. Don't worry, but a part of her stays numb, suspended. Mary wants to run out the door, find her daughter, bring her home to safety, lock everyone out. Yes, lock them all out.

"Lock the door, always keep the doors locked, always," another mother said.

"Who's there?" Mary says.

"Uncle Jim."

"Oh," Mary sighs, "it's you, but my mother isn't home."

"It's your Uncle. Let me in."

"I can't." The memory of his eyes comes back and the voice too, harsh, scathing like her father's.

"My, what nice tits you have," Uncle Jim whispers one day. "You are really growing up," and he follows her around with his eyes. She tells her mother.

"Nonsense, such nonsense, child, not your very own uncle." Her father looks at her, his eyes strange, suspicious.

"I can't open the door, Uncle Jim."

"You are a bitch. You know that," and he pounds the door.

Mary picks through the newspaper. Headlines seek her out. *Young Girl Abducted, Strangler Still at Large.* Girls, girls, young and pretty, advertise toothpaste, cars, everything, anything. Young, pouty, eleven-year-olds made up for seduction stare out from fashion ads with old eyes. Another time, another long ago memory creeps back.

When Mary walks by the cellarway on her way to school, she always remembers the girl, how she looked, Genevieve with long blonde hair. She was seven, the same age as Mary.

Destroyed. The word passes from woman to woman: the women on the corners with their babies, the women in church, and in the market place. Like the angel of death, "destroyed," the words spills on the girl's mother and family. The father drinks. Everyone says, why shouldn't he? His daughter is destroyed. How did it happen? Mary wonders. Nobody mentions her name, ever again, just "the girl, you know who I mean." She stays locked up in the apartment. "Destroyed," over and over they say it, but someone, a woman says, "I wonder, do you think she was asking for it?" Her father, who reads the headlines, the murders, the rapes, says, "She was asking for it," and he looks strange, suspicious.

"Don't cross your legs or go to places that are occasions of sin," the nun states emphatically, certain, as if she is revealing something at last, not like the usual flustering over the Sixth Commandment.

"We must strive to be like the Blessed Virgin Mary." Big words, pretty pictures, Annunciation, Assumption, Crucifixion, glisten, but the words stay strange and mysterious. The porcelain statue, white and ghostlike, the foot resting on a snake, frightens her, but Mary decides at nine to be a virgin. "What is a Virgin?" she asks.

The nun sputters mumbled words, Mary decides instead to be a nun. Everybody likes nuns and they are all protected with the habit and all, all locked in. Even her father likes nuns. Mary wraps herself in a mad frenzy of prayers and novenas and daily masses. She starts to forget that time, the room, her mother's cries for help. Prayers help but the saints seem so far away. She laughs with her friends, feels protected. But there are times a sharp scream startles her, makes her remember, but she prays it away.

"I'm going to look for her, she's late. She should have been home twenty minutes ago."

"Okay," his voice succumbs, and he worries openly with her. "I'll wait by the phone."

Up and down she speeds around the block, grasps the car wheel tightly, stifles a scream. Daughter, my beloved daughter, where are you? Her mind jumps back, forward, in fits and starts. The police will ask, "What was she wearing?"

"Brown shirt and jeans—no, yellow shirt."

"What does she look like? Have you had any trouble with your daughter, problems at home—boyfriends?"

"We are talking about a ten-year-old, Kathleen—my Kathleen—my daughter." She remembers the eleven-year-olds with their pouting faces, inviting, offering.

"Sorry, lady, just checking."

Up and down the street she stares at the preppy, scrubbed boys, wonders, is it one of them? She spies a long haired, spacy looking teen, circles around, watches him go inside a house. I'll kill him, I'll kill him if he's taken my daughter, if he touched her, if he even looked at her. *Destroyed*, the word hammers at her head.

"What will you do?" her mother will ask if the worst happens. "That's never happened to anyone belonging to us before, never in all the years." And she pauses, "It wasn't her fault, was it?" Another pause, "We won't tell your father." She watches as her mother twists her hands nervously, then goes to the sink and washes her hands again. Religion and hands, Pontius Pilate, the dismissal, all merge in confusion. Mary blinks back the thoughts, grateful she is only daydreaming.

Young mothers, happily married mothers stroll by, young children having children. She watches the couples, their hands jammed into each other's pockets, staking ownership. She stares at the girls, wonders what kind of girls they are. A radio blares "Do you want to make love or do you just want to fool around?" She looks into the car mirror, sees a woman with eyes that are strange, suspicious. The colors of autumn skim by, edging her vision. Brown and gold, brown and gold, she gasps, begins to cry. The picture she prayed away comes back.

"Mary, Mary," the voice pierces the darkness. "Help me, help me. Come and help your mother." She runs toward the door, but stops. Panic numbs her. She has come to that call often, but this is different. She knows, feels something different. She wants to hide. "Mary, oh my God, Mary, come help me."

At first the scene slips away. It's a dream. It has to be. She's there, but not really. No. No.

Her mother is against the wall, screaming. She's wearing a brown and gold dress. I've never seen that before, Mary thinks. Why, you can see through it. She stares at the left breast, big and pendulous. It's ugly, she decides, and watches while her father rips the dress piece by piece, the brown and gold silky material falling to the floor.

She turns her eyes, ashamed for her mother. Her father breathes heavily, and she realizes he too is naked, standing there with that thing. Her brothers have that, too. "You wouldn't touch me in front of the child," her mother screams. He rips away until they both are bare. The bodies seem fat and fleshy and the hair is in strange places. The air smells sweaty. It's not like the regular fights; it's not like the regular fights, Mary keeps thinking. She sees her mother on the bed, remembers her father going toward the bed. It is very dark; she likes the black that covers over her.

Morning and the eating, waking-up voices stir her. She walks into the kitchen. She stares. They both have clothes on. Her mother's voice is calm and naggy. "Straighten up your shoulders, comb that straggly hair," she says to Mary.

Mary wants to ask about being *destroyed*, about a lot of things. "Last night," but her father talks back and forth to her mother, around her, cutting her out. She watches them eat, with their clothes on. The picture of the brown and gold, falling in a pile, flashes again, but she starts to pray real hard, wills it away.

She pulls into the driveway, readies herself for the final pain. Fear tastes ugly, she thinks. Jim's voice sounds happy. He is on the phone. "Yes, little love, you're going to be right home. No, we weren't worried. You're only a little late. Forty candy bars. That's great. I'm proud, really proud of Daddy's little girl. Yes, I love you, too."

He smiles at Mary. "She's all right, hon. They lost track of time, stopped for a soda. She's at Sarah's now. She'll be right home. It's all right," and his voice wraps around her, the way it always does.

She still loves his voice and his eyes too. Wedding memories flood her when the pain and fear fall away along with the frenzied prayer. There are no more eyes that stare at her suspiciously, only eyes that love and a voice that gentles down the remembering. She comes to him freely.

"Mom, I'm sorry I was late. I didn't mean it. Mom, why are you crying?" She's wearing a green shirt, she thinks, not yellow or brown.

"Oh, nothing, love." She hugs her tightly. "Nothing really. Sometimes I get all mixed up. I just get all mixed up."

photo by Marilyn McLauren

Judith Johnson

Poet, playwright, novelist, mother of three daughters, Judith Johnson lives in Albany, where she teaches in the S.U.N.Y. at Albany Graduate Writing Program. She was born in New York City in 1936, and studied at the Juilliard School of Music, composing four operas while there, and graduated from Barnard College, cum laude, in 1958. Her awards include the Yale Series of Younger Poets Prize (1968, for URANIUM POEMS), a Playboy fiction award in 1977, and a National Endowment for the Arts fellowship in poetry in 1981. She served at President of the Poetry Society of America for two terms, 1975–1978. She is the author of 8 books; the most recent have been the WASTE trilogy (Countryman Press, 1977–79) and HOW THE DEAD COUNT (Norton, 1978). She has recently completed a new book of poetry, WHOOPEE, and a book of short fiction, MAINTAIN FLIGHT SPEED, and is finishing a novel, THE LIEBERMANN CATALOG.

Calling It Right

for Joel Oppenheimer

out my window there's grass. the whole frame shakes
with subway trains. sundays the children shout
the park up. i hear when the wood connects.
though i have work to do, don't care for ballgames,
don't mean to watch them hit and run, don't know
whose kids they are or whether they need watching,
my mind lets out an absent-minded whoop
when they do.
         anything that can take off
and go like hell or land on base will need
a cheer to fix it steady. too much can
fall short and does. the kids that i don't watch
whether they hit or miss may wind up hitting
or missing some time when i'll wish they hadn't.
go down past those split benches some dark night,
the quick plock of feet will count how they run
and run when the whole park shouts out past counting
someone's kid just been hit.
         tell me they'll strike
out or hit home whether i watch or not
whether i do my work or not. say others
will let them walk or call them safe. but still
i can't get by so lightly. something's out
there i should put my mind to if i knew
how i could call it right. for now, i'm not
all outside their game even though they're all in it
nor are they any less out, being in
here and on base.
         last night after the ninth,
the moon up, all kids home, the scramble over,
i turned my light down and looked past the field
to where something came up the wall and sat.
couldn't see what it was nor whether it
had scored, but only how it sat and sat
and looked past me while i looked out at it,
helpless to change its run of luck and yet
hoping it calls me right next time i hit.

Taking Stock

how shall you love me? if i come
in prudence and maybe a margin of pride
to count the ways, be deaf and dumb.
keep no tally, take no advice,
let nothing of interest build, don't sign
any notes. when our term's up and all's due
pretend an ignorance clear as ice
and reckon nothing i tell you to.

if we tax ourselves, as redlines crumble,
to stagger into a closure, wise
as brokers when all stocks fall / let's plunge
for killings we stumble upon. call us sly
bankers of life; market-letter and science
will guide our investments, not the crude
luck of the gambler. (but when foresight dies
take count of nothing i tell you to.)

if tomorrow you try the stock page to study
my curves and read out odds, think twice.
how many who came with a wintry judgment,
reckoning only their single sight,
played blind and justly lost. if tonight
the hand you hold doesn't measure true,
consider that measure and justice lie,
and balance nothing i tell you to.
client, how shall we end? if ever i light
the way, be sure no gains will accrue.
close out all holdings, like justice, keep blind,
hold tight to nothing i tell you to.

No-Name's Tale

(This is No-Name's Tale. My grandmother told it to me, and her grandfather told it to her when he was blind and old, although he didn't know the end. In each telling something has changed, for every hearer changes the tale.)

Now, when the child who was to become No-Name was five years old, he had a name. He had a warm, round mother, and a kind, proud father, three sisters, two brothers, and another child was on the way, for his mother had begun to walk heavily holding her shoulders back to balance the growing weight. No-Name was the next-to-youngest child to survive. Two others had died of the fever between his sister's birth and his own. They lived on a farm near a forest in a part of Bessarabia which sometimes belonged to Rumania but was now just inside Russia. On the same farm lived No-Name's grandfather, grandmother, two married uncles with their families, and one unmarried aunt. It was forbidden for their people to own land, so the Boyar was the titular owner of their farm, and they paid nine-tenths of their crop to him as rent. But still it was their farm and had belonged to them since before their grandfather's birth.

In the kitchen on the iron stove stood a large, brass kettle. The lid, the size of a gong, hung on a chain against the brick chimney. One afternoon while the sun hung high, the child who was to become No-Name stood watching his brothers and uncles in the north field. His job was to bring water from the pump, in the heavy pail. He had been doing this all day, turning his head towards the house, listening for a sound. The sound may have been the brass kettle lid being struck with the iron spoon his grandmother or mother used to call meals, although at this hour it was too early since the sun floated high. When the kettle lid was struck it would reverberate with a rolling, thunderous echo, and from the four distant corners of the boy's world, the fields surrounding the house, the western forest, the ditch separating their neighbor's fields from theirs, and the winding path of the village, people would drop their tasks and come running for the Holy Name of God and for their suppers. But he could not expect to hear brass so early, when the sun sailed warming the four corners of his world.

Maybe he listened for the first cry of a newborn baby, a high yammer he had heard twice before, when the little brother who had lived three days, and the sister who had lived almost a year, had been born in the high bedroom. But it was too soon for that cry. His mother had just that morning dragged upstairs, the women following hushed, and the harsh cries of labor had not yet begun to sound over the field.

Maybe that was what he listened for, looking over his shoulders at the house, then sideways at the path, the heavy pail resting just in front of his left foot. He saw a cloud of dust on the village path. A man with a rust-spotted rag around his forehead ran towards them, staggering, almost falling, and kept coming. The boy turned back to the house. There were no sounds of labor, so he brought the water to his brothers and his younger uncle. The older uncle put down his bushel basket and walked quickly towards the house. The younger uncle drank a large dipper of water, and dashed a second dipper over his head. Then he also ran towards the house. Just then the sound the boy had not expected rumbled and reverberated over the field. From the field's four corners people rushed towards the house. They dropped bushel baskets, pitchforks, pails, handles of carts, coils of rope, and ran as eagerly as to a feast across the golden field. The boy dropped his pail, and hurried towards the house, much more slowly than the others, for he was small and chubby and his short legs had to pump furiously to catch up. He saw uncles, aunts, and cousins, running out of the house towards the forest, the tallest cousin well in front, not waiting for the small ones, one uncle moving ahead, not pausing for wife or child, one aunt far behind with her baby on her back. The man with the rusty rag ran out the gate, onto the path, continuing towards the house after theirs.

A cloud of dust approached from far down the path where the man had first appeared. All this time the brass kettle lid reverberated. Now the boy's grandfather also trotted out the door on his arthritic, stiff legs towards the forest, with short, choppy steps, for his knees refused to bend. The boy ran inside.

Upstairs, the sounds of labor had begun. He could hear rhythmical bellows from his mother's room as he remembered hearing when the dead brother and sister had been born. His father stood near the kettle lid, holding the iron spoon with which he had struck it. The other children clustered near. His father seized the oldest boy by the shoulders and pushed him forcefully towards the door. "Run, run," his father shouted. "Don't wait for the others or for me. Let the strong not stop for the weak, the fast for the slow, the older ones for the babies. No time to save any but yourselves. Don't stop no matter what you hear behind, no matter what you feel touch you. Run when your heart pounds, when you cry salt tears, when the pain cuts your ribs. When you can't run crawl, when you can't crawl go down on your belly but keep moving. When you come out from under the trees you'll be in Rumania, where the pogrom can't reach you. By that time they will have killed us here, and they'll be sated. In that country make yourselves new lives, forget me and your mother and your sisters and brothers, tell nobody your names, where you're from, or what you are. Don't remember our names, don't remember your own name or the name of this village or the Holy Name of God, for these things are finished. They can never help you again." Or maybe he had no time to say these things, but the boy heard them nonetheless.

As the boy's grandmother staggered downstairs from his mother's room and made blindly for the door, his father gave him a heavy smack on the behind with the iron spoon, so strong and so hard that in pure shock and astonishment the boy jumped up and scrambled with his short legs out the door across the fields into the forest, never looking back although he could hear rhythmic bellows from his mother's room, men shouting, furniture overturned, wood breaking, metal ringing against stone, gurgling screams suddenly cut off.

Under the trees it felt cool. Vines between the roots tangled him, fallen logs tripped him, brambles stuck his ankles and knees, twigs snapped out to whip him across the face. One of his sisters fell. His older brother stopped to help. A tree smacked his other brother across the face. Blood blinding him, that brother fell. The boy ran past his grandfather who stopped, short of breath, leaning to one side, a hand pressed to his ribs. The boy ran, his heart pounded, he cried salt tears, his ribs cut. Far back in the trees he heard his oldest brother shout. There was a grunting, snuffling noise like a wild pig. He ran, his heart beat, the salt tears stung, pain cut his ribs. Far back under the bushes, his younger brother screamed like a horse. There was a floundering, crashing, and whinnying in the underbrush, like a steed pulled down by wolves. The boy ran, his heart beat like a huge, brass potlid, salt tears ate into his tongue, pain cut his heart. Not far behind he heard his sister whimper. Her voice changed to a high, bubbling squeal like a rabbit hung up by its heels and knocked on the head in the butcher's dark back room. Then the squeal choked off. The boy ran, his heart tore through his body into the darkness, tears burned his face, the pain pushed outwards till he felt he would burst. Right behind, at the back of his neck, close at his ear, he heard a small child whimpering, blubbering, and gasping like water sucked out through a drain. "Stop it, stop it," he screamed, but no sound came. "Shut up, I can't stop for you, I can't help. The strong must not stop for the weak, the fast for the slow, the one in front for those that fall behind. My father said to save myself. Let me go, don't follow me." But he had no voice. As he ran he heard the whimpering and the blubbering fall farther behind, until all that was left was his own gasping breath as he fell to his knees and crawled through the brambles tearing at him, snagging him, the vines knotted around him, the twigs snapping back, whipping his salted and bloody face. Much later he crawled on his belly under the vines, between the roots, through the cooling mud and moss. Still later he woke under the moon in a grassy field where a cool wind lifted his wet hair, letting it fall back over his eyes, and whispered, "Don't stop, never stop, save yourself, forget your father, forget your mother, forget your sisters, your brothers, forget your name, the name of your village, the Holy Name of God. Those things are finished. They can never help you again. But now they're gone, the pogrom won't follow you. You will be safe."

(*Is he going to die there? my daughter Miranda asks. You've told us this before. This time I hope he escapes.*)

(*You are the hearer, change the tale. In this telling, because you want it this way, he did not die. Listen to how he lived.*)

Then in that field very far away, from under the trees in the woods where he thought he had left them, the boy heard the snuffling of a wild pig, the crashing and neighing of a horse pulled down, the bubbling shriek of a rabbit, the blubbering and gasping of water sucked down a drain. He shuddered. Although he no longer remembered what those sounds meant, he knew he had to crawl or drag himself to where they could not follow.

(*This is a true tale, Julio Martinez says, staring at me as I tell it in a small library so many years later. I knew the man well. Only, you have lied about one thing. He was born in my village, not Russia or Rumania or that other place whose name I have forgotten.*)

(*No, says the black man named for the great king, Chaka. This thing happened in my village long ago. Only, the boy was taken by slavers and sold in your country, although he ran and ran to save himself. They stole his name and his language and made him take theirs instead, but we remember him still.*)

(*Listen, friends, the tale is old. My grandmother told it to me, and her grandfather to her when he was blind and old, although he didn't know the end. Who told it to him in what far country? Change it as you will, it will stay true.*)

So, in that grassy field, under the cold wind's fingers, the boy slept. He woke much later the same night or another night. Tired, stiff, his knees refusing to bend, he moved like an old, arthritic man. Something had crept out of him in the night never to come back, and it had crawled back under the trees to listen for a sound, what sound he did not know, so the sound could not follow him.

"Am I alive or dead?" he thought. "Who am I? What is this place?" (*See, you have changed the tale. Whatever name I thought he had he has lost.*)

"Do I have a mother, a father? What am I doing here? How shall I save myself? How shall I live?" But, since he knew the answer to none of these questions, he kept on crawling.

(*Now, that was how No-Name escaped death. Of all his family, he was the only one who escaped alive to tell the tale, and in his memory no names were left. How he found the gift to survive without a name in this hard world, this part of the tale doesn't tell, but another does, and that is the tale of the Survivor's Gift, which my grandmother told to me, and her grandfather to her. In each telling something has changed, for every hearer changes the tale.*)

Late one night, a five-year-old boy crawled into the Rumanian grasslands, caked with blood and salt tears, hungry, cold. "Where am I?" he whimpered. "Who will take care of me? Who am I? How shall I live?" A day or a week later, he crawled out, blood and salt dried on his cheeks, crusted on elbows and knees, his clothes tattered with brambles, vines, roots, twigs, so the wind ran through as through a dead man's fingers. He crawled under the lowest rail of a wooden fence, and dragged himself up a flagstone path to a door in a stone house with a well outside. There he went to sleep because he couldn't think what else to do. At sunrise, a man with a knit cap and a wool scarf came out to milk the cows. The man tripped over the heap of bloodied rags at his door, turned it over with his foot, and called, "Mother, what have we here? Is this the boy who stole the chicken last week?"

A woman big with child came out and stopped over the bloodied rags, whose eyes stared up at her through slow tears. The sight of a woman with child reminded him of something, although he could not have said of what. She looked carefully down at him. "No," she said. "This is not the boy who stole the chicken. I almost caught that boy. He was blond. This one is dark as a gypsy under the blood."

"Ah," said the man. "Is this, then, the boy who borrowed my ax when I was at market, and hasn't returned it, though he promised you he was no thief?"

"No," said the woman. "That boy was tall and thin, at least eleven years old. This one is a baby under the blood."

"Ah," said the man. He chewed the end of his mustache, then spat onto the stones. "They had a pogrom on the Russian side of the border. This boy will be one that got away. Give him water, then send him down the road."

No-Name began to cry, rolling onto his belly, digging his face down into the stones. "I'm not from that place, don't send me back. Let me work for you. I can milk cows. I can cut wood." But the man had already walked away.

The woman brought a dipper, and held his head against her arm, pouring water slowly into his mouth. She let his head down and brought another dipper, pouring more in, then wetting her handkerchief to wash the caked blood from his face. Then she pulled him to his feet, took his shoulders, and turned him towards the narrow, winding road. "Go, little Jew," she said. "In the village beyond the third field live your own people. Let them take you in. It isn't far. Go quickly, or my brothers-in-law will find you here."

"Give me bread," said No-Name. "I'm not a little Jew. I don't know who I am. I have no home. How can I go on?" He began to snuffle, then tried to stop because sudden terror stumbled behind him when he cried, like an animal grunting and snuffling in the woods.

"You must stand up and keep going," said the woman, grumbling but not unkind, and fetched him crusts and an apple. Eating the dry crusts, taking small bites of the apple to make it last, he stumbled down the road, his knees too stiff to bend.

A day or two later, No-Name came staggering and weaving up out of the fields to a small stone house at a village's edge. The house was protected by a dirty, grey, picket fence. Inside a stony yard, patches of ragged grass grew on a low mound, and a tethered goat grazed on the clumps it could reach. He pushed open the gate and came reeling in, his head spinning, little sparks dancing before his eyes. It seemed to him that he saw two or sometimes four of everything, four long, stone houses, four small shops attached, overlapping, a great clutter of iron wash tubs, rusty wheelbarrows, spinning wheels, broken rakes, handleless pitchforks, bent hoes, old rope, cradles without runners, constantly shifting position and color. As he leaned against a rake which began to slide sideways against the wall, four old women with big, gingham bonnets came out of the four shop doors and steadied the rake handle just as it started to fall and pull him down. The boy reached for the wall, wondering if it would slide too, and if he would then have to grab the old women to keep from falling.

"Ha," said the old woman in only one voice although he could still see four of her. She let go the rake, now that he was no longer leaning on it, and it promptly fell. "What a bag of rags here at my door. What's your name, baby rag boy?"

"I'm hungry," said No-Name, staring at the four of her. "Please give me something to eat."

"Do you think I can spare food when the Boyar takes nine tenths?"

"Is there a Boyar here too?" asked No-Name, looking away at the four grassy mounds. "I can paint fences, and yours needs painting. Does the Boyar paint your fence?"

"How can I feed a growing boy? My old man is away, I'm a woman alone in her shop without a man's advice. What will my old man do when he finds you here?"

"If he's away you need me to do for you till he gets back. I'm small, I don't eat much. I'll draw water, bring in wood, and move the goat's tether from one part of the yard to the next. When your old man doesn't want me, time then to send me away."

(*Does she keep him?* asks my daughter Alison, looking up from her picture. *I don't remember. Let's change it so she takes him in.*)

(*You are the hearer, you have changed the tale. In this telling, because you want it that way, she takes him in. Listen how it happens.*)

"Come in," said the old woman. "Bring that log from the edge of the pile. Let me see how you start a fire."

No-Name could not remember ever having lit a fire. He thought he had drawn water from a pump and brought in a heavy pail and stood in the cold dawn, watching another boy kneel at the stove and breathe on the embers. But when he tried to remember he felt a hand grab his heart. Far away in the woods a wild pig snuffled and rooted. This terrified him. So he knelt down to blow on the coals, hoping his body would remember the way with fire that his mind had lost.

(*I remember how it goes,* Miranda says. *But this time he's going to remember how to light the fire.*)

He breathed on the embers, blew on the waking coals, raked the embers and their nursling flames together until their closeness, like people embracing, heated them into light. The fire sprang up, the kitchen grew warm. The old woman gave him corn mush with last night's gravy, thick lentil soup in an earthen cup, black bread spread with chicken fat. He looked up through the haze. The fire smoked. He had not made it right. Through the smoke he no longer saw two or even four but five or six old women with twinkling eyes and bright red cheeks netted with wrinkles, an enormous crowd staring at him as he tipped sideways. His eyes closed and he slept with the empty cup tight in his hand.

When he woke up it was sunrise. He lay on straw in a barn with a goat tethered near him. The quiet, mountainous hulks of cows

164

steamed like bulwarks against the forest. He closed his eyes again. Later he got up stiffly and looked for a pail into which to milk the cows. He tethered the goat near the mound. He brought the milk into the kitchen, got wood, and made the fire, kneeling until it flamed, wondering what he was doing to make it smoke. "Maybe the chimney needs cleaning," he thought. "I'm small. Tomorrow before I light the fire I'll crawl up and clean it." He drew water, pouring some into the kettle, wondering where the old woman kept the mush and the bread. Just then she came down, her apron on, her eyes tiny and glittering. She cooked fresh mush, heated leftover gravy which she took from a stone jug, and they ate, the boy on a stool with his plate on his knees, afraid to join her at the wobbly table for fear she might think him too bold.

"What's your name, bag of rags?" she asked over her steaming coffee.

"I have no name," he answered. "Give me paint and let me earn my keep."

So that day he painted the fence. For supper he got black bread spread with chicken fat, and a slice of raw onion to keep away the rheum.

The next morning he crawled up the chimney to clean out the soot. He scrubbed himself outside in the freezing well-water. After he'd made the fire, drawn the water, and admired how the fire smoked less than before, he sat down on his stool, plate balanced on his knees, a little closer to the table, and watched the old woman sip her coffee.

"Bag of rags," said the old woman. "You're a willing child and a useful child and you don't get in my way. I know what you are. You can't hope to hide. Tell me your name so I know what to call you."

"Call me No-Name," he answered. "I can cut wood for you to last the week. I see your woodpile low, and your old man not back to cut for you."

"You're a small bag to wield a big ax," said the old woman. "I can't let you. You'll hurt yourself."

"If I don't hurt myself now, I will later," No-Name answered, turning so she'd not see his eyes. "Let me try what I can do. What happens won't be your fault."

So the old woman gave him the ax. Slowly, carefully, keeping his feet planted squarely and steadily out of the way, gripping the handle firmly, he stood behind the grassy mound and swung till his shoulders hurt. For supper he got black bread with chicken fat and a slice of dried beef from the larder.

He woke up in the straw with the goat snorting nearby and the comfortable bulkheads of the cows heaving between the cold dawn and his dreams. The old woman stood with her lantern high. Beside her stood a tall old man with a wooden leg and a battered hat.

"This is your ragbag?" the old man asked.

"That it is," she said.

"You want me to keep it?" the old man asked.

"It's useful and quiet, and doesn't eat much."

"Ah," said the old man, looking at the rising sun, then back down at the straw. "That will change. They grow."

"That can't be helped," said the old woman. "Feed little, they grow little."

"So be it," said the old man. "You, now, No-Name, let me see what you can do."

So No-Name milked the cows, tethered the goat near the mound, made the fire, which smoked less this morning, and drew water. After breakfast he cut wood till his arms ached.

"You'll do," said the old man. "Tomorrow I'll show you the right way to swing an ax and build a fire."

For supper he got thick black bread with golden honey spooned out of a stone jar. "I don't mind what you are," the old woman said. "We are of those who can own no land and hold no property. The Boyar takes nine tenths. What you are, we are, though we don't speak of it or pray to the Lord who makes it. Tell us your name so we can know what to call you."

"I lost my name in the forest," he answered, looking at the mound. "Call me No-Name, I've no other."

"I won't," said the old man, tapping his pipe out against his wooden leg. "Tell me your name or I'll send you away."

No-Name looked at the chimney he had cleaned. He thought of the warm, itchy straw and the comfortable hulks of cows drifting through his dreams, keeping away the grunting from the woods. He looked out at the mound with the goat nearby. "Give me a name," he said. "I'll take what you give."

"I can't," said the old man, striking his pipe against his leg. "Where should I find a name for you? Tell me your name or go."

No-Name looked out at the mound. "Under there someone sleeps sound. He hasn't lost his mother or his father, his home or his name, although maybe they've lost him. What does he need with his name under the grass? Give me his name, for he doesn't need it now."

The old woman turned away. She pulled up a corner of her apron against her eyes but said nothing. The old man tapped his pipe angrily against his leg. "Can you live with the secrets of the dead? A dead man's name is a heavy gift." The goat yanked up a clump of grass, and snorted.

(*Let them give him the name, my daughter, Galen, says. Last time they sent him away.*)

"Give me your dead man's name," insisted No-Name. "I need it if I'm to live. Who else does?"

(*This is a true tale, says Sita, standing over a kettle of curried rice, listening over the radio. I knew that child. Only, it was an eight-year-old girl and not a boy at all. She had been hurt by soldiers and came staggering and crawling with bloodied thighs into my village. She was dishonored and nameless. Not one would feed her, not one would keep her. They sent her to a camp.*)

(*No, says Nguyen, mending a net. It happened in my village. They were boys and girls, burnt, their hands blown off, sometimes the childless kept them, sometimes not.*)

(*The tale is old, I say. You change it at every telling. Shall we quarrel over the bones of the dead? What her name was, his name, how many names, how many tellings, who remembers? They have forgotten their names; change them as you will. The tale must change if it is not to go on the same.*)

"Pavl," said the old man, his memories of his own dead embracing his new son. "Your name is Pavl Liebermann. See that you use it well."

"That I will," said young Pavl. From that night on he worked for the old couple in their junkyard and their store, welding broken rakes and washtubs, buying and selling, taking their money to the Boyar each month, serving them like the dead son whose name he bore. But at night in his bed under the eaves where he had moved from the barn, he looked up at the moon. And each time he heard the snuffling of a wild pig, the crashing of a horse pulled down, or the squeal of a rabbit, he rocked back and forth and crooned, "No-Name, I'm No-Name, don't follow me. Don't take this name away. I'm No-Name, No-Name still, you can't touch me. Don't take this name away."

(*Now, that was how No-Name survived and took the name of Pavl Liebermann. He lived with that old couple. When they died they left him all they had. And how he carried the dead man's name and learned the secrets of the dead, this part of the tale doesn't tell, but the last part does. And this my grandmother told to me, and her grandfather told it to her when he was blind and old, although he didn't know the end. In each telling something has changed, for every hearer changes the tale.*)

One winter day old Pavl walked on the cobblestones in Galtz, blind, stiff, guided at the end of a gold-tassled cord by his eight-year-old granddaughter, Pavla. He had married twice and survived both wives. Not one of his first wife's babies outlived infancy, and childbirth killed her. He had worked long hours through poverty, hungry winters, war, his hand falling ruthlessly upon any who owed him money, for he had the survivor's gift. His mind grew twisted, tricky, shrewd, crafty, deadly, as he amassed wealth, leased ships, bought and sold grain, shipping to the four corners of his world. If the laws let him own no land, still, he could lease ships, move merchandise, borrow, lend. The Boyar took nine tenths. And from his second marriage, his son Lev and his daughter Thérèse survived. Thérèse married well, then divorced her husband shamefully and ran off to New York. Lev became Pavl's partner, married the wealthy Florica, then took control and forced blind Pavl out, as an ambitious young man with a proud wife must do. Florica gave Pavl three fine grandsons and two clever granddaughters, one of whom now guided him down to the docks.

(*Hold on*, says Julio Martinez, who has been listening. *This is a true story. I knew the man. But the name he took from the dead was not Pavl but Luis Casas, and the country was my own. I was there, I knew the man and his family.*)

(*No*, says Chaka, also listening. *This is not correct. I tell you he was sold into slavery. In my village they still remember the name he bore before your people took it from him.*)

(*It was not a man but a woman*, says Sita. *I knew her, she died dishonored by soldiers.*)

(*The tale is old*, I say, *told how many times. Change what you like. If you do not change it, who will?*)

So at last Pavl, who had been No-Name, grew tired of all this. Not even his health was left. He was as helpless in his son's house as when he staggered up bloodied out of the forest. He had nothing of his own. He stumbled down to the river, blind, weighed down under his long life, stiff with arthritis, unable to bend his knees, guided at the end of the cord like an unruly goat.

"Grandpa," said young Pavla. "There's the *Constantin*. She has three masts and a grey smokestack. Is she ours?"

"I don't want to hear about her," said blind Pavl, hunched down under his life.

"Grandpa, there's the *Heliodoro*," said young Pavla. "Is she ours?"

"Let me die soon," said blind Pavl, crouched under his life. "What I can't see and don't own I don't want. What good are these hands? What use my work? Why did I live when I should have died? Oh,

Something, Someone, You Who are like me and have No Name, change my life for me, let me go free."

(Oh Lord God, though he has forgotten Your Holy Name, he calls on You. Will you let him go now? His life weighs heavier than ever bucket of water or load of wood. How will You change it? Susan Molloy, you whose great-grandmother journeyed as a child in steerage after the Famine, if you were the Lord God in Her infinite mercy, how would you change this life? Surely you never wanted him to fight so hard to keep so little?)

(The tale seems true to me, says Susan. But I'd make him kinder to others once he'd earned his wealth.)

(That's asking too much, says Julio. I tell you, I knew the man. Who was ever good to him except for a price? How could he have lived except as a snapping wolf? I don't think he's what needs changing.)

(Julio Martinez, if you were the Lord of Life in His infinite justice, how would you change this life?)

(That's a hard one, says Julio. Maybe it was written that it should be as it was. It ends as all tales must, with death.)

(No, says my daughter Galen, glaring at us all. Nothing here is right, nothing ends as I want. I don't accept it. If God in Her infinite mercy gave me power, I would change it all, I would wipe it out, I would let none of it happen. Not from the very beginning, not the deaths, not the grunting and blood and fear, not the old couple's mercy, I should take all of it back, everything should go.)

(Now, thanks to you, Galen, to whom God has given Her wisdom. You have brought blind Pavl relief from his long life. Watch now, see the glory of what you have done, for the hearer has changed the tale. Because of you, it will not end like every other telling.)

Blind Pavl tugged at the tasseled cord saying to young Pavla, "Take me home." As he walked stiffly on the scalloped cobblestones, something loosened in his ribs the knot that had been tied so long ago. Slowly he limped home. His life dropped off. First the memory of this day fell. He forgot whether it was morning or afternoon, whether he had eaten or still hungered. What house he homed towards fell away. He thought he returned to the house on Constantia street where Lev and Thérèse were born. Lev's forcing him out of their partnership fell away. He thought it was time to check the invoices. Thérèse's marriage fell splat on the cobblestones. He wondered who this child was who tugged at his leash, why night lay so thick on his eyes, where his ten-year-old Deedee was, why she had not met him as he walked home. The names of children and grandchildren clattered onto the stones where they broke and were gone. His first wife's death and the dead babies she had born peeled away like torn rags. He wondered if it was time to court the green-eyed beauty who made such good lentil soup. The years with the old couple tore, the wind combed through them, pulled them gaily off his shoulders. What was this warm, scratchy straw in which he lay, keeping the grunting and the snuffling away? What was this blazing sun like a brass potlid? What was this salt and blood in his mouth, what were these red welts across his face? Who were these strangers who undressed him, pushed him, pulled him, forced him down, covered him with night?

(*Do You see the way of it, oh Lord God, in Your mercy? Do You see how gently You are undoing the long burden of blind Pavl's life, as if it had never been? Lord of Life, maybe You are tired of this long burden too?*)

Someone brought him tea with honey, someone spooned it into his mouth which hung witlessly open. Someone smoothed his hair, washed away the blood, stroked his forehead. Who were these people? Why did they call him father, not bag of rags? Why Pavl, not No-Name? Why darling, sweetheart, baby, not little Jew? The night lurched, staggering and weaving, over his eyes, two nights, four nights, how many nights, he was drunk with them. In the rich, shimmering, unfolding darkness, to the terror of his son, his daughter-in-law, his grandsons, his granddaughters, the blind old man began to snort and shout, tears glittering down his wrinkled cheeks, blazing like the points of stars out of his clouded eyes. He ran through the shimmering, manifold darkness. Far back in the trees a wild pig grunted and snuffled. "Yitzakh," the old man shouted, and nobody knew whose name he called. But his brother Yitzakh leaped up like a bright flame and brushed the dead leaves from his mouth which they had covered for so long. Far back under the bushes a horse foundered, crashed, and shrieked, pulled down by wolves. "Schmuel," the old man shouted, and his brother Schmuel reared up out of the darkness, nostrils flaring, flames in his eye-sockets, and sniffed the sweet air of life once again. Close behind a rabbit squealed a high, shrill, bubbling squeal, choked off suddenly. "Rivka," he cried, and they had to hold him down to quiet him. "Ah, Rivka." And his sister Rivka, the darling, slipped softly down off the sharp stake that had been pounded up through her not-yet-woman's body, and tossed aside the tattering winds of her death and her unlived life, smiling in the nakedness of her youth. Closer than his own ears, right there inside him, a small child whimpered and blubbered and gasped. Who was the child, whose the cry, the life sucked down the drain? "Chana?" he cried. "Rachel? Whose life? Whose death? Mother? Father?" But the hoarse gasping kept on. "New Hope Town, Flame Town? Oh Lord God of Hosts, Lord God!"

170

(*Is it complete? Has he given us back the forgotten names, told the secrets of the dead? Can he go free? Somebody help him so he can go free.*)

(*Is it life?* asks Reiko Shimazu, hiding her ruined face. *Must he give back his life?*)

(*He's given it back already,* says Susan Molloy. *It's unfair to make him give it back twice. Why is his dying so hard?*)

"Oh Azrael, Angel of Death!" blind Pavl shouts. "Come *now.*" But still he gasps, while a small child whimpers and cries.

(*Ah, listen, there's someone running and crying inside him right now,* says my daughter Alison. *That's the one whose secret he must tell to get free.*)

(*Now glory to God, hear her, old man, and say what you must. End your long death, give yourself back and be free.*)

And at last, in the multifoliate dark night, old blind Pavl hears our loving voices, the many hearts of God Who has heard his tale. "I can't keep on," he whispers to the thing that has sobbed with him through the woods. "I *must* stop and save you even though I die for it." He turns back, but where is the child who has been crawling through the brambles, whipped by branches, blinded by blood, gasping like water sucked down a drain? There's only a withered shadow, a dried-out husk twitching in the underbrush. He stretches out his bloodied hands to raise this husk, and the shadow grasps his hand tightly, wavers, melts, and pulls him down with it, sucked into the darkness. And suddenly, with a loud voice, "Emanu-el," the blind man shouts. "That was the name. Lord god of Hosts, Angel of Death, where did I lose it? Emanu-el, oh Emanu-el, my lost name!"

And turns his face from those whose names he no longer knows, and lays down the long names of his death, and rests forever in our collective mercy and wisdom, our peace which cradles him in infinite release.

(*Only young Pavla, of all those by Emanu-el's deathbed, guessed whose names he shouted so loudly or why. But she told her sister and brothers, and they remembered those names all their long lives, and gave them to their grandchildren, counting them over and adding to their sacred mysteries as we do now: Yitzakh. Schmuel. Rivka. Chana. Rachel. New Hope Town, Flame Town and your many dead. Julio's dead. Susan's dead. Chaka's dead. Reiko's dead. Sita's dead. Nguyen's dead. Menachem's dead. Yasir's dead. Lord God. Azrael, Angel of Death. Old blind Emanu-el. Grant us peace forever in this world which gives you back to us and which we have made. Let the story of these lives change next time we tell it. We swear to you the hearer will change the tale.*)

Ina Jones

I write in Cobleskill, NY, where I live happily with my husband and am a glad grandmother. When I took early retirement from my secretarial job, I thought I would go full speed ahead with writing. Full speed is harder than I imagined. I wish I were less diversified, not flitting from poems to short story to novel and back. Yet if I live long, I may yet complete my book of poems, my book of short stories, my two novels—all at once! Meanwhile, I try and I learn. My work has been published in Epoch, Blueline, Greenfield Review, Glens Falls Review, Sing Heavenly Muse! *and some others.*

One of the nicest things about writing is its associations. During the past couple of years, at readings and workshops, I've found many a new friend: young, no longer so young, older than I—age seems to matter less in any art than it does, say, at a country club dance. A number of people I used to see are retirees in Florida. I miss them. But I like it here, in our mountains, at work among friends.

The Fox

The first time Mildred saw the fox, she was alone in the house. Earl had gone to the village in the truck. Mildred had stepped to the screen door to let in Cleopatra, who meowed on the mat. Caesar ambled in, too — poor dog was getting stiff with age. Well, who wasn't? Cleopatra and Caesar, Mildred and Earl — all getting on. Mildred lingered at the screen, hearing the cicadas. And there on the hill, a ways down from the woods, stood the fox.

At first she thought it was some neighbor's dog — maybe the Bixby's. But no, the ears were different, the muzzle was longer. She and Earl had been living on the place only since spring, and seeing wild creatures excited her. Cautiously she reached for Earl's binoculars hanging from a hook. There, now she had the focus clear. A she-fox! For now the fox was sitting, and displaying, on her underside, a double row of swollen nipples. A mother fox!

"I wanted you to see her the worst way," Mildred said later to Earl.

"If she's nursing pups," Earl told her, "she's bound to be right in the area. You'll likely see her again."

Mildred hoped for this. In her mind's eye she kept seeing the fox standing in a blaze of sunlight. *The fox stood in an aura of light.* She said it over like that to herself.

Look as she might, Mildred didn't see the fox again for days. But one afternoon, there she stood. *Pert as you please*, as Mildred put it in a letter to their former neighbors downstate. She tried to make the letter enticing. *See how happy we are?* she wanted it to say. *See how wrong you were about our "burying" ourselves up here in our retirement?* For these friends had had a lot to say about her and Earl's buying this farm. Not that they were keeping livestock and growing crops. Just to own the acres was enough for Earl. That had been his dream.

Every once in a while, those next weeks, they saw the fox again. Earl even got several pictures of her. He had a camera with a telephoto lens, his retirement present from the bank where he had been custodian for lo-how-many years. "We'll send them a picture of the fox," Mildred planned. She was proud of how she had lured the fox into camera range by setting a plate of food scraps up in the field, half way between the house and the woods. She and Earl had watched from the porch as the fox crept closer and closer, then gulped the food and streaked off to the woods.

Yet now Earl commenced to complain about having a fox getting too familiar around the place. Arley Bixby had said a lot of wildlife had rabies.

"Arley Bixby, Arley Bixby," Mildred said. "Every time he opens his mouth you think it's pearls of wisdom."

"He knows the area like a book," Earl said.

"But never read a book," Mildred countered.

She and Earl had their spats, and Arley Bixby was one subject they didn't see eye to eye on. Mildred didn't care for Arley's cowboy hat with some kind of fur tail hanging off the band. Nor for his beard and showy belt buckle. About most things, though, Mildred and Earl agreed. But they had different ways. Mildred, now, when she saw a pretty sight, she wanted to talk about it. Earl was a silent one.

"See how she holds her head?" Mildred said one time of the fox, plucking Earl's sleeve. They were standing at the porch rail and it was sunset. Up there the fox stood, golden in the orange light. A funny thing: Mildred had a sudden memory of standing so, side by side with Earl, at plate-glass windows in hospital corridors. "See his ears, how nice and close to his head?" she had said then, meaning Randy's ears (their first-born, cute as a button in his little crib). And later, of Cassie, it had been, "See her eyebrows?" (That little bud of a face could just about break your heart.) "See how his hair comes to a point?" she had said of Clifford. "Make you think of anybody?" (It was Earl's hair, of course, that grew like that.)

Mildred's eyes got misty, remembering. "Doesn't her coat have a glow to it?" she said now of the fox, as Earl looked through the binoculars.

She decided to call the fox Lady. And she endowed the animal with attributes befitting the name. She imagined Lady lying patient and forbearing as her cubs scrambled over her and tugged at her nipples. What daily routines did foxes have, Mildred wondered, pushing her dust mop around the islands of braided rugs in the bedroom. What arrangements had Lady had to make for her lying-in? Mildred couldn't help but think of what fun she and Hazel Badgeley would have had, speculating on the habits and customs of lady foxes. Oh my, how she and Hazel had used to carry on sometimes, spluttering into their tea cups with laughter.

Mildred sighed. Having pulled the counterpane taut across the bed, she sat for a bit on the bed's edge.

"We've got something in common," she said, looking uphill through the window screen. Here, where pictures of her children and her eight grandchildren were aligned on the mantel, Mildred often felt like having a nice talk. "I nursed all three of mine, too," she confided. A breeze blew the curtains inward. Sun warmed her front. "It wasn't all that popular in the thirties and forties," she added. She looked down at herself, then cupped her breasts, now somewhat limp under her T-shirt, in raspberry-stained hands.

Mildred didn't let on to Earl that she was still putting leftovers on Lady's plate. To tell the truth, she started to cook a little extra, when it was something suitable—like chicken or lamb. Mildred had done some research. (A good thing they hadn't put the old encyclopedia into the garage sale.) *Foxes prey on woodchucks, rabbits, ground birds, poultry, and sometimes lambs,* she read under FOX. *They also eat rats, mice, frogs, worms, beetles, or fruits.*

My-my, Mildred thought. And thanked goodness that cats were not mentioned—yet felt nervous each time she saw Cleopatra mousing on the hill. And Caesar, though he was a German shepherd, retired—he still moseyed around some. Mildred didn't want him coming across Lady's children romping up there in the black-eyed susans. Pretty soon Caesar appropriated the couch, given such easy access. Cleopatra kneaded herself a spot on the antique counterpane, in the groove between the two pillows.

Mildred kept the F volume of the encyclopedia, open to the appropriate page, lying about like a good letter that bore rereading. *The female fox is called a vixen. Both parents watch over the young and carefully protect them until they are about two months old.* (Isn't that nice, Mildred always thought.)

One thing, she decided not to send a picture of Lady to their friends after all. Those pictures didn't begin to do lady justice. The colors weren't true. There wasn't the emerald green of the grass, nor the tawny gold of lady's coat. Besides, wouldn't their friends be likely to laugh—a fox eating off a china plate? (With a floral pattern at that.) Hazel, she would have laughed, too—but with affection. But there. Hazel had died almost two years ago, and Mildred ought to be getting adjusted. She blew her nose on some gritty tissues she found in her sweater pocket.

It was kind of lonesome in the house tonight. A cold wind whipped against the windows. The weather was getting fallish. Earl had built them a fire in the stove. But the stove was more for atmosphere—they had a good furnace, too. They would be comfortable here in the winter.

Actually it was all this kind of assurance Mildred had been feeling that day when she had first seen Lady. It had come to her then: we did right in coming here; this is the prettiest place in the whole world. Oh, hadn't she been afraid to leave their church, their friends, familiar stores, their doctor, and her flowering quince in the side yard? But that day, seeing Lady there on the hill—that sudden *beauty*, like—it had been a kind of go-ahead about their living here. Lady had been her sign.

But tonight Mildred felt low. Earl lay there across from her, tipped back in his lounge chair, snoring. Ordinarily she would have given him a good-natured shaking awake—offered to play him a game of checkers. But not tonight, thank you. For Earl had laid down the law. Apparently he realized that she still slipped a little something to Lady's plate now and then.

"Now Mildred, I mean it. Don't feed that fox anymore. Arley Bixby says it's not good to make pets of wild things." Mildred could still hear just the way he had said it.

Just for spite, she had gone up on the hill as soon as Earl had dropped off in his chair. Dusk had already been gathering. Caesar had whined at the screen door, seeing her start off. Once up there, she had felt kind of foolish, standing in the leafy wind swells. Serve her right if she twisted her ankle in the half dark. "It's not that I'm inviting you to my house," she said, scraping the remains of the stew to Lady's flowered plate. "I'm only trying to keep you from eating some nice rabbit. You vixen."

Mildred became adept at deviousness. Not only did she continue to feed Lady, she found a special surprise for her. At the village market they had baskets of Concord grapes. Instantly an illustration in a remembered grade school reader flashed into Mildred's mind—of a fox leaping before vines hung with purple grape clusters.

"I'm planning on taking some grape jelly down to Bixby's," Mildred mentioned casually to Earl. And she decided, while she was about it, she would also bake the Bixby children some applesauce cookies. The four Bixby kids seemed nice enough—though Mildred couldn't say as much for their mother, Charlene Bixby, who had this habit of addressing you through deep exhalations of cigarette smoke.

So here she was, sauntering on the hill to pick up apples under the tree by the stone wall, a basket hung on her arm.

The grass had now grown crunchy with dryness. There was a whirring of insect voices all across the fields—how Mildred loved that sound. Down home it had never been as jubilating. *Down home, down home*, she reproved herself. *Here's* home. And it was all right with Mildred. The mountains were turning gorgeous colors. She wished one or another of the children could have visited this summer—how the grandkids would love the place. Well, they were all far away. They all had their own lives. How peaceful it all looked—the Bixby place, their own, and on down the valley. *Apple time*, Mildred thought, when a cidery smell blew to her nostrils. Once, in her youth, a carnival fortune teller had told her she would have great joy in apple time. Mildred had felt keyed up every apple time since.

"I suppose your children are all grown," she said, approaching Lady's place. "They're gone before you know it." From her basket she took two grape clusters. "I'm sure you raised them well," she said, and stooped to lay the grapes, like an offering, on the plate.

In view of all this, then—what followed was hard to take. What devilment had been lurking, when all was so good, so peaceful there, as she had come down off the hill, walking in measured strides, bringing her apples like a harvest queen? What was there that hated to see a body get too confident?

"Mildred, now I hate to tell you this." That was how Earl started in, standing just inside the screen door, hat in hand. "Arley Bixby's lost two hens. A fox got 'em."

Mildred's heart began to race. "I don't wonder, the way they let their chickens scratch all over creation."

"No, Mildred, the chickens were locked in a coop. The fox got in from underneath."

"Why's it have to be *our* fox," Mildred said. "I imagine there's other foxes in these mountains."

"Mil," Earl said, and came over to shut off the water she had been running over the apples in the colander. "I'm sorry as can be. But it was a female fox. Mil, I fear Arley's shot your fox."

Mildred felt the blood drain from her face. She sat down on a chair.

"He's got the fox out there in his truck. He's—well, he's offered you the pelt. Or you could have the fox mounted, maybe, he thought."

"Get him off our place!" Mildred was up from her chair. She began to pace around the kitchen, clattering lids, banging drawers. Earl kept trying to reach for her, but she brushed him off with violent movements. She went into the bedroom to get away from him.

"Mil," Earl said, following her, coming up behind her. He tried to have his arms come round her as he used to do, leaning over to put his face into her neck. But she twisted away. "I want him off our place!" she said again.

From the doorway Earl said, after a silence, "Girl—isn't a thing I wouldn't do for you."

But Mildred did not turn. She began to cry now, rocking there on the bed's edge. Tears came from deep down, where things had been layered over. She bent her head, grieving, hardly knowing for what all. And no use to let her mind scurry around for possibilities. It was Lady all right. Lady was dead.

"My beauties," she said, calming herself finally. She stroked Caesar, who had approached on clicking paws, hesitant before such a storm. "My darling furred ones," Mildred said, pulling Cleopatra against her side. "It's just that I do so hate *relinquishing*."

Then she stood, looking up the hill. There was sunset light up there again. The trunks of the pines at the woods' edge were tawny. Asters and golden rod glowed like colors in church windows.

Why, at a death, did things in nature turn the more beautiful? Mildred had thought about this when Hazel died. Yet whatever sight she had cried about, thinking how Hazel would nevermore see it, always it had been as if Hazel herself were comforting her—were telling her it was all right.

"It's going to be all right," Mildred said, and wiped her eyes with Kleenex under her glasses.

Now where in the world was Earl going, angling crab-like up the hill? The foot of the hill was already in shadow, and Mildred saw Earl's red shirt blooming there. What was he carrying? A sack? And a shovel over one shoulder. Bless him. And only now did Mildred hear the sorrow in Earl's voice: *Girl—isn't a thing I wouldn't do for you.*

"Earl!" she cried, still from inside the house. "Earl!" she called again, running off the porch. And she flung her jacket about her. It grew chilly early now. The cold was coming. And they must take care of themselves, and of each other, she and Earl. She began to climb up the hill in the late light. Stones rolled under her sneakers. Grass tufts tripped her. She struggled for breath, but hurried on to close the space between herself and where Earl waited. Earl and she—it was only right that they bury Lady together.

photo by George S. Bolster

Laurence Josephs

Laurence Josephs, professor of English and resident poet at Skidmore College in Saratoga Springs, N.Y., joined the college's Department of English faculty in 1963. Since then, the New York City native's annual poetry readings have been highly anticipated events on the campus and in the surrounding community.

Each reading typically includes new poetry by Josephs, as well as old favorites, some of *which have appeared in the pages of* The New Yorker, Shenandoah, Southwest Review, Commentary, Blueline, Greenfield Review, Salmagundi, St. John's Review *and the* Greenfield Review, *among others.*

Additionally, his poetry has been featured in the anthologies Muse of Fire, I Am a Sensation, Counter/Measures, On Turtle's Back, Interfaces, Headway *and* The Honey and the Gall.

He also is the author of a verse play titled Free Fall, *which made its Skidmore debut in 1966 and was produced in 1972 at the summer theater of the Berkshire Festival in Lenox, Mass.*

Josephs's three poetry collections are Cold Water Morning, *published in 1964;* Six Elegies, *which appeared in 1973; and* The Skidmore Poems, *which appeared in 1975, when Josephs delivered the Edwin M. Moseley Faculty Research Lecture. The annual*

179

selection of faculty research lecturer is the highest honor accorded a Skidmore faculty member by his colleagues.

The owner of a farm in Greenfield, N.Y., Josephs uses his environment as a source for much of his work. The solitary life close to nature and the changing seasons as well as the natural rhythms of the year give him material and viewpoint, and much of his imagery and the recurring symbols of his writing come from his daily rural life.

Relating these universals to his own interior observations of self and others permits him to make powerful and affecting connections between himself and things beyond his control; and from such crossings and permutations often come the deepest meanings of his appealing and revelatory work.

He also uses myth, classical and Judaeo-Christian references to add another dimension to his perceptions of life and nature. His effort is to make the deeply personal somehow general, thus bringing his readers into his life by making that life seem something they can share.

Wild Geese Flying South

In the grey dawn—a good time
to start a trip—the geese
are flying south. Their vast
slim initialling of the air
announces it with a sound
almost of hunting dogs baying.

How my whole self fills with joy
at their beautiful safety! Here
below, unsafe, I yet rejoice
in their certainty imprinted
on the sky: my own dangers
forgotten: all the love

I have lost forgotten
for their sake, as one
rejoices in the good luck
of old saints, forgetting
for a moment of ecstasy
that one will never, never

be so sure of anything
as they have always been:
flying away and high beyond
mortality and the sad calls
of the flesh forever unanswered,
forever burning unslaked!

Lilacs

Last the heart breaks, and last their heart-
shaped leaves from some Persia of the mind
will rust and fall. Such promises as summer
makes but never keeps have dulled us down
as well: a scatter of memories, a drift
so heavy the air cannot support its weight.

See how the honest maples have healthily
reddened in their usual cheerful goodbye:
a weight loss unregretted as the branches
lift away from earth almost relieved
of that heavy greenness all absented now
by the departed birds: those fires burning south!

But the lilacs still rust and rust,
still cling, insisting, to the branch.
O, who can see color in the eye now blinded,
blanked by time? Who can recall that scent
dispersed now in the chilly dampness?
                                    At the end
of the driveway a tree killed by lightning

still stands in the crippled air. Such
monuments, such maps as love has made
above the indifferent earth remain sometimes
the nameless teachers of our own unteachable
griefs: like the dead leaves of the lilac,
heart-shaped, unspeakable.

Salting the Weeds

My young age in battle
with the father I truced
long after, was spent
salting the weeds of summer
down that road whose center
was wild growth.

Those salty pails of water
along with my own sweat and tears
fell upon an innocent scape
of insects surely drowned,
burned wet at my hand
in the deadly baptism

at his stern command,
day after day. O how I prayed
each night for sweet rain
to undo my carnage! As I dreamed
of a blessing to cancel
my sins while I lay

deep in my unearned sleep:
only to see the delicate
prey of my days return alive,
alive in spite of his
sentence upon them, and my own
unwilling obedience.

At the Cemetery (July 1983)

Coming back to a garden
of husks; a memory of plants.

Seeing what persists, that time
only hardens, preserves:

Sound of a slap, or no
sound but only the trace

of four fingers on a cheek
still whitened from the shock.

In the old way of remembering,
I bring some smooth pebbles

to place them on the graves.
A distant relative, coming

in worse weather will know
I was there without naming me.

Crabapple Hill

Let me tell too my wakings there.
It is too late for the sunflower
Image: patient
Follower of the indifferent master,
But for the Adirondack dawn

Where cobwebs are strung with easy crystal,
Not ever, never too late. O market
Of the prescient
Purchaser: all here to be taken and yet
How the heart leans in longing; as minstrels

Silenced by the yellow-tooth violet,
Unable to sing in that cold and all but
Too wanting!
Let me tell too my wakings there; forget
How the brook runs far to the sea, cut

Into time. And it is too late for the sun-
Flower image: of indifferent love
The haunting
Symbol. O turn away; turned from the gun
Of the seasonal death, now in the stove

Hear the voice of the applewood burning!

Schroon Lake

Thinking to rummage my life, the boy I was
(Alas, who still exists,)
Drove up to Schroon Lake through geography
Of time to seek it lying there under water
Where I had thrown back my first fish
Learning death as it could not swim again.
Pottersville is the town of my young summer
When I was given the Indian Brave, armless-
The-doll, beaded beneath his strict blanket;
Face tinct of iodine. A suitable companion
For the brotherless, he slept
With me grudgingly: he in his blanket, I in mine.
But going back found little to savor: the hotel
Smelling darkly then of cider and wood
Now eagerly possessed by Italians
Who have brought modern fixtures and loud cheese;
The general store, a supermarket now, where once
Were small hard pillows filled with the restless balsam.
I hung there until dark, kicking the pebbles
In a dry road, remembering nothing; never
Daring the lake, fearful to find it
Changed from what I could not recall
To what I would not; and left hidden by noises.
From nothing I had fled to nothing; had returned
To nothing, though I took and brought back
What alway lives inside the son:
Voice of his father to pour out
Over the night, grieving their distances.

Sherry Kearns

Sherry Kearns lives and writes in Cleverdale, New York.

Ice

Death lives under the ice
and tells it what to say.
Ice has a bass voice;
when Arctic air comes
it booms welcome
and cracks a deep door.
When it's stepped on
sometimes ice says
who
like a barred owl
which snatches up the field mice at night.
Other times it says nothing
like the hungry, silent fish;
or it will echo back footfalls
to an ice walker
who hears what is said
and who keeps glancing and glancing behind.

Snow

Snow is the beloved of ice
who lies with it winter long.
Snow muffles ice's voice
telling its own tales.
It says the rodents' paths
and what they ate;
it tells of dogs and deer
and whispers where the foxes' kits are denned.
In deep woods
where no sun or shadow is on it,
no speck to focus upon,
fresh snow is silent.
What a walker was told there
on snow's surface
was the blood's pulse
behind her own eyes.
When she left
snow said
who stood and stared here
and how long.

Fog

Fog is the final voice of ice
saying water's many names.
It repeats rain's persistent syllable
all night, all afternoon.
It calls down a cataract
which floods its culvert
in haste home.
Fog keeps walkers company
on a last trip over ice
saying to them:
there is no horizon
nor mountains,
there is not path
nor shore
nor each other;
there is fog,
this breath already breathed,
breathed again
and water spread underfoot.

Watching Fireworks on the 4th of July in a Boat off Bolton Landing

The ones I like best burst in chrysanthemum shapes
onto the heavens, then spread
and decay to ash that drifts softly down.
Yet the sparks losing form against night
confuse their light with the stars'
so I sometimes miss the fall of man-made fire
watching near-eternal heavenly light.
Again and again these tiny novas dominate our vision
while the running lights of watchers' boats,
bright and full, seem city streets lit by traffic.
Our own creations interest us most:
I watch for flowers and turn the water to asphalt.
At show's end, slapping the waves homeward,
I regard the constant stars.
There is imagined design for them, too,
what few I know:
Great and Small Bear, Orion, Cassiopeia —
but most, being unknown to me and sprawled across
so much sky, are stars
whose flames won't dim and fail under my watch
but extend in time past imagining;
they light the night above us
as they had over Egypt and Rome, the Kenya Basin,
holding their unthinkable distance above our celebrations.

Lake George

It is water that makes a wilderness here.
Fish edge front yards, the swamps conceal
turtles and waterfowl. In spring, cellars flood
and the breaking ice can take down docks.
The lake devours the land from underneath,
eventually gets the retaining walls, too.
A boat tied wrong to the wind can go
to the bottom like the old bateaux
the water covers and the French soldiers
we sail over, riding the surface, rough and smooth.

Calves Pen on Lake George

The waterfall wore a deep, smooth wedge
in the cliff. Now dry for centuries,
anyone can climb the rocks and jump
or dive into the lake from the top of the fall.
That's forty feet from the surface;
it's irresistible.
First from fifteen feet, then twenty—
soon the summit draws anyone who dares,
where first it's a jump, hollering
the whole way down.
But the urge is to dive;
to arch in silence from the rock,
to shape the waterfall,
echoing its line in air.

photo by Thomas Victor

William Kennedy

William Kennedy is a lifelong resident of Albany. Ironweed, *the third of his Albany novels, won the National Book Critics Circle Award and the Pulitzer Prize.*

An Exchange of Gifts

Quinn called Harriet Clancy the same day her letter arrived. It was two months old and had followed him across the Atlantic to Germany and back. The letter invited him to visit her and talk about Charlie Clancy. Is four o'clock okay? she asked. We'll talk and then go downstairs and say hello to Mama.

At five to four Quinn left his house on North Pearl Street and walked the two blocks to where the Clancys lived, across from Sacred Heart. The church had a new roof and a new coat of red-brick paint since he'd been gone. Also the Saviour had gained a splendid new image through the gilding of his statue. New faces passed, residents, probably, of the new housing project up the hill. But most things on this old street of shade trees seemed constant from Quinn's early childhood: the brick street, the buckled slate sidewalks, the old dogs, the pipe fences around the puny lawns, the thousands of fallen maple pods.

Harriet Clancy answered the bell, looking fine, with the same formation of teeth, the same brown eyes as Charlie. They were, after all, born only ten months apart: Irish twins. She beamed good will and clasped Quinn's hand in a way that clutched their common history, and she led him up to her flat. Everything was tidy for his visit: toys all in a box, newspapers in a neat pile, no lint on the rug, glass polished on the framed photos of a child and of the elder Clancys. No photo of Charlie.

"What about a cup of tea?" Harriet asked.

"Okay. Or maybe a beer?"

"A beer, sure." She laughed and brought two beers and two glasses from the kitchen.

"Beer makes you fat," she said. "I don't drink it the way we used to."

"The German beer's so good I put on twelve pounds."

"The letter you sent us from over there. It was a gift," she said.

"It seemed right to do after I met that fellow who knew the case. I guess there's still nothing definitive."

"No."

"It's a hell of a thing not knowing."

"It's worse than you think," said Harriet. Quinn waited for her elaboration, but she fell silent.

What was known was that Charlie was piloting a bomber into North Korea when he caught flak. Squadron members had a signal when someone was hit and had to bail out: When you landed, if you were all right, you fired one shot, paused, then fired another shot. If you didn't fire a shot, you were dead. Charlie's chute was blown farther north than anyone else's, the navigator remembering Charlie waving as he went out of sight over the horizon. After a while one shot was heard, just one. Had Charlie's pistol jammed? Had a gook shot him dead before he could finish the signal?

Nobody in the Clancy family knew even this much until Quinn bumped into Bobby Owens from North Albany in the sergeants mess in Frankfurt. Bobby had been with G-2 in Korea before being transferred to Germany, and one assignment took him to a hospital to interview people from the mission Charlie had been on. The navigator told him about hearing the one shot.

"Did you tell this stuff to the family?" Quinn asked Bobby.

"I made a report. I assume they sent it to the family."

"What I hear from home, the Clancys don't know anything about what happened. You ought to write them."

"I can't myself. Against the rules."

"Then I will."

"Leave me out of it," said Bobby, "and I'll put it through channels."

So Quinn, quoting an anonymous source, wrote Harriet with the news. Until then the only word the Clancys had had from the government was: Your son is missing in action. Then a year later: Your son is missing and presumed dead. The American Legion post in North Albany quickly added Charles Francis Clancy's name to those engraved on the marble memorial at School 20, which bore the names of all North Enders killed in action from December 7, 1941.

The Legion's memorial committee visited Mrs. Alice Clancy, Charlie's widowed mother, and asked her to be guest of honor at the service honoring Charlie. Alice Clancy listened to the invitation and then told the visitors she would take the matter to her ward leader, her mayor, her Congressman, to the national commander of the Legion, and to the President of the United States if necessary, to have Charlie's name removed from the marble. The Defense Department, she advised the visitors, damning their presumption and screaming into their confoundedness, had classified her son as presumed dead, and that is by no means certifiably dead and it is positively not dead enough to be engraved in marble. Don't you understand the difference, you lummoxes?

Rather than unengrave the name, the Legion officials chose to add the parenthetical comment (Missing) after Charlie's name. Soon thereafter Mrs. Clancy received a formal apology from the Legion's national commander, who hoped things had been resolved to her satisfaction. He added his admiration for her faith in her son's ability to survive war and captivity. "Hope," concluded the commander, "is one of the three great Christian virtues, and we must never forget that."

"What do you remember about Charlie?" Harriet asked Quinn.

"Everything. I could talk for a week. This tiepin, I wore it today because he gave it to me. I really couldn't shine his shoes playing golf, but one day I got hot and he was off his feed and I beat him for six bucks playing dollar-a-hole. He was so sure of himself that he wasn't even carrying any cash, so as a payoff he gave me the tiepin."

Quinn showed Harriet the pin, a golden golf club, a putter. Charlie had gone on to become a major figure in state amateur golf, then a pro who couldn't stand the heat, who double-bogied and three-putted under pressure. And after a bad day on the links he enlisted in the Air Force.

"I remember that pin," Harriet said. "My mother give it to Charlie for his birthday. It's solid gold."

"Is that a fact?"

"I'm surprised he gave it away."

"Well, he owed me money."

"Even so. He obviously didn't think much of it."

"I'd have given it back if he asked."

"That's what I mean," said Harriet, and she went for a second round of beer.

"You know what I remember about you?" Quinn said when she came back. "That pink dress you wore when I took you dancing out to Dinty's."

"You remember that?"

"It was like silk. Salmon pink. And snug is the word for how it fit you."

"Everybody liked that dress. I've still got it."

"No."

"You want to see it?"

"Why not?"

She brought it out on a hanger and he stroked it just above the hem. "Just the way I remember it," he said.

"I'll bet I could still get into it."

"No."

"What'll you bet?"

"You name it."

"If it fits you'll have to dance with me," Harriet said.

She went to the bedroom and when she returned she had removed certain garments whose absence confirmed Quinn's memory of the dress being cut down to Harriet's well-tempered clavichord. Quinn stood up to admire it from several angles and Harriet revolved as a model might.

"It's snug all right," she said.

"It'd command attention on any dance floor."

"They played 'The Tennessee Waltz' the year we went out."

"Right. And 'Mam'selle'."

"And 'I'd like to Get You on a Slow Boat to China.'"

"Wouldn't I, though," Quinn said.

He put his arms around her and hummed 'The Tennessee Waltz' and they danced. When she pulled her face away to look at him, he stopped humming and kissed her.

"This would be tough to explain if your husband walked in," he said.

"He's building a bridge in New Jersey."

Quinn, humming and dancing again, traced a finger on flesh that wasn't covered by the dress. As his incursions grew more familiar, she pushed herself away.

"That's enough for now," she said.

"It doesn't seem like enough," Quinn said. But she went back to the bedroom and returned in the dress she was wearing when he arrived.

"I really want to talk to you, Danny," she said.

"About Charlie."

"About my mother, who won't accept what happened. She got up in the middle of the memorial mass and said right out loud, 'You can't say mass for a dead boy when he's not dead.' And she walked out of church. She fights with the priests, she blames God for keeping Charlie hidden. She spent a fortune on a thieving fortune teller who kept telling her Charlie was in a peasant village, then in a pagoda. She gives my son the same gifts, the same clothes she gave Charlie. He's only two years old and he's already got golf sticks."

"What can I do?"

"Talk to my mother. Tell her Charlie's dead."

"I already told her all I know."

"Tell her you found out things you couldn't say in a letter."

"What things?"

"Say he was blown to pieces. Say he had his head shot off. Say anything, but kill him, for god's sake. Kill him. She'll go insane if she keeps on like she's going."

"It's really an obsession with her," Quinn said.

"Kill him," Harriet said.

They let themselves into Mrs. Clancy's flat and sat facing each other in rocking chairs, waiting for the old woman to come home from cleaning the altar at Sacred Heart.

"She was in church so often praying for Charlie," Harriet said, "that the pastor offered her a job."

With her shoes turned over, her elbows poking through her black sweater, her hair a bright white and clutching her bag of cleaning rags and brushes, Alice Clancy entered the house and came through the hallway into the parlor.

"Danny came to visit us, Mama," Harriet said.

"Oh, Danny, how wonderful to see you."

"I'm still not used to being home, Mrs. Clancy."

"We often talk about the letter you wrote us, don't we Harriet? It's nice that Charlie has such loyal friends. Let me put these things away."

She came out of the kitchen with a plate of macaroons.

"These are Charlie's favorite," she said. Quinn bit one.

"Shall I make tea?"

"Please no."

"Well, it's awful nice that you're back. It's nice that some of our boys have come home."

"Mama," said Harriet, "Danny has something to tell us."

"Oh?"

"Nothing, really."

"Tell her," said Harriet. "Go ahead and tell her."

"Tell me what?"

"There's nothing to tell."

Harriet stood up and took two steps toward Quinn's chair.

"Tell her," she said, louder than before.

Quinn shook his head.

"Tell her, goddamn you," Harriet screamed. "Tell her what you told me. He told me Charlie was blown up by the Chinamen when he landed, mama, that his navigator saw them blow him into little pieces."

"Everything I know I put in the letter."

"You son of a bitch. You rotten liar. He's lying Mama. He told me they blew Charlie's head off, but it was too terrible to tell us. Just before you came in, he told me. I swear he did."

Quinn and Alice Clancy stared at Harriet. Her chin grew bumpy, her entire body shook.

"She lost a son in the war," Harriet screamed at Quinn. "But did you hear her since she came in here? The first things out of her mouth, Charlie this, Charlie that. What about me, Mama? Am I your daughter? Am I nothing? I lost a mother in the war, that's what happened to me." She ran through the hallway and slammed the front door. Quinn and Alice Clancy sat looking past each other, listening to Harriet run up the stairs.

"I never knew she felt that way," Alice Clancy said.

"She's a high strung girl."

"She should've said something."

Quinn pulled off his tiepin and handed it to Alice. "This belonged to Charlie," he said. "I won it from him playing golf." Alice looked at it, then at Quinn.

"I gave that to Charlie for his twentieth birthday."

"Harriet told me."

"I thought he lost it. He said he lost it."

"He gave it to me because he owed me six dollars."

"Six dollars? I paid eighty-seven dollars for it."

"Harriet told me you spent a great deal for it. She's very devoted to you."

"The poor thing," Alice said. "Imagine her feeling that way and keeping it all to herself?"

"She's a very sensitive girl. She always was."

"Is there anything you didn't tell us, Danny?"

"Some things you just can't bring yourself to say," Quinn said.

"What do you mean? Do you mean?"

Quinn moved his head in what he hoped would be interpreted as a nod.

"Some things," he said, "you just can't bring yourself to say."

photo by Paul Rosado

Maurice Kenny

Born and raised in northern New York near the St. Lawrence River, Maurice Kenny currently resides in Brooklyn where he co-edits the literary journal, Contact/II with J. G. Gosciak and is the publisher of Strawberry Press. Mr. Kenny was given the prestigious American Book Award in 1984 for his collection, THE MAMA POEMS. A previous collection, BLACKROBE, was nominated for the Pulitzer in 1983 and did win the coveted National Public Broadcasting award in 1984. His most current collections are IS SUMMER THIS BEAR . . . poems dealing mainly with the Adirondack region, and RAIN, a first collection of fictions. Mr. Kenny's SELECTED POEMS: BETWEEN TWO RIVERS will appear in March of 1986 to be followed by ROMAN NOSE AND OTHER ESSAYS. Michael Castro, author of INTERPRETING THE INDIAN, has written: "His work is American Indian (Mohawk), personal and universal all at once." John Crawford, editor of West End Press, has written: "I reread THE MAMA POEMS today and it reconfirmed to me how powerful and sustained that book is. I think (Kenny) is alone in the current male Third World poets capturing a universal voice."

Sitting in the Waters of Grasse River

Canton, N.Y. - 7/1983

Swirling finch suck insects from the air;
a canoe paddles up-stream;
on the shore black-caps ripen,
and a girl trudges the bridge crossing the river.
Under the wings of a blue dragon-fly
Louie and I sit in the warm waters of the rapids
soaping our hair and talking of Molly.
One thought creates another,
one word builds a bridge between two minds,
two ages, centuries spanning Molly and us.
Surely she had sat in a river cooling
off summer heat maybe with William . . .
naked to their dreams, bare to the facts
of their history, progeny, shadows of the past,
to the horizon. Perhaps finch or hawk flew over
their heads . . . open mouths sucking insects,
or a bear stood on the shore, shores of the Mohawk
listening to the trudge of a new people
crossing the bridge from an old world . . .
not guessing that one day the Mohawk,
like the Grasse where we now sit,
would be clogged with rubber tires, beer
bottles, discarded trousers, so clogged
no bass can breathe, no turtle spawn
in the wastes and poisons dumped by a thoughtless
society.
What did Molly and William whisper:
love, the child maturing in her womb,
the war with the French, English expansion
into the far mysterious west,
the flood of aliens crossing the sea to this
unchartered map of rivers and watersheds
of an America older than they could guess.

We applied more soap to our hair,
rubbed furiously at our flesh
to clean off the stink of civilization,
the taint of poisons in the Grasse.

A gull flies overhead, pirouettes,
amazed to see such large beings
of shiny, flashing flesh. Convinced
we are not monstrous perch he disappears
high in the clouds. Up-stream we see the canoe
flowing towards us. The finch still feeds in the air
and black-caps continue to ripen.
Louie and I rinse out the soap, refreshed now
leave dripping water on the shore
thankful for the cool rapids.

Land

1976

Torn, tattered, yet rugged
in the quick incline of bouldered hills,
crabappled, cragged, lightning-struck birch, cedar;
wilderness muzzled; forests . . . kitchen tables and bedposts
of foreign centuries; meadows cow-ed
beyond redemption, endurance, violated
by emigres feet, and vineyards alien
to indigenous squash and berry,
fragile lupine and iris of the pond;
even the rivers struggle to the sea
while wounded willows bend in the snow
blown north by the west wind

1820

spring lifts under drifts, saplings
hold to the breeze, larks sing, strawberries
crawl from under snow, woodchucks run
stone walls of new cemeteries and orchards;
apples blossom, thistle bloom

(Madame de Feriet's ghost prowls the miraged bridge
spanning Black River and her mansion lanterns
glow in the clear darkness of the French dream,
hazeled in the richness of her opulence

the lands she would hold out to tenants for rent
have neither clearings nor plows;
the disillusionment loried her trunks to France,
her mansion to ashes, her bridge to dust in 1871,
her savings to pittance, her dream to agony

Madame de Feriet gave her French aristocratic manner
to a sign post at the edge of the county road,
tangled now by yellow roses and purple vetch)

1976

April lifts from under the drifts of grey
snow piled by plows ruthless in their industrial
might to free roads and make passage
for trucks and automobiles to hurry to the grave
with dead horses in the far pasture
that no longer sustains the hunger of bleating lambs

virgin spring lifts, its muddy face scarred
and mapped with trails of progress, its smoke
rising in pine, maple, flowering aspen,
chicory weed and clods, manure of waste, whey,
abandoned farm houses and barns shaking in the wind . . .
like blind old men caught without a cane in the storm;
spring bloody in its virginity, its flow corrupted,
raped in zoned courts of law that struck quarried hills . . .
a great god's lance thrust in the quickness of electric sun

rage of spring rivers, swollen with anger . . .
cold voice growling through the night . . . swirling,
swallowing the soft shoulders of shoreline;
the rage of the aged shackled to history
and the crumbling bones of its frame, fisted against
the night, shaking the cane against the dark, the bats
fluttering in the balmy summer eve, fireflies creeping
through the young green grass of the long fresh meadows

1812

the north, the north aches in the bones, the land,
in the elms' limbs gently swinging in that August
breeze, bereft of holiday and festival, ghost and voice . . .
tunneled by gophers; ticks and fleas stuck to an old dog's back

(General Brown marched his men to Sacketts Harbor,
struck the British in the red belly
and went home to lift a pint to his deeds
and captured acres, to ville a town, erect a fence)

1976

the gooseberry is diseased, and the elm,
stone walls broken, sky cracked, pheasants
and young muskrats sterilized, and fields

Sacrifice

For Joe & Carol

wolf tracks
on the snow

I follow between
tamarack and birch

cross the frozen creek
dried mulleins
with broken arms
stand in shadows

tracks move up-hill
deeper into snowed conifers

I hurry to catch up
with his hunger

cedar sing in the night
of the Adirondacks
he huddles under bent
red willow
panting

I strip in the cold
wait for him to approach
he has returned
to the mountains

partridge drum
in the moonlight
under black spruce

In My Sixth August

My father wades the morning river
tangled in colors of the dawn.
He drags a net through the cold
waters; he spits tobacco juice,
stumbles. Light warns the minnows
that hide under bullheads. Sharp air
smells of wild lobelia and apple.

In my sixth August a kingfisher
rattles from a willow; I am too
busy picking iris in the wet fields
to know a game warden shakes his head
above us on the narrow bridge to home.
The west wind has trapped our scent
and light prisons our mobile hands.

Picking Blackberries

Monday sun slants across the bush,
August brushes your hair in wind
off Lake Ontario; the watch
ticks at your wrist while the kids
squabble over who has the larger can,
the most berries, the blackest tongue.

Mrs. Anthony telling
stories in your ear
over berries meant for pie
to please your man
that might come tonight . . .
"the way to a man's heart
is through his belly."
You know that is a lie.

Your qualities were never baking,
but when you rolled up the sleeves
and baited your own hook,
or cleaned a mess of trout
or string of November rabbits
even when we demanded you darn
socks or heal blisters, fight
a cold . . . you spent years pleasing
what was not to be pleased,
darning where there were no holes,
picking berries more to gossip
with Mrs. Anthony than for pies,
forgetting teeth
needed tending, taking up
a glass of water in the dark
when Mary cried in fever,
or sitting at the winter window
watching snow in tears
telling us when he will come,
when he will go with no
understanding of what love is.

There's a plastic plant on his grave.
Yours is marked, name
chiseled into stone, the fence
around erected, prayer cards
about ready to be printed,
and still you have no idea
of what picking blackberries
was all about, you would bend
an ear to Mrs. Anthony
telling stories . . .
"the way to a man's heart
is through his stomach."

The end of the week, rain every day;
the lake is black in storm, Agnes' kids
are just about all married. You placed
the old watch in the dresser drawer,
and write letters to the family saying
how sorry you are to have missed sending
Christmas presents this year, and that
Mary's arthritis is getting worse.

Sparrows and wrens pick the blackberries.

North

In Memory of My Father

sun rises over mountain lakes
the fox breakfasts in the berry patch
mice tug grains into the burrow
grass has a way of growing

north by the old trail
north by the Susquehanna
north by the Freeway
north by the Alleghany or Mohawk
airlines that swept you into north country,
deerland, Thousand Islands;
north by semis that scoop up the north
and wrap its aluminum soil about
your Thanksgiving turkey
and freeze your pudding in the refrigerator

north by any path would be north
north . . . by north star, northern
northern country of villages and cowpens
cheese factories and crabapples, trout
diseased elms and sick roots
fenced meadows slit by snowmobiles
sky cracked by television wires,
and hunters blizzard to cabins
by dead deer . . . the last kept
them abandoned in the north snow
from home in Staten Island

north of strawberry fields, milkweed
north of maples running sap to boil
north, north country, northern New York
where corn grew to the table and squash
and bean covered the valleys

north of strawberry fields, north of sumac
north of smoke, north of tomorrow, today
of yesterday that was and is and will be
for strawberries grow forever
and wolves will cross the frozen river
under the flight of geese

sun humps over hills and horses
muskrats in the stream
swimming to shore with a mouthful of mud
the bee sipping honey
minnows in the creek

grass has a way of growing
north, north along the old trail

guard the eastern gate

James Howard Kunstler

James Howard Kunstler was born and raised in New York City, where he graduated from the High School of Music and Art. He earned a bachelor's degree in Theater from Brockport State College, but after a disastrous season of summer stock he veered into journalism and began a newspaper career with the Phoenix, a Boston weekly. Reporting jobs at several daily newspapers followed. At 25 he was a full-time columnist on the Albany Knickerbocker News. In 1975, after a year with Rolling Stone Magazine, as an editor and staff writer, he moved to Saratoga Springs to write novels.

His books include The Wampanaki Tales (Doubleday, 1979); A Clown in the Moonlight (St. Martin's Press, 1981); The Life of Bryon Jaynes (Norton, 1983); and An Embarrassment of Riches (The Dial Press, 1985). A new novel, Blood Solstice, will be published by Doubleday in the spring of 1986. His short stories have appeared in Playboy, Penthouse and Cosmopolitan magazines.

What Happens When the Light Goes Out

The summer of 1938 was a succession of disasters in our part of the country. A hurricane blew down barns and power lines; cucumber mosaic virus, wilt, cutworm and screwworm defeated the crops; timber fires raged through the foothills; and hardly anyone had any money. In Middle Grove, Sparky Payton's father, Junius, the town's only dentist, lay dying, and Grace Holt's teeth hurt.

This September evening, abnormally warm and alive with winging birds and bugs, Junius lay on his back in a first-floor parlor that was now his sickroom. The bedclothes were as crisp as restaurant napery over his frail body, while the cancer, which first appeared as a "smoker's cough" in April, had consumed nearly everything but his essential dignity. Sparky occupied an armchair next to the bed, the kind of chair a person could feel comfortable in over a long period. He was ten and a half years old, a dark-eyed, dark-haired boy, small for his age but socially advanced since he had just entered the sixth grade. This evening, as in recent days, Sparky read the newspaper from nearby Saratoga out loud to his father. He read skillfully and selectively, auditioning each story to himself before relaying it to his audience, and showing a marked preference for short items of a bizarre nature. Thus, he glossed over the report about Chamberlain's conference with Hitler in Munich (the mere headline made his father groan) and other demoralizing bulletins from Europe, and found what he was looking for in the lower left-hand corner.

" 'Insanity in State Rising,' " he read the headline, " 'Alcoholic Patients Increase.' "

"Great," his father said, with obvious effort. He had been known as a wry fellow, with a keen sense of the absurd. Sparky was a lot like him that way.

"Here's one for you, Pop: 'One Dead, Two Shot at Syracuse. Walter Bedarski, 54, pro . . . prietor of a West Side cafe, was charged with murder in the aftermath of a shooting incident that left one dead and two persons critically wounded.' "

Sparky stopped there. His father formed the word "why" with his lips.

"He saw some guy talking to his wife at the bar, it says. Hey," Sparky brightened, "guess what: one of the ones that got wounded was this guy's wife. He shot his own wife, Bedarski. What a crazy nut. Betcha he gets the chair."

"Sure," his father said.

Sparky's search through the news section paid off in two more stories of this type: "Galway Pastor Breaks Hip in Fall," and "Crazed Man at Rites for State Senator O'Brian." He read several comics out loud, "Myra North, Special Nurse," "Boots and his Buddies," "Freckles and his Friends," and "Alley Oop." On the sports page, he discovered with dismay that the Yanks had been rained out in Cleveland. Neither father nor son cared much about the daily doings in the National League.

"Want to hear the 'Thought for Today?'" Sparky inquired.

"Please."

" 'But shun profane and vain babblings, for they will increase into more ungodliness.' "

"Hear hear," his father said with difficulty.

"That's the whole shootin' match," Sparky said and lay the paper on a side table. The hall clock chimed seven times.

"Want to hear 'Amos 'n' Andy,' Pop?"

The dying man shook his head. Sparky drew his knees up to his chest and rocked himself in the chair. It was not a rocking chair, of course, and his rocking was not a social felicity. In a little while, he heard his mother's footsteps. She entered the room on a tide of appealing smells: butter, flowers, soap, coffee. Sparky could not bring himself to look directly into her eyes, afraid of what he might see there.

"I'll sit with him awhile," his mother said, and bent to run a finger along the child's hairline. "He likes it when you read to him."

"It puts him right to sleep."

"He needs his sleep," she said.

The boy did not wish to contradict her, but he saw clearly how his father's condition was tending toward a state of never-ending sleep, and at the same time he felt a wild uproar of anger and grief surge in the center of his chest.

" 'Course he does," Sparky pretended to agree and excused himself before she could read the truth in his face. Then, outside in the dooryard, it welled over, a strangled spilling of tears, vituperation, and half-digested lamb stew. He felt his world pitching, centerless, across the cold and empty expanses of a universe without a beginning or a middle, where all light dwindled to everlasting darkness. And in this transport of nullity, the boy reeled down the side yard to the rear of the house where the creek ran, flung himself out on a broad, flat rock (where he had launched "ships" of bark and paper years ago), and plunged his head into the water.

The dunking helped. At once, the fearsome voids of space con-

212

tracted in his imagination and he was back on Otter Creek in Middle Grove, Saratoga County, New York. It was here, in the shaded pool behind the house, where his father came to cast for rising trout after a day of drilling teeth. He always smelled of Lucky Strikes and oil of clove, and the combination seemed to work well keeping the bugs off. That Spring, barely a month before Junius's "smoker's cough" proved to be the life-robbing cancer, he gave the boy a twenty dollar Thomas and Thomas cane rod on the occasion of his tenth birthday, and spent a week of evenings showing him how to use it, how to construct gut leaders, how to tie knots of fabulous complexity. Sparky was proud, above all, that his father even comprehended these things since, for instance, Eddie Geiger's old man, a machinist at the Voight-Waldridge paper company, spent his idle hours drunk on cheap rye and snagging suckers with stinkbaits in the stillwater behind the V-W mill. What Sparky's father could accomplish with a cane rod seemed princely compared to that, and he had *never* seen Junius drunk.

Now, at a quarter after seven on a September evening, Sparky's father lay dying two hundred feet away in a parlor sickroom, while the ignoble Geiger would go on and on, boozing and snagging trash, for another forty years. And while, of course, Sparky would have no way of knowing this, an intuition to this effect may have caused him to angrily peg a baseball-sized rock into the pool. It kicked up a plume of water. Sparky was sorry that he had scared the trout and hoped that they had short memories. In a little while, he departed Otter Creek and made for the road.

"Let's go to the house," Sparky urged Hazel Holt, his friend who lived a quarter of a mile up the road. They were the same age and had known each other since near-infancy. Hazel was a pretty and athletic girl, a tomboy raised in the exclusive company of male children (including four brothers) and despised all the more by everyone except Sparky for trying to be like them. Eddie Geiger, Sparky's other "best" friend, especially disapproved of his liaison with Hazel. Hazel's father was a coal, ice and cordwood jobber with his office and warehouse in Saratoga, and the family lived comfortably in more bucolic Middle Grove. But the house Sparky had referred to was not the Holts's and certainly not his own. It was the Whalen house.

The Whalen house was a twenty-two room colossus on the far side of Otter Creek, reachable only by a private, rickety suspension bridge sixty feet long that had been the marvel of Middle Grove when it was put up in the 1870's. In the great house, the Whalens passed each summer for half a century. The founding patriarch of the clan,

Frederic, made a tidy fortune in patented wire fencing, and the last of the line, Jerrold, a romantic idler and bachelor, lost the remainder of the fortune in the crash of '29. For some years now the house had been a derelict. Sparrows roosted inside and out, bees made honey in a broken piano, and raspberry canes grew unchecked into a daunting briar patch on the lawns. A fire set by "persons unknown" – it was Hazel's brother, Frank, 15 – left a gaping hole in one side of the roof. Rain and snow got in and the west wing began to sag dangerously. Finally, the bridge was in such a state of decrepitude, its cables rusted and its planks shot up by frustrated hunters, that condemnation signs were hung on it by the county building inspector. Officially, the house could be bought for the back taxes, which now so far exceeded the property's declining value that the Whalen house's future as an eyesore and a fire hazard was guaranteed. Here, Sparky and Hazel came to play this September evening.

"Do you want to go to heaven?" Sparky asked her as they entered the music room with its honey-filled piano. The bees were already asleep.

"Sure," Hazel agreed. "Where'dja leave the lantern?"

"Hold your horses."

Sparky found the lantern stashed behind a fallen louver. He trimmed the wick with his pen-knife and lit it, adjusting the flame as low as possible. Heaven, in their private argot, referred to the cupola of the Whalen house. It was reached by two flights of stairs and then a ladder that Sparky and Hazel built themselves out of scrapwood and salvaged nails. Sparky let Hazel climb the ladder first, then handed her the lantern. Of all the rooms in the Whalen house, the cupola was the least damaged. All but one of the windows had even survived the hurricane, and through them the whole world that was Middle Grove could be viewed in its entirety at treetop level. The floor was neatly covered with carpet scraps. A three-legged card table was nailed to the wainscoting just under the window, making it as good as any four-legged card table. There was one chair (folding type) and one milk crate with a horsehair cushion on top that was, in many respects, more comfortable than the chair, lacking only a backrest, and Sparky had thought long and hard about putting one on. Finally, there was a mattress in one of the corners not occupied by the card table. It was covered by a water-stained blue cotton spread last seen on a Holt bed. This was heaven.

Sparky gazed out the window at his house, some distance across the red and gold-turning treetops. It was that time of the evening when electric bulbs glowed with eerie, otherworldly brilliance against the ambient twilight. His own porch seemed supernaturally vivid, perhaps because he knew the light burned for him. A dimmer light glowed in the window of the room where his father lay. Otter Creek snaked mysteriously into the distance, its green-black water partially concealed in veils of mist.

"How is he?" Hazel asked. Her voice had an appealing froggy huskiness, as if she was always on the verge of catching laryngitis. In fact, she was a healthy child. She asked the question from her seat at the card table where she was setting up a game of checkers.

"He's the same," Sparky answered her wanly. "No, worse."

"Isn't there something they can do?"

"Not a damn thing," Sparky said.

"Momma complained all through dinner her tooth was killing her."

"Then she should go into Saratoga and see Doc Demuth."

"She doesn't like Doc Demuth."

"He's taking Pop's patients."

"Momma doesn't like him. She says he's a horse doctor. She says she doesn't trust anyone drilling on her except Doc Payton."

Sparky turned to face her. "Then she'll just have to die," he said savagely and the tears followed instantly. He flung himself on the mattress. Hazel was more startled than anything else. The nature of his crying was an elongated, high-pitched drone, like a siren announcing not a warning or an emergency but the end of all hope. Hazel soon became aware of what she perceived to be a lapse of pure stupidity and she regretted it deeply. After a while, the siren stopped. Hazel kneeled down on the mattress.

"Hey, Spark . . . ?"

"Get away from me," he muttered into the blue spread. His own hot breath and warm tears nauseated him.

"Want to play checkers?"

"No!"

"Come on. We'll play some checkers."

"I don't want to play any checkers. Get out of here."

"It's just as much mine as yours."

"It's nobody's. Get out!"

"All right, I will," Hazel told him. She snatched the lantern off the card table and started down the ladder. With his face pressed into the mattress, it took Sparky a few moments to apprehend that he was about to be left alone in the dark, and as the foreboding seized him, he sat bolt upright. Orange light glowed unevenly up through the hatchway.

"Haze, wait!" Sparky cried.

"I'm getting out of here, just like you said."

"I didn't mean it."

"'Course you did."

"No, not like that."

"What's the matter? 'Fraid of the dark?"

"Yes."

The light stopped bobbling.

"I'm scared, Haze. Bring it back, please."

Once again the room swelled with light. Hazel's curious, fox-like face appeared. Sparky was ashamed.

"You're right," he said. "this place is just as much yours."

"No," she replied, approaching Sparky cautiously, "you were right. It's nobody's. We just use it."

"Who would want a rotten old place like this, anyway? You can sit down if you want."

"Move your fat rear."

Sparky rolled over to one end, leaving the corner for Hazel. She placed the lantern on the floor and settled in with her back propped against the wall.

"Happy now?" Sparky asked.

"Maybe. Who wants to know?"

"The boss."

"Don't make me laugh," Hazel said.

"Greenberg's got fifty homers now."

"No kidding? You think he's gonna break the record?"

"No. But fifty is a lot of homers."

"No one'll break the Babe's record."

"Sure they will," Sparky said. "Foxx almost did. Wilson came close. Greenberg could be the one. He could break it this year."

"You just said two minutes ago that he couldn't."

"I didn't say he couldn't. I said I didn't think he was gonna. He could though. It would take a miracle, but he could. He'd have to sock one in practically every game they got left plus a few extras. But he could do it."

"He's not gonna break the Babe's record."

"No," Sparky said. "Probably not."

The crickets were out. Their chirpings were slow, with long pauses between. One was in the house itself. Sitting on the mattress, Sparky and Hazel could see stars begin to appear through the cupola's windows.

"Want to turn the light out for a little while?" Hazel asked.

"What for?"

"To see the stars better. It would be pretty."

"I don't know."

"You could get used to it. I'll be here."

Sparky thought the proposition over. The deep, peacock blue sky with its familiar emerging constellations did seem somehow different from the cold and nullifying immensities of star-shot space that terrified him earlier. "Okay," he said. "I'll try it."

Hazel blew out the lantern. The night surrounded them like warm water in a farm pond. Somewhere not far away a dog barked.

"I'm gonna miss him so much," Sparky said.

"I know."

"I already do. He can't do anything but lie there and wait. It's like he's already, you know, gone."

"He was a nice man, your Pop. And a good dentist, too."

"Why did it have to be him?"

"It had to be someone."

"Why does it have to be anyone?"

"It has to be everyone, Spark."

"What a world," he said and wiped a tear from each eye.

"Did you ever see such a sky like that?" Hazel asked.

"Lots of times."

"This world's really something, don'tcha think, Spark?"

"It's something all right. Whatever it is, we're right in the middle of it."

"You think they'll ever figure it out?"

"Sure. When they break the Babe's record."

Sparky's mother sat on the edge of his bed and straightened out the boy's pajama collar as if he were going to church instead of sleep.

"Did you say your prayers?"

" 'Course I did."

His mother's lower lip trembled and she fell forward against him, her body heaving and quivering. At first, Sparky was confused, maybe even a little embarrassed, as if strangers might be looking in on them somehow. But he rapidly arrived at the conclusion that none of that mattered when her heart was breaking. So he held her until she had shed a sufficiency of tears and found the will to draw herself upright.

"Did you see what a beautiful night it was out?" Sparky asked her.

"Warm for September."

"It was really something out there. You never saw such a sky like that."

She kissed him damply on the cheek, wished him goodnight, and backed out of the room a little warily, as servants are said to do before royalty. But Sparky was not at all tired. He lay between the cool sheets in a rapture, thunderstruck by the sudden beauty of the world and, strangest of all, filled with nonspecific gratitude. Some time later, he left his bed and crept downstairs to the room where his father lay.

The lamp cast a dim yellow glow over everything in the room. His father's cheekbones looked like they were made out of old ivory. His chest rose and fell so slightly, and at such long intervals, that Sparky was not entirely certain it was moving at all. From the chair, Sparky could see into the next room where his mother lay asleep on her side, her back to him. He leaned close to his father's ear. "Pop?" he whispered. "Pop? Papa . . . ?"

His father's eyes rolled up like old, battered windowshades. They seemed to be the only part of him still capable of movement. Glistening moistly, his eyes seemed overflowing with eagerness.

"We'll always be here, Papa," Sparky said.

He was not sure his father comprehended until after he added, "Would you like it if I turned off the light, Pop?" '

"Yes," his father said faintly and with a maximum of effort.

Sparky kissed his father on the forehead, switched off the lamp, and went back upstairs to dream a boy's dreams.

Walter B. Lape

Walter Lape lives in Lake George and has taught English for nineteen years at Queensbury. His work has appeared in several publications, among them are: English Journal, Blueline, *and* The English Record. *He is one of the* Three Adirondack Poets, *a chapbook. His play,* Stage 1755, *a historical fiction presentation of the French and Indian War, is currently in production for its third season. He is one of the founding editors of* The Loft Press, *Glens Falls, N.Y., and he is an editor of the* Glens Falls Review. *Now he is working on a novel set in Alaska after spending two summers commercial salmon fishing on Cook Inlet.*

Bolton Road

Every morning I drag it up,
Empty it, coffee it,
Wash it off, dress it,
Pile it into the car,
And take it off to work.

Anywhere between the house and Exit 22
I meet you driving the other way.
We wave, we've never spoken
Never met, save for our daily nod.
I fabricate from where you come
And how far you go.
I tell time by you,
The season by your dress,
Not worn to mask the wonder
Of what's under your shirt.
It is the haste of the real day
That speeds our bodies past
After morning ablutions.

You passing up our trip today
Stripped the dream that rides with me
On the way to entertaining
What comes up after passing you.

You missing is no more than
A traffic signal change along the way,
Less in terms of turns of the world,
But it was an empty drive
For me missing you.

You do wave and must wonder who
Lifts his hand as you drive
To whatever is due you.

Do you ponder the body
That comes the opposite way you do?

Do you consider, after seeing it,
To touch it, think it over
Over you, to hold it,
Clutch it on the way past,
To fold in its arms,
To test it, press it,
And feel it when it's warm,
The body down the road every morning
Coming the same time you do?

Can two fellow travelers
Pause on a wave
To see what two can?

Should you come tomorrow,
I have mouthed you
This message, should you
want to stop, you'll know
You should.

Upstream

The water narrows upstream
Toward the wild spring
Where I was born.
A mild, abrading wind
Crisps my vision as I search
The clear shadows for grains
Of my lost past.
I tossed the stones of childhood downstream
To sail over and pass
When I let the pull
Push me southwest at eighteen and shining,
Angular and sharp like the Rockies
I crossed on the way
To the desert and stucco of L.A.
Time has tumbled the sunken rocks of myself,
Crystalized from my own blood-blue dawn,
Into gems I seek to pocket
As I plunge home,
Weathered for the current,
To bathe what I have left
In the honed valleys
Of upstate New York.

The Fisherman's Phoenix

When he was six, I said:
Snow falls from the hemlock
On Buck Mountain, it's told,
Because lake trout get lost
In dark, brittle water
Under new, ceiling frost.
They smash the granite base,
Displace their sepulcher,
And stir the hillside space.
Bruised snouts from crashing rock
Explain their fin flying
From cold, bolting and bold,
To escape their dying,
When April's waning lace
Melts to breed May's worst hatch,
And we make out first catch.

It's not so, it's a lie.
Winter waxes, trout die.
The young boy I misled
Has shed his shining face.
In place now, more involved,
Here the myth he should solve.

Gilled spirits brood; they lost their sheath.
Scouts hover ice, waiting, baiting.
Branches quiver with dust passing
And ring the casket as a wreath.
Beneath, corpses roll side to side,
Shifting spines by a froze-in tide
Until an arrow of sunlight
Ignites the char to rise again.
From sleep, the crust and soul unite.
This self-capture is seen by men.
Scaling the deep, they wake, leap, splash
When lake trout spring from winter's ash.

A *Teacher's Trilogy*

1. Tattoo Fighter

He cuddles the needle,
Wrapping thread around the tip
To form a reservoir for India ink.
He inserts.
He slaps his leather belt
Against the blood
To beat the ink into his skin.
The black blues.
Between the knuckles of his middle finger
He wipes the welted V,
Attacks it again,
Wacks the ink deeper.
It doesn't hurt to stab, he says,
Feels like being pricked by a rose or something.
He knows the shade he wants — navy dark.
He is a south paw
So that the faded cross and swastika on his left arm blur.
He works better on his right.
He is adding L-O-V-E to his right-hand fingers
To underscore two sets of initials and a "Jo-Lyn"
On the back of his hand.
Another, smaller cross above that wrist
Mingles with half-finished letters;
Interrupted tributes, mistakes,
Remain on his forearm.
A peace symbol curdles on the underside.

His mother dropped him off at his grandmother's
Some years ago.
This year he is fifteen
Repeating my class.
But he has a friend, an old man
Who trains him to box

In amateur competition.
In a composition he wrote:
When my trainer walks in,
You can smell cigar and hair grease
Which improves the smell of the gym.

Maybe I could train him some,
But he is not moved
To see other than the fight.
A fighter can be a very good thing.
I will fail him again this year.

2. She Has a Hand Named After Her

She plucks her eyebrows to bare skin,
Paints in purple outlined in black,
Shadows her eyes blue,
Heightens her cheeks with blush
She lifted from C.V.S.
She jewels the three holes in her left ear
Pulls at her breasts
The way Curt does with the hand
He tattooed for her.

She is glad her mother came home alone last night,
No stranger in the bathroom this morning
Eyeballing her.
She tells herself she will cut paperdolls
With her daughter,
Spread peanut butter at three in the afternoon,
Take her shopping for clothes,
And make up
Stories at bed.

Her mother says she is not old enough
To start work —
Finish school first.
But this year she earned her Christmas money
From the men at the mall.

Lunch Money

He hopes no one notices,
But he knows,
Even the teachers see
But turn away,
As he does when his parents argue
Hoping what he witnesses is not so,
Pretending, by avoiding, it will pass.
To make it right
Would make it worse.
He contends with the unavoidable,
As now.
But this is no fight.

He fishes his daily dollar from his pocket
Ready to hand it over
Between third and fourth period.
It is his lunch money,
But his stomach is knotted full
When he sits in class.
Even Jo-Lyn laughs
When she drops his folder on his desk.
He does not look up
Or answer to his name.
He is left alone.

But he is not the only one.
A fellow contributor hunches two rows over.
He wonders if he pays the same
Or more
(or worse)
Or less.
He would not ask,
To couple himself
With one as weak as he.
He has never seen the other's eyes
Or heard the voice
Silenced by the tattooed hand.

Lyn Lifshin

In interviews I've often said that in Eskimo language the words to breathe and to make a poem are the same and that writing for me is that central, vital, and necessary, that living without writing would be as suffocating and unnatural. That's why, tho I normally don't write anything, not even letters at this time of night—usually I work early in the morning, often before it's light, with the phone off the hook, dangling, with weeks as clogged and tangled with new writing workshops and 4¹/₂ hours of dance most days, I'm writing this now—the bed covered with envelopes, notebooks and coffee cups the cat's tunneling under, wind blowing thru the walnuts.

I let a lot of things sidetrack me before I began letting poetry be as central as it is: graduate school where I thought I wanted a degree so I could write and then found that by being denied a degree, I finally did, painting, strange jobs at ETV stations. Lately I've been working with a dancer and doing performances, classes and workshops that combine poetry, theater and dance, the same obsessions I had when I was younger than 12 so I feel terribly lucky to be spending so much of my time doing what's always mattered most. I teach a variety of workshops: poetry, writing, publishing, creative diary, diaries and journals, bringing forth creativity, using writing to reach those who withdraw, memoirs and mother and daughter workshops, where I'm always trying to get my students to trust their senses and to

227

find what is magical in the ordinary, something I aim for in my own work. Twelve years ago I wrote in MOUNTAIN MOVING DAY that "it seems to me a poem has to be sensual (not necessarily sexual tho that's ok too) before it's anything else so rhythm matters a lot to me . . . I want whoever looks at it, whoever eats the poem to feel the way old ebony feels 4 o clock in a cold English mansion or the smell of lemons in a strange place, skin . . ." I like colloquial language that sounds like the thought in progress, with all its raggedness, twists and spontaneity, not something polished over and over, all the edges smoothed away. I guess that's where the breathlessness several critics mention comes from. It's why I picked Wyatt to do my dissertation on—why I preferred his craggy, vivid language over Sidney's smooth, terribly smooth (to me) writing. I like Emily Dickinson's remark that "if I read a book and it makes my whole body so cold no fire can ever warm me, I know that is poetry. If I feel physically as if the top of my head was taken off, I know that is poetry."

I like rooms and my own work with a lot of space around it, pared down, like a Shaker chair. I revise a lot more than most people realize, write almost every day, except when I am finishing up a book or editing or doing marathon typing that turns verbs in my head to mush. I write long hand in spiral notebooks—revise then, revise when I type them up and often make additional changes when I read them in public.

Tho I was born in Vermont, in Middlebury (where I wrote my first poem because I had to, after copying a Blake poem out of Songs of Innocence and telling my mother I wrote it, having her run into my third grade teacher so by the next Monday I had to have my own poem with words like "rill" and "descending" in it) where I used to see Robert Frost wandering thru Main Street in baggy green pants (he'd buy at my uncle's store, only letting my father, not a Vermonter but as stoney and taciturn, wait on him) and carrying strawberries and where later he wrote on almost the first poem I wrote "very good, sayeth Robert Frost, nice images bring me some more I'd like to see others" and then was dead before I could or dared to, I've lived in New York state almost as long. I can't believe that, tho I went to Syracuse University for undergraduate work (where I majored at various times in art, radio and tv, theater and then finally English). Or that it will be the 12th fall in this house braided by walnuts and maples, hemlock, laurel, white pine, yews apple quince once, elderberry, plum and cherry. I always thought I'd live near the ocean. In many ways my life's been like the only kind of poems I feel really matter, the ones that take you someplace you didn't expect to go.

My most recent book, KISS THE SKIN OFF, winner of the Jack Kerouac Award in poetry was called "a delight and a refreshment" in Publisher's Weekly—and I think it gives readers a chance to see some of my longer poems, the ones probably less connected with me as does Hugh Fox's book LYN LIFSHIN, A CRITICAL STUDY which focuses on what he thinks are some of my overlooked pieces: poems about myth, history, what he calls the "serious" Lifshin. I'm looking forward to Mary Ann Lynch's documentary on me and to finishing up my collection of women's memoirs, a companion book to TANGLED VINES and ARIADNE'S THREAD. A book of my prose, prose poems and poetry is forthcoming from Applezaba Press, DOCTORS and I have had fellowships to Yaddo, Mac Dowell Colony, Millay Colony, a scholarship to Bread Loaf and Boulder Writer's Conference and a CAPS grant. My papers have been collected by Temple University and University of Texas at Austin and I publish regularly in a variety of magazines including ROLLING STONE, GREENFIELD REVIEW, APR.

Old Men   Hotel Brenner, Saratoga NY

they are like plants
put out on the porch
that only bloom at

night when the light
won't burn those
leaves that dissolve

by morning. Chairs
and teeth click.
Smells of garlic
roses   the word

yesterday like a
pile of bones a
necklace of stories
they thread with
their own hair
from these strings
they make a

harp to play
in the snow as
the holidays
blur. Those who

don't come back
next August are
added   become
strings for the
fingers left
to touch

Graceland Cemetery—Albany, NY

drivers on cold rainy
nights especially in
september with leaves
streaked across the
creosote see a woman
wrapped in satin
white in the gates
to the graveyard they
offer her a ride she
gets in but when they
get down to lark st
there's just a pool
of water a sleepy
woman at the door
who says it's nothing
it's my daughter it
happens in the rain
she seems to want
to come back here
you understand of
course that she's
been buried up there
for nearly 4 years

The Cat in the Tall Grass off Balltown

on a night rain
turns back to ice
upstate and gutters
fill like brooks
    trout could live in

that pulled the
cat to where if it
were dreaming the
blown sleet would
    form a cocoon a
round it he could
never leave

as it is   ice
crystals stud his
fur that blows
as if something
inside it was
moving

Saratoga

dark counter on
broadway early the
morning smell of
old wood a
woman her tight
lips scent of dark
cloth nobody comes
for the baths now
only these
gipsies monty
wooly would
sit out her
face looks
like it could
crack a charred
hole she says the
fires losses
there's nothing horses
now the beauty
gone smoke
her mouth
breaking
you know
but they lived then

Rooming Houses   Abandoned Hotels
Saratoga Winter

old mens dreams
in the bedroom

women who
held them once
in that cradle
their hips

rocking all
night shadows
sucking   the

walls pressing
on the pillows
like hair
empty cradles

down stairs
wet stone
ash blowing

back into the
room as if there
was something

outside trying
to come back
trying to

be that
warm again

Picking Tomatoes before the Frost

we pull up the long
tangles that all
summer everyone
was careful not to
walk on   Even your
denim jacket's
not enough i need
your arms kneeling
in the icy grass
that smells of
fire and a room up
stairs with a
stove   Love the
green we bring in
side will last will
get us thru winter
if we dont let
the fruit bruise

Elizabeth A. Lortie

As long as I can remember, I have been writing for and about children and have been fortunate to have studied with several published authors: Sister Mary Catharine O'Connor, Jean Rikhoff, and Johanna Reiss. Frank Hodge, children's literature specialist, prompted me to write my first novel for children, ages 8–12, F.B.I. Five Brainy Investigators, set in a small upstate town in the first summer of World War II.

My second novel, Steamship Summer, geared to young teens, tells of a girl struggling with her first romance and her first job. Neither book has been published yet, but I do have an agent. Between longer works I have been writing short stories for adults and children. "Tag-a-long" was published in Wonder Time and "McCrea Street Elementary" in The Glens Falls Review.

To earn a living, I teach English, and for the past twenty years I have been at Hudson Falls High School teaching grades 9–12 as well as semester courses in Creative Writing, World Literature, Short Fiction, and Twentieth Century Literature.

Since my three children have grown up and left home, I can spread my works-in-progress from one end of the house to the other, except for the spaces preempted by Ibn, my German shepherd.

McCrea Street Elementary, Room 1

Ada Crawford didn't know her sums and couldn't draw a circle or color in the lines. Miss Price didn't like her. I didn't like her, either. Sometimes Joyce and I chased her in one door of the pharmacy and out the other with Mr. Wilson saying, "Girls, girls."

"We were only funning," we told Ada. That was a big story.

Other times we were nice to her, like we didn't tell her she was adopted. My mother said not to tell because she might not know. Maybe that's why she seemed strange and cried so much. Maybe that's why her braids were uneven and came loose. Sometimes we let her walk with us; sometimes we didn't.

On the second Tuesday in November we had our first snowfall, and I got rapped on the knuckles for looking out the window instead of paying attention to the card chart. Paying attention was important to Miss Price. Ada was having a worse day than me. When we lined up for inspection, she was hunched over, Miss Price said. She pushed on the middle of Ada's back until Ada's stomach stuck out.

"No, no, no," scolded Miss Price, smacking her tummy. "Stomach in, shoulders back."

Next we held out our hands so Miss Price could look at our nails. Peter made a face at Miss Price behind her back, and Ada laughed her thin, high laugh. Miss Price stamped her foot. Another black mark in the book. Ada looked at the floor and twisted the ribbon on her braid. When the ribbon came off in her hand, she poked it into the puffed sleeve of her dress and pretended nothing had happened. I didn't tell.

Finally we sat down and got our arithmetic papers. Sums were hard for me, but I could do them if I counted things. I counted three pencils and one more and marked $3 + 1 = 4$ on my paper. Ada used her fingers. Miss Price rapped our knuckles for that, too, so I counted by the screws in the wood above the blackboard and by the legs on the chairs. The toes inside my shoe did not give me the right answers. Sometimes one of them would not wiggle. In the summer I used my toes to count all the time, and nobody ever knew.

"Imagine wanting to wear sandals in November," my mother said.

Ada couldn't count by using pencils. I know because I tried to teach her. "They're all yellow," she told me. "I forget which one I started with. Fingers is better. Start with the thumb."

They were, I agreed, unless you got caught.

Ada Crawford erased a lot. Every time I looked at her, she was

236

erasing again. I was up to $4 + 2 = 6$ and no erasing. I patted my paper. Nice and neat. Miss Price would like that.

"Daydreaming, missy?" The pointer landed on the edge of my desk and made my paper rattle.

"No, Miss Price."

"See that you don't. Four plus four."

"Eight." The only sum I knew right off.

Miss Price moved down the aisle. I could see Ada's right hand in the pocket of her dress. The pocket made little counting movements: one, two, three. She picked up her pencil in her left hand, saw Miss Price, and dropped it. She got it into her other hand before Miss Price raised the pointer. In Room 1 we wrote with our right hands. Ada's hand wobbled over a five. She waited until Miss Price turned her back. Then she rubbed it out. The eraser at the top of her pencil was worn down and made little scratchy noises in my ear. I tried not to listen. If I didn't hear it, maybe Miss Price wouldn't either. I looked at Ada. It must be hard to be adopted and a crybaby and lefthanded.

I wanted to tell Ada not to rub so hard, but the tap, tap, tap of Miss Price's black-laced shoes told me she was coming down our aisle again. Ada licked the end of her eraser and rubbed again. A hole! She covered it with her finger.

"Pencils down. Papers forward."

I turned around to take the papers from my row and pass them on. Ada was safe. She would have to copy her paper over tomorrow, of course, but I copied over lots of times. That didn't hurt. By the door stood a gray metal trash can, almost as tall as I was, and by the end of each day it was filled with crumpled sheets. "Trash for the furnace," Miss Price said.

Miss Price snapped the papers against the desk and held them on one palm like the grocer weighing leaves of lettuce and looked around the room. Who would dare to keep a paper back?

"I'm waiting."

Ada pulled her paper from her workbook and held it up.

"Bring it here."

Holding her thumb over the hole, Ada got out of her chair. Then she stopped and looked at her feet. They weren't working, I thought curiously. Ada couldn't take her eyes off her feet. I stared and saw it. Little streams of yellow crept over the pink roses on the tops of her anklets and down into her shoes.

"She's peeing her pants," Peter said.

"Ada Crawford, march to the door," said Miss Price. Her eyes were black marbles, her lips thin lines. Without my knowing, my hands clamped over my mouth. I was afraid I would say it out loud like Peter.

Ada walked to the front of the room, each step a little wet mark. Without a word, Miss Price leaned over and lifted Ada up and into the trash can. All I could see were her shoulders and head.

"That's what we do in Room 1 with children who wet their pants." Miss Price wiped her hands on her lace handkerchief and stuck it back in the belt of her dress. "The janitor will know what to do with her." Miss Price moved toward the first row. "Places for reading, please."

The Red Circle formed around Miss Price. Ada bent toward the circle.

Miss Price arranged her chair with her back to Ada. There was a little space between two chairs where Ada should have been.

"Close the circle, children." The chairs moved closer. Ada's place was gone.

I was in the Green Circle. We pulled our chairs around. If Peter looked down at his book, I could see past him to Ada. Peter was first to read. They wouldn't get to me until—I counted four pages—page 18. I opened to page 18 to be ready when it came my turn because I couldn't pay attention to the book. My eyes kept looking at Ada. She was listening to Benny read in the Red Circle and whispering along with him.

"Not another word!"

Ada stopped moving her mouth. She leaned her head on the rim of the wastecan. I could see her fingers hanging on the edge to keep her from slipping down to the bottom. The metal can rattled. When a sobbing sound like water gurgling in the pipes came out of the can, round and round the room, I stood up and took two steps toward Ada.

"Stop that!" Miss Price was saying. "Do you hear me? Stop that!"

Her head bobbed and I couldn't tell whether she was talking to me or to Ada. I stood very still. Miss Price rose from her chair, getting taller and taller, shaking her head. A hairpin fell to her lace collar. Another fell to the floor.

"No, no, no." She shook her head again and a strand of hair hung down by her ear, like a braid does when the rubber band snaps.

I felt like I was coming loose, too. It was my turn to read in the Green Circle and I wasn't there. The Green Circle stopped reading and waited. If I went back, I'd be safe. Ada sobbed and banged her head. I shivered and took two more steps.

Miss Price bumped against the Red Circle, waving her arms, her face stiff and white and her eyes flashing black. "Disobey me? Disobey me? How could you?"

My head pounded with her words. Ada's wail went up and up.

"Ada thinks you are going to put her in the furnace with the trash." My words came out so low that I was not sure I had said them at all.

A sound like a soft sigh came from in back of me. In the Red Circle someone started to cry. Miss Price turned toward Ada. I walked closer and looked over the edge of the wastecan at Ada slumped at the bottom. She didn't even see me.

The rustling in the room behind me and Miss Price's words got fainter and fainter. "I will have order. I will have order."

"Ada" I said, "hang on."

I pulled on the top of the wastecan. At first it only tipped a little. "Stand up," I commanded. Ada got herself partway up. I pulled again on the can and over it came, crashing down. Then it rolled over once and stopped. Ada crawled out.

"You hurt me," she said. Her face was puffy and red and she kind of hiccupped.

"I'm sorry." I picked up the papers and waited for the sting of the pointer on my back. Ada stood on one foot and then on the other. She smelled awful.

"Sit down," Miss Price said. "Sit down at once!"

I pulled Ada's chair to the Green Circle, sat down next to her, and opened to page 18. Pretty soon the bell would ring for lunch.

William Losinger

- *Born in Wellsboro, Pa., 1950.*
- *Graduated from the University of New Hampshire, MA in English.*
- *Was awarded the Lt. Albert Chariot Award for fiction, University of New Hampshire, 1973.*
- *Has taught at Adirondack Community College since 1974.*
- *Married, two sons.*
- *Publications include:*
    1) *"Taking Leave"* Colorado-North Review
    2) *"Harold Temmerman's Tender Liability"* Esprit
    3) *"Distant Voyager"* Kansas Quarterly
    4) *"Love On The Run"* Glens Falls Review
    5) *"Traditore"* Nantucket Review
    6) *"The Sick Rose"* Letters Magazine
    7) *Non-fiction article in* The Journal of Reading

Love on the Run

She was sixty-seven when Richard, who had been a fullback for the old New York Giants in the early forties, came into her life like a wide-end sweep, destroying any notion she might have of remaining the only woman in her graduating class of '34 who still managed to call her own plays.

It was her first marriage, then, and his second. He was sixty-seven, too. Years ago, they had been high school sweethearts at Saratoga High, and after they had quarreled one night over some inconsequential little thing she could never quite recall, he had left her, gone from her life forever, it appeared, yet now only to return, a lonely, pleading voice over the phone on a cool spring day, a voice from some dark, hidden part of her brain, a voice that said he had remembered after all those years. She was astonished at how readily she accepted his invitation for dinner, and when he proposed, only two weeks later, she told him that he was still the fastest athlete Saratoga had ever known.

They understood each other at once, and she soon discovered that the longing and love she had had for him forty-nine years ago was quickly rekindled. They grew intimate almost overnight. He was persistent, forceful, and loved her immensely. She felt seventeen again, and just as giddy and playful. When she ran her hands over his still-solid shoulders, tracing each sinew and curve with her fingers, she became aware once again of a certain delicate stirring, a steady contracting of time and desire, the special feeling that had belonged to them many years before. She gave herself to him willingly, without hesitation, and the migraines on rainy days and the chronic little flutter in her chest, a sudden, quick movement as if a small bird had been let loose within her, vanished altogether. The old love grew again, and within a month after he had interrupted her with a phone call that bridged the years, they were married.

Now he was hers, and after only two months of marriage, she feared he was tired of her.

He sat on the edge of the bed in their apartment in a renovated Georgian and rubbed his thin legs that had begun to hurt again. With much care, he massaged a long, white scar that crossed his left knee, the only tangible reminder of his three years of professional football.

It was late August, sun in Sirius, the air permeated with the summer smells of Saratoga during flat track season — warm beer, fried bread, pretzels, expensive perfume and priceless horseflesh. A perfect Saratoga summer, except that it was unbearably hot and, because of some mysterious worm that flew in the night, the roses had never fully bloomed. All summer their insect-incised petals had littered the streets and boulevards. Not that he cared. He didn't.

"What are you doing, Catherine?" he shouted.

He was in his undershirt and shorts and looked out their only bedroom window to the multicolored pennants attached to the top of the main grandstand at the track, visible just above the large, rotting poplar in the backyard. Blue smoke hung suspended above him and a crushed cigar lay in the ashtray next to the bed.

"I'm putting my face back on," she yelled from the bathroom. "You're a brute, you know; it's smeared all over my cheeks."

"Post's at 1:30," he said. "I don't know whether these knees will make it."

"We can take the car," she answered.

"Yes," he said, looking at his knees. "We can take the car."

She came into the room where he sat rubbing his knees. Her hair was a soft gray. She wore only a half slip and he stared at her wrinkled breasts thoughtfully.

"We don't have to walk, babe," she said. "We can take my car if your legs are starting to hurt again."

"My legs always hurt," he said, irritated that she should use the word *again*. His legs, their pain and constant care, were something private to him, something that belonged, he felt, to his life with his dear Anne, the woman he had been married to for over forty years. They had seldom quarreled in all their years together, but when they had, the days that followed were black and silent and the great void between them took up a formal and pained existence in his knees. They always hurt him when something had been wrong between them, and they had hurt him the most when he had sat amidst relatives and the putrid odor of gladiola at his Anne's funeral, listening to inadequate eulogies and the flapdoodle of friends who might console him. It had been there, the pain in his knees, the remote itching, during the lowest points in his life.

"It's not as good as it used to be," he said. "It's not as good as it was when we were first married."

She sat down on the bed next to him and covered her breasts with her arms. "But it can't always be like that, can it?" she asked. "It can't always be . . . blissful."

He buttoned up his shirt impatiently and then, with great care, slid his pants over his legs.

"Blissful? With these knees I'd settle for adequate. I think I'd like to cut them off sometimes."

"Richard," she said, "we don't have to go to the track today. I've been a hundred times and they'll be running for another week. We don't have to go today."

"Don't go and do what? Lie here and stare at this room? Anyplace is better than here, right now. I hate it sometimes. I hate these damned legs, and I especially hate this damned heat. You'd think for all we pay for this gaudy display of self-indulgence they'd install air-conditioning."

Because this was his fifth outburst in a week, she sat staring at the floor, trying to establish responsibility and guilt.

"Richard," she said, "do you think we . . . should have waited a little while before we married?"

Her frankness startled him. He fidgeted with his cuffs, adjusted his belt, then rummaged anxiously through his pockets for a match.

"Do you?" she asked again.

"Well, maybe you should have," he said angrily. "Maybe you weren't ready."

"Oh, no, dear. No. It's just that sometimes you get so down on me . . . on us. I just wondered if you think we rushed into something."

"Rushed into something?" he laughed bitterly. "How can we possibly rush into anything at our age? How can we rush into anything but death?"

Then, seeing that he had hurt her, and that she was crying, he placed his hand over hers.

"I'm sorry, Richard," she said. "I guess I'm still the nervous bride."

He felt he should apologize—he wanted to apologize—but the mood wasn't right, and so he couldn't.

"I'll get the car," she said, crying.

"No," he replied. "I don't want to ride. I want to walk. I want to walk on these legs."

In their walking his legs grew stronger. There was a fire along the sidewalk, a magnificent midday sun coming through the tops of the trees that lined the avenues and boulevards of Saratoga. Tourists— bussed in from the Island or Montreal, with visions of big winners down the backstretch or dramatic mile-and-a-halfs—scurried about to make post, to surge tight against the rail in anticipation of the first race. The push, the movement, the urgent, physical tug of the crowds seemed to rejuvenate him. He quickened his step, and the sun shone down on them, nearly dazzling them, squeezing them into an imponderable net of sunshine. They seemed possessed, in that isolated moment, with a clean, ready optimism. Anyone would have said so. She couldn't explain it. That's the way it had been for the two months of their marriage. It had happened before. When he was out among people, he was a different person. It was when they stopped, and were alone together, that they had their separateness to grind away at.

If they could only keep walking like this, she thought, then she could believe that his despair and lack of faith in them had been only his battered knees and the emotional ups and downs of early married life. Now, as she nearly ran to keep up with him, his legs seemed as quick and supple as any thoroughbred's and it was a delight to her when he led her through the park where they had been married.

She felt close to him then, seeing the ornate bandstand where the ceremony had been performed, right next to a famous fountain that spewed forth an endless stream of mineral water from the eroded bronze penis of a crudely cast cherub with tarnished wings. The town secretary—a curmudgeonly old woman with a gnarled cane and a malicious scowl—had served as witness, while old Judge Sullivan, sweating and fanning himself with yesterday's racing form, read them their vows. She had worn her mother's gold Florentine ring and as a wedding present she had given him her father's silver cuff set. He had looked glorious, so straight and tall. Nearby, the Saratoga Women's Chorus had sung an inspired version of "New York, New York" to a group of polite tourists gathered on the courthouse steps. Then, encouraged by the heat of another Saratoga summer, they had marched together down the sidewalk, past the flowering zinnias and marigolds and hollyhocks, to Richard's antique Studebaker Champion. Around the town they went, blowing the horn again and again in long, reckless, adolescent blasts. It had been the happiest day of her life.

Love on the run, she had laughed, waving her bouquet at the curious faces of the people on the street.

You'll have to run pretty fast to keep up with me, he had yelled over the blare of the horn. It was true. She had learned to run. That was the way he was, and she was quite out of breath when they finally reached their seats in the grandstand.

He was pleased with the view. The entire track was spread out before them. They waited anxiously, without speaking, for the jockeys to position their horses in the starting gate. The crowd surged tight against the white rail. The bell rang; the gate flew open. And when the horse he had bet on actually came racing down the backstretch, horse and rider one magical, rhythmic assault, a galloping wave of intent and grace in high gear, a winner by two lengths, he took her into his arms and kissed her, pressing his mouth to hers.

"And I thought he was nothing but a gelded no-show," he exclaimed.

She laughed. "You knew he was a winner. Tell me you did. You know a runner when you see one," she said.

"We're rich now," he boasted. "Forty-eight bucks richer."

He won eight dollars more and she made sixteen on a horse named Distant Voyager. They drank glasses of dark beer and shared fried bread in the shade of a large oak and listened to a small jazz group, and the sun shone down all around them. Later, they won ten more dollars on an Argentine stallion in the seventh and final race. She felt reckless and free, as she always did when they were out among people, and all the pomp and stuffy tradition of Saratoga during racing season was mitigated by their happiness and good fortune. She wanted the afternoon to last as long as possible. More than anything she did not want to go back to the apartment.

"Richard," she pleaded when they started back, "let's get something irresponsible to eat. Let's indulge ourselves on our winnings, celebrate our good luck."

They hurried away, away from the crowds and the net of sunshine, down the oak-lined streets, past the old Victorian estates. She knew a little specialty shop where they bought creamed raspberries and maple mousse in plastic containers. Then she led him toward the park, nearly running, holding his arm, determined to make them one again, to make them as close and assured of each other as they had been two months ago. As they walked, she wondered how she had ever taken a hard, fierce pride in her self-imposed celibacy, how she had ever believed, as she once had, that she was somehow morally better for her ability to do what few people ever do in their lifetimes — confront, and conquer, their aloneness. But she had, and it had been this special knowledge of her own superiority and quiet acceptance that had given her the courage to endure all those years alone, years she had secretly dedicated to the Virgin Mother, another courageous woman whose compassion and inner strength had been concealed behind the softly glowing eyes and the impassive smile of the Madonna.

It had taken Richard to show her just what a sorry solace her hard, fierce pride had been. She had been alone too long. He had offered her something else, and she found she had wanted it. Now she wanted him, forever, even beyond death.

But when they reached the park he was limping noticeably and was quiet again. They sat down on a bench near the bronze cherub. The sun was beginning to disappear behind a line of red pines and the evening was turning cool. Long shadows stretched out their fingers, absorbing the light that played over a carpet of pine needles and cones. Three girls in brightly colored dresses ran by them, followed by two boys in hot pursuit. She ate her snack in the rich odor of pine and earth.

"Cold?" she asked.

He did not answer.

He had set his container of creamed raspberries on the ground next to him, unopened. His face with its flat nose and thin lips looked small and pinched and sad. It was more the face of a stranger now than that of someone she loved, and she realized then how little she really knew of him. He had been born in Saratoga. He had been raised in the respectability and wholesomeness of upstate New York. He had spent nearly forty years teaching history at a small high school near Hartford. He had sired three children and had lived all those years with a woman she had never known. She knew nothing about the hours and days and years he'd spent apart from her, the still beam of his consciousness scanning the wilderness of his life. And during all that time—a lifetime nearly—he had never once thought of her until the anguish of his wife's death and a year of despair and loneliness had driven him to her. And she . . . had been only too willing. She thought at first that she could learn to touch that dark little corner of his heart, but now she knew that wasn't so. No one could, not even himself.

They sat in silence with growing weariness as if they had been married all their lives, the only sound the noise of crickets and tree frogs. It was clear by the strain on his face and how his jaw was set in grim determination that his knees hurt and that he was tired of her. Love on the run, she thought, was fine if you were seventeen or twenty or twenty-five. She highly approved of it, in fact. There was plenty of time then to remedy the mistakes, the disappointments, the unrealized expectations. But not at her age, or his. They needed time, and it was time, and love, that they didn't have. She only knew that where earlier there had been hope and desire, there was now only remorse masked with guilt and anger. But she couldn't feel used. She was too old for that. If anything, she told herself, she felt a mite blessed.

Then, because his knees were hurting, and because it was getting late, they started walking the remaining two blocks to their apartment. With resolution, she took his hand.

"It's not working, is it, Richard?" she said, the saddest moment of her life.

"No," he said. "It isn't."

Then he stopped, and with great relief, took her in his arms. He held her for a long while, the crickets and tree frogs in full chorus, and she clung to him tightly, pricked by the realization that she was alone, again, and moved, not by him this time, but by the little flutter deep in her chest, the tiny bird let loose within her.

Diane Lunde

Diane Lunde is an English teacher, a copy editor and a member of the Hudson Valley Writers Guild. She has given poetry readings and has conducted writing workshops in upstate New York, and she has published poetry in Washout Review, Groundswell *and* Blueline *among other magazines.*

The Hudson River

The trees that grow here
are vulnerable in their undress
and lace the sky more complicated
than a cat's cradle. Lacteal sky
seeps between branches, reflects
the ice and nothing of the substance behind.
Along the river is winter color. Reeds
dappled with milkweed. A close harmony
of sycamore, aspen, birch. With spring
I'll hang my ribbons and make a wish,
but now I'm anchored.

Adjusting my lens
I see an Eskimo fishing through
a hole in the ice; a fur parka
frames his face and he leans
to his reflection at the end of the line.
The ice seems to hold everything
in place, as if the arctic shelf might otherwise
give way and water flood fields and towns,
and all temples be submerged.

In the light of morning there is only
stillness, a smooth mask opaque
and solemn. It is a ceremony
of purification, this freeze expanding toward
the brittle rime that lines the banks.
I bend to focus each season
in its time, to accept the fullness of this hush
as transitory as ice on the river.
A kind of sabbath in my age of
unbelief. I wonder
will it be here when I return.

These Hands

Hands grow to
a bandaged cut,
a mosquito bite
scratched
and bleeding,
the scar
from a waterglass,
dry skin washing
dishes,
toilets,
floors.
Prominent veins
and tendons,
brown
liver spots.
Fingers twisting
caress
a child's face,
a cat's fur,
a feather.
Feel the earth
moist, dry,
crisp
lettuce and
ripe tomatoes.
Silk
and cotton
and wool.
Split wood,
hammer brass,
polish stone.
Fingers tasted
one by one,
your tongue
on my palm.

Main Street

Again
I walk this street,
balloons fly high
like a milktooth
under a pillow.

A dime in the slot
of a dream machine
carries me off.
That's the way to go,
I go

one foot dangling
the other
at the wall
hugging upright
with a tight shoe.

Shrill lights and
gaudy masks,
shadows
rutting cobbles,
grit between the teeth.

Automatic limbs fan
the fire of a red-tail street,
the roar between walls
between a ricochet
of dimes.

Catching Sight of Myself

Reflection in a shop window:
sandals, jeans and T-shirt stamped
with the circle of peace, my wild hair
the blossom of a scream beneath the skull,
I choke on the seeming revelation
I am growing old.

As I dance the round of daily errands,
cosmetically anesthetized, blood
still labors through my veins
red as anyone's stigmata;
fine tears crease my face as I snip
the stem of each rose.

Less than giddy, I see
my therapist each week,
that notary of buried treasure,
and at the end of my appointment leave
the salt of unearthed artifacts
beside the empty teacup.

On a timely diet of moderation, I
no longer yearn for a portable
canon, and layers of dust
collect on the stockpiled mortar
and bricks—I had wanted to build
a whole new universe.

I march to nuclear missile sites,
buy my bread in the health food store,
and still I dream of Katmandu
where climbers dump their empty
cans and bottles, middening
the slopes of the Himalayas.

Summer Projections: New England

Mushrooms break their cover, spores fly,
summer delivered to the northeast. The sodden
earth gives suck, the buds unfurl,
as automatic as a cat washing itself,
a dog pissing the limits of affirmation.

Amaranths, their tasselated blossoms, shape
the furred carmine where it grows
in beds of gaudy fuchsia and sweet william,
petunias, impatiens and touch-me-nots.
Only the narrow paths are overrun,
bindings we could do without—fear
to grant ourselves that latitude.

A footprint, a tuft of hair, a broken wing
are caught in the melt of tarred roofs and asphalt
as we learn to recognize even strangers, word
by word, across this great divide.
The spectacle rushing into space reaches
out to the edge and back, somebody listening,
taking notes for a book already written.

Any excuse will do, claiming we have
no expectations. But in our dreams we always
enter on the left, exit on the right,
like an old family recipe. It leaves
an after taste that is never enough,
something withheld, hidden beneath
the madding grass and careless spill of rain.

Ourland

A stranger in no country but
the one that we traverse
separately, I dream of some exotic
island, some Samoa of the mind,
as the earth revolves on its axis.

The pendulum oscillates between
red fields and green balloons,
held to the pivot of outdated
prescriptions, chimerical
promises of an easy paradise.

Like evening news you serve up your
facts: dates, places, other inessentials,
and I listen, testing the silences,
taking one step at a time to avoid
the cracks in the pavement.

photo by Jack Lynch

Mary Ann Lynch

Mary Ann Lynch was born and raised in Greenfield Center, in the foothills of the Adirondacks. "Before I knew television or the movies, I knew the fields and the woods, and the animals in them. I defined myself partly in relation to them—they had their territory, I had mine. In some transcendent moments, our territories came together. I always was aware when those moments happened, but could never quite verbalize what they meant. By the time I was a teenager I was filled with secret happenings that wanted to be told."

Lynch's poetry has appeared previously in Blue Line; her photographs have been exhibited widely throughout the country. She is currently in postproduction on two films, a documentary on the poet Lyn Lifshin, and a narrative, "The Amateur," which she wrote, produced and directed in Saratoga Springs in March of 1985. Lynch's documentary on Lifshin was funded in part with awards from the Helena Rubenstein Foundation and New York University's Tisch School of the Arts. Lynch lives in Greenfield Center with her husband and two children and also maintains an apartment in New York City.

255

Origins

Living in the country as a child I spent many long hours by myself. Our house sat at the edge of a field, a forest beyond, a stonewall separating the two. For the first few years of my life, I scarce dared tread a foot on the other side of the wall. While the familiar whistle of the train that cut across our back property line lay beyond that wall, so too did the bobcats I had only heard about, the creatures that I knew prowled every inch of that land where I did not go.

I knew well what a bobcat looked like, for I had seen them close up, very close up in fact, though lifeless, either newly-killed, as they were tossed on the grass in front of the shop that housed my father's taxidermy business, or, later, cleaned up, free of blood, standing mounted, or sliced and flattened to form a rug I could actually lie down on—though I wasn't supposed to. Those cats in the shop I loved to touch, to inspect, to be near. The others—in the woods—I watched for, sitting on the wall, peering into the tangle of trees, hoping for even the slightest suggestion of furred movement, or a glint of an eye in the setting sun. I longed for the sight of them, and more, for the chance to stroke their velvet backs, to hold their gaze while their fierce eyes looked into mine, just as I had gazed so deeply into the glass eyes of those in the shop.

There came the day I ventured out beyond the wall, slipping down from the rock, the rough edge scratching the exposed flesh of my thigh. It was just before supper, just the time when I should have been turning back to the house, and as I walked straight ahead into the thicket, stumbling on rusted cans from target practice, walking over protruding branches, my mother's voice was calling me in . . . but the trees called me more strongly. I walked a few minutes and then stopped, looked around, back the way I had come, ahead, to the sides . . . everything blended into a sameness and direction was lost. Overhead, the sun was going down, and as shadows moved across the trees a chill came over my arms.

A bobcat was nearby, I knew it. I stood motionless, listening intently, straining to hear the animal—but I heard nothing, save the snap of a twig under my foot as I shifted weight involuntarily. Annoyed, I took another step, stopped again. Night was coming on fast, too fast. I would see that cat if I just looked hard enough. Looking up into the trees, I tried to make sense out of the dense dark shapes. There! A feline shape stretched out along the branch, looking down on me quizzically. A blink . . . and it was gone.

But now, over there—a glint of white, the cat's claws in fact—betrayed the animal waiting for the right moment to leap down on me, enveloping my small frame in its warmth. If female, it might grab me by the scruff of the neck and take me back to its lair for mothering. That was silly, I told myself, knowing that at the age of seven I was too big to have that happen.

The night crickets further interrupted, with their predictable and insistent chirrups telling me to get on home to supper before I really got into trouble.

As I made my way back over the wall and then ran through the field I knew already what I would tell my parents at the supper table. I had stayed in the woods late because I had seen a bobcat in a tree and was afraid to move until it left.

They would listen patiently, knowing it likely that my story could be true, given the population in the woods. My father would tell me, as he had on many other occasions, that a bobcat wouldn't hurt a human unless it was first provoked. Soon the topic would be dismissed in favor of business of the day or family gossip, and my lateness would be forgotten. There would be no words for me to tell them that whether I had seen that cat or not, in my heart and in my mind I had heard a bobcat sing. I had held its furred body close . . . so close that its song had become my own, and would stay with me forever.

Rocca

We must have gone in the old Plymouth
Parked on Broadway
Walked up the steps to the second floor
And then down the aisle towards the stage
As close to ringside as we could get
That night
But don't quote me on that
I could be wrong
But not about you, Rocca:
"The Wrestling Wonder Out of the Amazon"
come all the way to Convention Hall
in Saratoga Springs, New York:
even then
you were my kind of man.

You sent my ten-year-old mind
somersaulting
every time you did your flying drop kick.

I had never seen anyone
like you
Rocca
Anybody could swing from a vine
or pin a man flat
But you alone
Had the magic in your feet.

Your act lit up that Hall
as even Caruso never
could.
Afterwards people jammed the aisles
argued with the refs
Me, I snuck back, waited.

You know
that picture of us
doesn't show it like it was
To me
you meant a world so far away
from Saratoga's chill
I swear
I saw
orchids spring from every kick
and never
a drop of blood.

Last Stop

She has left the City
far down the Hudson,
watched castles
recede into dark —

And then
A hum rises
from someplace near her shoulder
where the woman with the rough brown coat
and familiar European smile
had sat,
easing her to sleep
with the rhythm of knitting.

Now, a boy, eyes closed,
shirt askew,
rocks and sways
in his own space.

The hum,
got on at some distant dark spot,
will lie between them
all the way to the last stop,
warm as a secret
never to be shared.

Aunt Hannah

Hard by the stream that overflows its banks,
whirling eddies of white-tipped waters
across the back corner of our family lot,
Aunt Hannah lived, before my time.

Her hair fell in black undulations
to her waistline and beyond.

In a photograph she stands, right hand
on a chair,
her whole body slightly tilting back,
as if it were an effort
to keep her head erect,
the lengths of hair
draped over her left shoulder,
unbalancing her,
pulling her
earthward.

Walking down Mill Road, past the swollen stream,
past the place where Aunt Hannah's house stood,
there have been times when my shadow
leaving to the East,
has wrenched me to it,
pulled me back to water's edge,
to watch the currents on their way downstream,
so many years after Hannah walked this road,
so many streams
having passed between us.

Aunt Hannah Sears,

your skirts brushed trails
into this dirt road
that all these years have not erased.

Railroad Place

Across from where the old diner stood
Price Chopper has enlarged
its store
open twenty-four hours
a day

It stands
where trains
once roared
into children's dreams

Walking storeside I pass
geraniums wilting
two for a dollar
a shopping cart
overflows with mismatched shoes

There would be the doorway
where every week
my grandfather and I
brought my father's boxes
what large crates
every one to be weighed

The best always last
when I got on the scale
important as any parcel
marked New Hampshire or Maine

I rode those rails
through all the forty-eight
though I never stepped
a foot upon a train

It was enough
to stand
trackside
sound growing
in my stomach
traveling
with the train

March Monday

Tomatoes from the ice box
send shivers up my arms
rainy March Monday
my body lame

I turned the heater down
conservation-minded
no place was warm enough
that day

Outside the window
ice and snow
blanketed the garden
early peas still
two months away

Marriage Times Four

Three times failed
This was the one she would make work
They had sought this cool mountain air
Didn't care if they never saw another soul
Couldn't I tell about them
Weren't they such a pair
Did I ever see
Two such doves in a nest

She wanted to know
If I would have taken her
For seventy-eight
And if his smile wasn't
The cutest thing this side
Of Georgia

"Down there they grow such sweet peaches
Honey chile
But they don't grow peaches
Any sweeter than my Sam"

We stood roadside
Talking
Well she talked
And I listened
How I wanted her to take
The little kitten
She cradled in her arms

When she put it in his hands
And nodded yes
It was all settled
"Oh you can be sure
This one will get a good home" she said
"I'll put it to sleep with a clock
I'll make sure it never runs down
I know animals
I know how to keep a pet alive."

Judith McDaniel

I have lived most of my adult life in the northeast, the last ten years in these hills and mountains that are so much a part of the landscape of my poems and fiction. I feel the landscape as a physical presence within me, so that whether I am writing a story about a woman lost in the wilderness or about several women in their homes and kitchens, the landscape is equally a part of what makes them the women they are. In my poems the physical landscape becomes a character of equal weight with the narrator. "November Passage" is not a poem about a woman who moves to a farm; it is about a woman who meets the physical necessities of her environment and interacts with them. Now that I am living in Albany, I am removed from the daily presence of the mountains—which saddens me—but the poems return to that landscape in memory and refer to it as frequently as when I actually lived here.

I've published November Woman, *a book of poems, and a novel,* Winter Passage. *A novel for young adults and another book of poems are ready for publication. My current project is a book called* Sanctuary *to be published next year by Firebrand Books. It explores the concept of sanctuary in poems and essays and incorporates material from my trip to Nicaragua with Witness for Peace this summer as well as research on the Sanctuary Movement in the U.S. today.*

Snow in April

At noon you call
Feed the birds
you tell me robins
are starving they've
no place to land
and their food all
under the snow.

I carry out
the last scoop of sun-
flower seed, scatter
robinfood in the mud
tracks your car left
this morning and wade
back through ankle
deep snow while robins
hop awkwardly from low
branch to low branch.

Jacketless in April
sun I split two logs
at the woodpile. Squint-
ing at the too blue sky
one random cloud
a hawk's white coasting
belly circling sky high
watching for a hint
of red breast down
on the muddy road.

From my window I watch
robin's nervous hops
come to rest. She
wades her tired feet
in mud and pecks
at last summer's
final seed.

November Passage

1.

in early autumn darkness
I drive past the corpse   a deer   hung
by its antlers from the family shade tree
gutted   soft white stomach   slit
from crotch to throat   swaying
November remembrance   of summer breeze

a woman told me once:
"his oldest boy hung himself in that tree
they woke one day in August
found him there."

and as I drive
the country road   in each bare tree
my mind prints a boy   fifteen   hanging
by his neck   one hand tucked under the rope
as if to tug it away   the other hand
swaying   in the summer morning's breeze.

2.

we are two women
we live on this farm   without men
our neighbor   looks at our work
with the house   and the land
too bad   he warns   you can't find
a man   to do that for you
no locks on our doors   but we own
one splitting ax   three butchering knives
a sledgehammer   a chainsaw   and a rifle
tools of necessity.

3.

          every day in autumn
our cat presents a corpse   as the mice
come into the house for winter
when she doesn't return for days
I search and find her   lying in the mud
healing the wounds in her side
I see muscle and bone and grey
tissue   around each hole
and I wonder if she stalked this fox
or wandered into violence unaware.

4.

          last spring I got two dozen chicks
let them peck and grow   but now in autumn
I must choose to build a house
and feed them   or kill them
I read a book   go down to the yard
with my ax and knife   I read a book
and boil the water   take the bird
in one hand   the book said
ax in the other   lay the bird's head
on the chopping block   wild unmanageable
now insane   flapping   cackling   clawing
one hen's wings beat my face   rake my arms
her reluctance to die   heats me
in a fury   I kill four
and carry them in my scratched arms
to the bucket of boiling water   dip
hang and pluck   slit the still warm
flesh   knife tearing cardboard   and I
pull out the yellow and green intestines
the swollen golden gizzard   I kill twenty
birds   then give the rest to friends
the smell of blood and wet feathers
grown too strong   and all this winter
I will eat chicken stew made from birds I killed
and smell wet feather and see the ax
and the plucked yellowpink bodies hanging
from my clothesline.

5.

    our neighbor   brings us venison
to be served with turkey for Thanksgiving
two red-faced boys stand behind him
in my kitchen   their eyes slide
from me   to dill weed feathering
down a rafter   I cannot eat
the meat   nor refuse their gift.
I wonder   who killed the deer
and who will kill the bird.

6.

               swaying in the summer breeze
a piece of rope   two bales of hay to stand on
and kick away   one hand tucked under the rope
beside his neck tugging at the tightness
across his throat   white and soft
and his neck broken   the book said
place the head   on the chopping block
the ax in his father's hand   knuckles scraped
an irish drunk and a scotchman's fury
and he swung   in that tree.

Splitting Elm

Do your work in season, girl,
was all that Grandma said when
as a child I picked her apples green.

On a thawing day that voice
is dim as I hone a smooth
edge on the splitting maul, flex
my shoulders loose and slam
the wedged head into a reluctant
elm stump where tendrils grab,
wind and hold. I jerk the ax
and hack again, finally pull
the threaded halves apart by hand.

But when the wind is metal
cold at ten below I take the maul,
dulled and chipped by use, raise it
smooth and slice butter clean
through the long log length.

At ten below zero
even the elm splits clean.

November Woman

She walks november fields
backbone sharp to the wind
which races unimpeded down bare

november slopes. She is the woman
who cares for life's outlines, welcomes
this stripping down, keeps each moment

spare, sees the shape of the skull
pressing through skin at the moment
of death, waits for the comfort

of winter as she walks the harsh november
pasture. Her feet shuffle through bonemeal
leaves, dry bone twigs pruned from the lean

stark branch. She becomes as a bud
self contained along a bough; she holds
the leaf shape secure within. November

knows the opening of milkweed, the pod
scattered in soft white flakes, feathered
seeds which carry the tall stalk's form

but not the shape of winter. November
does not intimate the covering of snow
nor predict the softness of leaf, but holds

itself bone sharp and spare. In the dark
night she walks under a sky with no moon
past the silent shape of a white horse

standing on three legs, head bowed
to the wind, mane parted along the ridge
of a bent neck. Her bones grow long and sharp

as she walks among bones, shuffles
her feet through the dry twig debris,
becomes as a bud self contained on the branch

of a tree stretched out in the bare november
pasture, stands waiting with the white
horse in a dark field on a night with no moon.

Boundaries

Walking the boundaries
of our land   separating
hayfield   pasture   woodlot
we are bound together
by distinctions
our lives joined   by divisions
With a scythe we make a path
from house to barn
building patterns of repetition
the country demands.

photo by George Buggs

Gary McLouth

Gary was born in Batavia, New York, and raised in the nearby village of Corfu. He attended the local school and went on to graduate from Syracuse University in 1966. Gary holds masters degrees from Syracuse and Western Michigan Universities and most recently was awarded the Doctor of Arts Degree in English from SUNY Albany in June 1985.

I write in many genres but poetry is my first and most abiding form of written expression. The Adirondacks have been part of my life since my first visit at the age of four. I have missed few years there and recently Blue Mountain Lake and environs have been a second physical home and primary spiritual one. These poems attempt to join physical and spiritual experience in a voice true to both.

Recent work includes: Men and Abortion *(co-author Shostak), Praeger Publishers, N.Y. 1984. "Death and Other Frustrations", prize winning collection of short stories (dissertation),* Softball *(co-author, Nakell), a screenplay, and several poems published in* Earth Daughters, Blueline, The Art Department, Nadir, The Small Pond, *and others. Gary is a poetry editor of* Blueline. *He is a former college administrator and teacher and has worked in a number of colleges and universities in New York and Rhode Island. Gary has also worked as a farm laborer, bar tender, motel manager, handy man, and free lance writer. This summer ('85), he enjoyed a writer's residency at the Blue Mountain Center—"as close to paradise as I think I will get."*

Loyalty

Ancient voices bubble
in the wake of my gliding boat

Crisp Adirondack accents
alliterate secrets older than words

Through the lineage of Raquette
Ausable and Big Moose

Their submarine banter flows
among rocks and buried valleys

My probing oars sustain conversation
eavesdrop

. . . the translation is of
knowing waters

Waiting for my return

Labor Day

Over this half moon black lake
live all the points of heaven
I knew by heart in the sixth grade

Tonight the constellations
mock my memory
A bat's shadow flits
low to the water

I stretch my eyes into
that space I
once saw as a ceiling
curved over my bed
in my first room
with a window

There are no loon cries
no rustling chipmunks
Somewhere deep in the woods
beyond the lake
a logging truck groans
at a hill

In the water must be
a fish too cold to catch
a bug ready to be eaten
a rock too long there
to be just a rock

High in the top
of that pine on Bluff Point
to the North of a star
whose name I have forgotten
is its highest needle

And in the jewel of moisture gathering
at its tip
Life becomes personal

Blue Mountain

How can you hunker down
quiet purple in the dark and not want
the Big Dipper
to pour the Northern Lights
over these sleepy headed mountains
you commune with age after age?

Especially tonight, how can you
not spring up
and want to be heaven,
hunger in your ego of rock
to shake off your craggy trails,
your hoary face of tangle,
for once to tilt with stars
to commiserate
with all about you moving?

Standing at the edge of this blue lake shore
I think of an ant
wondering
shadowless at my bare toes.

I think I see the line of cedars along the moon shore
where deer have eaten as high as their heads
will stretch from winter ice.

Under your somnolent shoulder
the stars go cold in the lake
where you stand on your head
and wait.

Earth Quake Blues

Richter readings reverberate across the front page
America rivets her vertigo to the Adirondacks
No, not San beloved Andreas
We have our own Fault to fear and worship

The story rumbles out ubiquitous swarms of camera crews
their glass eyes magnify falling gilt edged leaves
mossy crevices
Hey, Wait! Where's the quake, steaming rubble, amputated
limbs? Did it really shake here at dawn? Look, we're on
live

Wool plaid and flannel survivors pad the lone Blue Mountain
    street
Summer sank into the city, Labor Day, but these news boys
reel at the lake, the fading red and yellow mountain ridges
Does it always seem so serene after a major tremor? Are we
embarrassed by no damage? This is live coverage

The natives are grim as mountains, clever as silver November
lakes. Damage resources are mobilized
How could we have missed it, 'cept it was real early
Here, this building almost jilted off its stone pillars
Yes, the camera zooms 6-inch cracks to New York, Sedona,
    Knoxville
The decrepit store finally gets attention

And, the mountain looks a little off kilter, yeah, leaning toward
Indian Lake, by God, more than usual. Sure as hell more than
when we went to bed last night!
Your name sir? You're a brave soul living up here next to that
monster and just taking daily menace in stride. Are you
married?

With the air time nearly gone, true havoc is discovered
A courageous little cabin lurching out over the lake shore,
pulling tongue and groove against fate, coughs up its cast
iron stove to the world. Sideways, cornerwise tossed from
its slate platform, grate shook mindless, stove pipe impotent
maligning the wall

What it must have been, here at dawn, to capitulate this anchor
like stove. These are brave people indeed
Video machines hum, groove the ass-up stove into history
and click off

The town surrenders to a mid-morning Canadian wind
Stubborn leaves blush against all odds of living
Two townsmen go about restoring the stove to useful condition,
neither remembering for sure who had pitched rum sotted against
her hot black belly in the night,
who had hung longer above the quaking hungry earth.

Good Work

Poetry don't pay much, does it?
The woodsman sighs to me
as he pulls the axe blade from
a near split piece of cedar
and cuts another arc over his head
like an Indian laboring over a log
he is digging out
and lets it slice the air silver
straight through the cedar's crack
to the chopping block

How much you getting for splitting the wood
I ask
He lays the axe on the block
steps into the edge of woods
that rake their late september branches
on the side of the shed

A man pissing in the outdoors
draws companionship
I step in and find a mossy rock
to aim at

The maples are flaming red, the oaks
reluctant to turn
A solitary yellow tipped leaf
meanders to the ground

Not enough, he says
but it's good work
and I can piss anywhere I want to
anytime

Memorial Day

for Marty (and Rosie)

1.

We have come up to this mountain lake
to give our knots back to the woods
to paddle at the surface of cold
rock bottomed secrets
we do not want to keep

The gray sky does not deter us
as we dip downwind
toward the scarred shoreline
that marks the foot of trail
up Castle Rock
Your brindle and white dog huddles
against the gunwale, against our sporadic
strokes

2.

She charges like errant electricity
through the beech trees, their delicate green
daring the tentative spring to retreat

On top, past the devil caves, above cliff slabs
the world almost falls away to ridges of fir
and forests succumbing to black rain
but we know it is all there, what we see
and what we know we could see
for some sun

There is no room for wandering men at the top of a mountain
The wind and water and fire have not made a place for us
One bent short root bare pine could say as much
We take a photograph and head back down

3.

On the water there is no ease
The east wind beats around tangled islands
to baffle the canoe
Digging up to our wrists we feel the surge
of inner muscle like dead wills awakening
as if by telling ourselves of Iroquois survival
we could taste the inside flesh of rabbit hides
talk in voices of the mountain trees and make love to supple lakes

The dog will have none of our rite
Plunging into the waves on her own fatal hunt
she brings cries from buried fears
Times full of times full of times
We flail into the wet, the cold, the wind
into the time of seeing this past
knowing there was nothing to save

Eugene Mirabelli

Eugene Mirabelli came from a town outside Boston to live in the Upper Hudson Valley area twenty years ago. He teaches fiction writing and literature at the State University of New York at Albany, and has written three novels, as well as some verse and non-fiction.

32

from Earthly Pleasures

The summer when I was sixteen my father took us all on a leisurely automobile trip into upstate New York, to the Rensselaer Polytechnic Institute where a former colleague of his was teaching, then next day we crossed the Hudson River to Albany to visit the State Museum, and then out to the great Helderberg cliff for the cool air and the view. But all I can recall of the trip is our excursion to that marvelous cliff. To get there we drove south from Albany, passing through farms and orchards to where the land was wide, empty. There the cliff stood across the hazy blue meadows like a giant green wall, rose a thousand feet and blocked the horizon for miles, the crumbled and terraced facade covered with trees except at those points where a battlement of white stone thrust up sheer to the top. The road ran across the fields to the foot of the escarpment, then turned abruptly and slanted up a long slow incline that eventually worked onto the table-land at the top. The view from up there is spectacular, even grandiose. The fields below are stitched together into a dense green blanket, the farm houses and red barns almost lost amid the gentle folds. Albany is farther off, a cluster of bright misty points under gauze; Rensselaer and Troy and Schenectady are gray pencil patches—the Mohawk and the Hudson are rubbed out, invisible. The far side of the valley is walled by the huge Adirondacks, and the blue space between the cliff where we stood and those mountains was once a frigid lake, formed when the melting ice of the last glacial era could find no easy path to the sea. And when its waters finally drained away there was left that powdery silken sand which, my father told us, rises like a cloud whenever you dig a cellar in Albany County. We explored the trails down the face of the escarpment and gathered rock fragments, then later that day we drove across the plateau—saw a stream whose bed was perfectly smooth slate—visited a quarry and came away with several chunks of fossil stone and some fossilized shells scavenged from the Helderberg talus. My own particular block of fossil stone, a magnificent specimen which I needed both hands to lift, stayed in my disused bedroom for years after I left home, then it turned up under the ferns in my mother's flower garden, and is now in my livingroom as a bookend, taking up about as much room as a one-volume encyclopedia. The stone is dark gray and has a thick layer of crumbly brown mud baked through it. The mud is packed with finely whorled sea shells, some fallen open to reveal the stony musculature inside; the gray part of the stone is surprisingly heavy, hard, jagged, its surface imprinted with scores of scallop-like shells, some prints containing a delicate little rim of white, like a finger nail, or an entire shell, pale bone color and marvelously fluted. At first I believed that the shells belonged to those clams and scallops and such which had lived in the ancient ooze of the glacial lake. But I was way, way off. The marine animals had been locked in their stones four hundred million years before the waters of that lake washed over them.

My father, gratified to indulge his children's scientific curiosity, had bought two little books on local geology at the Albany State Museum. The pages were dense with geological lore, charts, studious drawings of fossils, and there were gray photographs of the Helderberg escarpment and, on a ledge, a trio of young women of the 1920's in sailor blouses and bobbed hair. I didn't understand much of what I read, but the antiquity of the fossils—that I was able to poke my pencil into a stony cell three or four hundred million years old—fascinated me, induced me to work through page after page. I learned that the Helderberg formation is a deep flat deck of stone, but gently tilted so that one side is slanted down beneath the level of the surrounding land and the other is thrust up, exposed—and that exposed side is the cliff which rises like a wall across the fields south of Albany. The depth of the plateau is open to view this way, revealing layer upon layer of stone, each like the edge of a page in a closed photograph album. The stone sheets (limestones, sandstones, shales) must have extended across the empty valley to the mountains on the other side, but that was long ago and erosion has worn them back, split huge blocks from the escarpment, broken and heaped them until the facade is half buried in its own crumbling talus. The strata were laid down in seas of Devonian and late Silurian times. (I was entranced even by the strange lonely words: Devonian, Silurian, the earlier Ordovician, yet earlier Cambrian, and the fantastic Pre-Cambrian, vanishing backward into the foundations of the earth.) The occasional curious interleaving of sandstone with fine shale suggests the seasonal currents and tides running in those seas; other strata show a pattern of cracks such as you find in drying mud, and on others the surface is rippled, as it would be had it lain in the shallow water of a withdrawing tide. Most fascinating of all, there are coral reefs stretching blindly through the Helderberg cliff along with thin beds of limestone which hold the fossilized record of lagoons and tidal flats. I knew that coral lived only in warm seas, so how those reefs grew in our chill northern waters was a mystery to me. Was the world much milder then? Long ago, perhaps, wandering tropical currents broke where fir trees stand, or maybe the vast land itself had drifted north, ferrying its warm bones with it. But the museum handbooks were mum on that.

For the rest of that summer I collected stones, picked up some lovely speckled egg-shaped rocks from the beach at Cape Cod and found a muddy quartz crystal near a highway cut. But not many. My interest soon faded. I had been fascinated not by stones but by the record of passing time embodied in them. In my imagination the Helderberg cliff was merely the edge of the book, strata upon strata laid up like pages covered with the undeciphered scrawl of sea worms and the scarab-like signature of trilobites—a hieroglyphic history receding hundreds of millions of years. I was haunted by visions of that lonely coast with barely a creeping thing to move and no sound, no sound anywhere but the draining sea. Yet things did swim and crawl and spend their little lives, and some of them lay bedded now in that huge ossuary, waiting to be opened to my view. I fancied myself returning to the escarpment one summer day, climbing down the strata backward through millions of years to pry out some scrolled cephalopod and know its dumb history. But I had lots of other things to do first and never went there again. The implication of those orderly strata eluded me, and not until many years later (many years) did I come to know, to realize, that time moves only in one direction and that history is what happens only once.

photo by Jim Flosdorf

Kristen Murray

Kristen Murray was born and grew up in Schenectady. After living in New Jersey for eight years following her college graduation, she returned to New York and currently resides in Ballston Lake. An active member of the Hudson Valley Writers Guild, she served as secretary on the Board of Directors during 1985. She is currently on the editorial staffs of Groundswell *and the* Albany Tricentennial Anthology. *She holds a Bachelor of Arts degree in English from Wagner College and a Master's degree in English from the State University of New York at Albany, where she is presently working toward her doctorate in the Writing Program. Her stories and poems have appeared in various publications. She is employed as a staff writer for* The Research Foundation of S.U.N.Y. *and is the mother of three boys.*

My writing nearly always focuses on some aspect of a human relationship, whether it is woman-man, woman-woman, mother-child, or the relationship of the self to the self. I am interested in how a character reacts to the situations in which she finds herself, her ability or inability to accept responsibility for the consequences of her actions and decisions. Nature in one form or another frequently appears in the symbol structure of my work. Sometimes it is representative of the character's emotional or psychological place in the story; often it

285

functions as another level of meaning in the work. I enjoy writing what I refer to as the epiphany story, which I define as a story, usually very short, in which the character has the experience of self-revelation. It is, as the name suggests, a sudden awakening, usually triggered by something quite mundane, during or after which the character undergoes internal/psychological change which is often profound.

Another of my pleasures in writing is language. I like to play with it, make it work for me as much as I can. Many of my stories have begun with an interest in the language without any clear idea of where that will lead fictionally. It is often for me the single most important element in the story. If the language is working, if the words, sentences, paragraphs flow together, if the feelings and visions they evoke are powerful, I feel great satisfaction with the piece.

Trilogy

We are far out to sea on a small cruiser borrowed from an acquaintance, far from the shore, beyond the break of the waves. I make a pretense of fishing, dragging a large net along the side of the boat, which barely grazes the water keeping it wet. Margot's face is pink with the salt air and wind. Strands of hair cross her mouth like a horse's bit. She stands at the bow leaning slightly toward the ocean as she might lean to tell a secret to a friend. She leans too far; she topples. I watch her sink into the white foam and then I see him, her lover, and they are laughing as they entwine under the surface. He licks the salt from her bare arms. I pick up my fishing knife from the deck, lower myself on the side of the boat, plunge my hand beneath the water, the knife into his neck. He turns from Margot in surprise to face me, but I have managed to cut an artery and he bleeds too much to fight. He falls through the water as if a rope has been severed which holds him. His legs are perfectly straight; there is no struggle. Margot, alarmed, follows him, stretching her arms downward, moving them through the bloodied water. I climb the side of the boat. The afternoon sun is high over the water and red, like a pomegranate. My eyes eat the fruit and I doze to the buzz of horse flies and the ocean lapping on the boat bottom. When I awaken, it is to the rhythmic pounding of some object on the side of the cruiser. I investigate. It is the foot of Margot's lover beating against the boat with each movement of the sea. His body is caught under the craft's belly. I take an oar from the cabin to pry him loose. There is more bulk to him than I had imagined. When he is free he is not alone, but with Margot, the two of them naked and caught eternally in the love act. I set them adrift with my oar.

We have met Margot's friend by coincidence at a small lobster shanty in the cove which serves as a restaurant. We have all just finished eating and meet as we are about to leave. "Let's walk on the bridge," she says, a tall, muscular dark woman with tanned arms and legs and short frizzled hair. Her stride is determined, masculine, dykeish. I dislike her, but Margot smiles most alluringly and I am left to follow. The ends of the bridge by the land are wide wooden slats set horizontally. The middle third of it is steel: a drawbridge which opens for the tall masts of the fishing vessels which dock in the cove. Margot and her friend are ahead of me, their arms around each other, Margot's slim white legs in contrast to the woman's coarse brown ones. I am at once repulsed and attracted by the curling black hair which climbs her legs, brushing against the smooth skin of Margot. I linger behind watching them mount the slight grade which leads to the metal section of the bridge. They lean over the rail between the intricate steel spires of the draw machinery. Margot's skirt blows in the wind. A fishing boat appears in the distance and the bridge begins to hum without warning, and then a clanking, cranking sound like an unoiled wheel and the bridge lifts slowly to the sky. Margot and the woman are tossed into the water with startling grace, like cliff divers floating through the air down into the stiff sea. Margot goes under and does not rise. The woman's black head bobs about the surface like a dark gull. I run from the bridge, down the sloped bank, into the oily inlet water, and swim to Margot's friend. She is barely conscious when I grab her around the neck as I have seen done and pull her to shore. Her clothes have been ripped away by the force of the fall, and she lies on her back with her body exposed to me, the smell of the sea rising from it. I part her legs and make love to her, then leave her like a sea urchin to bake in the sun.

We are invited to a beach party at the shore house of one of the men Margot works with, a square, flat house on a grassy cliff overhanging the beach. Supper has been cooked and eaten on the sand and now the red coals under the hibachi grates are dumped on a pile of driftwood which we have gathered along the beach. Some of the wood is wet and spreads thick gray smoke where we are standing, but most of it is dry and the fire blazes up restlessly. Margot is the only woman present except for the pale fat wife of our host, who has been unpleasant all evening and who has just returned to the house after refusing to swim. The men strip to their shorts or bathing suits, remove their shoes, tuck their watches and billfolds inside. Margot unfastens the long skirt she has been wearing over her swimsuit. Surrounding her, the men propel Margot toward the water. I watch from next to the bonfire, listening to their voices. The host has an air raft large enough for two, and they have placed Margot inside it, her legs hanging over the sides as the men push. When they can no longer stand, they begin to tread water, holding the raft while one of them climbs in next to Margot. In a single quick movement he slips off her suit. He holds it high in the air like a prize ribbon, then throws it beyond the raft where it floats on the surface for a moment and sinks. The other men try to hold the raft still while he covers Margot with his body, but the raft sways and veers, fills with water, empties again. One by one the men join Margot in the raft, their taut, ugly buttocks wet with the sea, shining in sea light. The raft drifts farther out. They have misjudged the waves and one breaks on the raft, flipping it so that the men hanging on the sides are thrown off and Margot and the man with her are caught under it. The overturned raft bobs with the gentle rock of the waves, but no one comes up. The raft floats toward a stretch of land which juts into the sea a few yards away and catches on the craggy shoreline. I run along the beach to the jutting land, run along its length to the place where the raft is snagged on the rocks. It laps gently with the break of the waves. Margot's hair buoys out from under like a parachute.

Denver

Marion brought the dog home from the animal shelter and installed him in the kitchen. She spread newspapers on the floor and barricaded the entrance to the dining room with a two- foot high board she found in the garage. She took the blue dish she'd bought in Woolworths out of the bag and filled it with water, then sat down at the kitchen table with a can of Tab and read the typed-in line at the bottom of her lease: NO PETS ON PREMISES.

Ah, well, after all, she'd probably be moving to a cheaper place in a month or so. And he was a medium-sized dog right now, though he certainly showed promise of getting bigger. "Collie mix and other" the description on the outside of his cage had read. "All shots. Good with kids." He'd lifted his head and thumped his tail on the floor when she went near his pen. He had a kind of defeated look about his eyes, yet there was something hopeful in the way he rose from the cement and approached the wire door when she walked by, something that made her stop and go back to look at him.

"He's been here a month already," the grim attendant told her. "Tomorrow's his last day. One way or the other."

That was probably true for a lot of the dogs, she told herself.

"Is he trained?" She had promised herself that any dog she took would have to be trained.

"He's supposed to be, but he don't do too good with it."

"Well, does he sometimes?"

"Does it in the cage instead of outside in the run. Can't say how he'd be in a house. Maybe different. Maybe not."

As she walked away from him she heard him whine, just once, very low, as if he knew this was his last chance. She looked at all the other dogs first, but in the end, she chose him against all reason.

The kids were away for the weekend with their father. They would certainly be surprised that Marion had a dog. They had been asking for one for a long time, but their father always said no. Now that Marion lived alone with the youngest child, she found herself wanting a dog, for protection, she said. Every few weeks or so she would have a night of real terror, believing that someone had got in the house and was hiding in the cellar or in the crawl space of the unused room upstairs. She would just convince herself there was nobody and begin to drift into sleep, when something would bang or creak above her or below, and she would finally be driven to search the rooms.

It was during those sleepless hours that she started thinking about a dog. A dog would bark and scare off anyone who tried to break in; at the very worst, it would be clubbed by the intruder. A dead dog in the living room would be a sure giveaway.

She didn't know what to name the dog. There was no name on his card at the shelter; she was glad of that. He'd seem more like her dog if she could name him. She had thought of letting the kids give him a name, but she knew they'd come up with something like Spot or Blackie and the dog would suffer from ordinariness all his life. She looked at him lying on the cool linoleum, watching her. Maybe Hal would be able to suggest something when he came for dinner tonight. Hal would be surprised about the dog, too. "What do you want to get a dog for?" he said when she first mentioned it. "When we're in bed it'll be right there trying to play."

"Sort of a menage a trois," she'd said, and Hal had given her a funny look.

She thought the two of them, Hal and her ex-husband, had

convinced her that a dog was out of the question. In his practical way, her ex-husband had reminded her of how much the dog would be alone, how it would mess up the yard, how it would tie her down, the expense of feeding it. Hal with his disdain for pets had made her feel she was being foolish. But with everyone gone this weekend, and the house so quiet, she began to think of a dog again. Not that she was lonely, not that she didn't have things to do—that wasn't it. She imagined the dog curled next to her as she lay on the couch reading or following her to the kitchen when she went to make supper. Company.

The phone rang. The insistence of the bell made her nervous and she caught it on the first ring. Somehow she knew it would be Hal saying he couldn't come tonight. Just one of those feelings she got now and then, but she was right. He was being flown to Denver as a troubleshooter on some project snafu that had cropped up. He was sorry; he would rather be with her. In fact, why didn't she come with him? She was alone this weekend, right? What better time. He couldn't guarantee how much time he could spend with her, but she'd find things to do, and surely they could spend a little time together. After all, he'd have to sleep, wouldn't he? Ha. Ha.

"I can't," she said. "I've got this dog . . ."

He said, "Already it's tying you down. I'll bet you haven't had it three hours." Marion said, "One and a half."

She hung up the phone and looked at the dog flopped on his side at her feet. He had lost some of that nervous look he'd come home with. She thought of trying to board him overnight, but the nearest kennel was ten miles in the opposite direction from the airport. At least she had a name for him now. "Denver," she said, and he lifted his head. She could put him in the cellar and leave enough food. She would be gone only two days. But what if he howled and the neighbors complained. Hal's plane left in two hours; if she could figure out what to do with the dog, she could meet him at the airport. She really wanted to go to Denver with him. Marion was beginning to see that getting the dog was a bad idea. It was a little like getting married, a little like having children—sometimes you overcommitted yourself.

The dog stood up suddenly and whined, the tip of his tail dragging slowly across the floor. Marion hadn't bought him a leash yet, so she took hold of his collar and walked him to the door. When he was reluctant to go down the steps, she gave him a small push to the gravel driveway. Standing at the bottom of the steps, he lifted his nose in the air, smelling something. Marion tried to coax him to the grass, but he stood where he was, sniffing the wind, not moving.

"C'mon, Denver, c'mon." She slapped her thighs and backed away from him onto the lawn, but he stood as if he were carved stone, a monument to the porch steps. After fifteen minutes, Marion gave it up and took him back inside where he immediately lifted his leg on the dishwasher.

"Bad dog!" she scolded, hitting a folded paper against the table to frighten him. "Denver's a bad dog!"

He wagged his tail slowly and licked her hand, nudging the newspaper with his nose.

She got some paper towels and disinfectant cleaner and soaked up the mess. "Denver needs a diaper," she said, remembering that her youngest child had been out of diapers for about six months now and that she should be through with this sort of thing. She looked at the clock—an hour and a half until Hal's plane left. The dog was back under the table asleep. Quietly she moved aside the board between rooms and went down the hall to her bedroom. She began taking clothes out of the closet and dresser and setting them on her bed, bringing in soap and cleansers and shampoo from the bathroom and wrapping them neatly in plastic bags so they wouldn't spill in her suitcase. The dog must have missed her because suddenly he was whining and jumping against the board, and when she didn't go to him right away, the whine became a distinct howl, destroying any thoughts she had about leaving him in the cellar. She spoke to him quietly and he stopped.

She brought the suitcase from the upstairs closet and filled it with the things she had laid on the bed, changed her clothes, combed her hair. One hour to do something with the dog and get to the airport. She put her suitcase in the trunk. Taking the dog by the collar, she brought him outside, but he was afraid of getting in the car. He sat on his haunches on the gravel, whining, until Marion lifted him into the back seat. As soon as she got in the car, the dog jumped to the front. The pebbles that had embedded themselves between the pads of his paws loosened and rolled toward her white skirt. The dog was edgy and wouldn't sit still. He kept turning around and around on the seat trying to make a place for himself. As soon as the car started to move, he was up at the window, jumping against the door, sweeping his slow tail, whining.

Marion drove out of the city. She was traveling in the general direction of the airport, but slightly to the west where she knew it was rural and where she would be likely to find some wide expanse of field or woods. She was pressed for time, and she drove as fast as she dared until she came to a road which branched off to the left with a farm visible about a quarter mile on. She passed the farm and a couple of small houses, then came to a clearing with a heavy covering of trees beyond it and stopped the car. Marion went around and opened the door on the passenger side, but the dog wouldn't get out. She tugged at his collar and he whined a little and settled his rear on the seat so that Marion had to slide him along, then carry him out of the car. The ground was loamy and Marion's heels sunk into the soft earth covering her toes and the sides of her sandals with mud. The dog was watching her, his incessantly moving tail gathering bits of dirt in its thick fur.

"Go on, Denver, go find some nice people to take you in." *He can fend for himself*, she thought, *for a few days.* And there were enough houses around here that someone would find him. She imagined he'd have a better chance on his own than he would have if she returned him to the shelter. She felt guilty just the same. Irresponsible. It was like giving up a child that you decided you never really wanted in the first place.

She walked around to get into the car and the dog followed. "Stay. Stay, Denver." He tried to hop in now, although before she couldn't get him near the car. She had to push him away with her foot and slam the door before he could jump up again. With the door shut, she could hear his nails scraping the side of the car as he jumped at the door to get in. He began to bark, a high-pitched, desperate bark, and she was glad that the nearest houses were far enough down the road so that the people inside wouldn't hear him. She shifted the car into gear and began driving carefully along the edge of the road until the sound of the dog's nails on metal stopped and she could see him in the side mirror as he stood along the road. She felt a moment of misgiving that he might run out and get hit, but with twenty minutes until Hal's plane left, and the airport at least ten minutes away, Marion had no time for second thoughts.

The traffic on Route 60 was heavy but moving. She lost a few minutes behind a truck, but once she passed it, it was clear the whole way. Pulling into the airport long-term pay lot, she looked at her watch again: eight minutes. She locked the car, took her suitcase from the trunk, and hurried across the lot to the terminal. It took her a few moments to locate the Eastern reservations counter; when she did, she was in a line of eight or ten people. It occurred to her that she wasn't going to make it.

"I've got to get on flight 204 to Denver," she said to the reservations clerk when it was finally her turn.

The clerk looked at Marion patiently. "I think you're too late, but

I'll check." As she dialed the phone, she had that reproachful smirk of someone in control that seemed to say, "Why didn't you phone ahead? Why didn't you leave a half hour earlier? Why should rules be broken for you?"

"Is flight 204 still boarding?" Marion heard her ask. The clerk put the phone down. "I'm sorry Flight 204 is taxiing now."

"When is the next flight?"

Five-thirty p.m. tomorrow."

"Only one flight a day?"

"Yes, ma'am."

"Does any other airline . . ."

"You'll have to check with flight information. Straight ahead, turn right, third counter on your left. Can I help you, sir?"

Marion walked away from the counter and headed to information.

"Are there any flights to Denver tonight."

"Next flight out is 2:00 p.m. tomorrow afternoon."

Damn dog, she thought as she walked away. Damned stupid dog!

The long-term pay lot cost her four dollars, the daily rate, for the twenty minutes she was there.

It seemed to Marion that as long as the dog had already caused all this trouble, she might as well keep him. She drove back along Route 60, the damp evening filling the inside of the car with its earthy smell. When she turned onto the country road where she had let the dog out, the air yielded the scent of hay on the ground and tilled farmland and vast fields of new crops. The odor of the land soothed her, and she drove to the clearing where she had left the dog and pulled onto the side of the road.

There was no sign of him. She got out of the car and looked for his tracks in the mud, but the soil was so wet that even the tire ruts where she had stopped earlier had disappeared. She called to him; still he didn't come. She started into the clearing, sinking deep in the soft soil, heading toward the woods. She had an hour or so before it would be dark, so she searched the edge of the woods, calling to the dog, looking for him, in vain. The low brambles ripped her stockings, poked tiny, stinging cuts in her legs. The heels of her sandals caught in the dead leaves and underbrush, making it difficult to walk through the dense bushes. She looked for the dog along the banks of a creek that cut between the trees, following until it became a thin crevice of water and disappeared under some rocks. When it grew too dark for her to stay in the woods any longer, she drove up the road to the three houses that were nearby and asked if anyone had seen the dog.

"Black and tan, a little like a collie, floppy ears?"

No one had seen him.

She went back to the side of the road by the clearing. The night had turned chill and her skin felt the dampness underneath her clothing, a stark dampness not even her sweater could fend off. The moon was by now a frail gray light behind the moving clouds. Something barked far off in the woods, a fox or a dog. Marion stood by the edge of the dank field calling, hoping the dog would come bounding out of the trees. Occasionally a shadow darting through the bushes would make her think he was there; then it would turn out to be a branch or a bird skimming by the woods. A plane flew overhead, its headlights on for the landing.

"Dog! Where are you, Denver?" Marion ran into the trees again, catching her hair in the limbs, tearing her skirt, the sleeves of her blouse on the sprawling growth of the woods. Not until she fell exhausted in the mud of the creek bed did she know that the dog was lost to her, melded into that vast and nearly moonless night.

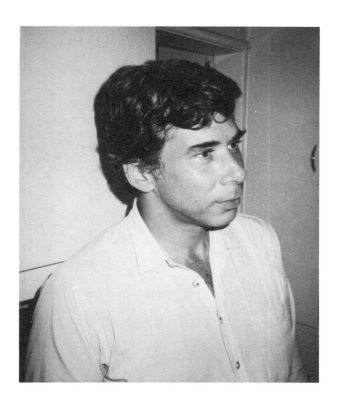

Martin Nakell

I have published widely in literary magazines, particularly in the Northeast. I received a Doctor of Arts from the State University of New York at Albany, and currently teach at Chapman College in Orange, California. I return often to the Northeast, and particularly to the Adirondacks. I have held residency fellowships at the Fine Arts Work Center in Provincetown, and at the Blue Mountain Center in Blue Mountain Lake, New York.

There is no region so inherently intimate as the Adirondacks in the scale of the landscape, in the way the light falls at different times, in the way the water responds to the mountains, the trees, the air, in the way, indeed, that the water stands on its own and commands our rapt attention to its breadth, its depth, its movement. There is majesty here, but there is always a measuring of the scale, a return to the minute and the close. Often you feel the true scale of your human smallness, yet it is not diminishing, nor even cosmic, for very little in the landscape is out of your reach, and it all seems to include you.

The Adirondacks increasingly have become a part of the geography of my poetry. "How It Will Be For You" was conceived among the lakes and takes cognizance of history, of Indian life, of indigenous ways of living.

I believe strongly in the music of poetry. I have often thought that if a poem sounds right, it's likely that it is right. Life in the Adirondacks has a unique pace, a special timing that has become an element of my poetics. Other things remain, the music of my strongly Jewish background, the rhythms of urban life, the sounds of other influential poets. But the rhythms of the Adirondacks, the sound of the water, the timing of birds, the tension of deer all are taking an important part in indirect and subtle ways. A poet cannot go out and swallow a landscape and then make a list of what he has ingested. A poet must live with a landscape, take it in, let it become a living part of all the elements of his work.

Thus, images of life in the Northeast have become central to my work, as I find increasingly that image, vision is the core of poetic structure. Together image and music and intellect make up the essence of poetry. So, in "Train" the image of the Amtrak hurtling up and down the Hudson River carries the weight of much thought. In "The Beast" the image of the beast itself, with its nebulous reality, carries our sense of anxiety, or fear, or knowledge. Those two things particularly, image and music, combined with landscape, and, for me increasingly the landscape of the Adirondacks, makes it possible to accomplish what Robert Motherwell says all artists do, that very primitive act of "making marks on flat surfaces with pigments" which express our condition.

Train

At first I dealt most
with the cemetery
laid down behind the house.
How do we live
practically on top
of the dead?
But the dead fade.
They are not even a winter's breath
compared to a train
at a hundred and ten.
When I talk
to a friend twelve miles
downriver, first
I hear the train,
south bound, hump the rails
gloat its horn,
then I hear it
from his phone.
First he hears
the north bound,
then he hears it
from my phone.
We believe that time is not an illusion.

296

Every week
on Monday's sick
morning lovers, startled
out of sleep's shadow
in the shadow
of another,
wave love goodbye,
board the train,
yield to its soft
cushions, its cold
windows, let it carry them
home to the City.
Every Friday, down there,
amid thick granite,
impenetrable spotted citystone,
at Grand Central
wiping soft soot
from the eyes they look
up north,
love's quiet love's
possible country.
Once a man was heaved
onto the traintracks
out the window of a bar
just as the train came
from the south; a cool, fall
night as stars began
that crisp shining,
bright points of stalactites
hung from the sky.
When the train came
and the man looked up in the midst
of his scream,
when he saw stars
and could not believe
either in time
or in the fact
that what was happening
that night was the last
thing that would happen,
and here, in this small
town on the railroad tracks,

the same train he had ridden
up and down, now
riding him home
to the star
to the ground of a grave
behind my house.

I didn't know him.
I don't know his name.
I wouldn't know it carved
into a granite stone
that shines like an earth-moon
gathering the sun's light.
I know only
his legend,
only his shadow cast
from that great non-action
of his life: to be thrown drunk
and terrified, laughing
a green hysteria,
no time to see stars,
no time to kiss trains.

Once, I stood by the tracks,
too close at a hundred
and ten the train whipped me
from my feet, bellowed at me
the enduring roar
no animal ever brought
from its belly.
I hollered mad
like a storm I railed,
Train! Train!
Then silence. Blue tracks
settling. The river behind
at my back humming cold water
to cold shore. Cold. Blue
cold. Steel.

Who was on the train
when it heaved by? What book
did they read to pass

anxious time or the time
of peace between two wars?
Was anyone I know
on that train? Was there
anyone thinking
one way or another
about me? What does the train
think? What is speed?
How fast is a hundred
and ten?
How cold the water?
How did he feel
when he became a legend?
How cold is the water,
blue, Hudson river water?
How slow is my hand
after the train passes
lifting water to sift it
through my fingers?

I'll tell you something, train.
I no longer fear
that at night
you'll run so fast
through my mind
you'll shatter
the skull. I used to.
But I've built a railroad.
It has tracks as thin
and delicate as your first
purpose. As my own.
They are laid through the white
bone of my skull. They are yours,
train, to run on.

How It Will Be For You

It's the moment
of appointments
when the hour is inclined
to twenty minutes past.
They await you
in boats and you go
smiling as at beautiful
strangers.
The grass you cross over
walking out
barefoot
is a foreign country.
The sun
who will some day flame out
is laughing
on the water.
They have a boat
with no names on it,
a broad canoe.
They have
their singing paddles.
They have your fear
wrapped in birch bark
though you carry
your own denials
in a pouch
sewn inside of you.
Time
prepares to close over
the gap you held open
so well
for so long.
As you refuse
to enter the boat
you are entering
the boat.
As you find yourself
in the middle
of the great lake

looking at the blue
quiet mountains
and whispering to yourself
"this is all a dream"
you are entering
the water you are swimming
without arms without
legs you are seeing
without your eyes.

The Beast

All morning the beast
wanders out alone and untethered.
Because of him
the birds sing insistently
sharp songs.
Because of him
the hills raise up the hackles
on their backs.
Because of him a few people
for a few moments
contemplate the walls
within which they spend
the fury of their infinitude.
Because he walks around
so freely
the trees cover themselves
with thick layers of green
needles and soft leaves.
Because of the beast's meandering
one man offers up his soul
as food sacrifice,
because of this daily walk
there are those who now return
to the pulsating silence
of their lovers.
One man embraces the beast
mistaking him for death.
The flagstones

nervously maintain their habitude
as pathways
and the animals
sleep through past noon
spread out
on the carpet of sunlight.

He walks around more free
than God
who is bound at least
to our suffering.
He walks around owning everything,
everyone,
and suddenly
he walks out of your eyes,
out of the tips of your fingers
out of your mouth like words.
Just wait.
Something in the mountains
will call him.
It always does.
He can't hear it
and can't know what it is,
but he'll walk up
through the foothills,
he'll drag shadows of fear behind him, he'll drag the knowledge
of pain chained to his waist
and cutting
a deep furrow in the earth
which will fill
later with fresh water.
We'll see him climb the hill
killing the air
on his way,
dust and dryness
flaking away from him in flames.
He's going to that voice,
that place
we can't imagine.
He's going to leave us alone again.

We turn over in our day.
We watch
the water flow
in a stream
or we see the smallness
of our sorrows
or perhaps we gaze
at our work and call it
by our own name, without despair.
We touch one another easily,
laughing.
And when someone says "Beast"
we say "what beast?"
We say, "we are alone here
on earth
and this is our country."

Mark Nepo

"Thoreau said, 'Moral reform is the effort to throw off sleep.' And I have come to believe the creative endeavor is a never ending effort to re-form, to re-claim the innate energies of life. And so, the pursuit of Poetry has become a perceptual way of breathing for me, a natural and daily process by which I test and break the urge to be all the things I was born to be, all the things I'm afraid of being, all the things I have no intention of being. The more I write, the more I create because I have questions, not answers. I create because I want to live as many lives as possible, as truthfully and fully as I can. I believe all human beings, secretly or openly, are searching for ways to be more than what they are. The presence of the earth and all things natural has always impacted our human sense of possibility, especially in vast, majestic regions such as our own.

"My Grandmother slept as a child under the relentless stars of the Ukraine. I was born in Brooklyn, was raised on Long Island, and have lived in the North Country since I was nineteen. Still, much of my exposure to the pulse and meaning of such a vast and quiet way of life has come over the last ten years in the farm life of my inlaws, especially Mary and F. Donald Myers, who own a farm in Wilton, New York, on which he was born. It is there I have done things I'd never do—holding down calves, medicating sheep, cutting up beef.

Many of my poems have been written on that farm, where nature's pull takes root in an inescapable search for the earth.

"*Through all of this, I've come to believe that all artists—be they poets, mechanics, magicians or farmers—all re-enact the moment of search, the moment of creation, pursuing what we can never regain, the instant of birth. And the search lands us in our freshest moments of living.*"

—M. N.

Mark Nepo was nominated for a Pushcart Prize in 1983. His work has been anthologized in THE INTERNATIONAL PORTLAND REVIEW *which showcased the work of poets from over 30 countries, and in the New York State Museum's anthology,* COLLECTED WORDS, *and will appear in Avon's upcoming anthology,* BLOOD TO REMEMBER: AMERICAN POETS ON THE HOLOCAUST. *His poems have appeared in many journals including* ANTAEUS, THE SOUTHERN REVIEW, KENYON REVIEW, SEWANEE REVIEW, SEATTLE REVIEW, DENVER QUARTERLY, NEW ORLEANS REVIEW *and* COLLEGE ENGLISH. *His previous books include a creative writing text,* ARENA FROM WITHIN THE I, *and a book of poems,* A MEMORY AS SWEET AS YOU MAKE IT.

During the summer of 1984, Nepo worked at Yaddo where he finished an epic poem centered on the life of Michelangelo. He has also finished his first novel, PRISMS, *and is at work on a collection of essays called* CLANDESTINE NOTIONS.

A Guide to Rock Climbing

Something makes me want to climb this rock
the way I sometimes get the urge
to step into traffic or lean
over the rail, 30 stories up.

Not much is said. I don't resist.
I lift my arms and he snugly knots the rope
around my waist:

"When I tug, push out
and walk right up her back."

I watch him scale the face in perfect rhythm
without a rope. He tugs
and I begin sliding my legs
in and out of thin cracks
long enough to hook my hands
on small angled juts.

Jamming knees and toes,
I test and reach with chafed fingers.
and wonder will the tug burn if I slip.
Will the rope cut sharp beneath a rib?

I can't find a foothold and I tremble
like a cancelled suicide teetering
from the top floor.

"Push out—"
He is distant.
"Push out—"

I quiver and stare at this piece of stone
which in years will be worn by the wind
from Whiteface over my shoulder.

I freeze. My nails go still,
no feeling to the knuckle.

I see nothing but small protrusions
and this hand-shaped rock leading with its atrophy
to my shaking wrist.

My soul has rushed to my fingertips
and to let go, to slip, would let it stream
like a punctured hose.

My feet scramble. I fall
and cling to the mass of rock
too big to hug.

I am spread, vulnerable.
The fear surges electric.
It forces me flatter.

I scrape a few yards
and then the snap, the tug
and I'm a dog shot,
hauled in on a leash.

I hug tight.
My cheek presses the stone.
It grows hot from my heaving.

I am seven or eight,
hit between the legs with a line drive;
falling to the street flush,
cheek pressed to the asphalt,
hearing feet and screen doors.

But the rockface is steep and I have just lost my soul
out my scraped cheek and I lie stiffly
being reeled in.

My palms flatten as they search the stone
like fossilized Braille

and there, just above
—the same arm's reach as before—
the jut of stone I slipped from.

The reach seems longer,
but I stretch and stretch
till I breathe like a fresco;
a naked figure spread on a wall
with nothing left to do but reach.

The Rusted Pail

We scuff the high dark grass
to fill the pail for the dying ram
too old to walk or bray.

The flashlights ring his saddened head and folded knee
with broken halos that neither hasten the end nor heal.

And we make sure there is no thirst
in his passing, a wish your father invokes
as he gives to sleep.

I want to touch the dying fleece.
But you say no and leave the ram
to the darkening crickets, and we stop
to hear him lick the pail.

I sneak back while you and your father sleep.
The horns feel brittle as he sulks up at me,
belly shuddering in weak rhythms.
I beg him to run the brook and die with the light.
He stares, glass-eyed, heavy beneath his crusty horns,
and I lift, palms thick and deep through his knotted fleece.

He does not fight or tense.
He only wants to drink and shudder beneath his flickering star
and I think of a thousand names to name his fall—
not one is him, not one is me,
not one the quiet white below his shedding chin.

He is heavy, too heavy. We fail
and the matted grass beside the pail
springs slowly up, while the grass beneath us now
grows warm and waits.

Artificial Intelligence

1.

Everyone is concerned where the satellite will fall
in which acre of geranium or stone
this clunker will burn its final pocket.
It is a marvel how far we can throw things
and as marvelous that they always return
sometimes as they were
sometimes smaller and gray
and scarred by the noiseless pummelling of space
colder, enlarged, damaged
or like the farthest Saturnal night,
untouched,
all this way
and still untouched.

At last, a vessel, after all these weary millenia,
that can re-enter without burning up.
But what earthly good, what organic virtue
remains possible, what hope
for the heart's rotation
if we can't burn
upon entry.

2.

We have, they say, done it:
engineered an artificial heart.
I'm sure it works: lub-dub lub-dub
but as echo as shadow as parrot to the divine.

As a boy, I watched my friend
hold a baby robin with a broken leg.
It was dying or so we thought,
and my little friend
took his jack-knife
and cut the robin's breast.

There was a slight shudder
and a tiny squeak
like the shutting
of a door
and like a piece of bark
the little breast of fur
peeled.

We watched
a pink almond
flutter
for seconds.

I looked away
and began to see it
everywhere
in everything.

I have found its image
in rivered stones
in the punky stem
of a single vertebra
in the underside of lily pad
the image of aorta
floating the surface
drawing blood of the sea.

Gravity was made
in the image of the heart
and when the heart stops, the blood
has no pull to keep it. It spills
without force from the ears
and eyes of a broken cave.

White Rage

The children, knee-high, are splashing in the lake
despite the abnormal quiet. The pines seem to stiffen,
the wind circling in a voiceless gasp. My dog, a setter,
at the water's edge, barks at the children's laughter,
his gold chain bouncing light about his neck.

My mother-in-law, barefoot, with a tray of sandwiches
heads for the dock. My wife in a sweatshirt reads in the shade.
The functions merely cycle: food, laughter, solitude. Is it
wrong that I feel closer to the pine and birch. I understand
the high branch, resilient, holding as the trunk creaks
and sways.

Clouds roll in.
There is a privileged glance of the others
without the glare. The squirrels have stopped, sidelong,
gray fur breathing in and out. There are no birds,
and now the lake is flat, the children
looking up, puzzled, arms dripping, hearts racing.
Only the dog continues, up and down the bank,
half-jumping, half-pacing.

A pink sheet cracks

I'm snapped from my feet   the breaking of wood

the falling whack of branches

my wife rolls the ground

her mother thrown flat as the struck tree falls slowly
for her legs.
                              I try to push off, to rise, to run
but cannot move, my skin hard. A spotted fire crackles,
the split birch steaming in the rain. I try to roll.
The dock has planks afloat, the children out of view.
The rain is fierce, the lake muddled. Mother
is pinned below the birch as men in boots run to her.
My face cools. A stranger steadies me.

My wife strokes my face, "I was afraid to touch you.
You were so still, and mama's hurt. I can't stop
shaking."

Slate from the cabin's roof covers the bank.
Some jut in the wet soil like thin slabs
of loss.

The children huddle inside,
the tops of their huge eyes pressed to the window.
Men swarm about the smoking log and now,
wet smells and dark skies will bring us more fear.

Nothing matters as the white veins flash
in the distance.

My setter lies in the water asleep,
his metal chain sizzling, his legs
bobbing in the rain.

I wade to my knees and float him to shore,
as if dirt were safer than water,
and the thunder fades, dancing to the crack
of a white and gaming whip.

Young Carlyle and Sloane

You understand Bill Sloane died Thursday
and the ground is hard, Mrs. Mckee, it's goin' on Thanksgiving
and the ground is hard like a fist in ice,
all gnarled and battered.
They want to hold him up till the thaw.
But I won't have it, I tell you.
Bill Sloane was a good man
and I won't let his bones wait till Spring.
The tombstone man — he's greedy with his time —
wants all winter to carve 'rest in peace.'
He's Carlyle's boy, a liar if there ever was and his old man —
worse than a hot day in December,
make you relax and then snap, cold as hell.
No, by Jesus, I had no use for Carlyle.
I wouldn't spit in his throat if his stomach were on fire.
The ground is hard, Mrs. Mckee, but Sloane was a good man.
I'll need a pick-axe and a spade
and the sweat'll dry as fast as it comes.
You understand it's right to dig a grave for a good man
and downright sickly to make way for a liar.
When Carlyle died, I had to dig all morning in the rain.
He had a solid brass box, solid brass and the mud weighed
as much as the brass. My legs ain't been right since.
I dug all morning and don't you know, Mrs. Mckee,
young Carlyle showed and started talking down to me
about some digger in Yurick. By Jesus, I'm no educated man
but I know the difference between a liar and a good man.
And Sloane was a good man, warm till the day he died.
Carlyle was a brain, cold like a fist in ice,
like the ground, Mrs. Mckee.
I never told no one, but two years ago in June,
the moon was bright, I dug my own, you understand
and put boards across. I thought I'd dig my own, you see
I'll be no burden and you needn't plant flowers —
just swear the box will be made square.
The dirt's in my garden. But the boards have rotted
and spiders and coon and possum and snakes
keep building nests and dragging straw
and bark, keep making home.

You understand, you can't keep the life out.
You understand, there is no rest.
The life above is gone and the life below can't wait.
There's no rest, by Jesus, and young Carlyle won't have all winter
'cause Sloane won't hold till Spring.
It's clouding up. I've let the sun slip again
and the ground's gonna be stubborn as your head.
You understand, the grave don't dig itself.

King of the Jews

I

Tonight Passover begins
and the loose piece of tin
rattles in the April gale,
and I want nothing but my stomach
against your back. The misplaced fly
buzzes about the headboard as you
seem restless. I think to wake you
and make wild love in sand,
though there is no sand.

You rustle and curl away
and I find little difference
in wandering a desert
or carrying a cross.

You are as holy as you sleep
in any robe clear enough to show your skin
below sky, tent or wooden roof.

You bring me your cross
and I will carve law into stone.

II

Today is Easter, and Helen bought you an orchid
and the priest, in the parking lot, pursed his lips,
"O' yes! We had orchids in the yard
in Miranda. The climate's just right."

The babes in the crowded pews whine.
They don't know enough to let the fears run
along the inside. They wail, and one or two—
as if some other voice takes hold their tongue.
They moan and drown the liturgy.

We wind the back roads to Ed's farm
and after ham dipped in glaze and a highball,
we walk my favorite brook in the lower field
and you remind me that old streams meander,
and I assure you I am not old.
But yes, you say, my eyes age before you.
They are not mine. And you do not own your tongue.

We think we speak, but guard our truths
from an angry world and all we ask will leave our lips
someday, quietly, and only dogs and cats will hear,
and they will cry likes babes in church,
like wolves on some Russian plain
howling prophecies to ice and grass
which know all
too well.

photo by Marjo Hebert

Kate O'Connell

I suppose a number of elements come together to create a writer—some of them may be mysterious. In my own case, I attribute my desire to write to several fundamental facts: where I was born, when I was born, and to whom I was born.

My parents were a young married couple living in Saratoga during the Depression. Because my mother was busy attending to sick relatives and working to ease our financial hardship, I spent most of my early childhood with my grandparents—my Polish grandparents in particular. Strong images of their farm and surrounding fields remain with me still: the crisp texture of grass and hay, the susurrous sounds of meadows, the stark colors of wildflowers in the brilliant sun, and especially vivid impressions of my grandfather, an immigrant peasant who could neither read nor write, but fascinate and charm with his storytelling, drawing pictures with words in the oral tradition.

It wasn't until I was in my forties that an urge came to me to write poetry. Although I had written short stories and poetry when I was in high school, now I was writing because of this mysterious urge, not because I had an English assignment.

Having taken up writing then, I have continued—writing both prose and poetry. This fall I will be collaborating with a photographer on a book about Saratoga.

I believe all the circumstances of my birth and childhood enabled me to become a writer—to be visited by the muse. I like to think that I have carried forward the oral tradition of my grandfather, that I have followed in his footsteps, and even perhaps that I am making footsteps of my own.

At Globerson's Corner

White paint spalls from the clapboards,
and the windows are boarded;
the old farmhouse still stands wayside
at East Broadway and Globerson's Corner.

Where my grandfather drove his droshky
on narrow roads, northward to town,
a freeway spreads its constant roar
over slow silences of the past.

Here I once summered,
listening only to quiet sounds:

> my grandmother's dress swishing
> through August grass,
> wildflowers whispering secrets,
> when bushes broom the house,
> winds flutter through murmurous
> meadows, at Globerson's Corner.

The sun sighs beyond the horizon,
and starlight echoes through darkness.
Even now I can hear hushed voices:
my grandparents humming a mazurka.

Autumn Elms

Tenuous
against rose-glow sky,
they stand
every evening,
on top of the tallest hill
in Congress Park.

When I see them,
I am reminded
of tired women
who have forgotten
to pull down the shades
before undressing.

They have shed their garments
thereabout;
their summer ornaments
detritus now,
heaps scattered on the ground.

I want to tell them
that they are beautiful,
still beautiful;
that their willowy limbs
are graceful,

ever graceful
as the arching arms
and tapered fingers
of Pavlova's dying swan.

Final Run
(The Cavanaugh Special)

August. The old D. and H. Station.
Night deserts the town, leaving shadows
orphaned in the waiting room:

light streams through windows
above the wainscoting, scans vacant seats
for bench marks, initialed, dated.

Save for the clock, emptiness echoes inside
the wood framed depot: cupola crowned,
long ago painted buff and brown.

Outside, shaded by its extended roof,
a solitary porter suspends his work;
the train calls in the distance.

Harbinger of the racing season
one time carried a carnival to town:
horse breeders, hot walkers, hawkers, grooms.

And stable banners were strung across Broadway
like gaudy clotheslines—elm to elm;
flowers flowed from hotel piazzas:

fuchsias, red and white petunias.
In Congress Park, Sousa's "Fairest of the Fair"
clamored through the crowd.

But louder than sounds familiar
grew the cadence of home town soldiers
who went to war from this station.

The porter now resumes his work
amid lingering ghosts of the past.
The train has waned to silence.

David Smith
(1906 – 1965)

Vulcan touched
his finger tips,
sparking the torch
in his hand.

Ignited,
the brawny Bolton welder
melded metal images
with geometric themes.

Fused flashes,
soldered sunbursts,
polished planes, points, angles.

Cut steel Cubi,
Zig zagged
a diagram through mid-air.

Silhouetted
in space
Hudson River Landscape.

Compositioned
Blackburn —
Song of an Irish Blacksmith.

Thrust upright
Tank Totem —
lightning striking
the Adirondack sky.

Suddenly steel and chrome collide
closing the Terminal Iron Works,
leaving wrought iron
rusting in the rain.

David Smith, a noted American sculptor, worked in Bolton Landing, N. Y., until he died as a result of an automobile accident in 1965. He called his studio the Terminal Iron Works.

Kate O'Connell   319

Listening to the Goldberg Variations

October. Late, late afternoon.
Slowly descending to the rim
of the horizon, channeling light
through a distant stand of beech
and maple: yellow, scarlet. . .,
the sun, lingering now, splinters
into gold dust rods that enter
the dim room where we sit
listening to Landowska play Bach.

Invisibly, the plangent keys
of the harpsichord pulsate
penetrating the gloom.
How familiar Bach's arias have grown—
those thirty variations.
How similar to love—
its disposition irregular
as the pulse of the heart
stammering through passages
of marriage.

Lately, I have come to worry that
there is always, always uncertainty
within love's vibrant invention:
a slight hesitancy in every beginning
before the heart beats rhythmically
through yet another movement.

Now shafts of sunlight flicker
out, and I am drawn to the window:
beyond the thicket, a light still dazzles
through fading incandescence:
Hymen in brilliant yellow beech leaves:
Hymen celebrates a wedding.

John Quirk

John Quirk has taught high school English for twenty-five years. He has at various times been faculty advisor to the high school newspaper and the literary magazine. Through Friends of Crandall Library he helped establish writers' workshops that currently are co-sponsored by Adirondack Community College and The Friends of Crandall Library. He has been published in Penguin, Expressions, The Glens Falls Review, *and* Descant. *He was one of the three poets featured in* Three Adirondack Poets *and he is one of the founding editors of the* Loft Press.

Skunk Hollow Time

In our tenth summer
when heat clung in our hair,
hung on our words,
riding them to the ground
before shimmering back
off the road again,
my cousin and I
snuck down to the Hollow,
wading in those
snow-cold waters
below Jakewise Pond.

We built a bridge
over green-wet blackness,
wedging posts
in a streambed,
locking them in place
with rocks that made
our hands bleed
as we cribbed
them against
swift currents
and summer storms.

We wanted to reach
past ourselves,
to have something
left over
at summer's edge
as we fumbled
under chill, flowing
waters that numbed
each separate moment,
giving us one forever
in a summer afternoon.

Eleven o'clock News, Channel 6, Schenectady

Cold air spills over the town,
Tumbling off eastern mountain slopes,
Nudging out whorls of heat
Hanging about our doors and yards.

The air pushes past leaves that hide
With reluctant fingers what the sun
Says behind the empty promise of
Indian summer.

It drags its sleeves across field
And rooftop, catching the wet and
Leaving its crystal mantle on the
New cleft, the chill-kept town.

Then it shoves its fingers down chimneys,
Around windows, across sills, poking
The weary, muttering with mute lips,
Brute lips about its zero condition.

And the stars, inexorable, untouched,
Watch this night life in the half light
Of cold past caring, miles past sharing
A small town's "scattered frost warnings tonight."

An End We Never Reason Out

If Frost's birch girls who are drying
Their hair in the sun were to stand up,
Pushing long tresses over their heads,
Stretching strong arms toward heaven,
They could mime the graceful elms.

But now they are a race apart,
Set loose in a Greek tragedy,
Destined to die in this century.
Once stricken or diseased, they are marked,
Chain-sawed, sectioned, shredded away.

If the town has money or people
Who care, surgeons attend them.
We see them wrapped in tape,
Unguents, incisions and tubing,
Bottles and bags draping their sides,
Suffering the quiet shame of Uncle Fred
Who has been given a little longer,
Perhaps even grows stronger
Before being hauled away to still
Another end we never reason out.

Spring Song

Anna plays her piano below,
The metronome marking cadenced
Runs of her sonatina.
Sound spills out onto the deck
And flows across the lawn,
Brushing over the spring wetness.

A chickadee dips into the still-
Drenched maple, darting up a branch,
Singing its two-note song,
Matching its crystal voice to her
Music in elemental harmony.

The bird is drawn to the music,
But never learns the source
And Anna, unaware, plays on.
A fourth time and a fifth,
The black-capped scrap of life
Sings against her notes,
Neither conscious of the other.

A chance glance out an upstairs
Window is all that marries them,
Songbird and daughter.
Such a modest audience.
For so soft a moment.
How can I tell one
And not the other?

It Never Snows the Way It Used to. . .

Lost in the wet mittens of years ago
Are the city snowbanks that lured us
Astride white mountains that shattered and split,
Dropping us waist-deep in crevices,
Locked tight and bright with laughter.
And when we clawed to the top again
Boots slid and spilled us into the road,
Cars blaring their warning.

When the snow left, there was that
Green top, scuffed and dented from street
Fights, a marble bag with chipped shooters
And winnings alike, and bubble gum
Heroes all living together in a golden
Brown cigar box.

And now, jumping fresh snowbanks, I
Can't recall where I hid that enchantment.
Has the dust of years covered those pleasures
Or are they carried by the child I passed
Some storms ago?

Marianne Rahn-Erickson

Now I mother, write, and farm on an isolated 100 acres in upstate New York. We raise boys, sheep, trees, and taxes. But I was born in Brooklyn, and raised by a lone pink collar matriarch. From our tight immigrant neighborhood we moved to "Stovepipe Hollow", a streamside log cabin in the Catskills. Old spirits of balalaika and soft fiddle music. Mountain laurel and huckleberries. Some trout, some bottom suckers.

Since then I've worked as a staff and freelance journalist and as an advocate for choice in childbirth. Toward that end I edited a newsletter providing access to alternative birthing opportunities and was a contributor to The Whole Birth Catalog.

Although approached from several disciplines, my academic work deals with the industrialization of American childbirth and the implications of bio-medical technology on women's health care.

Recently I've spoken at Skidmore, Yale, and the New York State Woman's Studies Conference on the politics of "natural" childbirth, and have presented Circle of Blood, Circle of Balance, which uses oral history to look at the metaphysics of being female, as symbolized by Native and Euro-American menstrual traditions.

And I have begun The Novel.

The Novel is based on the life of Mary Jemison, an 18th century Irish immigrant living on the Pennsylvania frontier during the French and Indian Wars. She was captured by a group of French and Shawnee at the age of 13 and adopted by two Seneca women, whom she calls her Nundawaho sisters.

Despite witnessing the massacre of her blood family, Mary eventually comes to favor life among the Iroquois, on several occasions refusing "opportunities" to return to white American society. Instead she chooses to remain with her new family, her new nation, and her own land—over 17,000 acres in western New York, the title for which she argued against vehement Iroquois sachems and the Congress of the United States. It was land she worked for over 60 years; land she would not have been allowed to own at all if she had stayed in her "own" culture.

The piece entitled "A Handful of Leaves" is a chapter from the novel in progress. It relates the birth of her first child, in 1761, in the Ohio River valley. Mary is 17 years old.

A Handful of Leaves

This river washed Ohio soil was smooth and not so stony as the dirt back in Pennsylvania. Even with weed roots grown through it was still loose and light to work. The morning's dew made it easy to hoe. Heavy into the eighth moon of her first pregnancy, Mary pushed a wooden hoe stick ahead of her through the corn, digging with the tip of it, loosening and flinging fragments of black earth and ripping white root threads apart, delaying the weeds.

It was the Moon of Green Corn. A hot, humid, no-breeze summer. The broad river sky hazy and ground drying. Too hot later in the day for Mary to work in the sun. She grew dizzy and faint and herself as languid as the August. So her habits were changing, separating her from the other women of the longhouse.

She rose earlier now, before the small diffuse sunrise fell through the smoke hole in the bark ceiling, before even an aura of soft light grew around the fire pit in the center of the room. The house still breathed heavily. None of the other bunk curtains were drawn when she woke. Mary dressed and pushed aside the supple deerskin veil that made private her own solitary bed, and tied it to one side, against the bunk post. She padded through many chambers, past sleeping relatives, toward the outer door at the far end of the bark house and crept out to work in the corn alone.

Outside the early morning ground was wet and the cold soil welcome to her bare feet. The air was chill and moist, damp as she breathed it in. But the sky was one thick pale grey color. There would be haze again today and no clear blue, no high thin clouds to lift and cool her.

It was the Moon of Green Corn. Soft white kernels just setting inside tightly bound green husks. And the air brought only the barest rustling of stalks, playing old patterns through the sheaves.

She no longer travelled lightly in the corn, this almost full pregnant woman. The weight of a baby held low in her abdomen made her thighs and crotch numb, achy. She was soft and loose there, rolling from side to side as she walked. The slim, now bulging figure, the long braid of hair, and the sand colored deerskin shift all shook with the short quick rhythms of weeding.

Already the stalks were higher than Mary. She could hide among them. Her hair itself the color of the corn's own silk, of the day's own light. She was herself a rank tassel, overgrowing and spilling beyond herself from hill to hill like some sister vine.

The strike of her hoe made dull thimp, thimping sounds. Wood hitting stone. Not the ringing anvil sounds of a metal hoe, but a softer, rounder, smaller voice.

Her weeding was just a light scratching of the soil, a shallow rilling of the surface, not a choppy raking. Not after the weed's very life, not out to turn over dirt over stone over roots, everything so deep or so downside up, putting air where air doesn't belong, til the succoring threads wither, can no longer water life. She didn't aim to kill by dryness, but just to scatter the top layer of weeds. To slow them a little, to make a small path for herself. We are all scattered, she knows, and still we grow.

And this sure was easier dirt than Pennsylvania, back home the ground so thin and rocky.

She was now active and fretful, nesting for the baby with an endless energy. Then remote and absent, sleepy like a cat on a warm stone. Sometimes on the Ohio, then back home, recalling things shut aside for years.

Her blood father came back to her in a memory. A springtime memory of hauling stones from the ground. Opening deep holes in the ground for fencing. Measuring and dividing the land by some ancient habit of rails and posts that made little sense to her anymore. The sun was coming in season bright again and her father's seeded field greening like the closest she'd ever come to seeing jewels.

"Just wait, little one, one of these days you'll top a fence post!"

Thom Jemison tried to make his daughter feel better about her lack of height. She was already 13, the fourth one, the sea-born youngest daughter in an immigrant family of six, but still a full six inches away from the flat part of any locust pole on their farm.

The child Mary was devoted to her father, and though she had her mother's pout and frown, there was no doubt whom she most followed. She was her father's keeper, this girl, and sought his company like a shadow. Mary set the next post up straight with such dark concentration that her father broke out with a laugh as he pounded the post tight into the soft spring soil.

"Oh, take care, Mamie, I'm just teasing."

He smiled the way he always did, the joy a light just below his skin, coming into his face brightly. The shine coming through his eyes, the skin around them wrinkling happy, and then his red beard spreading with a grin. Thom gave the set post another hit with his sledge and winked at his serious little daughter.

She remembered his face and closed her salting eyes against the sun. There was no need for fences along the Ohio. Nothing to trouble about keeping out or in. And this was not her father's land. It was her land. Sometimes, when she needed it. In summers. Winters the land kept itself and Mary kept herself. And her father was not here. This summer there was no man to keep. Sheninjee was gone, off with Cornplanter to meet Pontiac at Detroit. They should have been home already. But Mary kept herself this summer too.

Sometimes unsettled. She must make ready for her baby, but there was little to do. Other women would have spelled her from any heavy chores, but Mary would not be dissuaded from working the corn. Still she was often restless, circling between quiet and storm.

So she decided, in her driven times, to collect firewood. Anxious stacks of it. Save some ahead. Make ready. She went into the woods each day and collected armfuls from the dead and storm-broken wood on the ground. She snapped dry limbs from trees; trees rotting with galls and spongy, breaking at their centers from the canker. She pulled on them and pushed them down and cracked them into small pieces. Sometimes she brought an axe with her and patiently shaved down a crowded or bent sapling. All this until the door to their longhouse was tunneled with two high stacks of kindling.

The village laughed at Mary's obsession. Her friends urged her to relax.

"Gone! All gone! The firewood." Gwadanseh said. "You will pick up all the forest!"

The other women might tease her, but they all knew about the fevered small work. How the need for rest, for a deep space apart for herself, to hold on to these last days alone, opposed the need to be busy, to nest for the idea of baby. A still hazy dreamy idea, comfortable to hold inside and to speak to, practicing things to say in English, practicing having someone to say all those old words to so she wouldn't forget. Someone who wouldn't be angered by them.

"This is our corn patch. It belongs to Grandmother Onahada. You'll play here near me. We'll bring Pup and you can throw stones for him with Okeo." She laughed and twirled with the unborn round in a spin and laughed again.

The baby an idea to idly cradle. To think again the scarred lank face of the father made clear and round again. And to have that face accompany her for every day. Not to be alone. To have someone of her own always with her. To be never alone.

Thinking her blood mother was alone too in all that mountain forest every time she had one of her babies. No sisters or village of women to help her. Night after night in a windy winter cabin, spinning and knitting endlessly. Had Jane been alone even in that room filled with Thom and the breathing of children already born? Mary remembered herself as a willful child. Resistant and clumsy at knitting and hating every cramped attempt to learn until she'd finally refuse to have anything to do with it and would run outside in the snow and stand watching slices of light flicker from between the chinks, breathing in the sharp air til it cooled what was fighting in her and she could go inside again and be glad for the warmth and the tea her mother would have brewed. And . . . oh, to talk to her now in English words. . .

But she must stop and fill her person with fresh air, the air of corn and sun and dirt. Sometimes it was impossible now to draw a breath deep enough to fill both her and the baby. The air would catch within her, she couldn't open her belly enough to draw the full breath she craved. She coughed with the effort, could only take in shallow whispers.

Every day Mary carried a bucket with her to bring back full of water when she returned to the longhouse for soup. She left the corn before midday and walked down across a long low hillside toward the Guyandat Creek, through the low bramble growth, past alder sprouts and young aspen, to the spot where the village women drew their water.

Back-heavy and heaving a deep labored breath Mary stooped, half-squatting against the high creek bank, and leaned over to sink her bucket in the stream. It tipped into the current, sank full and was hoisted out.

As her legs straightened to lift her again there was a skirt-muffled boisterous rush and warm, soft, warm water spread from her sacred places and doused the insides of her legs.

Mary was shocked still; made nauseous with a quickening fear.

She spread her legs down into a squat and steadied herself with a hand to the brilliant greenweeds rank on the creek shoulder.

She was still, knowing an original half-dream, a half-understood recollection, a recognition of the way it had been for her mothers and sisters.

But it was the Moon of Green Corn. Too soon to have a baby.

There was much-dark womb water, blood too, spattered on the hard drought path of summer. The falls of fluid peaked dark spots in the dirt. Blood streaks shadowing her shallow mud like little fish stripes.

Caution breathed calm in her. Is this it? What next? When does the pain come? Should I move? Stay here? Will it be now?

Her skirt was soaked in spots, dark damp rivers along the cloth wrapped it heavily to her legs. She waited. The Kingfisher came to shriek along the creek channel, as he always did when someone came to the water's edge. Then the questions left her and she relaxed, still on her haunches, resting into the belief that it was indeed her time. A new smugness arriving, nestling in the woman. Is this what they say is so painful? The others, those who hate weakness, warned me of this? I'll have my baby right here by myself and carry her home just like one of the old Nundawaho mothers. They'll see a white woman just as strong as an Indian.

So she stayed there. And waited. And stayed in that expectant squat. For minutes. And more minutes. Time enough to begin to feel restless, for she did not notice any further changes. Then a little while longer still. Time to admit maybe she was wrong and time enough to feel embarrassed by these generations of trees around her who wait so long to grow. They might be laughing at this foolish girl human who sits and waits for her baby to come to her as lightly and easily as the wind blows late summer down away from the parent thistle. But the trees are gentle and they say, Do you think it's been easy for us, girl? Because we don't speak to the air, don't tongue our labor with every leaf? Can you feel yet what every stretching twig growing tight along our bark is to us? We too rend ourselves with life.

Mary took a slow breath and stood up. No new feeling but wet between her legs. No pain, no parting, no opening. Just the same dull heaviness, her thighs once again yielding to the pressure of this low baby heavy between her legs.

She returned to the village. And though it was too soon to have this baby, Onahada knew the sign had come and sent Gwadanseh and Nediyo down to the creek to prepare the birthing hut for Mary's labor. The two sisters spent the afternoon carrying supplies; a kettle and bowls for warming water, parched corn for soup, fresh berries to make a juice for the laboring mother, and fragrant medicine plants. They carried skins and trader blankets, and some of Mary's firewood, in case her birth lasted into the chill night.

Then Mary was sent to the birth hut, although there had been no further signs since her water broke.

The hut belonged to the Onahada family and had not been used in the three years since Okeo's birth. The path there was overgrown and thick with raspberries, brittle grey canes and spiny new red ones. Thorns scraped at her ankles as she passed through them, but Mary was glad of its private location. Glad too of the clouds gathering, welcome of the darkening weather to fold around and embrace her, to give a cool dark sleep, for she had grown weary anticipating a labor which did not come, and felt the animal need to crawl away and rest.

The hut was that crawl away space; in a small brushy clearing, set in the woods at creek's edge. It was small, holding only three or four people. Its circle woven of elm saplings, sharp cut points driven into the ground, thin trunks arched, held with roots and covered with sheets of bark like a tiny longhouse. There was a small door on the creek side to crawl through. Inside was a depression meant to hold a small fire. Beside this Gwadanseh had spread a mat for Mary to lie on. It was a crudely scraped hide, one Mary fleshed herself that first winter with the Nundawaho at Sciota.

"I brought this special one," said Gwadanseh. "I know you like it."

"Yes I do," Mary laughed, recognizing her first forlorn attempt at tanning. "Thank you! But look at it. . .I scraped it so thin!" In several places the membranes had been too diligently removed, where by now the hide had stretched into small holes. "I'm glad I'm better at it now."

"It's special for you, still," smiled her sister, who looked at Mary closely and added, "You look so tired already. It will be good now for you to rest here."

By nightfall some small clenchings had come, but oddly, on occasion. There was no pattern, and no strength to them. But with each one she became excited, ready, she thought, to have a baby. And after each one she was alert, waiting for the next pinching spasm, and the next. But they were sporadic, and as the night became late she grew tired with the waiting, irritated by the long circle of anticipation turning to boredom.

The spasms came less and less often and then she slept, not much disturbed by the few cramps that did come until just before dawn, when they became stronger and more often, so that she was again excited and chose not to sleep. But after eating, the pains were gone and Mary slept, again, deeply, until halfway through the day. When she woke this second time, the air was dark, the stifling and humid weather was broken. It had rained and now a fine drizzle moved through the clearing.

Labor did come on that afternoon, still slowly, but in a more certain path. The character of this birth had worried her sisters, and Nediyo went back to the village for advice.

Deyugaho was emphatic, "Tell her loosen her white woman's hair." So they untied her braid and between contractions the sisters combed her waist length hair out in a thick fan shape down her back.

Gahnegadesta had said, "Untie her clothing and let the river loosen that baby."

And too restless to stay in the hut, Mary walked out through the thin forest toward the creek's edge. The moist air struck her face and freshened her body. It was no longer raining but there was a mist running around and ahead of her along the creek. It travelled quickly, so that only brief patches of forest were visible, an acre here or there, the vision changing; a lean sense of space, a dark focusing around her. Ranks of black-wet tree trunks, canopies obscured, seemed themselves to be moving through clouds of hanging water. The mists through the forest made her feel small and hidden, held by something strong, the way she felt in the corn.

She moved slowly, a few feet at a time, waiting from tree to tree between the grasps of labor. When a pain did come, it weakened her legs and drew her down close to the ground in a squat, clasping her hands around a tree for support, resting her forehead against its bark. Spreading her legs and centering her thighs low toward the earth dulled the pain and she could be comfortable. It was good to feel something there besides that heavy tingling she'd been carrying for the past month, that always ache and soreness. Now stretching the soreness and the oddly cold thin twinge drawn inside her belly became a kind of relief, her legs carrying her so close she could set a new person upon the earth. And in concert, the child within her twisted through each contraction, seeking its own right position.

The mother left her shirt and skirt at creek's edge and waded into the Guyandat to bathe. The river's color had changed, no longer the thick clay green of hazy days but a fast black, colored by the shadow not the reflection of trees. No birds, no animals, were speaking. Just the silent force of stream.

The current split around her back in a cradling vee, like the crotch of a tree grows apart, holding something we can't see of the sky.

Mists gathered over her skin and her broad bowed waist was wet. The sky's water warm to that of the chill creek. Her hair thickened with mist, blonde hair darkened with rain water like the corn tassel itself will turn after a soaking. Droplets of mist saturating her hair so that each strand caught, clung hair to skin, and wrapped and twisted around her shoulders and waist with each movement. Her body held in its own reverent web of wet bronze.

Caressed so by her own hair in the waist deep swirl of river, Mary's hands skimmed the current, loving it, and cupped the flow, bathing first her shoulders and arms, now her belly and hips, her pale girth stretched and colored with stripes like the belly of a trout. The hands dipping into black water, raising up clear fluids to roll off her skin. She warmed her breasts in her arms and cradled her own softness, relaxing into the flow of strong water between her thighs.

The contractions became steady now with the rush of the river. Sometimes almost breathless, hard twinges in a place so strange it was almost never imagined; a low slow stabbing with an immense dull stone. Breathe, close her eyes, to breathe through it. It subsides and an almost giddy feeling is left. She is light. Easy to be weak, to be taken by the current. Easy, this opening of thighs to let a baby out. A delight at the gurgling water, a river through her legs, streaming a thrill that first tensed her crotch then eased her like the games she played with Sheninjee, private and terribly quiet behind the skins in the longhouse full of sleeping relatives. Looking, always looking in his eyes, or somewhere behind her own, breathing, kissing and breathing, smelling his lips, wetting his lips. Mary enjoying the tightenings of her labor, learning to relax around them as she had learned when to soften and when to hold her husband.

But as more contractions passed, she could no longer find a graceful rest. Her legs would not support her during tightenings. She tried to float her body between pains, and immersed herself slowly, completely, for the last time as two people, for the last time as one person. The water chilled her breasts and shoulders, shivered her neck and turned her mind from private pleasures to the chore of getting into the hut to lie down. Only to lie down, that was all she could tolerate. She became fragile and heavy to herself. To get to the bank, to be wrapped warmly and dried in a blanket by her sisters. To get to the hut. To lie down. All this a strife in her body. The passing of waste and vomit overtaken by pain during which she could not move but only shudder in ill caught agony.

Inside she was not allowed to lie down as she felt to, but asked to sit up, leaning her back against the sapling wall. Mary's bare feet dug into the soft bed of humus as she shifted between contractions. Against the creak of the dry elm poles she shifted herself, searching for a more comfortable position.

The wet evening brought mosquitoes thick to the hut. A small fire smudged them away but also made the air close and smoky. Nediyo rubbed handfuls of sage plant between her palms and dropped them into the burning twigs, filling the air with a menthol bite.

The deerskin padded Mary's back but the night air came through at the base of the lodge and was cold on her hips. White slices of moonlight fell through the limbs of river trees, through gaps in the old elm bark, and finally dappled lattice patterns across Mary's body.

Her breathing was fast and uncontrolled. It did nothing to relieve her. She was too excited, gasping at her own efforts.

She searched for the remembered speech of English. Her Nunda-waho sisters did not understand her words. It was her blood mother who spoke to her thinking, and Mary, remembering, gave her own voice to Jane's parting words, breathing them around her pain. "How can I part with you. . .how can I part with you, my darling. . .no hope of rescue. . .no. . .remember your name. . .she said remember my name."

"Be quiet!" scolded Nediyo, who felt she'd been patient enough. "That does no good."

But Mary was delirious. "I heard you mother. . .didn't believe. . .you were calling me. . ."

Again she was silenced by Nediyo, more sharply this time. "Stop with that language. Now you are here!"

But Mary was not there. She was with her ghost mother.

"You're sending your energy too far. . .out to the wind. . .where? To Sheninjee? He doesn't need it. Send your energy out through your bottom, to his baby."

But Nediyo was far mistaken. Mary wasn't thinking about Sheninjee anymore. And she wasn't thinking about the baby. The baby least of all.

"You're doing well, Dehgewanus." Gwadanseh was speaking to her. "Soon your baby will be here."

But the baby least of all. Baby? Mary had forgotten about having a baby. There was no cause, no reason for this. It just was. It will always be. No cause, no end, no reason. She didn't care to have a baby. Let it stay where it was.

336

Her mother spoke again through a grimace, "I wish you had died an. . .infant. . .in my arms." Her last words circling again and again in Mary's mind. The sorrow of their separation returning to the stubborn birth of this child. "The pain of parting. . .then. . .pleasing to this!. . .see the end of your. . .troubles."

"The pain of parting is now, Mother." Mary gasped, her body shivering, quaking from her thighs to her neck trying to release a great agony.

She continued on in delirium, for there was no rest now between contractions. . ."is now Mother. . ." and the breath was gone again, and the agony silent.

Mary fell limply back against the sapling wall and sighed deeply. Pausing now, eyes watering and chest heaving, she let dribble the mouthful of water Nediyo insisted she swallow. The trickle cooled the skin of her neck. Mary breathed a smile at the sensation, murmuring lowly to herself, for she was still above the presence of her sisters, "I remember your English words," surprised by her own language.

But Gwadanseh touched hold of Mary's hand and reached her with her own dark eyes, collecting her Irish sister back from the white spirits until Mary was only there in the little elm hut with her Nunda-waho sisters again.

"Dehgewanus, it is almost time to be carried open. Open your mouth but do not speak. It will soon be over."

Mary heard the words. She was grateful but could not respond. Another wave of labor was coming.

"Now. . ." she groaned, wearying, tiring of it all. Again, "now. . .", and then a new strength came to her and she became silent through a clenching that threw back her head, that opened her throat like an ecstasy, that swallowed her breath, but slowly, barely, separated her and burned and begged to be touched and pushed further and harder and then rested.

Her breath would not be caught from one pushing to the next. It raced ahead of itself out of some new tunnel inside her, and finally, some sense of movement, now a huge purpose pressing down, burning her, rushing her over the edge of fear for its own delight. Never before so open, so taken by her own breath, not with any man a joy so far, so self-full, a joy so never to be stopped.

Gwadanseh's hands, her two hands, two fingers, the barest aid of separation. No pain in the stretching, a strength to be pushing, to be finally almost open, to force open, baring the lips of her crotch til it was full of slick new hair, a wet pasty silvery slick of new hair. Touch this slowly rotating head, a face turning on its own axis, a new face circling up between her legs.

The sound filling the hut, the breath, the rhythm, the ecstasy, cries in her throat, repeated, repeated. Sounds of her sisters. Coaxing. Laughing. Singing "it's coming, it's coming, it's right here!" The shoulders squeezing, body turning, baby sliding quickly, purple, into Gwadanseh's hands.

Mary's breath still coming fast, trilling "oh, oh, oh. . ." and her face tearful, light, watching. Watching. . .Why the face of her sisters? They are waiting. Too quiet. Clouded. Watching for the first breath.

But this baby does not breathe.

Does not move.

There is no wiggling scream at this world. No indignant shock. No frightened tuck of her legs.

The hut is quiet.

Gwadanseh holds the daughter over her own knees, face down toward the earth again, and rubs quick circles around her back. Still the dark color. And the mother is silent, her breath caught now and hushed. Gwadanseh grasps the baby through a slippery coat of blood and dips her feet quickly up and down in a bowl of night cool water. The infant shudders, a wind of cold air filling her. She pulls her legs up, startled, curling them tight to her body in a fragile but complete protest. A breathing of fluids murmurs in her chest. Her color brightens and she cries weakly one time. Her body convulses and her tight featured head shivers until she is placed and clings on her mother's body.

The mother lowly coos to her daughter, tentatively, "you are here, my baby. . .my baby." Soothing, amazed at this creature.

"It's over!" hopefully, to her sisters.

But the sisters stay quiet, to themselves. It is a too small, too young baby. A handful of leaves. A breeze too still.

Blood in dark clots and cream from the womb slathers this child, curled now in her mother's arms beneath a cover of deerskin. No, don't wash her yet. Hold her. Just hold her. She's had hard passage. Let the little girl rest.

Her limbs still and thin, she is a rubbery blue stick of a child. Not moving more than her breath. But already one eye open, peering steady at her mother, fist up against her mouth. One clear black eye asking the new and eternal question: Is this it? What next? Why does the pain come? Is it up to me?

She must be helped to nurse. Mary is so new and awkward with the baby as she tries to shift her from her arm up toward her breast, but the limp infant slips back down her belly and into a quiet ball. Nediyo positions the baby's bottom a little higher with one hand and with the other holds Mary's breast away from the baby's nose as it meets the nipple, the swollen still soft breast covering too much of the wincing little face, covering her air.

A disinterested mouth weakly forms over the nipple. She makes a few sucks so feeble that her mouth slides off into the pale part of the breast and she makes no attempt to find suck again. The three sisters try again, but it is the same thing. Hold her. Just hold her. She's had hard passage.

The eyes are closed now as the child curls to find sleep, sometimes catching a fitful breath, sometimes its small legs pushing against the mother's stomach as if to climb, to shift, to make something more of this sleep.

As the child rests, her placenta is born and her cord is tied and cut. It is smudged with ground deerskin to clot the blood and dusted with spores for healing. Gwadanseh bathes Mary, washing her with goldthread water, its acrid smell clearing the warm blood and fecal birth sweat. Mary's legs are padded between with torn rags to catch the flow they tell her will continue, and she lies on fresh blankets, the baby still in her arms.

Privately she tries to rouse the child and have her nurse, but the girl sleeps through her efforts. Mary is drawn by the smell of her. "Janey. . ." she calls the baby, trying the sound, seeing if it moves the infant. "Janey. . ." But every move with this child is so tiny and fragile, she does not disturb her again.

She lets the baby sleep. And wonders at the dark face beneath the blanket. Such a dark face with black hair she has never seen on any of her family's babies. She doesn't look like Sheninjee, she looks like a stranger's child. But such a perfect little strange face, tiny puckered lips and black eyelashes. A seedling this girl. A touch would fold her; too fragile to transplant.

Mary keeps fierce vigil, not wanting to miss a breath of her daughter's life, and only closes her eyes every few minutes, when she can no longer resist their weight.

But she starts awake. It is morning now and she must have slept. She is roused by the baby's choking cough. It sounds more rumbly now. There is a cry and a painful look on the baby's face that wasn't there before. A weak shuddering cry no stroking, no holding can appease. This child is hungry, but cannot eat; is fevered, but hasn't breath. Her throat strains for air, her small belly pumping madly after it.

Gwadanseh steeps thistle plant in boiled water and dips her finger in the mixture, trying to dribble some into the baby's mouth. A few drops go in but the baby chokes and spits it out, the effort hurting her.

"A little more," the sister urges.

"No. That's enough!" Mary cries, holding her baby away. "It hurts her!" And she huddles herself forward over the baby, her long hair hiding it like a shroud, as if to protect it with the shadow of her own body.

Gwadanseh coaxes, "It helps the breathing, Dehgewanus. It brings the mucus up."

But Nediyo grasps the bottoms of Mary's hands and makes her hold the baby up so Gwadanseh can give her more medicine.

Another few drops make the child choke again and spit. An awful, wincing, tight look gasps on her face and she wails a cry that is silent. She is suddenly still, that one eye open, searching after her mother's face. But the clearness has faded now, all light is gone and there is only a grey world in that eye. The baby is going far and deep, and Mary holds her, carrying her there, losing her.

The child shudders once and convulses, her breathing becoming excited. The baby struggles, but no breath comes. She draws no air and turns a white no Indian baby should ever be. The stillness comes back and stays this time.

And the night air comes in to the elm hut too fresh, too fertile. Something is growing out in the lush green night, but not in here.

The words of her mother come back to Mary again, practiced, in a prayer, in a curse, touching her own daughter. How can I part with you, my darling? I wish you had died an infant in my arms. The pain of parting then would have been pleasing to this. I would have seen the end of your troubles. . .the end of your troubles.

Things are growing out in the lush green night. But not in here.

Jean Rikhoff

I was born in Chicago and brought up in Indianapolis. I graduated from Tudor Hall, a girls' school there, went on to Mt. Holyoke (B.A. English) and to Wesleyan (M.A. ditto), worked for GOURMET magazine as an editorial assistant, spent seven years in Europe, part of the time teaching for the University of Maryland Overseas Program. My daughter was born in Spain.

While abroad, I helped found QUIXOTE, an Anglo-American quarterly that lasted six years (I am also the editor of Grosset and Dunlap's QUIXOTE ANTHOLOGY, a collection of the best fiction we published during that time. I have published ten books — seven novels, the anthology, and two young adult biographies. The so-called Timble trilogy, my first three books — DEAR ONES ALL, VOYAGE IN, VOYAGE OUT, and RITES OF PASSAGE is set in the midwest and roughly (very roughly) based on my eccentric family. Three novels in the Buttes/Raymond series are set in the Adirondacks (BUTTES LANDING, the first book, is meant to suggest Bolton Landing, though the site is on the other side of the lake in the book; ONE OF THE RAYMONDS and THE SWEET WATER continue the saga of these two families, and I always meant to go back and finish up the books, bring them up to the present. I have finished half a novel in the next part of the story, but didn't finish it because I got sidetracked on what you could call my obligatory woman's novel, WHERE WERE YOU IN '76? At present—and for the past five years—I have been working on a very long book set in the slate quarries around Granville in the nineteenth and twentieth centuries. I hope to finish this—at last—this summer.)

For twenty years I lived on a farm on the New York-Vermont border; currently I live in Glens Falls, where I am a Professor of English at Adirondack Community College and an active editor, and one of the founders, of the Loft Press, which also publishes THE GLENS FALLS REVIEW.

I have also published short stories, poetry, and articles at various times in my life, but my real passion is the novel.

David Smith, I Remember

Well, the *New York Times* made it official, I guess, David. They put your picture on the cover of a Sunday magazine section and called you "America's greatest artist." Characteristically the *Times* showed only your *back* in the cover shot and the caption was in error: "David Smith working on a sculpture with an acetylene torch in his studio." It was not gas acetylene at all, but electrical arc welding you were using in the picture. But then. Also, they put the *America's greatest artist* in quotation marks. In other words, Hilton Kramer's comment, not theirs. Not for the *Times* to go out on an artistic limb.

How you would have banged the table. All your life you had been puzzling over your place in the pantheon. You knew well enough where you belonged. What was the matter with the other blind boobs that it took them so long to see? "What you really want is your face staring off the cover of *Time* and a big nice write up on how great you really are."

"Go back and write those books about those horrible people in Indiana."

It takes one to know one. You'd come awake yourself out in Decatur, Indiana, and who better recognized the portraits etched in acid, the faces and twangs, and hangups of my Hoosiers? "Write about something healthy."

Healthy? Is that what you'd call the "Medals for Dishonor"? Possibly. Isn't the optimist the only one who can know how wrong things are? Out in the shop banging away on steel, welding (one way or another), scribbling out sketches—and bugged by the ladies who hired busses to come up and gape at the eccentric, run around your grounds like it was a public park. They *picnicked* among the great monoliths and threw their wax sandwich bags and apple cores under the Cubis. It did no good to put up signs. Those kinds of people can't understand *private*. And how about that lovely lady from Albany who stomped in to ask you to run up a little garden thing in plaster, chaste Diana or Pan among the Naiads? To their faces you were polite and perplexed—always trying to explain. Finally, the wooden barricades. The ladies climbed down from the busses or out of expensive automobiles and moved the wooden horses, the 2-by-4's, the big messily-painted sign, PRIVATE. DO NOT ENTER. They entered.

From the cinder-block house that you had built yourself up on the hill, we would gaze out over our brandy and sodas and see them peeking in the shop, picking flowers out of the gardens and the only deterrent to denuding the masses of blueberries out in back was Jo-Jo, that evil-tempered horse who chased anybody who came over the fence.

The trippers helped themselves from your garden (you were, after all, something of a public institution even then, your Bolton Landing house with all those mammoth sculptures in front mentioned "as worth a visit" in the sightseeing guides to Lake George). They had their pictures taken laughing fit to be killed in front of those great cosmic pieces that would later make such moving problems for the Tate and Guggenheim; the ladies saw no problems at all save for the angle of light required to keep them in focus and the sculpture in the background. While we watched, they ran in and out screaming, "Look at *this* one! Isn't it killing?"

Fighting the refrigerator door (which always stuck), you were full of anger and indignation. But isn't rage really the result of disappointment? Once you banged out onto the porch and hollered, "Go home, get out!" They paid no attention, too busy having their screamingly funny pictures taken.

You raged against this, against that, some of the anger rightfully focused, much of it simply against the way things are. A good deal of that is of course rightful, too, but most of us wear ourselves out reshaping over and over our bent lances. You put yours to work in sculpture, a good use of bent weapons, but lord, you wanted the human things of life, too, didn't you? What artist doesn't, even Proust in his sealed room, even the big pirates like Morgan, walling themselves off from the world in private palaces on Fifth Avenue.

Well, we're all misunderstood. Others let it go. You didn't. On the phone in one of your monumental stormings against life: "I'll hire paid killers and—"

"David," I screamed, "you're on a party line."

Sometimes slumped over in a chair, agonizing over your sketch pad, you used to look up. "Do you ever get away from it?" you'd ask.

And understanding too well that It, I said simply, "No."

We would sit in silence, and think. We were working as well. Most of the kind of work we do is done slumped, silent, in chairs, exhausted and agonized.

All right, we would forego for a day the crushing schedule, the endless pursuing visions, and go r-e-l-a-x. I shudder now, remembering. Let's take the skiing. At age fifty-something you decided to do the slopes. Of course on only the best. HEAD had considerable trouble running you up a pair of proper skis, but months later you were hoisting yourself aboard the longest pair of slats I ever saw in my life. No one could have managed them but of course (again) you were determined. The novice on the Jay-bar with the children, humility the taskmaster. An unlikely role for you if ever I saw one. I made the mistake in pity at greatness sunk so low of getting you on the T-bar and nearly killed you. "Give me a push, will you, girl?" and down you flung. It was impossible to watch. How many spills did you take getting down? "My god, girl, what if I'd broken my arm? How would I *work?*" Snow was blowing over you like a shroud; naturally we'd gone during a blizzard and ran off the road getting home. But in the truck I always felt safe. It was the Mercedes that was rigged for death. That car had more malfunctions and evil ideas than any instrument of industrialization I have ever encountered. And, naturally, you loved it. It was your badge of honor, your own award of achievement, like staying at the Plaza Hotel where you left behind your dirty shirts and rumpled suit and expected the staff to look after them until you came down again. You expected your wardrobe to be hanging, clean, pressed, and perfect, in a closet anticipating your next visit. Raw anger again: the Plaza had misplaced one of those enormous shirts or hung your suit in someone else's room. Letters, telephone calls, frustration, the Plaza polite but mystified. The *Times* hadn't yet given you the accolade that allows you to leave dirty linen around the world to be taken care of. You would come back and tramp up and down my house with your great outsized boots and make me listen to lists of grievances you had drawn up against that great hotel and go home in a rage if I dared even smile. But all I could ever think was what a perplexity you must have been to the Plaza.

The Mercedes was utterly ill-equipped also to give you the love you anticipated, just as the Plaza was ill-equipped to give you the kind of adulation you needed. For one thing, the Germans had not put together a car to lie about idly for weeks and then start off in thirty-five below zero weather. Thus would begin one of those sessions in which you and the car pitted your stubbornnesses against one another.

The pattern had commenced from the first day you bought the motor car. Having purchased a Mercedes, what to do but show it off? That first trip ought, lord knows, to have been forewarning enough. Up to the Hermans to dazzle Frances and young Katherine. Spinning along in triumph, you neglected the proper angle of a curve. The glorious chariot went in the ditch and you and it had ignominiously to be pulled out, Frances and Katherine witnesses to the first disgrace. Of course there were others: batteries that gasped and went dead, a dashboard whose lights went up in a blue shower of sparks and burned out. That car was constantly relaying the message: DANGER. BEWARE. I dreaded riding in it, trembling on the handsome red leather upholstery in anticipation of another brush with death.

One dreadful night you decided we would have a "nice" night out. We were to drive to Glens Falls to dinner and a movie, a perfectly straightforward expedition for normal people, but we were planners and plotters against normality, born losers out in a white, cold December night trying to make the Mercedes and ourselves behave as other people did.

David Smith in his good suit (I have forgotten my own attire, yours was always far more memorable than mine), that black suit, huge, that shimmered green and dead under certain slants of light; a silk shirt, custom made; an impossible tie; a "good" overcoat: you had also put on your gentleman's manners, elbowing me along awkwardly to the car, seizing the door and flinging it open magnanimously, hoisting me onto the car seat as if I were an invalid, fussing about getting me "seated." I thought for a moment you had gone mad but, no, you were only showing me what a man-of-the-world you could be. And I was struck absolutely dumb. I didn't know what to do with you in this role. We were the two who ate and talked and drank all at the same time, arguing, accusing, interrupting, expostulating, demanding each other's attention. We had never never in all the time we'd known one another been "nice," and all this elegant attention made me feel as if I'd lost myself and was suddenly without any place in the world. You, on the other hand, gave an impression of swimming straight for your element. It was baffling, but I accepted. What else was I to do against such belief?

We commenced toward Glens Falls. You were going to show me how a really first-class night on the town might be run. It was all there, I am sure, inside your mind, the whole perfection of the plan laid out before we even began the long faltering drive, the Mercedes blinking and coughing, hunching itself up, springing for snow banks. At the restaurant, grandly you ordered Lobster Americaine and an impeccable white wine of absolutely correct vintage. You talked vineyards and labels happily; oh, it was going to be such a memorable occasion.

Neither the lobster nor the proper bottle of wine was of course on hand. I thought to have scallops. *Not nearly fancy enough.* Seizing the menu from out of my hand, you ordered—I've forgotten what; it was scallops I got. And you something (at least you thought) wrongly turned out. Then began one of those restaurant scenes where things go back and forth from the kitchen to the table, the table back again to the kitchen. I couldn't eat. You didn't. It was all wrong wrong wrong. The Lobster Americaine and the right wine, life should provide at certain times, in certain places.

There was no time with all the trips of food back and forth to the now-frantic kitchen for an after-dinner drink. We made a dash for the movie. *Dr. Strangelove*—which was the reason for this whole expedition—had gone off the bill the night before; we were left with a bad Western. Not just mediocre, but utterly, unbearably bad.

Squirming in a seat fashioned under specifications to suit a normal man, you fought for an inch of space for your legs, your huge coat, elbow room for arms thickened from wrestling with enormous pieces of steel. Someone tapped you on the shoulder and asked you to scrunch down. Short of decapitation, I could see no place for you to put your head; all the available room was already taken up with arms, body, coat, legs.

Nothing to do but have a drink after the show in the "best" spot. Here you stretched out, relieving aching muscles, and promptly appeared to inhabit the whole room. The waitress had no idea what to do with you. I don't think she'd ever seen such a big man, and vast size obviously made her inattentive. The third time you gave her the order you began to shout. The rest of the room gaped at us. On a dais a man played hit tunes and sang semi-risque songs. You were obviously pained but tried to make the best of it. *By god, this was going to be an evening to remember!*

We drank brandy and didn't even try to talk. Tongue-tied with dismay, I was; I imagine you were just worn out with the effort of the whole thing, but you ought to have been resting and recharging yourself because more was of course still ahead. The Mercedes waited.

When we got out, it was about one o'clock in the morning, one of those steely still frigid nights where simple sounds seem like squeals and a faint blue glow hangs over everything. We got in the car, crushed with cold. You put the key in the ignition and went to turn the engine on. The key remained locked, *frozen, goddam it*, you roared, and I just sat there, the world in ruins, paralyzed with cold, horror, and the belief I would never get back to Bolton.

"What are you doing?" I finally managed to get out.

"What the hell does it look like I'm doing? I'm pounding the goddam steering wheel. With both hands."

After the steering wheel had learned its lesson, you got out and lumbered around the chassis beating the fenders, kicking the wheels, hammering on the hood. The low ache of tin vibrated in the cold; your fierce voice carried everywhere. One thing no one would ever say about you, I thought, was that you had cultivated caution until you had lost the power to feel intensely.

Then a moment of silence; back in the car, fiddling with the key. It remained locked. Corporal punishment taught the Mercedes no lessons. We sat side by side, speechless, shivering, until at last you said, a big man beaten, "Let's get out the goddam manual."

You were a man I was used to seeing work easily and knowingly around the most intricate, complicated pieces of machinery; a man who moved gracefully and serenely through masses of steel and iron; a man who every day of his life twisted and turned metal and made it do what *he* wanted. In that bitter bitter cold, by flashlight we pored over diagrams, read off lists of standard and extra equipment, studied graphs of performance tests, looked at meaningless drawings of internal systems, but there was nothing at all about anything so basic as a key that wouldn't turn in the ignition lock. I leaned over and touched that key wonderingly. And of course it turned, quite easily, at the merest touch.

We drove home without one single word passing between us and, at my cottage, you leaned across me and opened the door. I could get out and up to the house on my own. The night of the gentleman was finished—forever, it turned out; we went back to being ourselves, workers who at the end of an exhausting day often phoned one another to come down (or up) for a drink or dinner or an argument to relieve the tedium of an Adirondack winter evening.

"But you *painted* that beautiful thing!"

"Of course I painted it. It's my sculpture to paint if I want, isn't it?"

"But orange and black. My god, it looks like Halloween."

"You would say something like that. You just don't like *any* of them painted. You're against paint in general."

"Because they look *better* when you leave the paint off."

"That's a"—sarcasm you could hardly breathe in—"writer's point of view."

Usually the words came out oblong from either side of a huge cigar. You were banging around the kitchen, which was too small for a man of your size, doing something exotic with shallots. A fabulous cook, but no good at cleaning up or for those moments when things went wrong. You threw disasters out the back door and started all over, snarling, swearing, downing brandy. You hated women fiddling (your word) around good food. They turned it froufrou; the whole goddam world was made treacherous by women. Men made better food than women. They did *everything* better.

During the spring thaw I came upon you beside the back door shovelling up an awful mess of broken crockery, old rusted pans, bent tablewear. Belligerent before I had a chance even to ask, you explained, "I got tired of doing the goddam dishes all winter so I chucked them out. The goddam snow covered them. But now—"

Now you had to clean up. It was spring and spring was a time of frenzied activity for you. The garden, for instance—you had a mammoth garden beautifully laid out, lovingly tended. All summer long you carried armfuls of vegetables to friends; they augmented the baskets of wine, the lobsters you brought back from Albany, fish fresh from the lake, a beautiful roast you just couldn't resist buying but that was too big for one man alone on his own, the Sunday paper, books and magazines, always something, you never came empty-handed. The givers: do they do it trying just to show love or to find love? Why always be the kind who asks the inanswerables? We were both born that way, I guess.

There was, also, the horse to deal with. My job, it turned out, was to tame Jo-Jo so that when David's two daughters arrived for the summer holiday the animal would be placid and pleasant.

"Now, listen, this horse has got some bad habits—"

"I should say he does. Do you know what he did when I went out to get him? He ran at me all teeth—"

"The thing is, he needs a lot of work—"

"He tried to bite me, David. Horses have sharp teeth. I don't think that's the kind of animal you should have around young girls—"

"It's just a bad habit. Now, the thing is—"

"*You* get on him first."

"I'm way too big for him, for crissake. I'd stove him in."

"Not that horse. He looks to me like he could carry any—"

"I thought you loved animals—what about all those cats you've

348

got? Would you sit on one of them? Well, if I sat on this horse, it'd be just like your sitting on one of those cats of yours—"

"He tried to *bite* me, David. He ran right at me with those awful teeth—"

"Put the saddle on. Here, I'll put the saddle on. Just try him. It won't hurt just to try him, will it?"

Jo-Jo took off down that field in front of the house and in and out of all those wickedly sharp sculptures bucking and crow hopping, plunging sideways, sitting down, rearing up, and over all my screaming and Jo-Jo's heavy breathing, the clatter of hooves, and the rattle of steel as we rushed by, I could hear David roaring, "Hang on, *just hang on.* He's going to settle down. He's bound to settle down—"

Jo-Jo stopped dead, planted his front feet squarely and lowered his head. I sailed fifteen feet over his head barely missing an outstretched steel lance. While I lay stunned on the ground, he came at me with that menacing mouthful of teeth. Oh god, I thought, and shut my eyes.

"Ah—ha—you goddam no-good gelding—git—git—GIT—"

Jo-Jo sailed over me. There was hair—fur—all over my riding pants as David picked me up. "Why didn't you hang on? My god, are you *all right?*"

"He's ruined my good Kauffman pants. Look, they're all hairy and torn—"

"Oh, pants," he said. "You might have hurt your hands. You write with them!"

Arguments about the horse ended—Jo-Jo went—but the incessant nagging about the company I had down at the cottage continued. What I needed was a tighter schedule, less friends, and more work. *It's only the work that matters:* only the work. . .only the work. . .

I did have too much company. I didn't work the way I should. I made promises and resolutions, promptly overlooked, forgot, or abandoned them. David, in his exasperation, would stand in the midst of my small cottage and point dramatically to the limitations of space, the demands of time, and the practicalities of husbanding energy.

My cottage *was* exceedingly small—the largest room was the kitchen, but it was crowded with manuscripts, beer-making apparatus (I was poor and all my friends thirsty; homebrew worked out to about five cents the quart and even a moderate amount was practically guaranteed to put you under); I had a small child and the toys, books, abandoned shoes and shirts that go with small children; I had seedlings, pictures, a piece of (small) sculpture David had given me, three stone heads I'd picked up abandoned in a previous apartment, skis, and so many books the struts under the floor groaned when you walked on them. There was a small living room, almost all bookcases, and in a corner one bed on which my young daughter usually slept, a tiny bedroom, and a tinier bath. But the view, twenty miles down Lake George, was stupendous, and guests usually sat on the porch and read, drank, played chess, argued, and chased wasps. One afternoon we arrived to find the place a complete mess. Since we had left only a little more than an hour before and the cottage had been reasonably tidy, David was aghast.

"My god, people have been living here while we went down the street. There are clothes all over the place. Books, glasses, tennis rackets, swim suits —"

"It's probably just Tom and Joe —"

The notion people came, let themselves in, settled, and went their way to turn up again at will mystified him. "You mean you *allow* this?"

"It's no worse than the ladies picnicking under the stainless steel."

"At least I put up signs."

"But, David, these are friends."

My friends all seemed to him dangerous interlopers who would assert themselves and demand attention which (now) I realize he regarded as rightfully his. Once an old friend from literary quarterly days turned up. I was sure David would like him, and I spent a week of preparation with humorous anecdotes. Cut no ice at all: I got in return the well-known Smith sulks, a very large man on a very determined pout. About eleven o'clock the first night of the visit, my young daughter and I had gone to bed in the miniscule bedroom. Dick was lying on the living room bed in his pajamas reading.

Suddenly the house began to shake. David was such an enormous man and my cottage was so small that when he tramped up on the porch the whole frame of the cottage went into a seizure. Then I heard voices, banging, more talk, the house shuddered some more, and my friend Dick at the door announced, "Rick, the fishman says to tell you he's here."

David just happened, he explained, to be passing by (at eleven o'clock at night) and he just happened to have all these perch and he just happened to remember I loved fresh fish: big and belligerent, in the doorway with an enormous pail. Then he began to laugh. Decatur, Indiana, approved the sleeping arrangements. He thundered back out to the Mercedes and brought in wine, salamis, bread, jars of preserves, pickles, olives he just happened to have with him in case we felt like a snack.

He stayed until four o'clock. My friend Dick was as puzzled by David as David was by him. "You mean he does this all the time?"

Well, yes, he did. A lot.

The very first time David ever came to the cottage he arrived at ten-thirty at night with a *Life* photographer. I had been introduced to David once years before, but had been abroad; taking the cottage was my way of coming home; I heard David was still in the area and had dropped him a note asking him if he still had that small piece of sculpture *The Puritan* that I had admired years before. A couple of months went by and I had forgotten the letter when one night the house began to rattle. I opened the door on David and an exceedingly tall thin man identified as the photographer from *Life*. David had a quart of whiskey in one hand, and he uncorked it between his teeth, spit the top out, a characteristic entering gesture I was to learn meant, "It looks like a good evening ahead."

Fifteen minutes and two drinks later he disappeared; he was on his way, he informed the *Life* man and myself, to get some lobster he had up at "the place." An hour passed, then thirty minutes more. We had just had a blizzard and the *Life* photographer and I gazed out on a world of endless drifts, speechless. We had exhausted all small talk, and god alone knew what had happened to Smith. The *Life* man began to prowl about restlessly. There wasn't much room to prowl and finally, anchored at a window bleakly looking out at all that white, he said, "Got any candles?"

I handed over my supply. He bundled himself up and went out into that winter wasteland. He was running from drift to drift scooping out altars in the snow, then setting lighted candles in the niches. Presently a world of flickering snow altars lay outside my kitchen window while inside, the prodigal returned, David was at the skillets doing something unbelievable with lobster, wine, shallots, and rice. Nothing, but nothing, has ever tasted as good as that dish which David tried unsuccessfully time and again to duplicate. At the funeral I ran into the *Life* man again—the first time since that evening years before—but he had no recollection of it at all. Too many other, more interesting evenings had intervened, I suppose. But for me it was the beginning of a memorable friendship. We never stopped, David and I, save for that one disastrous evening being "nice," arguing from then on.

"You absolutely cannot expect to consider yourself an intelligent human being if you don't know anything about jazz."

"But, David, I don't like music, not at all. Most writers don't. It offends some inner ear they keep for dialogue, it—"

"Just listen to this. *Listen.* It's great—just great," tramping about, jabbing the air with his cigar. All that noise, I would think, and steel myself for another lecture on New Orleans, the Five Spot, Monk and the other legendary jivers.

Once, in the midst of a great cacophony of drums and brass and god knows what, he thrust a small statue at me. "Here, you like it so much, take it. But just, for chrissake, listen to the solo. Don't look like that—you can develop an ear. If you *try.*"

Generous to the end, the very end: the opened bottles with the tops thrown off into the shrubbery, lobster and books and thick bundles of the *New York Times*, a gift of sculpture, a greater gift of friendship. He could be outrageous, angry, a battler, muddle-headed, incompetent, wrong, but generous, clever, fun and full of the juices of life. He was never never small or petty. He retained, for instance, love—real love—for his two former wives. They angered and exasperated him, or at least one did, and the other I don't think he ever really understood, but he still cared for them. He was the sort of man who couldn't take love back. Bonds for David meant forever. He was a vast concentration of rebellion beating against the imprisonment of the limitations of his own body and mind. He was like a man raging against his designated fate. Above the law, but confined, consigned to it; reveling in trampling on social mores and distinctions, but after the revels, alas, the ruin. He knew it all. But, then, don't we all?

Death now always means May for me.

On that May morning a little before seven the phone rang. It was a friend. "Have you got your radio on?"

"No—"

"David's been killed, Rick. In a car crash."

"It's the Mercedes," I said. "I always knew it."

"No, it was the truck."

I put the phone down slowly and stood looking out the window on the beginning of growth. I kept shaking my head. Somewhere in the back of my mind I was prepared for this death, but it was the Mercedes I had feared. Wrongly. Of course. When the truck—the truck that I had always trusted—left the road, David had been flung against the struts. That big head I had also always trusted had been crushed against the overhead struts, the truck itself scarcely damaged. Later it was sold—almost as good as new. But there was nothing, Albany-bound where the live lobsters came from, to mend the man. The skull that had had so many visions was broken bits of bone.

David's death took place just four days before my birthday, in May of 1965. That is quite a number of years ago, and yet I still feel that it is utterly and absolutely impractical that he does not come up on the porch and rattle the house. Did he not shake everything he touched? It's no good, I feel, the *Times* vindicating his beliefs in himself now. It's too late. He wanted to know when he was alive.

David, never go in peace. Nothing became you so well as the manner in which you shook the places you lived.

"I don't know why you want to *paint* it. . ."

"It's mine, isn't it? I can paint it if I want, can't I?"

No, not any more; no, not ever ever again, you can't.

So what is left?

I know, I know. The work. Always the work.

Michael Rutherford

Michael Rutherford is the founder of Alternative Literary Programs (ALPS). He is the author of two books of poetry and a novella, The Tale and Its Master (Spring Harbor Press, 1986). He lives in Voorheesville with his wife Kathy and their daughter Eve.

From *Lives in Flight*

Craft

There are places dominated by one sense, places bonded together by the eyes, the tongue, the nose. My Nana's home lives in the airy memories of my nostrils. Hers was the first home I ever knew soiled by the fumes, the breath, the floating juices of good cooking. Entering by the back door, (we never entered through the golden oak door in the front) I'd glance down into the cellar to see what new vegetables were waiting in the dim corners of the basement. The perfume of apples would float up, the delicate aroma of pears, the golden pitch of peaches. From the pipes hung scallions, nets of onions, strings of drying wild mushrooms. Then up the short stairway, open the door, and into the kitchen. The door would open toward you, seemingly pushed by the welcome of whatever she had in the oven or cooling on the stove. She'd hurry our coats off, offer cookies or pastries, scoot us out of the room with promises of imminent food, and return to her cabalations. I'd peer around the corner to watch her, fascinated by her intensity, her communication with her materials: talking to each pot, exhorting the vegetables, coaxing a pie to fruition. She moved with the economy, the surety that I came to recognize in all artists: truck drivers, pilots, ball players. The innate recognition that there is really no repetition, that acts must be brought to perfection through constant trial. That, above all, deeds without joy lose meaning, lose quality.

Things with Wings

The bees came with the house, like the green paint that peeled and dribbled over its gothic body. My parents probably never even noticed the bees as they looked at the house with the real estate agent. The agent never mentioned them.

Once we moved in, we found them quickly enough. They had their hive in the attic, over the second floor bathroom. The first week we lived in our new home, bees dripped through the lathing onto the bathroom floor. My father, hung over and oblivious with morning, stepped on one that first week.

He lies in the bedroom, the shades pulled down, the day slucing in in dust muscled beams. The doctor talks to my mother:

"He's allergic to bees. He'll have to carry pills in case he gets stung again. Meanwhile, try to get the hive out of the attic. Didn't you know that he was allergic to bees? I'd thought he would have told you."

"No, he never mentioned it. He's never been stung since we were married."

The tiered black medicine bag folds shut. The clasps click. The doctor and my mother walk out of the room and gently close the door.

I come around the hall corner, where I've been listening to the truth that my mother will dilute for the children's ears.

I pull the door quietly towards me, tight against the frame, so I can turn the knob without the snick of the tongue in the latch. I insinuate myself into my parents' bedroom. There on the bed, my father dreams in a honeyed coma. His leg swells taut as a red sausage. His face is plaster of paris, the texture of a damp wall. He breathes like he is climbing a ladder.

The house hums like an engine. The whole house is suffused with the sound of bees. Thousands of them crawling through the walls in the unity of the hive. The floors shiver slightly beneath our feet. After a few weeks, we go through our daily business, aware of the house throbbing as we sleep and breathe.

My brother Sandy and I come out of the house after the first snow of the year. In the white carpet of snow, hundreds of bees rest like cigarette butts. Drones thrown out of the hive with the advent of cold; the attrition of workers burnt out by summer labors. We pick them up and bring them into the kitchen, cradling them in our palms with the reverence that boys give live bullets. We find an empty ice tray and fill it with bees; stash it in the freezer, hidden behind the ice cream, a dessert to sample later. After school the next day, we bring them out and, fastidious as jewelers, spread them delicately on the dining room table. Hundreds of Hairy legs, the obsidian tears for eyes, the tawny fuzzed abdomens. Some thaw and awaken, rise clumsy as fawns, speed their wings invisible to flight. Summer temperatures. The pollen sacks on their legs ache. They fly into the walls, expecting flowers and greater space.

Toiling in the Vineyards of the Lord: I

After five years behind a desk at the library, I chuck it for Poets in the Schools. I scout up jobs, work two to three weeks at a succession of schools, take over classes and teach poetry. If the school likes me, they hire me back the next year. Cultural Darwinism. Barnstorming with language.

Strangely, most problems come from the teachers. Many feel I don't teach poetry. Poetry, after all, rhymes, is deep, obscure and terminally dull. Compounding this, many teachers ask for the program to get out of teaching a class. This is the world I enter. Mr. Milltown's class is no exception.

"And now class, here's the poet, Mr. Rutherford."

Clutching a pack of cigarettes and a pile of ungraded papers, Mr. Milltown eases toward the door. The ninth graders groan; some slump in their seats; others lean heavy heads on crossed arms. Flies buzz against the windows; rows of slack, video-scarred faces.

"Any questions?" I ask.

"Yeah, Poet, flex your arms," a greaser calls from the back.

I pull up the sleeve of the T-shirt, give them a biceps shot. Whistles, cheers. I silently thank my years of pumping iron.

"Now before we get going, do you think Mr. Milltown should do the work with us?"

Mr. Milltown slips out the door as I propose this. Shouts of, "Yeah, come on, Mr. Milltown, get in here, do it with us," draw him reluctantly back into the room. He pierces me with a venomous glare as he slides into a seat.

"All right. I'll explain what imagery is for awhile, then give you a specific theme to write a poem on, then we'll read them aloud. Mr. Milltown and I will write too. And I'm sure Mr. Milltown won't mind reading first."

The Inner Space Expedition: Mr. Milltown's class

The poet appeared each morning, gave survival tips, clicked his heels three times and vanished into a coffee cup.

Lynn found a mirror in each page she wrote, leaned too close, fell in and drowned.

Amy sucked the hearts out of lilacs and spit back bees.

Chink picked his teeth with a switch blade, pried the top of his head off and unleashed a meteor shower.

Monica wandered away one night and came back with a husband and three gingerbread children which she shared with the class.

George switched channels until he got static, greased himself with electrons and got a tan.

Vic climbed a female pot plant into the clouds, stole a singing harp, ran back and cut the plant down and smoked his poems.

Amos kicked a football until it burst, autographed on both sides and diagrammed plays he hoped were poems.

Fred slept.

Elvin went hunting, married his gun, grew a pelt and worshipped the moon.

Lloyd went hitch-hiking, got picked up by Bonnie and Clyde and punctuated Bonnie's poems with dum-dum bullets.

Julie brought Jesus to the campfire one night. He had fish breath and he left blood on her blouse when he touched her breasts.

Katie drew pictures of horses each day and rode them away whenever she saw smoke.

Nancy wove Navaho poems spun from a drop spindle and nailed them to the wall to exhibit them.

Ron ate the centers out of oreos and tossed the black cookies as poems.

Kevin painted his face, drank pig blood, chewed betel nuts and stared through his paper as if it were a window.

Nelson sucked the ink out of dictionaries and sweat poems as he did bench presses.

Gina grew gardens of poems that ate insects and strangled birds.

Chris rode a van or images with illuminated doors, mag wheels, side pipes, a water bed, stereo 8 track and inflatable dreams.

Tina threw paper mache hearts at all of us. We wept and threw them back.

Frank bathed in K-Y jelly and the class woke up.

And we found Mr. Milltown's bones in the forest, scored by the teeth of innumerable animals.

All in all, a typical ninth grade class.

At the end of my last day, I walk slowly out into the parking lot, my briefcase stuffed with poems from the kids. Three burlies from Mr. Milltown's class lean on my pickup truck. They cup their hands around furtive cigarettes. When they spot me, they straighten and give me lop-sided grins.

"What's up, punks?" I ask.

"Hey, Mr. Ruggabugga," Vic opens, "we decided to, uh, chip in and get you something."

"Yeah," Elvin adds, "for a poet you ain't a bad guy."

"Before you came, I never knew you could be an artist and still beat people up," Chink says.

"Here, Poet, take it," Vic pushes a paper bag into my hand. "Open it up."

I pull a carton of Lucky Strikes out of the bag. Smiling, I shake everybodies' hands.

"Guys, you should've spent the money."

"We're really sorry, Mr. Rootie," Chink explains, "we know you like cigars, but this was the best we could do. Over at the Grandway, they got all the cigars locked up in a big glass case, not like the cigarettes here, which are sittin' out in the open. Even after Vic knocked over the toilet paper display, we still couldn't . . ."

"Shut up, Chink," says Vic and pounds him in the shoulder.

I brush away a tear. "I don't know how to thank you guys. This is really touching."

Toiling in the Vineyards: II

Mrs. Abbadabba nears the end of the list of spelling words. I sit on her desk and shift through posters, valentines and thank you notes the kids have given me in farewell. Even a few perfumed dinner invitations from mothers. Some of the third graders glance over to me, anxious for the test to end.

I hood my eyes and daydream. The third graders shoot up, fall in love, marry, buy my poetry books, have children, go to my poetry readings. I teach their children. Some even become writers who acknowledge my influence and write with slightly less than my skill.

In the field by my thatched cottage, we are all having a picnic. The bees are loud in the glen. Ants crawl up my white beard. A beautiful woman walks over to my chair:

"You probably don't remember me, Mr. Rutherford. You've taught so many of us: me, my parents. But I just wanted you to meet my children. Come here, kids; don't be nervous. Here's my son, Michael Rutherford Grabowski, and this is little Michelle."

I tousle their hair and reach for my tumbler of Jack Daniels.

"And now children, here's Mr. Rutherford."

The teacher's abrupt introduction snaps me from my reverie. My vision clears. In the front row, Amy picks her nose and sticks the snot under the seat. Fortunately, enough kids are applauding to give me time to re-orient myself. I'll wrap up my visit with a round of questions that'll impress poetry onto their malleable souls.

"And before I leave . . ."

Groans. A shadow passes across their faces.

"Let's talk about what we've learned."

Hands flash up before I can phrase a question.

"Can any of you tell me things you found out about poetry that you didn't know before I came?"

The phrasing sounds a little phony as I hear the words float off my lips. So what. I point into the anemone of pink arms.

"All right. Brent, what did you learn? Tell all of us in a loud voice."

"POEMS DON'T HAVE TO RHYME."

"You're right, Brent. Very good. The rest of you can speak a little quieter than Brent did. Amy, what about you?"

"Poems can be funny and silly like you, but they don't have to be," she offers a random-toothed grin.

"Thank you, Amy. O.K., Carl, what else?"

"Poetry comes from inside us, what we feel," he reads from my invisible script.

"Great, Carl. Good job."

I see a hand covered with white paste. Jill hasn't said much in class. A breakthrough.

"Well, Jill, I'm glad you have something to tell us. What did you learn about poetry from my visit?"

Her serious little face squeezes, "Until I met you, Mr. Ruttaferd, I thought all poets were dead." She smiles with the release of words.

Humbled, I silently thank her for the gift of life.

Toiling: III

The cafeteria has been constructed with the universal architecture of institutions: just enough lighting to strain the eyes, the acoustics of a sewer pipe, the ordered multiplication of identical chairs and tables and rubber garbage pails with green plastic liners.

"And now teachers, here's the ballooning poet, Michael Rutherford. Mr. Rutherford will tell us a little about himself, explain what he'll be doing with our classes over the next couple of weeks and answer any questions we may have." The principal sits down in the front row and eyes me expectantly.

The place has begun to work its usual magic; the faces of the teachers are somehow losing their features; a slide that will end with the gathering slurred to a host of mannequins.

"I guess I'll start by answering questions," I offer defensively. My voice, normally loud enough to talk over a jackhammer, wanders the room, whispering to those before me, chortling with its echos in the corners. I watch my audience through a thickening haze of cigarette smoke. Heads lean into palms. "Does anyone have any questions?"

"What do you do for a living?"

Already I am tumbling away, out through the ceiling, leaving my lips to fend for themselves with a zen apathy honed in hundreds of rooms like these. My mouth moves. Phrases exist. The hand falls. Silence. Another hand rises.

"Where does inspirational come from?"

Spread out in the raddled glow of early evening, the balloon struggles to inflate itself. Into it I throw warm words, fables, fairy tales, necromantic incantations.

"Do you sit by a stream to write?"

Somewhere the balloon rises. I have tied each person in the room to a gossamer line of light. We trail beneath the balloon in a long kite tail, a skein of mandrake roots. A great mouth opens in the clouds and we slip in on an inspiration of breath. Vistas waver in the distance. I point out to my fellow drifters the infinite geography behind the eyes, the ribcage.

"What will we have to do in class?"

The line of light parts. The dolls sift towards the ground, as slow as thistle fluff. Beneath each, a pack of poems bays and barks, waiting, sniffing the shadows of the spinning figures, homing inexorably on the individual scents of darkness.

"Do you ever get lost when you're writing?"

The balloon grows flaccid and wheezes down toward dark meadows, towards arms raised to me for prophecy. My throat clots. I spit lumps of gibberish. The villagers raise their fists in silent curses. The balloon swings down through tree tops. Branches whip.

"Just from what you've seen, how does our school compare with others you've visited?"

Like a bladder of dreams, the balloon finally deflates in an empty alfalfa field. I lay still for a while, pick my sore self up and begin pushing the warm fabric upon itself to pack it away. I walk up and down the vast insubstantial bulk, squeezing the last air out, flattening it. People appear on the margins of the field, strange faces with a familiar curiosity. Gradually, one by another, they join me in folding the balloon up. And as we work, I answer questions about what has landed in their midst. We finish and separate, the taste of sky shared, taken home to leaven sleep.

"Well, we all feel a little clearer about what will be going on, Mr. Rutherford. Thank you." My lips stop. The principal walks over to shake my hand. The teachers clap, get up and go to their cars. The spring sun melting a sheet of ice to a dark stain in the parking lot.

Joanne Seltzer

Joanne Seltzer was born in Detroit but has lived in Niskayuna since 1960. She has published several short stories and a number of literary essays, in addition to scores of poems which have apeared in a wide variety of literary journals: POETRY NOW, THE VIL-LAGE VOICE, THE MINNESOTA REVIEW, BLUELINE, *and many others. Some of her poems have been anthologized and a few are used as classroom texts.*

In May 1983 Joanne Seltzer was elected to the National Steering Committee of The Feminist Writer's Guild. She is also a member of The Poetry Society of America and Associated Writing Programs and is recognized by Poets and Writers as both a poet and a fiction writer. Her biography is included in THE WORLD WHO'S WHO OF WOMEN, INTERNATIONAL AUTHORS AND WRITERS WHO'S WHO, PERSONALITIES OF AMERICA, *and other reference guides.*

The Loft Press of Glens Falls, New York published her collection, ADIRONDACK LAKE POEMS, *in the spring of 1985.*

The Island

Near the north shore of Piseco
the island stays forever wild.

No-trespassing signs are posted
To Whom It May Concern

but I beach my boat
and walk along the trail.

There are flowers—trees—
fallen branches—

a hill—a rocky cliff—
the world in miniature—

if you disregard the signs.
Disregarding the signs

the chipmunks crossed the ice
last winter

and will be trapped
and will be nesting here

no matter how bored they are
until the lake freezes again.

Paradox Lake

On the fourth day, I begin to see
all that was invisible to me.
Distant ducks. Frogs at my feet.
Among the strands of marsh grass, forget-
me-nots appear—pale reflection
of the sky. Damselflies and dragons.
Arrowhead surrounded by water.
Boats that cross the lake and disappear.

The paradox is this: ebb and flow
are multidirectional. I row
both with the current and against it,
and I drift—I am casually thrust—
wherever fortune takes me. Love,
you are the boat I have lost sight of.

The Sacandaga Campsite

Here at this dammed-up river
the public ignores the social war.

Women haul water.
Men build fires.

Parents share the common chore
of watching their children

not trusting hired lifeguards
to count drenched heads.

Each couple brings exactly two
green-webbed lawn chairs

softening the afternoon return
to the sand.

The river falls down a vertical wall
beyond the swimming hole.

It hits the rocks with a roar.

The Case of the Pickled Woman

She is known as the lady of the lake
last seen alive at mystic dusk
alone in a wood canoe.

Her fractured head at wet peace
prayed anchor-bound to rock.
Her noose held fast to the fraying years

while dry rot cracked her name
until she was found on her water ledge
by skin divers who chanced to touch

a perfect female mold.
Her green-tinged vegetable body
was portaged up for the resurrection

but her surface disappeared
at the charmed kiss of remembered air.
Her cord broke and her anchor fell

to the bottom of Lake Placid.
Her logbook closed on self-affliction:
caught by the deepest depression

she jumped (it is said) to the cold chapel
under the shadow of Whiteface Mountain.
Only the high peaks know

if that pickled woman
cast her weight, like a magic sword,
to the great stone slab.

Waiting to Watch the Bears

They come to the garbage dump
here at Long Lake
almost every night.

If the wind blows right
the bears
can pick through trash
without suffering the odor
of humans.

But if the wind blows wrong
or if too many humans come
for the evening show
the bears
remain in the deep woods
empty-bellied.

I stand
among this comic throng of man
on a cliff above the landfill
near the road to Newcomb

trying not to smell the garbage
trying not to smell human.

At Big Moose Lake:
The Scene of an American Tragedy

A female duck
somewhat slighter than a mallard
glides toward the dock
lights on the water
and quacks
she has arrived.

Without a metallic violet-blue wing-patch
she's as drab as that blue-collar woman
spilled into this elevated water
by the desperate social climber
(her boyfriend)
who almost married Elizabeth Taylor's
wealth
prestige
and violet eyes.

I remember how Shelley Winters
stared greenly beyond the tamarack bog
and sank two thousand feet above
the distant
humdrum
sea.

photo by Malie Smith

Jordan Smith

Jordan Smith was born in Rochester, New York, and grew up in the outlying town of Fairport. He was educated at Hamilton, Empire State College, the Johns Hopkins University, and the University of Iowa. He is an assistant professor of English at Union College.

Jordan Smith's poems have appeared in AGNI REVIEW, ANTAEUS, ANTIOCH REVIEW, CHELSEA, GEORGIA REVIEW, GRAND STREET, NER/BLQ, PARIS REVIEW, IRONWOOD, POETRY, and other journals. His first collection of poems, An Apology for Loving the Old Hymns, *was published by Princeton University Press in 1982. He is currently completing a second collection, "Lucky Seven," with the assistance of a grant from the National Endowment for the Arts.*

Constable Hall
Constableville, New York

Here, simple description is not enough. These are cut stones rising
  through an August drizzle, gray gables, great cornices,
The roofline harsh against the sky, and the weathercocks rusting,
  swinging in a changing wind, the iron pickets darkening.
The door bolted, its paint etched away. And on the shutters, a
  patterned, elaborated journal of weathering. . .

But there is no one to read that script now. No one to bend the
  corner of a visiting card, and turn again toward the carriage
  drive,
Or to notice if the windows have taken on the steely air of rain in
  deep woods, if the brambles have moved closer.
Who will recall the small jets of the gas lamps; who will count the
  grain of oak stairsteps, the yellowed invitations on the mantel?

And how should I describe these rooms truthfully? You will not
  walk through them, nor will I. Or if we should, on a wet day, a
  day for failing sight,
Then we should see as I have always supposed spirits must, as if a
  great weight pressed against each eyelid, and the world had
  changed
To streaks of rain-water on an antique pane, something withheld
  in flaws and swirls of the glass, something given back:

A single lamp, perhaps, still burning in a room where so many
  years have been forgotten. But who could speak of that and be
  believed?

Vine Valley

There will be nothing left to forgive. The inn
failing along the canalside, lattice-
work of beams and splintered panes. Beyond the lakes,
already there is the sound of windows breaking,
that vision of cold. So the landscape grows
deeper, a dryness in your throat
aging with the wine, marriage of spirit and bad weather.
On the hillside, two men with hooks work
toward each other along the vines. They've built a fire
by the road of leaves and blackened grapes,
and the porch shudders in the autumn sun.

This is what you meant by grief: a stroke of charcoal
lost against the dark weave of the scarf. That sorrow
is a spring seeping through matted leaves,
these roughened planks. The journal entries
thread their heavy weave around your throat,
and there is nothing left to say. Or only the white
script of fast water on the creek,
how her tears fell on the purple dress, darkening
rosary of amethyst and widowed fields. Early winter
reciting the year's last testament: the old man
is sick again, and the farm up for sale.

All you remember is the trellis of moonlight
over his face. He abandoned the fences
as the fields grew more difficult, empty as a house
without a single vase, or what a vase can hold:
Ash. The veins of each leaf
give up their vintage at last, simply and in flame.
You put your hand on my shoulder, and say it's past
time to thin the vineyard down. And we go out
where the firs reel like a farmer gone
half-blind from his glass of bad whiskey. If the shadow
of his hands tangled in your shadow as he fell,

if he only stood where the barn walls met, background
of shade and cracked siding, it was still the same: a fate
passed to us in the dim tracks cobwebs leave on stone,

gray weathered into a fainter gray. On the doorpost
you carved a tree nearly swallowed by vines
and two deer gnawing at the root. We called it home,
sweet interlacing of hunger and the world.
There was nowhere else to go. A house surrounded
by the fullness of grapes, of leaves turning the light
back from their stalks. Promise of early harvest
and a deed in your hand, settling all claims.

But out here the land is only a clearing, the sickle's
cry and passage. A failure of trust. The house
falls as if winter went on like a father
dying before your eyes, dying into himself, a brother
who won't step out of the shadows seen finally
for nothing but a slur of half-light interrupted
by the window slats. It would be so easy to let the snow
take everything now, take you, the way you wanted
even your elegy to blame itself for how you stood
between silver maples on the hillside, your arms
crossed with the white sun. I gave you up,

and there was no one left to speak. Once you wrote
all we are given are the steps of a mower
coming home in the evening along the sheaves.
The shaded lantern in a window marked with frost,
how it fell and shimmered as he passed between the trees.
That blame is a way of twisting another's death
into your own. So I confess I've taken you
into this field, as a foundling becomes half-kin.
You come toward me now down the rows of vines,
and we are so alike we must share even
this grief: that sorrow is original,

a fellowship of loss lying at the root of things.
You put the scythe in my hand, and we walk
where the smudge rises slowly from damped fires.
We will bury him together, before the early squalls,
while leaves still smoulder in the ditches. Because wine
tastes bitter without a trace of ash at its heart.
Because this is what brothers must do: forget,
as an empty house settles into its legacy of knotted stems.
As hearing the end of a father's story let us sleep, arm in arm,
at last, let even our sleep deepen into this curve
of night and the first snow, turning, gathering us in.

A Lesson from the Hudson River School: Glens Falls, New York, 1848

(for Dale and Stewart Davis)

> *It falls by no rule at all; sometimes it leaps, sometimes it tumbles; there it skips; here, it shoots; in one place 'tis white as snow, and in another 'tis green as grass; hereabouts, it pitches into deep hollows that rumble and quake the 'arth; and thereaway, it ripples and sings like a brook, fashioning whirlpools and gulleys in the old stone, as if 'twas no harder than trodden clay.*

James Fenimore Cooper

Look, above the mill-race bridge, the turning wheels. . .
   see how, as the spray flicks, the air
turns bright, laughing, grim and turbulent at once:
a certain blustery quality of light
   not accounted for in paintings
of the old masters. No gothic radiance

   half-hidden by ruins and mist
fills our work, my friend, no glory-haze of Rome
   or Egypt or Greece betraying
some old world's felled stones to our eyes.
No, an American light, as if time stopped
   in the midst of an explosion,

a glass factory, say, and all those splinters
   still hung in the air: hints of death,
to be sure, and hints of a powerful life,
and something more. . .brilliant, scattered reflections,
   as if unfettered souls burst out
to fill this vastness, and the aim of our art

was but to recollect them. Here,
those pines, if managed with a more precise stroke
    and a greater fidelity
    in your choice of greens, will soon make
the perfect type of *Perseverance* or *Faith
    in Nature*, which is a near thing

to faith in man, faith in yourself. You will learn.
    A style that will become you well
may be found with the same fine taste as your marriage
of a suit and cravat. It is mostly technique,
    though you must still maintain that love
of the unsummoned, unexpected Sublime,

    that trust which has enabled you
to withstand some long hours of eloquence
    at the Lyceum or a jar
    of hard Vermont cider: your hope
that the dregs—of apples or oratory,
    both are dull enough at first taste—

will bless you, as all true gifts bless, suddenly,
    a drunkenness when common hours
seem common no more. You have seen the painting
Sailing above the Narrows, Newburgh, New York?
    I cannot recall the artist,
but he has painted the pleasure fleet racing

    before a line of wooded cliffs,
water and sky both gleaming. It is fine work,
    and particularly because
    one cannot tell if that great glow
comes just before sunset or just after dawn.
    There is a sheen to the sail-cloth

that is almost ghostly, as if the granite
    were some half-forgotten spirit,
his sacrifices gone, his altars broken,
his prayers and hymns unspoken, who yet persists
    in this local revelation,
filling taut canvas with his strong, dappled

presence, his endless stillness
reflected even by the Hudson's waters.
  Some days the river seems to me
  a rutted cemetery lane,
all those fair sloops running headlong for the rocks,
  the patient watchfulness of shoals. . .

But, to say more of that landscape. . .It recalls
  what Emerson once remarked
we must observe in all the works of genius:
our own rejected thoughts come back, a certain
  alienated majesty.
Although it was not majesty struck me most,

  but a sort of desolation—
all that light caught forever in the pine boughs,
  bound between the stones and current,
  the boats still in their still motion—
nothing like the elegant testimonies
  of the great English Romantics

to time's equally elegant ravages.
  (No, I suspect the truth is this:
that for the Europeans no thoughts remain,
concealed or otherwise. All their pictures
  may reveal to us are remnants,
split husks, forms without the mainspring of spirit.

  Theirs is an art of spectators,
as if their society had reached its height
  with the invention of the clock,
  and then consecrated itself
to the observation, classification,
  and collection of bits of gear,

the torn dials, bent hour-hands littering their hills.)
  But, to return to our painting. . .
to yours, I mean. If you would sketch the full strength
of these rapids, you must not omit the shades
  of slate, blue-gray, even black,
which are not adequately explained away

374

as reflections of the mill-wheels,
or as traces of the ore-flecked stream bottom,
   but must be some strange property
   of the river, an illusion
caused by the speedy passage of the current
   through our more constant line of sight.

The source of the Hudson? It lies further north,
   near Marcy. No, I think no one
has yet lugged his paintbox and easel so far,
though to sketch the famous *Opalescent Gorge*,
   as it is called—the whole spectrum
rushing toward you as long as the sunlight lasts,

   and at night, or so I have heard,
a varied glow, like a thousand true moonstones,
   a never failing light—that sight,
   rendered for good on your canvas,
would be worth a few difficult miles of trail.
   I heard once of a man who tried.

A Boston man, he was neither an artist
   nor a woodsman, just a dabbler
in trade, in shipping, in stocks and capital,
who, after losing his townhouse in a fire,
   decided for no clear reason
to purchase a rucksack, paintbrushes, a gun,

   and start for the Adirondacks.
He took the train this far, then started on foot
   and, within a day, lost himself.
   You've seen how the turnpike dwindles,
first a clear trail, then a deer-path, then nothing
   but brambles, windfalls, rippling sounds

that no one has quite explained—they make you think
   the stream must still be near at hand
when you may have strayed far from its banks. He strayed,
stumbled on stumps, fell headlong in a ravine,
   which he followed in the late dusk
until a light began to flicker nearby.

Jordan Smith   375

Through the pine boughs he saw a house,
which, even at some distance, seemed familiar.
   There was no path, no sign of life,
   except, hanging from the front gate,
a lamp, which he recognized as an heirloom
   by the initials in the brass:

his initials, his father's, his grandfather's.
   He stepped back, and saw that the stones,
the brass door plate, the angle of the chimneys,
even the hinges and shutter bolts, belonged
   to his ruined Boston mansion.
He was a practical man. He went inside,

   lit the parlor lamp he purchased
not two years before, pulled a few unread books
   from his shelves, and went up to bed.
   He felt some slight apprehension
of ghosts of his servants who died in the fire,
   but he slept soundly all the same.

What frightened him at last was this: next morning,
   on a tray of antique silver
which had once held the calling cards of his guests,
he found an unbound, half-tattered manuscript,
   written in a hand like his own.
It was *his* history. He read it twice through,

   shuddered, and threw it on the fire.
It was not what was written there that scared him—
   if that volume told him the truth,
   he would return soon to Boston's
wealthy, complacent bosom—but what was not.
   There was no first or last chapter,

no accounting for his birth or for his death. . .
   No, I could hardly swear to you
that the tale is true, nor can I remember
where I first heard it. From my father, perhaps,
   or in that tavern in Glens Falls
where we stopped last night. Maybe it came to me

as I was walking, a day dream
given in the mesh of branches, root, and sky,
   reflected in the rushing stream—
   the branches gnarled, heavy with moss,
ancient, broken roots, and the current frozen
   in their web. You see, what scares me

about this landscape is that nothing is new,
   nothing forgotten, nothing lost,
and nothing changes. There is no end to it.
Even our ghosts are not souls back from heaven
   or hell. No, they are the stories
we have once heard or told and cannot escape,

   those poor, wandering vestiges
of our thoughts, those accidental reflections,
   illegitimate brain-children,
   whose conception we may deny,
but whom we cannot ever disinherit.
   Well, I have strayed far indeed

from the subject at hand. You do the mill-wheels
   well enough; with more persistence
they may become symbolical of something,
if only of your native strain of talent:
   endless gestures pointing nowhere
but toward yourself. You may rely on that.

Guy Johnson: London, 1788

And in their train, to fill the press,
Come apish Dance, and swoln Excess,
Mechanic Charme, and vicious Taste,
And Fashion in her changing dress.

Hoadley, lines after *The Rake's Progress*

Move the lamp closer. No, no. There. Turn the wick
lower, let there be more shadows. Let them play
across Sir William's portrait. I would see him
    dimly even now,
    as I best recall him,
  his face, part soot and part flame,
  an endless strife. My dead uncle.
Though I say he was like a father to me,
I mean only that he had a father's face,
  if, as the old Greeks proposed, war
  is the father of all things.
    Sons must take their fathers,
    good or ill, whereas

a nephew is free to prefer the comforts
of a blaze to its rage, or features mottled,
like mine, from gin to. . .Boy, another glass here.
    Look, there in his eyes,
    how the paint seems to scale
  and reveal flecks of dull white
  below the green. Those were his eyes,
like snowfall in a deep forest, unsettling
a dappled world of sunlight and earth, setting
  new boundaries, breaking the peace
  between trunk and root. Genius. . .
    he had the Englishman's
    genius for measure,

surveying, just apportionment, stone fences.
He was like a great boulder, run nearly through
with a thousand dark fissures, and yet loving
　　his splintered brightness
　　more than any clear gem.
　　Boy, go to the tavern now,
　　fetch another bottle. . .He's gone.
That is what servants do, and nephews, all such
lackeys. They give you a few sidelong glances,
　　pilfer a few trifles, and leave
　　you to the less than tender
　　　mercies of memory.
　　　But, Uncle, perhaps

it is providential that we are alone.
What I could never tell you straight to your face,
because I could never find there one still point
　　where my eyes might rest,
　　I can say now at last
　　to this portrait you so loathed.
　　("The painter," you said, "has made me
seem the worst of all men, a man of fashion.
Stooped, round shoulders. . .and smooth hands! And just look
　　　　　　　　　　　　　　　　　　　　　　　　　　here,
　　how my features almost dissolve
　　in the speckled wallpaper.
　　　No this is hardly me."
　　　You left it to me.)

If there is one thing I shall never forgive,
it must be that what you valued most in me
was my least gift, my knack for cartography.
　　What was my great *Map*
　　of the VI Nations but
　　the journal of your exploits
　　and intrigues, a fresh division
of your life from the lives of lesser mortals;
what were the Iroquois but your household gods;
　　the Mohawk clansmen but your hand
　　outstretched. What has my life been
　　　but one endless survey,
　　　your private preserve.

Hardly a life at all, that of a province
whose glory is the capital's radiance
broken, diffused, into rumors, bad weather,
    poor houses, worse taste.
        And what of my portrait?
    One Canajoharie wit
    said it resembled a certain
baronet's favorite chair: well-stuffed, yielding
to the slightest shifts of your great lordship's weight,
    and that the Mohawk brave standing
    behind me might as well be
        some upholsterer's man
        come for spring cleaning.

Well, had I never forsaken the pencil
for my current retinue of cane, corkscrew,
and catarrh, I'd have drawn my likeness better,
    a death-bed portrait
        in the style of Hogarth:
    a chamber much like this one,
    the chairs broken up for kindling,
empty bottles, the bed groaning on three legs,
a thieving servant, a master with nothing
    left to steal. And a few touches,
    more fanciful, but still true
        to the subject's spirit:
        above the mantel

a caged monkey, half-starved, half-bald, yammering,
and beside him two portraits, paired like Greek masks,
comic and tragic—a stern, elegant Lord,
    and an oversized,
    obsequious fellow,
        whose splendid red uniform
        now graces a Cheapside pawnshop.
A third picture too, I think, a real Hogarth,
Plate V of *The Rake's Progress*: the wastrel heir
    wedding an elderly widow
    for reasons too obvious
        to require my comments.
        Notice how his eyes,

dear Uncle, turn with equally obvious
intent toward the young bridesmaid, and notice too
that a crack runs through the Sixth Commandment's plaque.
     (I suppose the girl
     is the old bride's daughter.)
     I am no stern moralist,
     nor a 'specially moral man
but is this not a fair representation
of your lust for Molly Brant? She is the girl,
     I mean, who must play the harlot
     while her mother—the Six Nations,
          if I may extend
          my allegory

from the sensual to the political;
you pretended to keep such affairs distinct,
but took your pleasures wherever they might come—
     while her dear mother
     is swived quite royally,
     if, because of her age
     and frank distaste for novelty,
more in spirit than in fact. Her true father—
the longhouse fire, symbol, in my parallel,
     of the ancient fidelity
     of the Iroquois—spent, doused,
          buried by your desire
          to measure her charms

against profits in furs, the King's endless thirst
for allies against the French, the newest wing
of Johnson Hall. You won over the Mohawks,
     sent Joseph to school,
     made him a strange mongrel,
     part Mason, part hatchet-man,
     made Molly your good English whore.
You took their most private gift, the great Valley,
grasped it tight, stripped it, and with a few harsh strokes
     on a royal grant made it yours.
     And, Uncle, even in death,
          you trimmed them down farther,
          dividing their wealth

among us, your will true to its own nature
from first to last. You were true to nothing else.
And your legend, what of that? Well, I have learned
     that it is not myths
     reveal a man, but facts,
   those broken relics of you,
   who were never all of a piece,
you, who always severed ties yet sought firm ground,
made new alliances to see just what lay
   now within, now without your reach.
   A division on a ground
     the musicians call it,
     that was your true style:

a chord, then endless variations, hinting
now at this new modulation, now at that,
and each more refined, more rigorous, more stale.
     So your heirs have turned
     on each other in court
   over an inheritance
   long gone to ruin, rebellion,
and drink. So too, your lordship's reputation,
cheapened by the tarts and wastrels of Saint James's;
   there is not one of those weak-kneed
   bastards who—when drunk, dreaming
     of lost empires—will not
     bore me yet again

with that tale of how you outdanced all the braves
in the Seneca longhouse, so they might break
friendship with France, and further your British scheme
     to hold the Valley.
     And they tell it badly,
   beginning, like poor painters,
   with the atmosphere: smoky walls
of birch bark and ash staves, false faces hanging
in the murk with lips twisted and cheeks bulging
   as if they chewed a bitter root.
   Perhaps the tribal elders
     curse your high, frantic steps,
     or stare angrily

as, one by one, their young men rise and join you.
It is all so common. An artist would show
what moved you so: you wanted to be the fire
     kindled in their hall,
       you wanted not to cast
     shadows, but to be the source
     of all shadow, source of all light,
source of the very difference between them.
Decline, decline. . .The fire always less than God,
     and the dancer less than the fire,
     the shadow less than the man. . .
       And what of the shadow
       cast by the shadow?

Just how distant a relative would that be?
A young nephew, say, from Ireland, with his pack
full of pencils, brushes, signs of his longing
     for his own new world.
       It was yours already,
     the world I found; it required
     not artists, but artificers,
inheritors of established tracts, old deeds,
old visions, old vengeances, who pawn these off
     as their own. I, your mapmaker,
     recorded how your shadow fell
       on such and such a date,
       how it grew or shrank.

I'm at it still, a portraitist whose subject
escapes him, except in certain odd effects
caused by a shaky hand, or in mannerisms —
     defects in the style,
       a critic would call them —
     in which an old bitterness
     turns habitual elegance
against itself, turns light to half-light, darkness
to a shifting composition where nothing is clear
     except that you are present there
     and will never go away.
       You, who are the silent
       ground of all my speech. . .

Still, I must ask you this. Do you remember
how, when I first saw your country, I proposed
to paint its full extent, not in a series
    but as one great work?
    You laughed, and would not stop,
  except to say I must stay
  content with the place you set me —
my maps, my great house, your daughter in my bed,
a son's share of your estate — and not seek more.
  I knew then I must never hope
  that the Valley might be held
    in any hand but yours.
    Yes, and I know now

a son's portion is to starve, if he should fail
to consume his father, if he should not seize
the whole world for himself, and so learn to scorn
    all gifts but his own.
    I was too weak for that.
  I took what was offered,
  and I became the offering
the past demands. No one will remember me,
Uncle, unless they remember you as well.
  But will they recognize you,
  those who've not seen how I lived?
    I am your legacy.
    I am what is left.

Joseph Brant: Niagara, 1804

I have seen so much of Christian knavery and policy, that I am sick of
Europe, which loves war and hates peace, therefore I want and long to
have a wigwam near Great Pontiack.

Samuel Peters, LL. D., in a letter to the Mohawk chieftain Joseph
Brant, London, 1803

My Dear Samuel Peters,
I fear you do your continent and yourself
some small disservice. Europe,
as your letter suggests, may hardly seem a true home
to one whose birthplace (or birth-
right, as you would have it) includes the wild shore
of Memphramagog and those peaks

along whose bleak chalk crests
Rogers fled after his raid on Saint Francis.
(He told me some years later
that only the passing shadows of his rangers
gave the boulders of White Face
their famous appearance of a sinister
watchfulness. Viewed just at twilight

or noon, they were as blank
as a clean skull, and so filled his men with fear
that as many were lost there
to madness as to the French and their Algonquin braves.)
But perhaps your banishment
is more a blessing than you have acknowledged?
Birth assures a man of only

one final rite, and homes
are always fatal to those poor voyagers
whose inclination it is
to return, who forget salvation lies in the hope
that they need never come back.
No world is fallen but in our sad efforts
to recount it, as if the sum

of broken trails, faint lines
on parchment, could somehow equal your first sight
of a long stretch of rapids,
a rocky shore, gray water at dawn as the haze lifts,
or as a late mist settles,
as memory settles when we come too near
some original thing. Better,

I think, never to speak
of what we glimpse beyond ourselves, for fear
we will lose everything
to windings that share nothing in common with this world.
You ask how I liked London.
I best recall the masked ball to which I came
simply as myself, a Mohawk

in full war dress: leggings,
half my face painted, bearing a scalp axe, &ct.
This caused such astonishment
(till then I had worn my well-cut crimson uniform,
which is the prerogative
of a British officer and gentleman)
that the Turkish ambassador,

who had mistaken me
for some fop from Saint James's done up in plaster,
dye, and gauze, twisted my nose
to see what lay beneath. I let out the same war cry
that began the harsh battle

at Oriskany, and as the dancing stopped,
and the peers and the musicians

sought refuge where they could,
I raised my hatchet and leapt. The Turk's ladies
fainted, he fled, and the ball
was judged a success. But later, in my room, I knelt—
though this was not my custom—
and prayed aloud, not for the King's great, failed cause,
but for Sir William Johnson, Bart.,

who was, as you must know,
   the first royal minister to my people,
      my brother-in-law, my friend,
yes, almost my father. What I had shown those good lords
      in jest—that one must either
   trust appearances or trust nothing at all—
      I had learned from him years before.

   You recall how the French
and their Huron allies seized our northern forts
      one by one, the white ensigns
settling like fog over our forests, the ivory
      dress uniforms spilling down
   the St. Lawrence, as if even the dead rose
      against us and scattered the trails

      with hungry, wakeful bones.
   I was not yet sixteen. I still remember
      the horror of my first view
of a dead soldier's white leggings, white jacket, white face. . .
      a pale, empty face, nothing
   staring open-mouthed at nothing, at the world's
      foolscap wiped quite clean away.

   I marched with Sir William
and his company of Mohawks to relieve
      our last stronghold on Lake George,
which was not called by a king's name then, but by a saint's,
      a French saint's. How proud we were
   to rechristen it. How little the water
      changed, ready always to reflect

      any man's glance, a whore
who, seeming to return our embraces, gave
      nothing that could not be had
by all comers, who forgot us as we turned away.
      But who can say if truly
   we knew ourselves there at all till that one glimpse,
      our features rippling, flickering,

made our blood lively with fear,
with hatred, for the solitude waiting
past her quicksilver surface.
Near Ticonderoga, we met a British platoon
whose chief officer refused
to join our advance, so great was his terror
at the thought of a strange forest

blooming with savages
(those were his words) whose *murderous treachery*
(or skillful native courage)
was the distorting echo of his own cowardice.
Johnson beseeched him softly
at first, but soon he knew the coward's nature
beneath that imperious red

husk of a uniform.
He did what great men do when the matter lies
very near the heart. He stood,
and in the same quiet tone he asked, "You will not come?"
Then he untied one legging
and threw it at the officer's feet. Each brave
did likewise, and again Johnson's

"You will not come?" again
his Mohawks flung their leggings, again he spoke.
Each time the English captain
refused, and grew more pale, like a lost hunter
who stumbles into the rock den
where the copperheads shed their skins. "You will not. . ."
It was no longer a question.

Johnson stood naked there
with his men, raised his hatchet with theirs, his arms
and body painted like theirs.
Once more: "You will not come." The officer fell backward,
still shaking his head, trembling,
and all the blades were thrown to the ground. All our just
and civilized censure, all laws

binding men in honor,
had been invoked, had failed, and were now cast off,
leaving the spirit revealed
in its pure rage. Dear Sir, can you wonder if I thought
Sir William a great prophet
after that night. He showed me the prime mover,
first cause of all the civilities

and gestures of mankind,
of the world we make for ourselves: a hatred
for what would slip from our hands,
the cowardly, shimmering fabric of foreign things.
If we love appearances,
it is because this anger finds its best home
in opposites—courtly manners,

peaceful towns, ripe orchards—
so immanent is it in every detail
of our lives. He taught me trust,
piety, and devotion, and what I saw unveiled
in him, I took for gospel.
As I had taken his Christian god for mine,
I now saw this acrid spirit

reflected everywhere:
traced in firelight on a friend's face, on my face
shining in a sharpened knife. . .
or in those features I thought were mine. I knew myself
no longer. I was possessed
by the desire to carve the world's forms away,
to know this demon more purely,

to hoard all his power.
So my life went on, a litany of death
repeated over, over,
leading nowhere. Or should I say it led me always,
like a trail of ill omens—
blank skull of a wolf, footprints circling your own—
nearer to what I most regret:

dawn at Cherry Valley,
Butler smiling, unsheathing his sword, crying
"Let my bloody angels play!"
There is no need to recount that slaughter, to place blame,
    or to lead you, my patient
friend, much further through those horrors that changed me
    from acolyte to a mere man.

I found no vision there,
only human shards, only an empty lane
    where a dead man's outstretched hand
pointed toward a building as yet untouched by flame,
    except for one stain of soot
on the oak door, a dark trace, like a profile. . .
    Sir William's, I thought, or my own.

If I was startled then,
it was nothing to what followed. Within the house,
    someone sang, a low voice,
almost like that of a stream, its sweet, unending song.
    In the parlor, a woman
sat spinning, and when she looked at me I saw
    neither fear nor astonishment.

She went on with her work,
and although I begged her urgently to flee,
    to hide, or else to prepare
for death, she continued to sing. When I fell silent,
    she wound the thread once again,
and said there was no danger, that Joseph Brant
    was leader of the raiders

and a great friend of hers,
and he would surely come to find her. Dear Sir,
    I was streaked with paint and blood
so that Johnson himself would not have known me, but still
    her lack of recognition
so unnerved me that I was doubtful even
    of my own being, or of hers.

I did not know her name.
  Yet as her twisted thread reeled out, as her hands
    shone and vanished through the wheel
and she sang again, I knew that I stood near the hub
    of all things, alone with a force
  far beyond either my hatred or my awe,
    an outpouring so endlessly

    patient as to seem still,
  a pattern running through my life, a pattern
    which was all of life, changed now
as my vision wove it in her image. This was home:
    not the heart of the world, but
  the world itself, emptied of desire, waiting
    for me to create it anew,

    to wind its stiff fibers
  and feel my own strand passed around the spindle.
    So our homes find us, my friend,
when our spirits dwindle, when our shadows no longer
    quicken the earth's reticence.
  If you are that tired, you have earned your passage.
  There will be no need to seek it.

Your servant,

Joseph Brant

Mason Smith

Mason Smith, 49, grew up in Gouverneur. His first novel, Everybody Knows and Nobody Cares, *was published by Knopf in 1971. He taught at UC Santa Cruz 1971–73, returned to join his brother Everett in building wooden boats and began writing for* Sports Illustrated. *In 1975 he received a fellowship in fiction from the National Endowment for the Arts. He has written for* Gray's Sporting Journal, Esquire, Outside, The New York Times Book Review, Quest/79 *and* Quest/80, Yankee, Adirondack Life, Wooden-Boat, Small Boat Journal, Nautical Quarterly *and other periodicals. He now lives at Lake Ozonia, in the northern foothills of the Adirondacks near St. Regis Falls, where he writes and restores boats.*

The story is pretty young and hokey but I notice that it comes out of some of the same springs as my present work. You have these older voices, in bars, in chorus of coots with their sedentary wisdom, and in front of them vivid younger men, baffled by women. Even the artist who surrenders to the wish to live a life. And of course the North Country with my usual grudging admission of its hold. What's to be said, biographically, after that? We're so thin, here, that each of us probably thinks he owns the place; and in trying to write universally, we make regional literature, folk literature, maybe. So I'm wedging myself a new county, Olmstead, in between St. Lawrence and Franklin, and trying to write regional literature on the chance that that is way to hit the other mark. It's the same scene that Philander Deming couldn't stop denoting: where the land slopes down northward from the plateau to a blueish haze with glints of the St. Lawrence in it. Why one gets fixed in such a place I don't know, but I think it is that river, and Canada, and the woods and mountains to the south; yearnings and tensions because there is so much, and so little, of the world at hand. I'd give up, and I guess I have given up, all the possibly smart moves of a career for the poetry of a life here in these seasons, by this lake. Though not without migrations and raptures elsewhere which are salvations. Story of my life. If you are not just graced, you have to be intransigent, and get your credence out of going whole hog.

Loss of Isabel

People sodden down into comfortable habit have their losses. They suffer from change. They regard themselves as personages of fiction and see each other driven by demons they fondly suppose to be the products of their own fertile and generous appreciation—until those very forces produce an astoundingly real breach in their obscure ritual. Then they have nothing but themselves, and they fume and rage over their fate as we did over the loss of Isabel.

Lord knows we regulars of Harold's Restaurant live passively through enough awful tales, and passionately through enough others, without anyone's telling them. It has always been understood, too, how well such tales deserved to be put in writing, and who would do it. We all enjoy fine reputations amongst ourselves, which we jealously guard each other from ever having to prove.

This time, though, it is different. No one has said as much, but whether from the profundity of the outrage (for we are, as we would never have thought, subject to outrage) or from some wretched irascible perversity of humor, we are smitten, we feel mean, and I have sensed our compact broken and this indecent demand made of me to write. On account of Isabel.

Or on account of a pair of men known half-spuriously as the Chittenden boys, who lived among us in some inscrutable, stallionish, no doubt absurd combat—locked in it, inseparable. On account of them and Isabel.

While I write, Lijah Ayers, who passed with us for the world's best driver of draft horses, dies of injuries from the crash of his old pickup, which he never could operate—a fact, we used to say, that added to his credit with animals. Safford Haskell stays drunk, having at last provoked our legendary deerslayer to shoot his wife (in the arm). And our outlaw, the Indian John Sinohese, who was always too frightened of punishment to get caught, waits trial in the Saranac jail, for petty thievery. Scum we've been called; and scum we are. It's the end.

The Chittenden boys were regulars, like all of us, of Harold's Restaurant Hotel. Not a hotel really; a place with uncountable and uninhabitable cold empty rooms overhead and a faithful family of ruffians at the bar. The Chittenden boys were our own. It isn't too much to say, in fact, that they were the most ardently pondered, most reverently appreciated devils among us, which is saying much in any such rough-spoken pack of woods and country workingmen. We were a family there, fatherless and motherless (well — no; we had our duchess) but of an understood solidarity, and these boys were our pride and joy, the most confounded tragic disgraces of us all.

They were different enough. Seth, the dark one with the gleaming eyes under his harsh black brush-strokes of brows, had the rugged make and the lithe, self-sparing motions of the hereditary dairy farmer. He was reticent, even morose, and yet his words, the few that there were, fell into curiously startling figures. Where you or I might say we couldn't swim any better than a baby, he'd say "no more'n an anvil."

The other one, Dick, was physically a case of hard work laying lean muscle on a frame that had grown up loose and longboned on the presumption that it would never have to fold down next to a cow. An awful error. His red face, where it wasn't burned, was freckled, and his sun-bleached eyebrows gave it a cheery openness which his pale blue eyes, lit by the faded blue workingshirt he always wore, warmly confirmed.

Shuffleboard (Harold keeps a marvelously waxed, idiosyncratically leveled table) is an individualist's game; you can hate your partner and rival him bitterly, all to the good of your score. Well, those two incorrigibles were our champions. They never played each other, never played apart, and almost never lost. Seth shot either handed with the sides of the board for guide, and Dick shot freehand with the left, and we all said the reason was that neither could stand to do anything the same way as the other.

Together in open hostility they farmed the Chittenden place. That is to say, the Elthorpe, the Donovan, and the Delaye places that were, along with the original Chittenden homestead. Just the two of them — all that land and a herd that, taking in young stock and dry cows, would go over a hundred head. Of course they had big machinery. And then they were young fellows, both of them.

They lived alone in the big black house on the hill just above where the 'pike crosses the Sugarbush brook, and they let it go to the devil. They weren't in it but just to sleep and scramble eggs, so to say.

We speculated Dick—Dick whoever he was, for he wasn't actually Chittenden—must have done the meals, so far as they were done. Because we noted what can only be called an air of moral superiority on the side of Seth, one to which we could just faintly see Dick giving way. We pictured him, flushed a little, wordlessly turning his hand to the job, and we were pretty certain that he made Seth pay for it in some other coin.

To think how we wondered what prevented them from having a woman there! There were plenty of cooks and housekeepers hereabout who would have been glad of a chance to queen it over that fine old house, in return for stuffing them three times a day. Even a wife, or wives (for the sake of their jealous equality!)—why not? If their personal attractions hadn't been sufficient, they were well off; that was a good farm, which goes for much around here. Mightn't we have thought, we wonder now, of our tainted, feral, amorous, fattish, bizarre, of our quite mad Isabel?

To see ourselves as the playthings of some demonic fictioner, I have told you, was our way of living with our own misshapen lives. It is a kind, innocent maybe, a time-beguiling way. But after the loss of Isabel, sensing ourselves molested, we found it wasn't enough to say, "Ain't them two the drivenest devils ever?"

In the first place, we knew about Abby.

Abby was Seth Chittenden's sister. We regulars of Harold's knew Abby to look at only. She took the snug tavern to be not her province. Oh, she put her braided head in the door once in a great while to call the boys to milking. That was in the days when "the Chittenden boys" meant Seth and his real brother Hoyt, who used to incline to forget the cows.

She had the Chittendens' strong dark eyebrows, their long lashes and their shining eyes, except that hers were green, not brown. She was young, hardy, clear-skinned, handsome; and she blushed to the roots every time she looked into Harold's place.

Well, old Sewell Chittenden, with a lame back from his milkhauling days, got ready to retire. Hoyt, the real brother, quit. And Abby went up to the lake to waitress at Corinne Belliveau's little resort. All this happened pretty near at once, so that we in Harold's were saying, that spring, that "Seth had the summer to get himself a wife."

He didn't. He probably never intended to, never could bring himself to try, because it wouldn't have required trying. There are some good wives around here now that would sooner have been his than whose they are. Anyway, what the trouble really was, was that none of them remotely measured up to Abby.

There are farm girls and farm girls, and some of them could spoil a man for life.

Abby would ride her pinto for the cows and count it entertainment. An ice storm meant she got to milk by hand. And if a calf was coming backwards in the night—it wasn't fun perhaps, but it was duty: she'd tie baling twine around its feet and heave on that, in time with Seth, however long it took the cow to freshen. You've seen sisters put their brothers' marks too high.

Our jests on that interpretation only turned him black. "She'll be back by silo-filling," he would say; he never used her name, but the pronoun *she* meant Abby.

The summer wore on, and several women waited. His days were filled with work, and one by one they passed. *She'd* be back in the fall, *she'd* tend to him, feed him right, talk to him, make him talk. . . . Who can say how he anticipated her return?

Meanwhile, though, Abby Chittenden was serving, cleaning, making beds and so forth, at Corrine Belliveau's. And staying at Corrine's was one gangling blue-eyed painter named Dick. The last name is forgotten. It fell to our inclination to use that old phrase we had used for Hoyt and Seth: the Chittenden boys.

Yes, he was a painter and at that time apparently put together some kind of a living by it. He had come to the North Country to paint Adirondack nature—had done such things before: gone to some different place, to learn it and paint it. Corrine says he would stand on the end of the dock, and look, and look, and look. At what she knew not. And then, hardly taking his eyes off the haze down the lake, he would move, head forward but upright as if he were being dragged by the eyes, slide a canoe into the water, and with awkward long-reaching strokes propel the craft crazily toward his vision.

He came to dinner in awful old tennis shoes, his usual faded blue shirt, and khaki pants which looked, the laps of them, as if he had mixed paints on his thighs. He rolled his sleeves above the elbows, certainly not out of vanity over his arms which were brittle sticks at that time. But the almost white, sun-bleached hair over his mottled burn offended nobody, nor even his smell of turpentine and tube-colors.

Abby had to serve this painter. Our dairymaid Abby had to approach this big beguiling child-of-another-nature. At first, they say, he struck her funnybone. He would be telling some wild story—his tales were apt to be supernatural ones, about whispering winds and communication with porpoises and the like—and he would be waving his long arms around, so that Abby would have to tap him on the shoulder or even lay hold of one arm for a minute to put his pie down in front of him. Then she'd just barely make it back to the kitchen to do her laughing.

Later on it changed. I've heard of a picture of her by him. Nobody seems to know where it is. Nobody even describes it. I mention it here in place of all we don't know and don't want to know.

For, some way or other, he didn't behave himself.

"She had to be operated on." You heard that phrase and this one: "He was gentleman enough to marry her."

Neither phrase is enlightening, and believe it or not we do not speculate on them. They are Corinne Belliveau's words, who says nothing else, but put Dick out and refuses to abide where there is mention of his name.

Apparently it was when it became clear that Abby was not quite right, afterwards, that Dick made his "gentlemanly" offer. Offer, for she did not marry him. What do you think? She could not. She was not permitted. Seth Chittenden refused to allow it. Stricken, doomed, her fidelity to Dick her last and best possession of faith, she pleaded with her brother, and he repulsed her. By the violence of his oath, he froze his sister's will.

She must already have been shaken in it. She can only have surrendered herself purely and unfathomably with a sightless optimism, a thoughtless confidence; but the whole visible world was the painter's darling, not Abby alone. She must have been shaken to learn this, and her plea to Seth have been, itself, an act of resignation. She accepted and became proud in her brother's pride.

She stayed. Seth had, in a way, won his mate.

But incredibly and yet inevitably he was cheated. Dick was there, Dick heard the oath, and he would not leave. Seth could shoot him if he liked, but he was staying. Abby could send him away, but he would go no farther than the barn. Seth broke up and burned Dick's paint-box. It made the painter wince, but he lingered. Then Seth just simply beat him with his fists till he could only crawl, and shut him out of the house.

The artist crawled into the barn.

Next morning, swollen and scarred—but clean: he washed off the blood in the pump-house; and fragrant: of ground oats and corn instead of turpentine—Dick silently watched Seth go through the chores, and started in to breakfast behind him. He didn't get there.

If he ate, those two days, he ate what could be scavenged in a barn. One can survive there without any great resourcefulness. He drank raw milk and did not attempt the house. But he made careful note of what Seth did, and in the morning when Seth came out, the chores were finished except for the milking. And then while Seth ate his breakfast, the phantom of the barn was wheeling silage to the herd and throwing down the bedding.

The second morning, while Seth lingered with his Abby over breakfast, even the gutters were being cleaned, and when Seth came out again to face the old rigors of dairyfarming, he found nothing left to do but drive the tractor out to the meadows with the spreader.

You put together for yourself what he must have thought as he steered over the chopped stubble of that summer's corn-land. For that night they ate together. They stayed up late, silent, the three of them. Finally the men both went to bed. And this became the pattern of their life, while Abby lived.

Between two mistrustful loving men, a brother and a seducer, Abby's life faded out. In torture? That is a pretty good case of what torture is, I should think. With her death we got our first good glimpse of Dick. The two men stood side by side at the grave, Seth looking down into it, Dick away off at the leafless trees.

Not so long after, they appeared one night in Harold's little bar room and, pacing each other carefully, engulfed two equal and prodigious rations of beer. Dick had hardened. You could see that with his greater size he ought to be able to beat Seth into the barn for the night if he ever took such a notion. Seeing a certain vicious bitter respect reciprocated between them, we guessed he had done it. And then had proclaimed his intention of having a drink. Seth wouldn't have let him go alone. Out of tenacious habit he pursued the ruddy giant. They drank without talking. They watched one another's eyes. When both savagely drunk, they left together.

After that they came regularly. Still the two of them! We got our heads together when they'd gone. What was up? He, Ryder – Raeger – whatever his name – could have left. He could have walked away from all that. What should keep him to this endless antipathy now that Abby was in the ground? And him such a painter! Why should he linger on the farm, striving dawn to dusk in all that unlovely –! giving up even his own name for that of Chittenden, and living in ugly bondage with the strange, manful, antagonistic Seth?

The only answer was that neither of those men intended to let the other return to a normal life. Abby had been the only hope of them both, or the only honor, and to give her memory up to the other would be for each a curse. Who's to say that Seth wouldn't now have decided to take one of the women that were just waiting for him to ask? except that Dick silently forbade it? Love for Abby, we said, possessed them still, and it bonded their mutual hatred with ambiguity, so that their jealous watchfulness took on the glimmer of comradeship.

They farmed together for those two or three years—and *farmed*; they didn't drift. They seemed to have, together, these two vengeful enemies, a genius for running a farm at the same time as each bore up, with bitter gladness, his end of their everlasting warfare.

Let one of them glance at a woman, and as relentless, coarse, and bloody a shindy as you would ever want to see was on.

Not that it didn't get to happening now and again after a year or so. Oh, no.

By this time Dick too enjoyed a position with the women, like Seth's, as a man to pin one's life to. Abby? They were both forgiven for Abby! And then some! Their story itself was like secret wealth, noble blood, magic power; and there were women who might have thought privately that proud Abby's life (since did she not share the guilt? did she not have them both a while?) was not too high a price for it. Oh, their story made them priceless!

If that were all, it wouldn't be told.

Year passed year. They might have gone on forever the same, but that a cap had been set for those boys. Caps had been set many times for one or the other to no avail. But this was different, for the cap this time was Isabel's.

Never mind the last name, even though her people are all gone. A woman decent enough looking underneath that ludicrous attire and those wiry-curled permanents, but kept a maid by the suspicion of a dangerous insanity that persisted around her; a scent, as it were, a feral scent that gave predators concern for their own safety. Isabel, female as all the circles of hell themselves, whisked freely among us unharmed, greeting with alternately chaste and passionate kisses ten or twenty unmerciful scoundrels from out of the Seaway and the farmland and devil knows what dens in the woods who wouldn't think twice about undoing the Holy Virgin. I mean, our tastes are catholic; get drunk, buy a bottle, and any living thing with the proper places under her clothes will do; off we go to a chilly cabin heated by kerosene, where half-wild dogs share the bed. But never any mischief done to Isabel. Do you see? No one thought it safe! That gives you an impression. A dreaded whirlpool she seemed, a vortex of delayed, mad passion to which it may be none of us felt himself equal.

Then there was the class distinction. On the death of her parents, an immodest sum had been invested for Isabel, which yielded her a modest check every month or so. This she disbursed with heart-stopping arbitrariness. No one would have had the audacity to claim her for himself.

And she bore herself like a middle-aged dowdy duchess; the benevolent kisses, the shawls, the heavy knit sweaters, riding boots — never mind!

She, it was she! who made us all feel like tragic men. She who defended and praised, gave each his shame and torment, told us all how we were damned souls and cursed from high and low! She who cemented the compact between us! Who couldn't be touched, couldn't be known, whom we worshipped for our own wretched reflections in those tattered-iris's eyes!

How shall I tell you now that it struck us as comical when Seth and Dick would go out on the hard-packed snow and spatter it with each other's life's blood over our ward and protectress, beneficent beer-buying Isabel? How shall I tell you there was nothing we liked better?

We might have wondered, might have prevented, might have saved her, might have — what? There were signs for us to see.

Isabel greeted Dick with a different kiss from the rest. It had a tinge of — of abandon, you know, as if she were trying to match souls with him. And he would respond with a jolly pat where most of us thought there might be thistles or a fox-trap. Then off she would run to Seth, transforming herself on the way; and Seth submitted to her sisterly treatment with a minor flush of his cheeks. She insinuated herself with each as his partisan against the other and their team partisan when they played shuffleboard. Dick often set her on his knee after a victory and, stuttering loudly, would try to convey to her some far-fetched tale over the throbbing din of the juke-box. Over it all would rise her laughter, and then suddenly it would stop, she would leap to the side of the embarrassed Seth and they would whisper fondly and privately.

Seth, now a somber, affectingly sad Seth, awoke her sympathy, her warm motherly womanhood — or ought one to say her sisterliness? She sat by him steadfastly, touching his shoulder with hers and not looking at him but, as it were, defending him with a warning in her eyes for anybody who approached. But we would also see her fix her crazed eyes on Dick with a violently suggestive gaze, with that same gaze that used to fill the rest of us with dread of some irrevocable mistake, that wild, engulfing gaze, and draw him like a vision into an intimate, forbidding threesome.

Isabel, who claimed to be, sometimes, the duchess of a kind of — is it cheese? — duchess of Camembert, in Normandy — who held all our stories somewhere in her bulky garments, somewhere on her careless person, who turned herself for each of us into just the thing we wanted to be terrified to find —!

There were signs, God yes, but still the outrage stung us when Isabel vanished from our midst.

Vanished. Without warning. So did the Chittenden boys.

Oh, I fictionalize, I am irresponsible; them one might see in the morning if one was out that way, one or other of them, spreading manure, riding the high tractor over the snow-covered meadows. But not Isabel. No one ever saw her again, to say he had seen her for sure.

After a time the boys began coming, sometimes but not always together, to the tavern. They drank heartily, and they swore heartily at everything under the sun but each other, and their shuffleboard game went to the dogs and they didn't care. They were positively genial. They never mentioned our loss of Isabel, and no one mentioned her to them. And when a report reached our ears, once upon an afternoon the following summer, of a woman splashing happily "in all her natural splendor" in a secluded turn of the Sugarbush brook — which presently old Farnan, who takes trout where you and I would swear there are none, swore off as being utterly barren of fish — we gave up our duchess, without a qualm.

I say without a qualm. What in hell *am* I to say? That we were outraged? A woman shared, that's nothing. A surrogate sister shared by brothers? That's a little something. But *Isabel*; it was, it had to be, it could not be our Isabel.

Look! I commit this horrid groan. Lijah burns out his clutch and drives into a tree — the best man with horses in the woods! Adultery is suddenly real reason for murder, robbers rob, and Roger Cooke is off in Potsdam marrying a waitress — talk of your surrogates — see! How could they catch her, how could they dare, how could they make flesh of that mad virginal untouchable mother of us all?

No harm came to them.

And all is indecent and tame.

Barry Targan

Harry Belten and the Mendelssohn Violin Concerto *received the Iowa School of Letters Award in Short Fiction.* Surviving Adverse Seasons *received the Saxifrage Award from the University of North Carolina.* Kingdoms, *a novel, received the Associated Writing Programs Award. I teach at the State University of New York, the University Center at Binghamton. My main interests are building boats, boating, gardening. Besides reading and writing, that is.*

As for my fiction, I see myself as working within the oldest tradition of story-telling, where narrative provides a pressure out of which character can develop.

The Garden

He hammered the sharp, stinging sound into the thick, wooded hills that cupped his land in a bowl, driving the large #16 common nails into the new joists and rafters and studs and then into this terrain. He meant to stay. He had taken the inheritance and had put it down, like a gambler, perhaps, but not like a fool: there had been method, if not system. And his father would have approved. It was not the taking of chances that got you into trouble, it was the bad odds. So he had played it safe enough. He had learned what he needed in Rhode Island and then in Sweden, and now, with what was left of the money, he had bought this place and the tools and machinery for his work, and the important wood. From now on whatever happened was up to him.

He drove the nails with the heavy framing hammer. With each two-pound blow the nail sang higher, as the length of the steel short-ened into the lumber: first a percussive thud and then three rising notes, thin and vibrant as harmonics on an E string. The weather had been good for building, had rained little. This extension to the rickety house would be finished by the weekend; not the casements or insulation and wiring, or the painting and trim, but the framing and sheathing and siding. He could take his time with the rest and with fixing the old house itself. He had all the summer that was coming after this good spring. And more. But by Sunday he could set up his tools and machines and benches in the extension, and then begin to think of the cabinets and chests and tables he would build out of the planks of pearwood and beech and cherry that he had stored in the air under tarpaulins. But now he kept his mind to this task, saving the promise of the cabinets and tables as once he had saved the promises of dessert.

He turned the last joist on edge and tugged it a fraction until it dropped into place, the notches he had cut in the two-by-six sliding down firmly and exactly. He sighed with small pleasure as the pieces of wood melded. Heavy rafters or dovetail joints along the edges of elegant boxes, it was the same to him. He handled all wood the same way. He spiked the rafter down at either end and in the middle across the central beam. He stood up. This was done. He would stretch, go down, drink some coffee, and then begin to cover the roof with the plyscore. He looked around at the rimming hills and picked out birch and maple and white oak that he would take down someday, to be sawed into material by a mill. And the air was still dry. It would not rain. It might not rain for a week.

The battered Volkswagen popped and shuddered its way up his hill, kicking stones out of the loosened gravel road, the sound of the car rolling around more and more quickly as it came closer until it was directly down from him, next to his truck in the rough driveway. It stopped. The last of its banging waved back over the hills. She got out of the car.

"I'm Jane Friant," she shouted to him and then ducked back into the car and hauled out a paper shopping bag, *Pricechoppers* printed on both sides of it. She picked her way through the flotsam of the building site. "I'm Jane Friant," she said next to him, quietly. "I live over there." She pointed widely to the entire east, to the horizon, to the Green Mountains of Vermont. But then, more precisely, "On Christie Road. I live about five miles down. A small house, a few acres, a loaf of bread, a jug of wine. And a view. Hi." She put out her hand. They shook. "I heard you were here, but I've been traveling a little and working a lot. And the gardening this time of year takes what's left and more. I would have come sooner." She looked around. "Where's *your* garden?"

"No garden."

"No garden? But what are you going to talk about?" She laughed, thrush-like, watery and quavering. "Whenever we get together, that's what we all talk about, our gardens. Whose peas have come in, how heavy the Japanese beetles are this year, what to do about slugs, blossom-end rot in the tomatoes, strategies to foil the woodchucks. I think you should put in a garden in self-defense. Oh here." She handed over the shopping bag. "Welcome."

"How about some coffee?" he asked, taking the bag.

"Sure." She followed him toward his house. "Can we have the coffee in the new room? I love it, the skeleton of a house, where you can see how it all works. There are very few things you can see that way, clearly, all at once, what makes it all work. It's a shame you have to cover it up."

On chairs that he brought out of the house they sat under the open rafters. She had brought him homebaked bread and jars of jelly, jam, and preserves, all her own. They ate the bread and jelly and drank the boiled coffee that he had quickly made. She drank the coffee and winced.

"This coffee is awful. The bread and jelly are terrific but the coffee is awful." She made her thrush-laugh. She looked about at the strict intelligence of the walls of studs with the headers set for the windows, the wide sills, the tripled two-by-fours that made up the corner columns.

"I guess you don't want more?" He held the camping pot up by its long bail, offering.

"Oh well, why not. Half a cup." He poured. She looked into the cup. He watched her face. Her skin was very smooth. Even in the April chill, her skin did not tighten across her bones.

Then she said, "I feel like something in a *New Yorker* ad." With her hands she placed the caption for him in the air. "Frame up." She started to write the copy, then stopped. "Guess what the ad is selling."

He shrugged. "The house?" He did not read the *New Yorker*.

"Oh no, the ad never sells what it first seems to be about. Go ahead, guess again." She sipped the coffee and puckered. Then, "Oh," like a gasp. "Look."

She pointed up with her finger, but did not raise her arm. "The hawks. Red-tails. He's courting her." They looked up. One hawk swung slowly up and up, in infinitely small increments but in a widening gyre. It did not appear to be rising. All around that hawk the other hawk, the male, barreled and looped, racing unimaginably high and then dropping like a diver tucked tightly into himself, hurtling past her and then in an instant braking and pulling up before her, throwing wide his wings, the pinions still streaming, in a massive display. Then he would fall back and begin again to thread through her slow, tightly banked spiral.

They looked up through the rafters, so they could only see the hawks slatted, chopped as in a strobe effect or like stop-action photos put on film run quickly. The hawks were here and then here and then here.

" 'The achieve of, the mastery of the thing,' " she quoted. He chewed her bread slowly. "Hopkins?" she offered. The hawks had sailed away.

She was Jane Friant. She lived on Christie Road and took care of herself and was trying to succeed as a writer of fiction here in the hills of Washington County in upstate New York, hard upon the border of southern Vermont. She had graduated from Bennington, not far from here, three years ago and had been busy ever since, writing and raising food and putting it by.

"How's it going?" he asked.

"Which, the writing or the garden?"

"Both."

"Well, I haven't missed any meals yet. But writing? How can you tell? I'm happy with what I do. I get stories published in good little literary magazines often enough to make me think I'm alive and well. I get myself invited to colleges to give readings and to be on panels. I apply for grants. I review books for twenty-five dollars and the books. I write letters to editors. I keep in touch. Is this an answer?" She reached out and put her hand over his. It was hard and calloused like his own, a laborer's hand, a field worker's hand. Was she asking him this, or only demanding his closest attention? "I'm writing well enough to suit me. I know I'm not kidding myself. I've got a right to do this. I'm not living in a romantic fantasy. I'm working hard at what I want to do." She released him.

"Is that enough?" he asked. "For a writer, I mean? Isn't there more? I can make these chairs and sit on them and that's enough, except I need money so I'll try to sell them. But a writer can't do that, can you? You can't use a story. You can't just stop with the writing."

"No," she said. She stood up and walked about on the rough sub-flooring, as on a stage. Her work boots beat upon the flooring. She stuck her hands into the back pockets of her jeans, tightening her plaid mackinaw shirt across her flat chest. "No," she said. "You're right. A writer must have an audience. *Must!*" she shouted the word. It circled up like the hawks had. At the opening for one of the large windows that would look out to Vermont, she turned and stood like a painting in the frame. Her hair, long and black, had fallen free of whatever had held it. She hoisted herself up onto the window sill and braced herself against the jack studs that would hold the casement, wrapping her arms around them as if they were the chains of a playground swing. "And there's more, curse it. There's fame and fortune. And praise. Adulation. Immortality."

She was laughing now, shouting and laughing, telling the truth and stepping back from it too. "I'm twenty-five," she shouted to him from her window seat across the work room. She leaned forward, straining, as if she would force the sill to swing high into the room. "I've got thirty-five more years to win the Nobel Prize." She whooped and clapped her hands and tottered a little on the window sill.

"Look out," he said. He reached out his hand as if he could reach her to steady her.

"What?" she shouted over her own noise, over her own ebullience.

"Look out," he said again. "Don't fall."

"Oh no," she said. "Not me." She hopped down from the window sill and came back to him.

They finished half the bread and a good part of the jar of jelly. It was a jelly made from violets. She talked to him about where he was, what it was like here in season, where to buy things that he might need, who lived hereabouts. Then he stood up. He had half a day's work left, the roof to sheath and more. He explained that he would do the roof before the walls, so he could use the large room for storage right away. He had wood waiting for him at Hartley's in New York, rosewood and Brazilian mahogany, and there was ash and butternut that he would pick up from a friend outside Poughkeepsie. He needed the storage. He walked with her down to her car.

"Thanks a lot," he said. "Thanks for the welcome. I'm sorry I can't sit longer. We'll do this again."

"Why don't you come for supper?" it occurred to her, and she brightened to the idea. "Sure. Come on. I'll have Jaeger and Mara over. They're painters from further down the road. Come on. Start to meet the folks."

"Like this?" he said. "I stink. I haven't had a shower in a week. The hot water's not hooked up yet." But he did want to go to her supper.

"Come early. Take a shower at my place. Come at seven. I'll tell Jaeger and Mara to come at eight." She started the car and turned it around, the noise of it a conclusion. As she started to drive away, he shouted for directions.

"Christie Road," she barely shouted back as the car started to skid and twist down the driveway. "You'll see the car."

He fell. He reached to pull a sheet of the heavy three-quarter-inch plywood into square across the rafters, and the brace he had laid down to stand against snapped under him. He slid three feet down the incline of the roof and then into the house, between the rafters that he had set on sixteen-inch centers—close enough to bear the heavy snows he had been warned of, wide enough for a man to fit through. As he dropped, he fell against the jagged end of the broken brace. A large slivered end stabbed into him, a knife of wood thrusting up into the large muscle over his left shoulder blade. He landed softly, bending into the shock, taking it the way a spring compresses; then he let himself out and up like a gymnast coming off the high horse. And then he flattened himself quickly on the sub-flooring, the pain sparking in him, up through his neck and down his entire left side into his ankle.

He let the pain alone. You could not fight the pain. He closed his eyes and waited. The pain was like a sound in him, a roaring. He tried to think what the sound was, if it was a locomotive, or the wind, or a waterfall. He gave it up, letting the sound increase until it began to block itself. When the pain finally receded from the rest of his body and settled into a throb in the actual wound, he sat up slowly and reached around to touch. He could not reach the wound, only the end of the spear of wood. He took the end of the wood in his fingers and yanked it out quickly. His blood ran a little but clotted in his shirt and against his back.

He climbed back up onto his roof. He established a firmer brace, squared the four-by-eight sheet of plywood and nailed it down. And then another sheet, and the next, through the afternoon until the roof was covered. The shoulder would hurt more in the morning than it did now. The bruise would be worse than the cut. Now he hardly felt it. What he felt was the house tightening, coming into being accurately. He went about with his four-foot-long straightedge, testing the plumb of the studs and the corner columns to see if he had skewed them with the roofing, but nothing had moved. The bubble in the leveling tube floated unvaryingly between the scored lines. What he felt was a future coming into a shape. For the rest of the afternoon he worked at cutting the hole in the roof and boxing it where the metal chimney of his wood stove would emerge.

At six o'clock he stopped and came down. It was darkening. Next week daylight saving time would start again, and he would have more time to work at the end of the day. And it would be warmer. Winter had not altogether gone out of the land. There were cracks and pockets all over with ice still in them. And in the clear, cloudless high-pressure weather the night temperatures would drop far down, to two or three degrees Celsius at the least.

He rummaged in his sleeping room in the old house for clean clothes. He wrapped underwear and socks in a heavy cotton shirt, and those in a pair of clean denims. He took out of the closet a thick and intricate poncho designed and woven for him by Heldogras in Sweden.

Heldogras. He would look at her from the woodworking shop, across the courtyard. She would be working at the great loom, with the beater swinging from the overhead beam. At ten o'clock each morning, never sooner, she would turn to look for him and then wave. One day at ten o'clock she had held up the finished poncho and waved it like a flag, a signal, and then she had put it on. It fit her as well as it would fit him. He understood. He left the workshop and went over to her in the weaving studio, sawdust and wood shavings trailing after him. Heldogras's teacher had scolded him for his dust.

They left the weaving studio right then, Thursday morning, and they did not return to their classes until Monday noon.

The Konstfackskolan was fixed on the far north edge of Stockholm, just where the city begins to flutter off into the endlessness of the Swedish coniferous forests that wash unbroken into the northern snow fields. They left the Konstfackskolan and stayed together wherever the next day, the next hour, would lead them. They made no plans, needed none. By Sunday they were in Gaule, 185 kilometers from Stockholm. Heldogras had friends in Gaule, and, all of them drunk, her friends drove them back by three o'clock in the morning to his apartment, to his room in the apartment that he shared with Kurt and Bjorn. When he and Heldogras had awoken at seven, he had gotten out of bed and put on the poncho to go to the bathroom. The wool on his bare skin was like Heldogras had been—not rough at all, but surprising, a sensitivity like loving itself. Unbearable. He had taken off the poncho and gone naked past Kurt and Bjorn in the kitchen.

Peter Martin. She had contrived his name into the poncho on its inner side at the back of the neck. She said she had done that because now whenever he wore the poncho he would feel his name there and remember her. And that was true.

He put the poncho back carefully on its special hanger in the closet. From one of his duffle bags he hauled out a dark brown crew-necked elbow-patched sweater, his freshman football sweater from Brown. In Sweden he had removed the numerals from it. But, as with Heldogras's poncho, when he wore this sweater he remembered that past, too.

His history was a history of leavings. He had gone to Brown for a year—his father's school, and what would have been his father's choice for him. But Brown had been his own choice too, as much as any other. He had no argument for or against Brown. He went. It had been a satisfactory year, but it had not meant enough to him to want to return. In that year he had found the Rhode Island School of Design: the shops, the machinery, the skills, the lucidity of the purposes, the elegance of the India ink on the white scrolls—it all alerted him. He was admitted to RISD and stayed two years, increasingly centering on woodworking until the dean had called him in to talk about his "overwhelming exclusivity," the dean had called it. The dean was sympathetic and helpful. He had seen it happen often, young design students falling into love with the making itself, finding themselves as craftsmen first and maybe forever. It was a good discovery to make. Better happily now than miserably later, when it was too late to do anything about it. The dean had told him about the

Konstfackskolan. He told him that it was the best of all possible places to learn his craft. His art.

He had stayed at the Konstfackskolan for two years, twenty-four continuous months with only small vacations. He could have stayed another year to complete the three-year program, but there was no more that he needed to learn. The third year would have been a year of refinement.

And it would have been a third year with Heldogras. Then he had thought that, if he had stayed with her for that year more, he would never leave her. He would either stay in Sweden or bring her back to this country. Back to what? He had thought that then. Now he did not know.

He knelt down and reached far under his bed for a pair of shoes. He hadn't worn shoes since he had sat with the lawyers and closed on the property. From then on he had worn only his usual work boots. As he reached far under for his shoes, the wound on his back split apart slightly. He had forgotten it. The chill had deepened. His sweat had caked around him in the cold, stiffened, so the wound had opened more like a break, a fracture. He had left Heldogras and he did not want to think about it.

The water streamed over him in vines and cords and ribbons. His week and the April coldness washed off and out of him. He had shaved first and now he was showering, turning the water hotter and hotter each minute or two. He remembered the sauna heat of Sweden, him and Heldogras in the sauna in the basement of her apartment house, where sometimes there would be seven or eight men and women mixed together. He had never gotten used to that. But he had learned heat. Dry or wet, he had learned the pleasure of it, the heat working through the flesh down to the bones and then into the bones themselves. The bathroom was blank with steam. The water cleaved his skull. He looked down, and around his feet the water swirled pink from his blood.

He reached around his back to feel the wound, but everything was too wet. He turned off the shower and watched as blood ran down his haunch and his leg. He moved his left arm. There was still a piece of wood in him. The heat had worked it loose enough to hurt. When he moved his arm, the bleeding quickened.

He dried off as much of himself as he could and then wrapped the towel around his waist and tucked it into itself. The blood spread in the towel. He would owe her a towel. He opened the bathroom door and called her. In the small house the bathroom was on the same floor as the kitchen. He called again. When she got to the bathroom he explained before she could be surprised.

She was very efficient. She ordered him to lie down on the floor, on the towel she placed over the rug in front of the Franklin stove with its small fire. She brought over a professional-looking box of assorted bandages and bottles, pins, tweezer, clamps, cotton gauze and other things in plastic bags. It looked like more than first aid. She sponged the wound and examined it closely. She felt around it with her fingers.

"Does this hurt?" She pinched gently.

"Haah," he arched with the pain.

"Yes. Well, the problem is that a piece of wood is lodged in there at an angle. It's got to come out. Whenever you move the wood saws away in there."

"Take it out," he said.

"Me?"

"No. The cat. Get the goddam cat to do it." He did not like to be hurt or sick. More than discomfort, he would feel anxiety, a low-grade infection of panic seeping through him when his body did not work right.

"Listen, it's deeper in there than you think. I'd have to fish around to get at it. That would *really* hurt. And you need something to prevent infection anyway, and probably a tetanus shot. Come on. I'll take you to the hospital. We can get there in fifteen minutes. It's over in Cambridge. I'll leave a note for the Jaegers." She continued to sponge his back.

"No. Just do it. Clean wood is safe. You don't get infected."

"That's an old wives' tale. You can get infected by any unsterile. . ."

"Will you just *do* it? Will you just shut up and *do* it?" He tightened all over. He rose up a little. The pain was severe in that position. It knocked him down.

She went to work. He felt the cold tweezer like a branding iron on his skin, but that was all he felt there. What happened now was like the splinter had turned into a large spike and was driving into his heart through his lungs. He could not breathe. He squirmed and arched up. She put her knee on him and forced him flat and still.

"I've got hold of it. Don't move. Here goes." She pulled it out. He screamed and crawled forward nearly out of his loosened towel. The heat from the Franklin stove quickly warmed his exposed rump. She drew the towel back up over him. He sobbed once, a great heaving out of the rest of the trauma. She stroked his neck and with her other hand continued to sponge the wound. Then she held a large gauze pad to it.

"It's stopping," she said. "You could probably use a couple of stitches, but I have some butterfly bandages and they might work. I'll try to stop the bleeding first with surface pressure. That's the best way."

He was exhausted. The long day of work, the accident, the relaxing shower, this tension and pain. But it was more the release that had drained him. He could have held out, but he could not contain the giving in: he swept down the backwash, grew bleary and vague and thick under her hands.

"You know all about this?" he said.

"This is the country. I'm a member of the Volunteer Emergency Corps. They give you a good first-aid course. Do you want to join? We always need people." She rubbed an antiseptic salve over the wound and replaced the pressure pad. She continued to rub his neck.

He was falling asleep. His voice was drifting away from him. "Are you taking notes? Are you going to write about this?"

She was surprised. "No." Then, "Yes. But not how you think it. Did you ever hear of Trigorin, the character in Chekhov's play *The Seagull*?" She guessed that he had not. "He was always writing things down in a notebook that he carried with him. Whatever caught his eye or his ear he would write down. He would make his stories out of what he saw or heard—nothing less, but nothing more. He would never be a great writer, and he knew that about himself. He allowed life to determine beforehand what he could imagine. That makes your own life count for too much." She had stopped rubbing his neck. "You've got to be free of your own life if you're going to do something great. Do you understand?"

"No," he said, mumbling into sleep. "Just don't write about me. I wouldn't want to find myself in a story."

"Why not?" she asked him, but he was gone. She sat a few more minutes, holding the gauze pad tight to his back until she was certain that he had stopped bleeding. His breathing evened out. She put her free hand softly on his back across from the wound. He shivered through all his muscles, his entire body rippling like a horse shedding flies. She dressed the wound and went back to preparing supper.

"My god, she's killed him!" Jaeger said as soon as he came into the house, Mara behind him. The outside cold scuttled in across the floor and shook him. He rose like a diver kicking up into the air; out of his depths, he popped awake and gasped. Now the three of them stood around him. He looked at their heavy shoes.

"This is Peter Martin," Jane said. "The body down there on the floor." They all laughed, Peter too. He worked his towel tight around himself and stood up. "Peter, this is Mara and Bob Jaeger, but we call him Jaeger." They all laughed yet harder. Peter held onto his towel and shook hands with them with his free hand.

"Talk about a compromising situation," Jaeger said. "And you only met him this morning you say? I think I need a drink to handle that." He walked off to the kitchen to help himself. "And you," he said back to Peter, "you had better get dressed."

Jane had been right. Without a garden he would have to listen more than talk, but it was good listening. Their gardens were calculations, *acts* as much as necessities, arrangements with complexities and resolutions, like war or art. Jaeger was going to move his tomatoes this year to lower ground and his onions higher, where the drainage was better. The seeds for the French squash, the courgette, had arrived, and he would give Jane five of them. She gave him the address of a good and inexpensive supplier of shallot bulbs, a secret to be kept. Mara would try once again to raise celeriac to a size that made it worthwhile.

But they brought him in, talked about Washington County to him, who and what and where. And then beyond. Jaeger told them about New York, Paris. Galleries. Sales and near sales. Jaeger was fifty-five, florid, effusive, squirish in his ragged patchpocket tweed. He had come to his small success as a painter only about five years before. After nearly thirty failed years, as simply as it had formerly been difficult, a gallery in Paris accepted some work which immediately sold well. Now he could not paint fast enough. Each year he would have a show. For thirty years he had lived on Mara's trust fund, and now this. Mara herself was a watercolorist, successful within a fifty-mile radius of their studio-home farther down on Christie Road.

"And you?" Mara asked him. He told them what there was to tell about how he had come to settle here, and what he wanted to do with wood. He told them about RISD and the Konstfackskolan in Stockholm. He made some sketches for them of his designs. They were delighted.

"No one else around here is doing that," Jaeger said. "You should do well."

Jane's house had delighted him at once. He followed the homemade invention of it quickly, noticing the off-balanced dimensions of the rooms, the odd placements of doorways, the windows higher than usual. It was a well-built house but differently constructed, a house made by a good carpenter with a strong will who just might have been in a hurry. He asked her if she knew the house's history. It was quite small for a country house, built as it was in a time when houses were made three generations large.

The house had been built in 1868 by Frederick Whinney for his grandmother, Freda Mattheu Whinney, " 'who would not live with us,' " Jane quoted. She took him to a small panel in the band of wainscoting that cinched the entire interior of the house and removed the panel. There it was neatly carved: the information and the statement. Frederick Whinney had signed his house and given his reasons or explanation. The rest was up to posterity.

Jane had made her house bright and do-daddy in authentic country style, with starched chintz curtains, old gray crocks and jugs with blue eagles on them that she still used, implements and bowls of lustrous wood oiled and burnished by decades of use, cast-iron cranks and wheels and three-legged pots and hooks and hinges and latches from the century before.

The gold-rimmed glasses she wore now fogged up slightly in the change from the cooler rooms to the hot kitchen. Her smooth skin gleamed in her own warmth, and she was rouged by her exertions as she bustled about.

When they ate it was from her larder: Leeks, potatoes, onions, stewed tomatoes, brussels sprouts. Pickled cucumbers. The last of the Belgian endive from the crate of sand in the root cellar under the house, and carrots still crunchy and stiff. A few small leaves of lettuce already from the cold frame in the back yard. Her own heavy, wheaty bread. Two small roasted chickens (from a neighbor) stuffed with apples and nuts. Apple pie. Freshly ground coffee.

The Jaegers had brought the wine. Jaeger explained the fine points of what they were drinking and told excited tales of his discoveries in the back road vineyards of France, as he styled them. Now that he visited France so often, he could make and keep contacts, he said, getting in on the good things like this 1965 St. Emilion from Monbousquet that they were drinking.

"It's as good as anything from Château Cadet-Bon and half the price." He had poured for them again. And again.

Jane's house, the food, the wine, the gardens, weather, terrain and history of Washington County. Fragrant apple wood in the Franklin stove. The rising tax rate (on his land too), the new bridge over the river at Battenville (the childhood home of Susan B. Anthony), the layoffs at the paper mill in Center Falls, the good guys and the bad. Sweet. A savoring. The sweetness of this possession.

414

This all belonged to him. Now he belonged to it. It was the first of anything that he had. He leaned into it, full. Already the wound in his back was beginning to itch, a sign of healing. He had always been quick to mend.

"Do you know what a hutch is?" Jaeger asked. "A colonial hutch? If I showed you a picture of it, could you make it? In pine?" Jaeger was a little drunk, but so was he, and he was tired too, heavy with his contentment.

"Sure," he said. "I can make anything."

"Can you make this hutch if I show you the picture?"

"Sure."

"Don't talk business at dinner," Mara said.

"OK. OK. I won't talk business. A trade. I'll talk a trade. A trade between gentlemen and artists." He turned back to Peter. "You make the hutch and I'll give you a painting. I'll pay for the materials. Deal?" He reached out his hand. Peter reached across and took it.

"Deal," he said.

He did not want to make the hutch. He did not want to make something from a picture of something that Frederick Whinney's great-grandfather might have made. And he did not want to work in pine. Anyone could work in pine. You could nearly punch pieces out of pine like the pieces in model airplane kits printed on balsa wood. He could make a pine hutch with a penknife. Even maple would have been better, but maple was dull. Hutches were dull. "How about a trunk?" he said. "How about an elegant wooden trunk with brass straps? For traveling to Europe?"

"Only if it can fit in our stateroom on the 747," Jaeger said.

It took Peter time to understand. He had better leave. Get good sleep. He stood up.

"I'm off." He thanked them all.

His own house was icy. The fire he had left in the chunk stove had smoldered down to nothing. He built the fire up quickly and stayed near the stove until he could bear the dash to his bed. The cold there woke him for a few moments. The nails sang up their scale, the hawk called, Jane glistened. He slept.

He returned from the city and Poughkeepsie with his rosewood and mahogany and ash and butternut and racked it up carefully in the new room, shimming each piece of wood up so air could circulate all around it. In time there would be a special shed only for the wood, where he could dry it for years and open it up and discover his ideas in the wood unhurriedly.

The warming came. He finished the sheathing of the house, the siding and the shingled roof and the casements. He completed the wiring and got the hot water working. Arranged his tools, aligned his machines. Began. The harness he had chosen to pull in was softening into his shape, his sweat annealing it, making this life pliable. And he fished early and late in the legendary Battenkill that flowed out of Vermont all across his country to empty into the Hudson. He had been a warm-water fisherman, plugging for bass in the weedy ponds and lethargic lakes of the Ohio he had grown up in; but he had learned about trout and salmon in the spuming rills of Sweden, and now he would fish no other way. The water of the Battenkill was dropping quickly without the wet spring of other years, and the warm May had spawned hatch after hatch of the Ephemerida on schedule. He had taken many large browns with predictability. Twice he had driven to Jane's house to give her fish, but she was not home.

By the end of May, for all his work on the building, he had still completed three pieces. A large box-like drawer within its own stand for holding a silver service, and two extremely narrow bookcases, eighteen inches wide by five feet high. The box for the silver was done in pearwood, the bookcases in lemonwood. Every morning he rubbed them with oils of his own device. And he had completed the pine hutch and delivered it to Jaeger.

Jaeger had offered him his choice from among twenty canvases. They were all broad, feathery abstractions in flat, pastel-light colors. Each painting seemed as if it were one piece of a large, endless roll. Twenty pieces. Nothing appealed to him. He pointed at random. "Yours," Jaeger had said. There was also the bill for seventy dollars for the wood and the stain and the varnish. Jaeger was surprised at the cost. Now the picture leaned against the wall across from his three pieces.

He heard the car coming up the road. Even over the whine of his bandsaw he heard the car exploding up the hill. He turned off the saw and watched as she stopped at his mailbox and took out his mail for him and then started up his driveway.

"Who is Heldogras?" she asked, handing him letters, catalogs, *The Wise Shopper*. She walked by him into the room and turned around and around in it admiringly, and then she saw the three pieces. "Oh," she said, and went to them. Her hand moved to touch them, but she took it back. She wanted to touch them but would not.

"Go ahead," he said from the doorway. "Go ahead."

She reached out her hand and drew it across the wide top of the box for the silver. "I've never felt wood like this," she said. "It's velvety. Softer. Is this all one piece?"

"No." He walked over to her. "It's two pieces. I joined them. You can't even see the line. The joint mostly follows the grain. You can't even feel it, the joint."

"I know," she said. She rubbed the piece again.

"Not that way," he said. "Here's the way to tell how close a joint is. With your tongue." He bent to the case and touched the tip of his tongue to where the joint should be. He stood up. "If you can't feel a joint with your tongue, then there is no joint any longer."

She bent to the case and licked it. "Peuh." She made a face. "It tastes terrible. It tastes like your coffee."

"You're not supposed to taste it, just feel it."

"Peuh," she said.

And then they stood on either side of the furniture.

"How have you been? How's your back?"

He told her how he had been and where he was now, getting his motion, moving well. Sixteen hours a day. By summer's end he was certain he could fill the shop with pieces. And he was going to do a harpsichord case, the wooden work, all in yellow Andaman padouk. He had heard from a friend in Sweden that the Andaman padouk was being sold. It was wood that had belonged to an old cabinet-maker in Sigtuna, northwest of Stockholm, as rare as wood could be. He and his friend had often tried to buy the wood, but the old man would not sell it. And now he was dead and his daughter was going to sell it and between the two of them, him and his friend, they had bought it.

"There isn't that much of it. I couldn't afford it if there was. I'll only get about 300 board feet, but even with a good ten percent wastage, fifteen even, I'll have enough for the harpisichord and a bench. And I already know the wood. I know just what I can expect from it. It's being shipped next week. This is very exciting, do you see? Getting this wood? I never thought it would happen." Could a writer understand this? "You don't know about this kind of experience," he said. "This is a different kind of reality."

"Is that your friend? Heldogras? The one who is buying the wood with you?" It was not a question. It was something else.

"Heldogras is a friend, but a different friend. A different *kind* of friend, all right?" His voice had tightened.

"I'm sorry. I pry. It's not personal. I pry. That's my kind of reality. A letter from Sweden. A woman's handwriting. I go on from there. I'm sorry. I really am."

"Like Trigorin?" he said.

"You listened to that?"

"I listened. I just didn't understand."

They were silent again. She turned to the thin bookcases. "Are these expensive?"

"Two hundred dollars."

"Where do I lick them?" But he did not answer. "Hey," she said, turning to him. "You aren't really angry, are you? Don't be angry. I've got me some good news and I'm delivering it around the countryside. I'm bursting with self-congratulations. I sold a story to *Sewanee Review*. $400." She flared up. "I'm going to eat all next year." She punched him on the arm. "Come on. Let's go to Saratoga. I'll buy you lunch. I'll show you the town. Come on."

"You're always feeding me," he said.

Then she saw Jaeger's painting. "Did you do the hutch? But of course you did. Jaeger wouldn't have given you the painting first." She walked over to the painting. "What do you think?"

"No more trades," he said.

She turned and ran over to him. "Good. No more trades. No deals. But this is different. This is a treat. A celebration. I *need* it. Come on. Come *on*."

They drove to Saratoga, twenty miles westward, and she took him to an elegant lunch at Lillian's on Broadway. And after lunch she walked him about the town like a tour guide, showing him bookstores and the coffee house where young musicians played and poets read their work, galleries and leather shops and bittertasting springs. The library, the bakery, the museum in the park.

She was tall, nearly as tall as he, and a little slouchy in a loose, big-boned way. She moved quickly, the quickness of energy and not nerves, so she seemed to take up more space than other people, to live in a kind of swirling. In Lillian's, along the streets of Saratoga, in its stores, she captured wherever she was. Crossing one street she took his arm unconsciously and hugged it, a gesture out of the general exuberance that fueled her, an affection for the world coming out according to her plan, which was no plan more than to go on as she was. "Oh Peter," she said across the street. But nothing more. She dropped his arm. She smacked her fist into her palm and walked on in seven-league strides, her peasant skirt caught against her long, driving thighs, her black hair free again. He trotted to catch her.

She gave him advice. He must advertise. Seek outlets in Albany and Glens Falls. Go to the important crafts fairs like the one at Rhinebeck. And above all he would have to contact interior decora-

418

tors. They were the people who really sold the hand-crafted furniture. And he would need an accountant to do his taxes. An accountant could save him a fortune. She would recommend the accountant that she used. She seemed to know all about surviving.

The day turned longer, exfoliated. She took him to antiques and to a lady who raised and sold African violets from under the fluorescent lights in her basement. There were hundreds of plants and Jane bought six of them. And one for him. "They're good plants for taking care of themselves," she said.

They drove six miles down to Ballston Spa so she could show him some special buildings, cupolas that would never be built again and upper stories that overhung the sidewalk. And back to Saratoga. They decided to stay for a six o'clock movie at the Community.

"The country mice come to town," she said. She did not want to stop. Nor did he.

The day was good for him. Other than fishing, he had been working all through the week, free from days, on the house and the furniture. And on his ideas. Only the ideas were difficult, insubstantial and without a grain to consider or a place to cut into. A few days earlier he had hiked up to the top of his land to think about his strategy and his checkbook, but the day, just then, just there, kept him on the hilltop and away from the future.

He thought about his future just enough to get by. There was money to finish off the extension and the repairs to the house. There was about five hundred dollars for incidental pieces of equipment and supplies that he might need. He had wood enough for now. And there was a few hundred more for food and gas. The money for the harpsichord had come out of that. Sooner or later he would sell something, and then something else. It would take time. He had no illusions that way. He would achieve solvency after he was ready, prepared. First things first.

But it was good for him now to be listening to Jane. He did not know his details and she did. His future took on some of her heat and exactness.

"Can you do restorations? You know, replace missing legs, heal cracks or whatever, that sort of thing? Can you make fancy picture frames?"

"Yes. I can carve wood, too, but. . ." She pushed him aside.

"Well, there you are. Get people to know that. Get people to know that you exist. Listen, I've got an idea." She pulled him into a store on Broadway that sold pottery and woven pillows and cooking gear and baskets and everything else of those kinds of things in those kinds of stores. "Ask him," she whispered sharply to him after she had told the salesgirl that they would like to see the owner and the girl had gone off to get him.

"Ask him what?" What had she done?

"You know. If they want something. *Something made of wood.*" She poked him hard in the ribs, his conspirator.

The owner appeared. Peter explained that he was a furniture maker: chairs, chests, music stands, anything else. His own designs, the best of woods. The owner of the store asked his price range.

"Look," the owner said. "I don't sell that kind of thing. People come in here, they're looking for a present. Ten dollars, twenty. Maybe even fifty. What about bowls? Can you show me some turned bowls?"

"And boxes?" Jane asked. "What about boxes? He makes terrific boxes."

"Yeah, I'll look at some boxes, too."

"Would you consider taking a bookcase on consignment? Two hundred dollars?" she asked him. She nodded at him to encourage him.

"On consignment? Why not?" the owner said.

Peter said, "Wait a minute," but Jane dragged him out of the store. Outside. "What are you doing? I don't want to turn bowls. I don't want to make a lot of boxes. And I don't want to put the bookcase in a knickknack store."

"Why not? As long as you make it well, what do you care who buys it or how it's sold? This way people will at least get to see your work. They'll see the bookcase in the window and ask who made it. What's wrong with that? What's wrong with *you*?"

"Would you write bowls?"

"No," she said quickly.

"So?"

"So *what*? I don't follow you."

"You don't follow *me*? *I* don't follow *you*!"

"It's different," she said.

"Why, because you sold a story today? Because you're going to eat all year?"

"It's different," she repeated.

"How?"

"You don't care," she said. "It's all the same to you. You make something and you sell it and it's gone."

"That's outrageous."

"It's not an insult, Peter, just a fact."

"It is *not* a fact, and it's still outrageous."

"Well, what do you want, then?" she said. "And anyway, you don't have to do any of this. All you did was find out something, that's all."

And it was good for him to find out something. He had always known that he would need to know more than wood and his skills to live from them, but he did not know what more. Out on his mountain he would never find out. He needed the ballast of this marketplace, some lead in his life, a chance to come down from Sweden and the harpsichord into the valley. A chance to come down from his hilltop, up where he could not care.

After the movie they had a beer in a downstairs bar on Caroline Street in the center of town.

"I'll make some boxes but I won't turn bowls," he said across the table to her. She leaned back hard against the booth seat, shaking it. Laughing, she reached out and put both her hands on top of his, nearly spilling the beer between them, and squeezed firmly.

"Is that what you were thinking during the movie?"

"It was a lousy movie."

She had put on her glasses in the movie and wore them still. Looking at her, he could see himself reflected in the lenses, and that small reflection stuck within the background of what seemed her gigantic eyes, his head and shoulders and chest fixed within her dilated pupils. Her hands were rougher than ever from the gardening, and her face, still smooth as ceramic, was darkening from the sun.

They drove home. In two days she was going to Shreveport, Louisiana, to be part of a creative writing workshop sponsored by the state university. Ten days. The minor leagues. Her fee would cover travel expenses and she might clear a few hundred beyond that. It was thankless work but part of her life, the steps before the giant steps. Shreveport before Bread Loaf. My bowls, she told him. Not even boxes.

They drove back through the soft night off the uplifted limestone strata of Saratoga down onto the sandy plain by the Hudson and then across the river and up the rising, enfolded shale hills eastward. They talked on about what they were doing, would do now. Their tempos suddenly leaped in a coda to their day, quick recapitulation, intense upward modulation. Ideas of shape, of ordering so clearly etched occurred to them each that their hearts raced separately toward the morning, when they could work.

At the bottom of his hill she slowed in order to make the acute-angled turn up his road, but he told her he would walk it, take the night air. She stopped the car; the engine running down chattered the loose body. In the silence the peepers still chirped, but bullfrogs called now, too, up from the light streams feeding the Battenkill. He did not get out. She waited. But their metaphors came between them, just then, and bound them like the indenturing vows of apprentices to tasks and to other glories.

"Thank you," he said outside the car. "A great day." He turned and crunched off into the darkness. The car exploded and shuddered away.

He followed as much of her advice as he could. He would wait to advertise when he had more pieces to show, but he checked out interior decorators in the Albany area in the telephone directory from the Greenwich library. He called some of them and sent letters to others telling them what he had to offer. He turned three bowls out of some blocks of cherry that he had, and he constructed three clean and simple boxes, three by four by seven inches, out of scraps of various things. He took them to the store on Broadway and sold them immediately, eight dollars for each bowl, six dollars for each box: forty-two dollars. The owner said to bring him more, and asked about the bookcase. Peter said he would bring it in next time.

Forty-two dollars and a painting. His gross profit. Something had begun, but what? He would drive by Jane's again. Often now when he was out he would drive by her house on Christie Road to check on it. He supposed that Mara fed the cat. He would stop his truck at her house and try both doors and walk about. Three days after he had expected her to return and she had not, he began to drive by the house each day. At the end of a week he stopped at the Jaegers' to ask if they had heard from her. Could something be wrong? Should something be done?

"Jane can take care of herself," Mara said. "She probably stopped somewhere to visit friends. She often does." Then she said, "Are you interested in her?"

"Interested?"

"Oh, you know what I mean."

But he had left that alone and driven off.

And now, two weeks past due, she was back. He pulled into the driveway to tell her how he had earned some money at last. She was in the garden, hoeing furiously, desperately, he thought. She swung the hoe like a pick. The dirt splattered. He meant to say hello. Instead he said, "What's wrong?"

She looked up at him from under her wide-brimmed straw

fieldhand's hat. It set off her face nicely, pulling her features into a frame, holding them together as they were not naturally held together.

"Well, the garden for one thing," she said. She was tired. She was trying to drive her tiredness into the ground. She would stay in the hot garden all day until it was dark, and then she would be exhausted and would sleep and would wake up tomorrow and start again, and maybe after she did that for enough days she would be able to be still again, in balance.

"And for another thing?" he asked. He had wanted this to be a greeting for both of them, a returning.

But she was not through with the garden. "Look at the lettuce. Didn't it rain here at *all?*" She dropped to her knees and straddled the row, her fingers scurrying like mice through the wilted stems, plucking out the hopeless.

"It's not my fault. I can't control that."

She looked up at him. "What are you talking about?"

"The rain. I couldn't make it rain. I'm sorry, it's one of my weaknesses." He was shouting.

"Stop shouting. Don't you shout at me." She shook her fist at him. She stood up and took her hoe over to the cauliflower, away from him. The pastel-green leaves were erect and firm. They had set well. She worked between the widely spaced plants, scraping the low-sprouting purslane off the dirt like icing off a cake. He followed her.

"I only stopped by to tell you I sold some bowls and boxes. To that store in Saratoga. He wants more." He waited close behind her. She did not turn.

"That's fine," she said in her smallest voice. By her left foot he saw a bead of water drop in the dust on a waxy cauliflower leaf. A tear.

"Go away, Peter. Leave me alone for a while. OK?"

Instead he put an arm around her and walked her out of the garden to her back porch and sat down with her. He put his other hand up to her face. Her hat fell off. He eased her head down to him and let her sob into him. The cat purred by, rubbing against her. Back and forth the cat went, purring louder and louder until they could both feel the cat vibrating against them.

"How much did you get for the bowls and boxes?" she asked.

"Forty-two dollars."

"That's not bad, is it?" She sat up from him. She began to figure. "You could almost live a week on that, couldn't you?" She pushed her hair back.

"Maybe. If I had a garden," he smiled.

She took his hand. "I've got more than enough. I grow enough for a dozen people. You can't just grow one tomato plant. Get a freezer. I'll show you what to do."

"Sure," he said. "OK. And next time I'll water the lettuce." She squeezed his hand and let it drop. She picked up her hat and put it on.

"This hat does wonders for me. I don't look half bad in this hat, you know." She went back into the garden and he went with her. She got him another hoe and showed him what to do.

Shreveport had been terrible. What she had expected, but worse, too. The heat, the impossible food, the ship of fools she had been sent to sea in. What most depleted her was the pretentiousness and vulgarity of it all. She had not expected talent or skill; only a reasonable willingness to talk intelligently about fiction, about how people thought and felt their way through the human predicament. She had not been even remotely close. They had come to strut and to pretend. A retired doctor who was going to cash in on forty years of his patients' confidences. Cash in. That about summed them up. On the fifth day the doctor had propositioned her, had actually offered her money.

"No kidding? Wow. What did he offer? What are you worth on the open market?"

"That's not the end of it. Michael Lerner, the poet who was doing the poetry part of the workshop, he wanted me for *nothing*. He was going to do me a favor, the vain asshole."

"He was going to charge you, huh?"

She hacked at the weeds and the dirt.

"Maybe you're angry because he valued you too low. The doctor didn't offer enough, the poet didn't offer anything. Your feelings are hurt."

She refused his joke. "Then there were two creeps taking the fiction workshop who were always hanging around me, too. Fifty-year-old men in tight blue jeans. They had to alter the jeans to get their guts in. And it was like they just read Kerouac, for godsake. Long hair, sunglasses, grass, fat men in blue jeans drinking beer and talking *street* in Shreveport, Louisiana, in the good old summertime. Damn. Every time I turned around, there they were."

"I don't know. It sounds kind of flattering, all that attention."

"Does it?" she said, sharply enough so that he looked up. She had crossed over into his row and now confronted him. "Does it? The only bitch in town?"

"Hey, come on, will you. I'm making a joke. I'm trying to cheer you up." And he tried again. "You know how it is with you arty types."

"You're such an innocent?" The air between them cracked open. He did not like the smell of this talk about the men around her, and she knew it. In the broken air between them he saw her looking at him just as he was looking at her, the sunlight silvering them both like mirrors. "What about Sweden? What about Heldogras?" she said.

"What?" It was shocking.

But she turned away and went back to cultivating her row. She was past the cauliflower now and into the broccoli, moving fast.

He recovered. That she had remembered Heldogras had surprised him. Confused him. She imagined things so differently than he. "Heldogras was something else altogether. You can't compare. . ." But she was not listening. She would not hear. Even in the briskly rising heat of this day, she was huddled coldly in her trouble, larger than Shreveport.

They worked without talking, with only the sound of their hoes slurring through the dirt connecting them. He tried to match his stroke to hers, catching her rhythm, so they were raising and dropping their hoes exactly together. She finished her row and waited for him.

"I stopped in Washington," she said when she was next to him. His blue shirt was dark with sweat. "I visited good friends. College friends. Bill and Helen Wells. We were all together in Bennington. They got married right after college. The week after. Now they're talking separation. Divorce. It was ghastly. They're living together and they're thinking about divorce. They still sleep in the same bed, use the same john, and any day they might split. I didn't know how to handle it. I was in agony. There I was on the living room couch, like whenever I visited. Only it was like none of us belonged there any longer. We had gotten stuck together in the past and couldn't get loose in the present."

"Why didn't you just leave?"

"They wouldn't let me. I had to listen to one, then the other. Alone. And then together. Over and over. Like it was their hobby. And maybe I was fascinated, too. I'm not allowed to turn away from anything. Anyway, it was all quiet and urbane. Civilized. It was so civilized now that I couldn't understand how they could have married in the first place. Where was passion? Where was the anger in their disappointment? Peter, shouldn't they have been hurt or angry?"

"There aren't any rules," he said.

"I think there are," she said. "They just didn't play by them."

"It comes out to the same thing," he said. But she shook her head against that, dull and heavy.

"Do you want some iced tea? I do. I've got it ready."

They sat on the edge of the back porch and drank the tea, thick and minty. He had taken off his shirt to the sun.

She said, "Do you know what I saw this morning? I saw a Canada goose. Just one. It was flying south. Incredible. That really upset me."

"How do you know it was a goose? They fly so high, you can hardly tell it's a goose from just one bird. You need a flock in a V to tell."

"Oh sure you can tell. You can see the wing beat. Nothing flies like a Canada goose. I could tell."

"Maybe it was just flying around. South for just a little, but then it was going to turn back north and catch up with the flock. You can't tell."

"I could tell. It was going south. All alone. It was very upsetting."

"You *couldn't* tell," he insisted. "Anyway, animals are always doing strange things." He turned his head to her. "Breaking rules." She was staring out across the garden to the long arbor of grapes that marked the north boundary of her property. "And why should something like that upset you?"

She put her hand, her fingers, on the scar on his back. It was white and twisted like a mealworm, and the skin beside it was pink and tender. She rubbed it absently.

"Oh Peter, I can't get an agent to handle my novel. A third agent turned it down." She rubbed the scar softly, as if she would make it go away. Her hand was not as calloused or tight as it had been before she had gone to Shreveport.

"Can't you just send it to a publisher yourself?"

"Yes, but novels never get bought that way. I need an agent and I can't even get one."

"You've only tried three."

"Three's enough. That tells you something."

"That's silly. You can't just give up."

"I know. I can't give up but right now I feel like I can't win. Like my friends in Washington. My life's a Mexican standoff." She was rubbing his whole back now with two hands, massaging it, but she did not know how. He had learned how in Sweden.

"You're tired, that's all. You're just down. A little depressed. You need some rest and then you'll go on. You know that. Rejections are part of the game. Your whole life is going to be like this. It won't stop, you know." Her hands stopped. He turned completely around to face

426

her and put down his glass of iced tea. She looked at him dumbly, her mouth half opened to say something, as if she had been struck across the face. Her eyes were wet again, and her dark hair framed her face within the frame of the hat.

"Hey, Janie," he said quietly. "It's just not so bad. You'll be OK. You'll see." He put his hands around her neck and slowly worked his fingers into her muscles as Heldogras had taught him. Finding the knots, he kneaded her and she loosened. Then her tears came slowly.

"Goddamn bird," she said.

He unbuttoned her shirt and opened it and bent to her chest and kissed each small breast. She closed him in her arms and rocked back with him onto the porch. He kissed her all over her face, gently, over and over. Then, "Peter," she said. "Don't do this now." She was hugging him tightly. He tried to push up from her but she had not released him. "Peter?" She was asking something. "Are you going to be angry?"

"No," he said. "I'm just going to be mixed up." She opened her arms.

Standing by his truck she said, "It's not you. I like you. It's just that I can't rest now. Yet." He started the truck. "I'm not making this clear, am I?"

"No. You're not. Do you think *you've* got it clear? What do you mean 'rest'?"

"Peter, it's just that I suddenly saw my life, just then, about to turn into something I might write."

"Trigorin again?"

"No. Not Trigorin. You. You said it yourself. You didn't want to find yourself in a story. That's what I felt back there."

"Janie, I really don't understand what the hell is going on." He started to back out. She had to step away.

"You'll come back here, won't you? You won't stay away because of this, will you?"

"Sure. I'll come back whenever you want." He backed out onto Christie Road and drove off to his own work.

But after a week he had not heard from her and he went back. She was gone again. He walked around the house and checked the doors. The garden was getting weedy again. Before she had left she had mulched the tomatoes and heavier plants, but the seedlings were shaggy. He unwound the hose from its reel against the side of the house and watered the lettuce soakingly and wetted down the rest of the garden as well. He finished watering as Mara drove up. From the road she called.

"Here, I was heading your way." She waved an envelope at him through her car window. "And Jaeger wants to talk to you. He's up at the house now. See you later." She drove off.

The note was from Jane. She had enclosed it in a letter to Mara to save time.

Peter, I am on Long Island doing work, would you believe it? Got called away urgently. Great possibility. Will explain when I see you. Do me a favor? Save my garden? Water the lettuce like you promised. And remember, half of everything you save is yours. The Law of Salvage, I think. The key to the house is on the ledge above the back door. I like you a whole lot.

Jane

He went back into the garden and weeded in it for an hour. He picked some radishes and lettuce for lunch. Then he went further up the road to Jaeger.

Jaeger wanted to add a small room to his house, a breakfast nook off the kitchen. He wanted Peter to do it.

"You can do it, can't you? This sort of thing?"

"Yes, I can do it, but not for paintings."

"Oh no no no, of course not. Draw me some pictures and give me an estimate. When can you do it? I'd like to get this done as soon as possible."

"Now. I can do it now."

"You can?"

"Sure. Get me a ruler and some paper."

In an hour he had sketched out the addition and shown Jaeger what his options were: windows here or there, baseboard electric heating or not, lighting possibilities, built-in seats. He figured he could do it for about three thousand dollars, half material, half labor. Jaeger said go ahead.

"Shake," Jaeger said. Then Peter thought that Jaeger must also have had the job estimated by someone else. He had underbid.

"You'll have to pay for the materials first," Peter said. "I don't have the money to lay out. You can put a check in the safe at Curtiss Building Supplies and I'll draw materials against it. OK?"

"Fine. I'll do that today. When can you start?"

"Tomorrow."

But tomorrow it rained. It rained for two days. The lettuce would survive without him. He stayed in his workshop and turned bowls and worked on some boxes. A hundred dollars' worth. On the third day he started the addition to Jaeger's house. He contracted for a back-hoe to dig the foundation trench, and by the afternoon he had set the forms for the concrete footing and had called in the Redi-mix truck. By the end of the day he had finished the footing and was ready to lay up the concrete blocks of the foundation. In three days he would have the deck down and completed; the rest of the building would be easier, closer to making furniture where you could work on a piece at a time, measure and cut and fit precisely. The rest of the addition he could work in around his own work. And his garden. Driving home that night he stopped at Jane's house, but only for a moment. Then he returned to his hill.

On the second night he stayed at Jane's. It saved him the drive home and back to Jaeger's in the morning. He sat on the back porch and drank a beer and watched a large woodchuck circle up to the fenced-in squash, the courgette. It sniffed the fence and then waddled back into the field. He thought he should get a .22 and sit here and drink beer at the end of a good working day and plink woodchucks. The thought rode over him pleasantly like sleep when it is good. He finished his beer and then worked in the garden until the mosquitoes began to come up too quickly. Then he went into the house and showered and made himself a tuna salad.

When he had come to his hill the first thing he had had to learn was what to do with his nights. At first he had been too tired out from his work and excitement: his days and nights did not break up into busy-ness and loneliness, only into light and dark. But soon enough he found his day ending and then nothing else. He had expected that. It was part of the overall equation—the money, the land, the tools, the wood, the loneliness. And the time to work on it all, that was part of the equation, too. It would take time to blend everything into a life, to make the accommodations that would be needed, and to add what he would find as he went along.

He got a TV. He hooked together his tape deck and equipment and speakers. He read more. And he worked at his drawing board on his designs. Some nights he would go over to a roadhouse in Salem and listen to good hillbilly music and to the people, farmhands and millworkers mostly, getting slowly and happily drunk. But most of all he waited.

His first night at Jane's he examined Frederick Whinney's house closely, happier even than the first time to discover unexpected intricacies and details. Had Whinney done this because of his grandmother, or to spite her? After the eleven o'clock news, he got into Jane's bed and slept.

Days followed days. It rained more than he had counted on. He turned bowls and sold them. Closed in Jaeger's addition. Took off a bright day following the rain to bring the garden up to prime. Blossoming was everywhere. Fruits were forming—beans, early tomatoes, broccoli, cauliflower. Jane sent a letter instructing him to harvest the peas, how to blanch and freeze them, which were the snow peas to be treated specially. How to tie the cauliflower leaves up around their heads. To hill the potatoes and the onions and the leeks. And more.

I'm into the planning of a huge writing project. Who knows when I'll return, but very soon, I hope. Oh, I miss my garden. Do take care of it, and I hope it isn't taking up your life. In haste.

Jane

Three weeks. He sat on the back porch drinking beer. The woodchuck came up to the fence in its ritual of hope. It had dug down, but Jane had set the fence deep. And after that the woodchuck had no other strategies, only patience and hope that one day the fence would be gone.

He drank his beer. The addition was finished. A friend of Jaeger's wanted him to turn his one-car garage into a two-car garage. Another friend wanted him to fix a leak in the roof. The store in Saratoga wanted as many bowls and boxes as he could reasonably produce. They were selling well. August was coming. The racing season. The tourists.

He sat on the back porch in the sun's long rays, drinking the beer. Already the summer had started to break up into a hazy layering, the diminishing curve of spring's excited becoming flattening down into methodical and even growth. A tree in the hills across the river had burst into accidental autumn fire, while the dark and vital green of all the trees grayed down beneath the wax thickening over their leaves to protect against the dog-day heat to come.

He heard the car. At first he thought it was a memory, a trick of memory in a daydream, but it was real enough and approached. Even before it arrived, he went around to the front of the house and waited.

She threw her arms all over him. She hugged him and then came back to hug him again.

"You look great," he said. She was deeply tanned. Even her dark hair had tinted auburn. "You really do. You look like a piece of well-rubbed beech." He reached and rubbed her cheek across the bone. "Come and see your garden." He took her hand and they ran to the rear of the house into the field. He showed her through it, explaining what he had done with her instructions and what he had contrived on his own.

"Oh you've done well," she said. "I couldn't have done better." She examined everything, the distance he had thinned the carrots, how he had trained up the cucumber vines, if the melons were finding themselves enough sun. She pinched the soil to see if it was friable and yet damp. "Should I be happy or jealous? You've done so well with it."

"You could be both, I guess."

She took his arm and pranced him into her house. He was everywhere in it. His clothing, his books and papers, his slight rearrangement of pots and dishes and knives in the kitchen. His impress was upon it all. A chair shifted, the cat's dish placed to the left of the door, the TV moved a foot nearer to the sofa. His smell. So quickly he had possessed her house, assumed her garden.

"What are you doing?" she asked. He was hunkered down before the open refrigerator, considering it. How broad he was across the back! She had forgotten that, or perhaps never remarked it. How tight limbed!

"Making you something to eat," he said. "I'll bet you didn't eat all day. I hardly ate all day myself." But then he stood up from the refrigerator and closed it. He came to the table and sat down across from her. "I'm just so glad you're back," he said. Then he sat and watched her, smiling and still.

"Me too," she said. "Me too."

But she was not *back*. For the weeks that she had been gone, she had not wanted to be gone, had wanted badly to be here, to come back. She had counted on it through the tiring collisions of the work sessions on the project, and even more through the shrill excursions of the talented and skilled people unfurled in their flags and ensigns of social array, drinking and talking hard, as strained as if they were always sailing close reached, stiffly, in an endless race. But what she had come back to now seemed gone, moved forward to where she had just caught up with it, a goodness, yes, but of another kind. *What kind?* She fluttered at the answer.

"I'll do it," she said, getting up. "It's been so long. I miss my kitchen."

"I'll help. I'll get things from the garden. You get settled."

From the kitchen window she watched him move about with the woven ash-split basket, picking delicately through and across the long rows. She put her knuckle between her teeth. She had imagined this, exactly this scene, at night in Amagansett after the restless, nervous house of her hostess had subsided and still she could not sleep. She would look out her kitchen window at her rich garden and then he would be in it, working in it as she had told him in her letters, moving about in an inland light so different from that of the sea. Even today, driving the long trip home, she had imagined this again. She trembled, actually grasped the edge of the table to still herself.

She had made something come true.

They worked together. He had gathered cucumbers, early tomatoes, baby carrots, a small cauliflower, young broccoli, Swiss chard, lettuce that he had shaded from the sun, tender yellow wax beans, scallions, a cutting of chives. He stripped cold chicken from bones in the refrigerator and made the salad and a hot and garlicy French dressing while she steamed the beans and stir-fried almost everything else in olive oil. They heated frozen rolls in the toaster oven.

"This is good, this is so good," she said. "They eat so badly out there. Good, but bad, you know what I mean? Everyone's worried about their health but they eat steaks like this," she showed him how thick, "and pounds of lobster in pounds of butter. And the drinking. Wow." She ate quickly. "This salad dressing is terrific. Oops." She dribbled some food out the side of her mouth. He got up and snapped a paper towel from its roll for her. She saw him watching her. He ate slowly. He is ruminating, she thought. What a word.

She was repossessing nothing. He had jumped her claim.

She told him what had gotten her to Amagansett. A college friend had landed a contract with Hawthorn to do a book on American regions. The subject wasn't new, but the approach would be. The approach had sold it. The idea was to build a grid of universal activities and then to lay it on the seasons and the place. "For instance, road-building and maintenance through the seasons in all the regions of the country. Do you get it? You can't see America unless you see its people at work against the backdrop of their two most important influences, terrain and weather. How about that?"

"It sounds like a good idea. Where do you fit in?"

"I'm going to do this part of the country. Upstate New York and thereabouts. I'll have to travel sometimes, but mostly I'll be here."

"I thought you wrote fiction."

"I *write*," she said. "Mostly I write fiction, but sometimes other things. It's not either/or. And if this works out I'll make some real money, which I can use. It's a good experience."

"You don't have to defend it. Not to me. You're defending it and you don't have to."

"Yes I do," she said. "A little. Sometimes a lot."

"No you don't. You're too up or down. You should level off."

"There goes my Nobel Prize."

"See. See. All or nothing with you."

"I was just kidding, Peter. I thought all about this project before I accepted. I'll *like* doing it, honest. I'm OK. I'm all right."

He told her about building the addition for Jaeger and the work he was going to do on Jaeger's friend's garage. He was also producing an easy one hundred dollars' worth of bowls a week for the Saratoga store. He would work on his fine pieces in the winter, when the tourists were gone and the weather closed off his construction work. He would build the harpsichord then.

They had chocolate ice cream for dessert. She told him stories about the high life far out on Long Island. He brought her up to date on Washington County. "In some ways it's not all that different," she said.

"In the meantime, I'm rolling in money." He showed her his accounts scribbled on a piece of paper in his wallet.

"You shouldn't do it that way. Here." She showed him her carefully kept account ledger and the envelopes of specific receipts. "You'll need these for the accountant. Did you call the accountant yet?" He hadn't, but would. He was thinking of buying a mortar mixer. What kind of write-off could he get? The accountant would know.

He had left the mat in the tub after showering and it had gotten moldy underneath. He had mixed meat and fish scraps in with the vegetable trimmings for the compost heap. She found an empty beer can under the sofa in the living room, and small plaques of dried mud in the hallway, even though he had swept from time to time. He was all around her, like a fume.

At ten o'clock he said he would go. He went to gather his clothes. But even if he took everything of his away, he would continue in the house now, like a stain.

"Peter," she called after him through the short L-shaped hall. "Stay."

She woke early. The redwings and grackles were signaling to each other from the verges of nearly dried-up streams. Sparrows, wrens, thrushes bubbled about. It would be a hot day. Already the heat had stirred enough insects into flight that the barn swallows sailed about, plucking them out of the air. The birds were in place. She awoke and stretched out and bumped him. He stirred but slept on, deep, completed, creasing the bed downward. In the room's dim light his white scar glowed. She rolled toward him and kissed the scar and fell back.

She smiled at the ceiling. There was so much to do. The garden would need harvesting in earnest this year. And she did not want to lose the summer interviews for the book. She had thought of enough likely possibilities already to get her going, and once she started she could keep on. She would find the others. There was so much to do. She should get up and begin. Still, she waited in the day rising, waited for them, by degrees, to dwindle into lovers. And maybe less.

Edward Tick

I began as a Bronx Jewish street kid. When I was 6, my family moved to Queens where I spent the rest of my childhood. I first came to the North Country in 1968, to study at SUNYA, and spent the Vietnam years here. In 1975 I sought, like others, to green America, and so moved to Columbia County, where I spent the next 9 years. America's narcissistic decade ran its course and I returned to Albany in 1984.

In my part of the North Country — the Hudson River valley and the small metropolis straddling the plains of Albany — I have gotten to know people of every kind — from Native American to 97% Puritan, from Christian Buddhist to Jewish atheist, from deputy sheriff to fifth generation alcoholic to eighth generation New Englander. The setting for these meetings is a stunning ecology in which each month is its own season. The hills and waters, sun, clouds and winds, cities and villages are among our most dramatic actors.

On the North Country stage, the clash and combination of souls with each other and with the land still enacts the violent and tender drama of America's melting pot.

My offerings in this anthology share a few of my small glimpses in search of the larger picture through the windows of my North Country home.

On Regionalism

Painters view the world. Musicians, dancers, actors, singers perform in concert with others. But the writer withdraws. Because of the depth of this withdrawal, writing has been called the loneliest art.

The struggle to shape language into art is, of necessity, solitary. It demands withdrawal from the noisy, fragmented world of our workaday lives. It demands deep concentration on the inner tumult to sort through all the sounds, picking a note here, a line there until, beneath the chatter, an essential voice is heard. When the writer is either lucky or inspired, what the ancients called visited by the muse, s/he can wrestle the divine song into words and forms that will appeal to the language community in which s/he dwells.

In contemporary America, writers' withdrawal is made even more severe, more isolating, by the economic, social and political conditions under which we must exist. The publishing industry today is oriented toward blockbuster sales. As *Newsweek* reported when William Kennedy won the National Book Critics Circle Award, "Good reviews won't dent the book publisher's rising indifference to quality. The promise of money is all that matters to most of them now."

It is not only publishers' hunger for megabucks that alienate the writer. In recent years in Argentina, Chile, both Chinas, Cuba, Greece, Turkey, the Soviet Union, Central America, South Africa writers have been harassed, imprisoned, even assassinated. But worse than being persecuted and thus knowing that someone hears your voice, is feeling that your life's work is not worth the paper it is written on. In America, a deadly form of censorship is practiced. Here writers are ignored. Thus their spirits are broken.

These broad concerns may seem to have little relevance to the Hudson Valley in which we live and write. But that is not true. As long as we writers believe that major publishing is our only goal worth striving for, as long as we count New York City as the center of the flat literary world, as long as our fantasies of blockbusters block the clear and honest voice of quality that can rise from within, as long as we do not listen to the voices of our neighbors that call to us from over the hill, as long as any of these conditions exist, we have been successfully censored.

We can refuse to pay unjust tithes to fantasies whose realization is inaccessible and unattainable to all but one in a million of us. As an alternative, we can hold before us the model of literary regionalism.

Traditionally, regionalism referred to qualities in literary works, such as dialect, character and setting, that marked the work as a product of a particular geographical area. Today, regionalism has come to mean more than that. With the growing inaccessibility of the major publishing outlets, with the actual decrease in writers' fees paid by the major magazines, with the subtle form of censorship practiced in America today, regionalism connotes not only a literary quality but also a literary comradery — a banding together of writers in a particular area to support, explore and critique each other's voices and to help each other develop audiences and outlets for their creative works.

This kind of regionalism argues at least three components: a comradeship among local writers; a sense of community with the people and areas among whom the writers live, including a commitment to local audience and quality of life; and a commitment to develop publishing outlets, both locally and beyond, not only for oneself but for all the writers in the region.

Major models of literary regionalism can be found in the San Francisco, Chicago, Western and Southern writers groups. These groups have been most studied not as societies of writers but as representing styles of writing. But if we look to the Imagists, Surrealists, Dadaists, Bloomsbury Group or Generation of '27, we realize the importance of writers living and working in concert. In fact, the evolution of literary style is bound up with people, places and cultural epochs. The above groups evolved because a burden of historical urgency was shared by writers living and working in intense proximity.

Some of the burdens we have inherited as late twentieth century Americans are deep senses of isolation, fragmentation within ourselves and our social structures, alienation, terror and numbness. Literary regionalism represents one of the important grass roots movements that have evolved since the 1960s as efforts against these trends in our civilization.

Gore Vidal said in a recent interview that he never votes for president but would not dare miss an election for a local representative. His comment underscores the idea expressed herein. One man or woman can do precious little when s/he seeks by him or herself to change the world or the language. But when we band together with common goals and when we set our eyes on the hills, valleys and neighborhoods in which we live, when we listen to the voices down the road, in the next town, in the earth beneath us, when we give these voices the opportunity to speak, then, in fact, the quality of life does change. The life we live. The life we write.

Edward Tick   437

Migration

From off the turning earth
a thousand blackfeathered bodies
spring through brambles and leap on boughs.
Their chattering is the clatter of the bound.
Their wings are not yet ready.

Many gather.
Their noise is great.

A cloud of birds
call and leap to each other.
The winds they will challenge are strong,
their goal long and far.
The paling autumn sun
splatters against tired tree crowns
thick and dripping in silhouettes
of ready black angels.

They are strong and numberless,
the ones that will fly.

Silence invades their throats.
A fury creeps into their wings.
In a burst the sky is blackened.
The trees are left alone.

Countless and powerful in the night,
their wings, their unseen wings.

The Fall

The two men wear dark glasses.
Behind their backs their van is packed
with camping gear and beer. With every bump
their mess kits rattle. The rain
plinks on their roof like a piano
out of tune with the blaring country music.
They stare without talking
past the swishing wiper blades.

Behind the van a trailer.
Out of it, like empty flagpoles,
rise the sleek brown legs of a deer.
Its black hooves shine.
On the trailer's hard bottom
its eyes, soft, glassy,
stare without seeing
and drip
and drip.

Paul Weinman

I've camped and excavated early Indian sites in the Lake George Valley. As Education Supervisor much study and work deals with teaching activities concerned with the interrelationship of people and environment of the Adirondacks. In 1982, I received the CAPS grant for poetry and the Center Press Innovative Fiction Award in 1983 for works dealing with Adirondack life. Recently, Samisdat Press published the chapbook—He Swings a Straight Stick. . . a collection of baseball poems.

Traced by Blood

Back by the raspberries, he stands
and stares where a path had led to spring peepers.
Out by the pond choked thick
with alga and leaves rotting brown.
When his feet were smaller, he had followed
his father's steps so quiet through the moss
and throbs of amphibian nightness.
Tried to imitate his easy stride
and twists through brambles grown long
in flowers all white.
But he'd always get scratched at least once
in that thinnish manner of raspberry thorn.
Skin would part so clean —
leave a line slow
to be traced by blood.
They'd sit at hickory roots along the shore.
Watch some ducks and talk over each day.
Share what both saw first . . . a star,
splash of small fish taking a moth below.
A ripple of turtle about to surface,
what mom had been like.
Father'd been buried
back by the raspberries.
Next to her where the path
made that smooth bend,
then straightened again.

Got so Grandma

Got so grandma creaked up such a violence of wood that we cracked her chair so she couldn't keep rocking like she would. Crashed it to splinters that burned near as fast as her tongue snapped angry.

Bible words they were to be sure. But in such bursts we'd jump at tables thinking crazed chickens just broke through the door.

When that her chair had gone to flame, grandma fell to listing our sins. Saying them fast and full of whichway and every what had gone on. Missing not one of us and for certain remembering each to whom.

No one much spoke, what with her about to fill us with guilt. Embarrassed we were to know each of the other and that to them of us. So we took her false teeth and snuck them to a hole she'd never know. Mumbled she did. But we hardly minded it a bit.

That's when she took to cornhusks. Collecting them dried brown in a box of cardboard. She'd set them careful this way thick, thin way that. Her box stuffed full to the top with lids tucked tight for wait.

At night when we sat to some hand-chore or sloe gin. . .maybe play cards with what pennies we had. Then she'd take that box of husks to lap so frail. Wait till some special time she would. Lift up lid and thrust her thin hand in deep.

Crunch, crunch and it'd send shivers to spine.

So we set her upstairs where she couldn't come down. Legs all gnarled from mountainsides and so many kids of us. But she thumped her fists all boney at boards of floor. Or gummed moist noise through slatwood cracks.

Couldn't stand that. Her being overhead and all.

Put her out back with sacks of potatoes and herbs hung to dry. But she'd wheeze and spittle when we passed through. Whisper sounds of sons deceiving and daughters not being the ways they should.

When she we buried by the stone wall at last, the woodchucks took to coming. Dug holes deep with tunnels that would whistle mournful sounds all night. Wind it was and more.

Words were hers and we knew it well. And no matter that we'd shoot a chuck or two. . .fill each hole with stone and sand. None of that would stop the noise we knew were of her muted mouth.

Finally we set her teeth to one tunnel. Layed in some flowers and read Bible words while the sun was up high. Night sounds stopped at that.

Cept when we did a little sinning.

Logs Jammed

Caulked boots I'd wear no more. Swore to Christ hisself and cast them worn thin to bunkhouse floor. Let the logs pile high onto the heavens themselves! I won't walk another skinned spruce, lay peavy pole to hemlock spinning in springtime fury.

Pete had gone under, his mouth split wide as thunder. Screaming sounds of despair while wood danced demonic steps in meltwater flood. Crashing to rock, splashing jammed piles twisting in groan.

I'll no more drive trees to mill. No more, after begging for some celestial hand to snap him from that thrash of death. Not with me seeing his eyes full open in fright and me to shoreside knees praying Lord, Lord!

Let him to water walk.

Days after the jam had been blasted free, his body bobbed in woolens thick. Caught against the very rocks those logs had enmeshed themselves unto. We pulled him bloated to boat, buried him graceful where some flowers had sprung in blue.

Words were read from the book he kept. I now the same. And though my boots are no longer caulked in spikes, I pray that my steps will hold to the twists I'll take.

Who Died to Who

I'm too old in dying, he'd say. Things ain't the way they should be seen by me. I'm not denying any of them gadgets to you—inventions and all. But my God was back where you couldn't touch finger tips in hugging a tree. When there was a good chance at bringing down an elk and you had to keep watch for mountain cat.

Now I can't walk without an automobile barking for running me down! And there's hardly a deer to what woods are left.

Course we'd heard him growing with years and adding in ways. But being one of the few old-time guides who'd done so much never to be known again. . .why we'd keep him at the hotel. For tourists to talk to and take his wriggley name I taught him to scratch . . . .autograph.

Only catch was him being convinced that God beat him in getting to be dead. Now that caught people up short, though for sure added some sort of character to his being. Especially when he'd get at thumping his foot for more whiskey and adding elaboration to tales already a fabrication.

But he was a money-maker to take down into big-sized towns. Set him up in shows with a stuffed bear he'd claim to have felled from a tree and struck him death with but a knife. Kept sticking it, too. Till we had to get another—so's the stuffings didn't all spill out, you know.

Only when he started that God stuff did we have to close up the booth and drag him to a sobering sleep.

When we started taking him in the bigger cities, sure he drew folks like flies to deer hides. And didn't it start to get at his head—swelling it up like such does. But instead of keeping to tales of cliffs and trout, wild storms and running rapids with gaffing logs—he'd get off farther and further into God's dying with the civilizing of them woods.

We'd tell him it wasn't true—but then, he knew we never did believe—nor did most of them he talked to. In God, that is.

He got real bad one night. Cussing in a way it wasn't so funny. Cursing people for what they did—till I asked him what was he doing when all what started wrong kept growing till now it was done? Took gut for me to ask him that.

Stopped him short—for he shot many's the moose and elk that's no more. Cut timber and guided investors to great tracts of mountain to develop.

Well, shut up he was. And walked slow to his room. Blew out the light, but forgetting it was gas that brought bright—candles had long passed.

In Early Driving

In early driving of logs to mill, it wasn't but a crew of a few hardy men. Walking them winter-skidded trees from freshet of dammed-back smaller streams. Then to those broader. . .till finally they'd float in the wide ones.

When more men were hired out as the mountains were getting theirselves clear-cut clean, why teams of each lot-owner were riding timber amongst each others. Soon, all them big sticks were getting in mix and them river-type fellows quick to fix things up each in his own way.

Up to fourteen a day we toiled in hours. And there were no weeks to have a Sabbath between. You drove that wood from the first spill at water life until they'd move no more to sawmill jaws.

Course the owners, being in woolen suits trimmed with silk, wanted none of their cut lost to another. So they devised a brand for each. And as logs were pig-yoked from the banking ground, a stamper stroked every one. . .setting mark seen in sorting.

Now them with golden watch from pocket and well-clipped whisker chops wouldn't want the men they paid to walk wood, piking another's problem without the same being done for them, you know.

And so it was, even written and read to each crew that it was cooperating we'd all do. No matter from whom you drew pay—only exceptions there'd be was from whom put food to tin plate. Though the camps would all serve about the same kind of mashed-up stew.

Flimsy rules they were for certain and us always wet with freezing spray and spill. But so frantic at poling and jumping log at log from before dawn till not long after day, that glad we'd be to lay body at shore for rest.

Tempers, they weren't as long as a pole. Nor was it watched with a—well, well—if any one man tracked at his showing of strain. Sleep, sure it was short, but enough to allow time for many's the sorting of them thought to be slackers.

All went the same, excepting this one twelve with their river boss. These men had no special looking about them, but workers like that weren't seen even amongst our best. Leaping and poking with pikes; laughing together and in song harder than the ram of pine against jam.

No hedging for them in mixing with any of us to break a pile. Fast that they'd thrust a peavy pole to wrest a sawed tree from putting others in a fix.

At night—no swearing. . .only songing. Their grub was more like food and for sure some of the best of it would find way to being heavy at each of our plates. Their driver? No spit at your feet or jacking higher from him. Wasn't but the worst of us that wouldn't have worked with them.

The excepting being their morning prayer-talk while we'd still sleep. And that no whiskey business. . .too much for me.

photo by Mary Ann Lynch

Ron Welburn

Ron Welburn is a native of Berwyn, Pennsylvania who grew up in Philadelphia. He is of Cherokee-Conoy Indian and Black descent. He attended college at Lincoln University in his native Chester county and holds graduate degrees from the University of Arizona and New York University. Welburn has taught at the U of A, and for several years at Syracuse University. He's taught as an adjunct in the New York-New Jersey metropolitan area and in the New York Capital District.

Though he attended art school for several years as a teen, Ron Welburn did not begin to write or study music until he was 19. He is a self-taught cornet player and saxophonist and has composed over twenty musical compositions. Since 1963 his jazz reviews and essays have appeared in Walt Shepperd's Nickel Review, the Syracuse New Times, the New York Amsterdam News, Jazz Times and of late Down Beat. In 1975 the Smithsonian Institution and the Music Critics Association co-sponsored Welburn and nine others as Fellows in their Summer Institute in Jazz Criticism seminars. . . He co-founded and edited a jazz/newmusic magazine, The Grackle, and from 1980–1983 coordinated the Jazz Oral History Project of the NEA at the Institute of Jazz Studies, Rutgers University–Newark.

Welburn began writing poetry and fiction while at Lincoln, twice winning the laureate's Edward Silvera Poetry Award. Over the years he's published poetry in over 63 anthologies and magazines and 19 short fictions. His books of poetry include Peripheries; Brownup;

The Look in the Night Sky; *and* Heartland. *He currently lives in Albany and was the 1985 Writer-in-Residence for the Schenectady County Public Library. He is a trader at Indian pow wows selling books by Indian authors. Also, Welburn was, in 1972, the first to teach a grant-funded creative writing workshop in a New York State Prison (Auburn).*

MOHAWK MEMORY: *Schoharie County, N. Y.*

atop this mountain ridge
I can glory in the night
the shooting stars spear
through the sky like lacrosse balls.
the Mahican are having a little fun
tossing orbs from the east.
under the dark of the moon
the Haudenosanee must cover
all goals and can
throw back nothing.

all other stars resting
above us tend to their business:
the hunter, the family of sisters,
the two bears before coyote
tricked them of their tails.

above the trees to the northeast
Place Beyond the Openings
a light show proceeds and
heavy drums filled with water
overwhelm the sounds the winds make.
this is a distance from Skohar'le
but there is a mixture of sounds
and glows on the horizon
like the redcoats and their logs
spewing fire, moving
westward to Cherry Valley.

the show is a thing of power and beauty
from where I stand;
the night but a comment,
a story told in summer
of how we once lived.

Into the Helderbergs
(Rensselaerville, New York)

Soft cool flames drenched
in sunlight cover the hills.
Witness, wont you, these baskets
of oranges, grapefruit, apples, and
you'd think no green ever lived here.
I walk paths absorbed by
the oldest ritual I know;
the trees clustered on the hillside
like strawberries.
I taste the yellow brilliance
of the afternoon and stroke my hand
along the quill patterns the birches make.

Wont you come with me this autumn
and bathe in the leaves
as we make our way toward
the settlements around Vroman's Nose?
I know a road up a mountain
that a barred owl stubbornly sits in,
blandly amused by any headlights
and soft as a still night in its flight.

The Moment of Prayer

While not forest bred
I know the trees as more than foliage.
I believe in the power and the glory of the sun
and have never felt the same about prayer
seated or kneeling, my hands clasped,
in a brick structure serene with lovely glass
as I do amidst ash and birch and pine.
Perhaps it was that hill rising
behind the house where I lived,
a hill my short legs ventured to climb
that seemed so far, so upward and eternal,
its floor carpeted with the oldest leaves.
Knowing this begins the moment of prayer
that takes us through our lives
to our longest journey.
My grandfather lives in the sun
the greatest of stars
the oldest of ancestors whoever I am.
Yes, I have sat in storefront churches
and in cathedrals, and have prayed in my home,
kneeling or standing,
and I know there is no prayer
as full as that which can brush the sky
and the leaves of grass, and the moss.
Sitting across a fallen timber beneath
redstarts and sentinel jays,
I attain the strength of peace, and then
I know my grandfather's knowing
as I stand tall before him,
my feet in the earth's hair
my arms raised high with the trees.

My Son's First Kingfisher

See, he flies
like he wants to stop
in mid-air,
has a tic in the wingbeat.
Most of all, something's tickling him.
Maybe he thinks we're funny-looking,
or it's just a private joke
showing off here along Tawasentha.
He was the one made that big splash
in the creek we heard —
must have a fish in his belly.
That's what it is.

Pitching Coups

The arc of the pitching arm
unwinds a circle of dreams
and corkscrews out behind a kick
to release a flying head,
in whose face coming towards
the men with the bats
is a leer and a laugh.
The stitches of the sphere blur
into war paint and the head's
ecstatic yell echoes
throughout this canyon of battle.
It flies as straight as an arrow or
whirls like a tomahawk;
sometimes it just jumps off a ledge
the way lovers are said to do
in secret ravines all over this country.
It always comes ready to count coup
and tease and intimidate.
The pitching arm belongs to coyote
and so does the flying head.
The arm belongs to Chief Bender
from yesterday, then Allie Reynolds,
and the next time to Cal McLish,
and now to John Henry Johnson and
Fernando, the Valenzuela.
Pitchers all.
Coyotes too.
'Skins.

Russ Williams

A Whitehall native and resident, Dr. Russ Williams is Director of the New York State Senate Student Programs Office, State Capital. A hunter, fisherman, and voice for ethical outdoors skills and uses, he is the father of two girls, a member of the New York State Outdoor Guides Association, the Adirondack Conservation Concil and the National Grange, and is Director-at-Large of the New York State Rifle and Pistol Association. He writes an outdoor column, Ancient Adirondacks: Arts & Arms.

Howard Has Never Been to Brant Lake

I have   a sister there
who has a husband who
loves wood   work   too
like Howard   not stone
labor   has two children
who are girls growing up in wood

when last I was there
unloading lumber into
this brother's home   black cherry
Howard was home   alone
in his workshop sanding wood
keels with the heels of his hands
while I was laying cinder blocks
was working half-model boat hulls
under unseen seagulls
wheeling overhead
while I was leaving Brant Lake in the dark
along the Adirondack Northway
my sister's daughters
were sleeping in the tired arms
of her husband, their father
while Howard, living on Long Island
worked Tru Oil into his
late night model boat   Howard
was rolling over in bed
to embrace his wife
who wishes for children
while I was pulling up the driveway
gnashing my teeth with fatigue to be
so far from Brant Lake
all of a sudden
Howard was sanding his wife's shapes
into storm, wind, and wrack
enough to unload lumber all night
along the mountainsides near Brant Lake
working himself into lather
well under sail
while I was trying to remember

where I had been
slipping into bed
while Howard was just beginning
to sail down the lake
and into the trees
at the far end

LONG ROD:
the Mettawee at Dawn

damp grass longing downhill
slope in darkness past mullein
beyond chickory
into sand
pebbles
tumbling in darkness
pushing soil
feet caking
in clay
the steep

                                            man descending

baffled by uproar
cloudhead of water
rumbling
into the Mettawee
green river
billy of waters
draining woodland farmland
fish feeding
into Lake Champlain

                                           river descending

hemlock darkness
beyond the river skyline
branches wade in the water
phantom fish at the ankles
birds in the mind
wade in the green
fly tackle soaking
the current between, the cave of hemlock
sunrise, the sudden
yellow flowers on the slope behind

454

Night Fisherman

It was still light when we pulled off onto the gravel to park. We could see the men through the trees, gathered in a group toward Pringle's section of the river, standing away from the embankment. They were smoking, trading stories, coming and going from wherever they had set down a Thermos bottle beside their buckets and nets. Behind them the river roiled into Lake Champlain where, out near the middle, the last motorcraft of the afternoon were curving away toward docks on the Vermont side.

Dad closed the trunk, crossed the ditch into the trees, and came out into the open. Henry Crawford, a new man in town, younger than Dad by several years, kind and friendly toward me, was with us, following behind Dad. I was in back, carrying the long nets.

The group of men turned a bit, flashed hands in quiet salute toward us, nodded, and Dad nodded back. Henry tipped his head too, but the group seemed not to take notice and began to close up again like a murmur. I stumbled with the nets—but only Nate Whitbeck saw me, and he kind of winked before closing with the group again. By the time I came under the bole of the old cottonwood at our usual spot above the roar of the falls, Dad and Henry already had our gear down and were lighting up.

After awhile, Pringle stepped over. There was another man with him, Busty they called him, a kind of sulking character whom I saw only whenever he was hanging on Pringle.

"Dick," Pringle mumbled, nodding to my Dad, but his eyes were turned toward Henry. "You must be Crawford," he said.

Henry started to swing out his hand, but it was clear Pringle wasn't going to take it, so Henry kept on reaching until he took hold of both nets I had leaned up against the tree. He laid them on the ground.

"That's right," he answered. "Henry Crawford."

"Ever been smelting before?" Pringle asked.

Henry looked down at himself and gave a little chuckle, looked up at Pringle. "Can't say I have," he said. "Can't say I ever heard of smelt until Dick here told me about them. Best damned eating in the world, he said—and that they come by the bucketful. That's why I'm here—and because Bobby promised to clean 'em up for us," he laughed, ruffling my hair.

"Clean 'em?" Busty butted in. "Best way to clean smelt is right off your plate."

"Well," said Pringle, "just remember them smelt are damned shy critters and awful nervous when they're running. Walk soft on the ground, don't go near the river 'til after dark, and stand still in the water when you do go in—or we'll all get cleaned."

"He knows the situation, Bill," my Dad said. "Everything'll be just fine."

"I hope so," Pringle responded, and he turned, tapping Busty on the elbow, and walked off toward the group, Busty gesticulating in small emphatic strokes most of the way, circling Pringle as they went across the rough ground. We watched them go.

"Friendly sort," Henry said.

"Generous," said Dad. "That's why he stands the place at the mouth of the river. He gets 'em when they begin running in from the lake, and again if they panic and turn out. And if none of 'em do get more than twenty-five feet upstream, well that's all right with Bill, too." He slipped the suspenders over his shoulders and moved forward to help Henry with his.

It's the moon, Dad always said, that draws the smelt—the ideal magnet and light of the moon singing like a beacon, drawing the smelt in from the lake to spawn in frenzy up the stream, rattling the water, dancing by thousands beneath the old light. That's why it's supposed to be best to go smelting when the night is a bit overcast, the light uncertain, and the tide of the moon strong overhead. Feeling its gravity, the fish come up after its light, searching it out, squabbling up out of the depths and into the river. The sudden light of a strong flashlight stuns them at their weakest moment in the practice of their oldest religion; a net plunges to scoop them out of their darkness and into the waiting buckets.

Summer evenings, Dad would take me in the car after dark, drive the old road out to Pangman's Hill, kill the engine at the top, and coast down the long hill past the Horton place, off the road beyond the barns, and deep into the high grass of the meadows.

We'd sit a quarter of an hour or so, not speaking in the dark, and then he'd touch my arm, lift the flashlight, stick it out the window into the night, and touch it off. The meadow would explode into daylight and the grazing deer be riveted alert in the glow. The green eyes of other deer beyond the sunrise of the light would blink like stars. Then, the light would go out and the darkness cave in around us again.

I would try to guess how many deer we'd seen and hear Dad trying to control his excited breathing beside me. Once, I saw tears glistening on his cheeks in the moonlight.

We were drinking coffee from the Thermos, creamy-sweet stuff, the way Dad liked it. Henry was holding Dad's flashlight and they were talking about how best to use it. I watched the panorama of the far shore of the lake in the dusk, while they spoke quietly behind me, waiting for the dark. Suddenly I realized it had happened, the far line of the Green Mountains had become a great darkness, indistinguishable from the night sky above it.

More men had moved in on either side of us, and the glow of cigarettes marked the various spots up and down the bank from which one could smelt. I curled my feet inside my old sneaks the way I knew I'd do in the water and tried to imagine the cold rush that would come through the canvas, my woolen socks, and into the spaces around my toes. Soon we would begin to move, holding our breaths.

Our spot was on the last curve of the river before the lake, on an outcropping above the falls, from which we could either net the smelt as they scrambled uphill in the heave of the current down the channel of the cascade, or where we could wade into the pool above, from which the river fell away over the rocks into a tumbling current.

I saw Dad stir.

"Get ready," he spoke, and lights began to open up downstream near the lake. Then I could see it, an applause of splattering on the surface, the splashing shape of the cascade in front of us, and then we began breaking into it with our nets, dipping, interrupting the flow, lifting, emptying into buckets, turning back to dip again.

Someone was shouting something above the excitement, and I realized it was my own voice, exultant, and Henry laughing behind me, shaking the light. Our buckets were filled, and the flow was beginning to ebb as the smelt entered the quieter water above us. Now Dad was laughing, shaking the water from his net at me, turning to take one last dip, and Henry was shouting, dancing backward into the darkness.

The flashlight cast a.wide circle of light from the end of Henry's arm as he fell back over the falls, landing full on his back in the water, his head striking an upthrusting of rock that emerged just level with the surface of the boil beneath the cascade.

I saw and heard it happen, all of it, the way Dad lunged forward and then froze, the way Henry's shout turned instantly to silence, the way his boots filled with water and fell suddenly, pulling him down, and how the light floated from his wrist and slipped back into the depths behind him, shining upward, as he took in a last unconscious breath of struggling water.

The rock came alive with fishermen, shouting, flashlight beams striking haphazardly at the night. The voices grew muffled and then stopped. One after another, the flashlights were extinguished as Henry, a startlement on his face, began to slip downstream in the shaped darkness of the pool, half silhouetted, half dappled in the damp glow of father's flashlight below him.

The fish were gone and only the men were left, standing still, staring into the water, caught up in the darkness. I saw tears on my father's cheeks, the long net dripping from the end of his arm, and turned away from the terrible beauty of the thing I had seen, the dark thing I was seeing, and headed toward the car.

I heard a voice downstream shouting to Busty somewhere in the darkness to get a blanket, and turned to see. I watched Pringle in the distance, step into the water, moving toward the shallow part of the rapids where Henry's body would soon wash up.